tunnel vision

SUSAN | ADRIAN

tunnel vision

THOMAS DUNNE BOOKS | ST. MARTIN'S GRIFFIN | NEW YORK

This is a work of fiction. All of the characters, organizations, and events portrayed in this novel are either products of the author's imagination or are used fictitiously.

THOMAS DUNNE BOOKS.
An imprint of St. Martin's Press.

www.thomasdunnebooks.com
www.stmartins.com

Library of Congress Cataloging-in-Publication Data

Adrian, Susan.
Tunnel vision: a novel / Susan Adrian.—First edition.
pages cm
ISBN 978-1-250-04792-2 (hardcover)
ISBN 978-1-250-04791-5 (e-book)
1. Psychic ability—Fiction. 2. Undercover operations—Fiction. 3. High schools—Fiction. 4. Schools—Fiction. 5. Dating (Social customs)—Fiction. 6. Family life—Virginia—Fiction. 7. Virginia—Fiction. 8. Science fiction. I. Title.
PZ7.A273Tun 2015
[Fic]—dc23

2014032376

St. Martin's Griffin books may be purchased for educational, business, or promotional use. For information on bulk purchases, please contact the Macmillan Corporate and Premium Sales Department at 1-800-221-7945, extension 5442, or write to specialmarkets@macmillan.com.

First Edition: January 2015

10 9 8 7 6 5 4 3 2 1

For Michael, for always being on my side,
and for Sophie, for saying what I needed
to hear, every time. And for all the hugs.

1

"People Following Me" by Phunk Junkeez

The man is there again: long black coat, pressed pants, spit-shiny shoes. He leans against a spotless black Durango, phone to his ear. Eyes trained on the big double doors.

I stand behind the cafeteria windows and watch him, rubbing one finger over the edge of my phone. Back and forth, back and forth, the edge smooth and familiar.

The guy's a sore thumb in a parking lot full of kids and beater cars. He's not a high school student, or a parent. But he's been squatting in the same spot every damn day for a week. He stays until I come out, watches me get in my car. Then he drives away.

I don't want to think about who he is. Probably is. He sure as hell looks government, flattop to regulation shoes. But if he is—if they know about me—why is he here? Why am I still here?

I text Chris, stuck in the gym for *Oklahoma!* rehearsals. Chris claims he does theater for the girls. Considering the girls (Rachel Watkins, cough), I can't argue much.

He's here again. Am not insane.

It buzzes right back.

u r total crackpot. New nickname crackpot jake. Y/N?

Then:

Don't you and your paranoid ass have to get M?

Myka. I'm already late. She'll be sitting out front waiting for me, freezing her butt off. I drop the phone in my pocket, staring at the man. I stalled as long as I could, hoping he'd be gone when I came out.

I have to be rational. He can't be government, at least not after me. Dad said if they found out my secret I wouldn't even know what happened. They'd swoop down in black helicopters or whatever and that'd be it. I'd be gone.

He's not doing anything like that. So even though he's stalkerish, and my alarms are firing all at once, I have to shake it off. He probably doesn't have anything to do with me. I have to walk past him and go get my sister like every other day, take the exit to reality instead of Paranoia Land. I'm getting as bad as Dedushka.

Or . . . maybe the guy's from Stanford, and he's scouting for the tennis team. They were so impressed with my video and my application, they sent someone to check me out . . .

Okay. That's just a different kind of delusion.

I push the door open and walk, easy, not looking his direction. It's cold, the February wind slapping at my face. This is the tricky part, a narrow passage. I have to walk right next to him while he gives me the stalker eye. Muttering into his phone, like always. I can never make out what he's saying.

Except today.

"Permission to take him?" he says, in a weird, soft British voice. "It's perfect. Right now."

I stop dead and look at him. Hair like a bristle brush, stubble, muscle-thick shoulders. Eyes set on me. I scan the parking lot. It's dead, between the normal rush and the after-school groups. Nobody there but me and him, and a few kids smoking way at the end. They probably wouldn't notice if he knocked me on the head and threw me in a trunk.

Take him.

Jesus. This isn't in my head. They do know. I fucked up, and someone *knows.*

I have to get away, or it'll happen like Dad said.

My car's too far—and he knows where it is. I give him one more look and take off down the path to Bennett Street, pound across it. I hear him behind me. I got the jump, but he's following.

There's only one place I can think to go. I cut across the corner of the Episcopal church lot and dive between traffic on Dranesville, heading for it. Half a block more. I pant, not looking back, my pulse booming. Focus on the goal: the open iron gates of Oak Grove Cemetery.

Past the gates I skid to a stop. Now where? The cemetery's empty, sad with dead grass and heaps of gray snow across the graves, the trees winter-bare: not much cover.

Heavy footsteps smack across the road behind me. He's still coming. Damn it. I can't confront him alone in a cemetery, and I can't fight a guy that big—even if I could fight. I need somewhere to hide. A fat tree, a tomb . . . there's a small mausoleum to the right, but you can see behind it from the gates. I trot farther. *C'mon, Jake. Now.*

The Miller angel. She's huge, six feet at least, marble wings spread wide. The only thing big enough. I dive behind her and dare to look back.

He steps through the gate, deliberate.

The marble is icy under my fingers. I grip it, my mouth shut tight so my breath won't show. He keeps coming, step by slow step, head darting every direction. Hunting.

It feels like I'm in a *Death to Spies* game, this is World War II, and

I have covert information he's after. Except this isn't a game, and I didn't imagine it. He *is* following me. But not for what I know. For what I can do. Who I am.

He inches in a few more steps, hand in his coat pocket now. Wait, does he have a gun? I've got a backpack full of books, and keys. And no ninja skills at all. Once he gets as far as the angel I'll be obvious; a dead, stupid duck. The cemetery is massive, twenty-five acres, but it's enclosed by a stone wall and that gate is the only entrance open in winter. There's no other way out. If I run for better cover now, I'll be in range of any gun.

Poor planning. If I was playing *Call of Duty* I'd know the map, where to go, the best vantage points for hiding, for shooting. I'd never have trapped myself like this.

I crouch lower, trying to force my frozen brain to think of something. My phone buzzes in my pocket and I slap my hand over it to keep the sound low. Probably Myka wondering where I am.

"What're you doing, fool? Huntin' for treasure down there?"

I spin, my back flat against the angel like I've been shot.

"Pete!" I swallow, but don't get anything but air. "Hey."

Pete stands a few feet away, striped sweater and wild brown beard over overalls, a shovel in his hand. It'd be disturbing, a grave keeper sneaking up on you with a shovel, if I didn't know him so well. And if I wasn't *almost* positive he was only shoveling snow.

He raises thick eyebrows. I turn and peer around the angel, back toward the gate. The man isn't there. Pete spooked him.

But he might be waiting for me outside. I'm not clear yet. I'm determined to be smarter about this from here on.

Pete eyes me funny. "You doing drugs, kid? Did they finally break you down?"

I laugh, sort of. More like a bark. "Not today. I was . . . I was looking for you."

One eyebrow up. Pete's a master at that language. That means *I don't believe you* and *you're a bonehead* and *explain,* all at the same time.

I press against the marble with the tips of my fingers, considering. I need to get to my car. I need Pete to come with me—whoever the man is, I'm betting he won't mess with me with Pete right there. There has to be a way to get Pete to come with me back to my car.

And then there's Myka, still waiting for me.

I try to look embarrassed. "My car won't start. I don't want to call AAA again or my mom will kill me. I thought maybe you could look at it?"

"That's why you was squatting with your nose pressed against a gravestone?" Pete grunts. "You looking for a mechanic? Wrong place, buddy. Ain't no good at cars."

I bet I could get him to do it without breaking a sweat if I were a girl. If Rachel asked me—even Lily—I'd sprint right over to help, even if I had no idea how to fix it.

No, not Lily.

Not being a girl, all I can do is push. "C'mon, man. If you looked at it, we could figure it out."

He's silent for a full minute, twisting the handle of the shovel into the hard ground. Then he rolls his eyes. "Fine. But only 'cause you're a good customer."

"Not a customer yet." It's an old joke between us. Part of my senior project is researching the families buried here—Pete sees me a lot. Today the joke leaves a bad taste in my mouth. I check again. Still clear.

I let Pete go ahead out the gate. With his shovel slung over his shoulder, he looks like a mountain man, or a mini-Hagrid. I stay a step behind him.

The man isn't anywhere in sight on the street, or in the school parking lot. The Durango is still there, hulking. With the tinted windows he could be sitting in there watching and I'd never know.

I don't want to turn my back on him, but I have to go through the motions of fixing my car. I pop the hood of my white Civic, let

Pete lean his big belly over the engine, and get behind the wheel. Then I start it up, right in his face.

Pete jumps back, swearing like a maniac. I don't worry too much. Pete thinks everyone's an idiot anyway. In ten seconds flat I drop the hood, jump back in, hold up a hand to Pete, and speed out of the lot.

I hang on to the steering wheel, getting my pulse under control so I won't stroke out. There, whoever you are. You're not taking *me* anywhere. And it's Friday. I've only seen him at school—so if all goes well I should have till Monday to figure out how to deal with this problem. There's got to be something I can do. I don't see any black helicopters yet.

The clock says 4:20. Twenty minutes late already. I have to deal with Myka before I can even start to think about it.

She isn't outside when I get there at 4:53. Good: she's not freezing her butt off. Bad: I'm late enough that she had to go back in. Now I have to venture into Genius School looking for her.

Officially it isn't Genius School. The sign says Nysmith School for the Gifted. Same thing, in my book. The kids in here are probably years ahead of the ones I just left at Virginia High, and this place only goes up to eighth grade. They come here from all over the East Coast. Physically it's impressive too—all glass and white walls, marble floors, cutting-edge equipment and computers and labs. If my sister had a choice, that's where I'd find her—in the chemistry lab working on who knows what, some god-awful mixture of foul-smelling chemicals that could blow up at any second.

I guess she didn't have a choice. She's sitting in the admin office alone, swinging her awkwardly long legs off the edge of a maple bench. Glaring at me through her hair.

"You're late."

"Ungrateful. I could've left you here." I smile so she knows I'm teasing. "Besides, I'm only . . ." I look at my watch.

She pouts. "Fifty-four minutes exactly. Mom's going to slaughter you and toss the pieces."

I pinch her arm lightly, and she jerks away. "If you tell her. You won't tell her, will you, Myk? Brother/sister bond?"

She narrows her eyes at me, rubbing her arm. She has gorgeous eyes, huge and green like our mom's, with thick, dark lashes. They make up for the horsiness of the rest of her face at this age, the big front teeth. Twelve isn't kind. 'Course I wouldn't tell her any of that, good or bad.

"All right." I sigh. "Music choice is yours. Today *and* tomorrow. And since we might hit rush hour traffic, that could be like the whole *Twilight* sound track."

"That's ancient," she scoffs. She tucks her hair behind one ear, looks up at me. "When you didn't call me back, I was worried." Her voice goes small. "I thought . . . I don't know. Something happened. Like . . ."

Like Dad.

I want to tuck her up in a hug, like I used to. But that won't help in the long run. She has to be tough. We all do. Especially if something does happen to me—no. No even thinking like that.

I fake punch her in the arm. "I'm fine, dorkus. I'm here, everything's okay. Now let's clear out. What do I have to do to spring you?"

She sighs, stands, and pulls her backpack (Little Einsteins—my joke last Christmas, but she uses it anyway) over her shoulder. "Principal Evers," she calls. "My brother's here."

The principal, a stern woman with fluffy hair like a poodle, pops her head out of the big office in the corner. "Fine, Myka. Have a great weekend. I'll sign you out."

That was way easier than I expected it to be.

Until we walk out the doors, and I see the black Durango idling next to my car.

2

"Police on My Back" by The Clash

I grab Myka's arm, staring at the Durango. Trying to work out a better plan this time than trapping myself in a dead-end cemetery, or getting one of us caught while we try to make it to the car. Maybe the world won't end if he "takes" me in, but nobody's taking Myka anywhere.

He must've followed me from school, and I never even noticed.

She pushes my hand off. "What are you *doing*? It's subzero out here! I'm still cold from waiting for you." She steps forward.

"Myk," I say in a low, tight voice. "Stop."

She freezes. She knows to trust me when I sound like that—to a point. She's also giving me a wide-eyed look like I've grown another head. We have to do this fast. Screw a brilliant plan. I don't have one.

"We need to stay away from the man in that black car, okay? He's dangerous." I try to keep my voice calm, reasonable. "Here's what we're going to do. I'll get close enough to unlock the car. You stay here. When I say go, you *run*. Dive into the back, lock the door as soon as you get in. You got it?"

She shakes her head slowly. "You have *got* to get some meds. You're delusional."

The driver's door of the Durango clicks, swings out. "Have you got it?" I repeat through my teeth. "I'll explain later. Trust me."

"If this is one of your games—" She sees my expression, frowns. "I got it. Stay, then run."

I step forward, eyes on the Durango, clicking my remote. He probably could reach me if he tried now.

Two more steps. His big hand—Jesus, his hands are big enough to strangle puppies—slips over the edge of the doorframe, and he starts to leverage himself up. I take another two steps, click click click. Damn lame remote battery. Another. Click click. He's standing, propped on the edge of his door, watching me. Awful eyes; small, like a pig's. Step, click. Finally it unlocks. I press it again to get the back.

"Myk? *Go*!"

We run. I gotta give it to her, nerd or not, she's faster than me. She's already in as I slam my door—just as the man gets to it. I slam the lock down, shove the key in the ignition. He's outside the door bent toward me, his face three inches from mine.

I don't know what I expect him to do next. Maybe bang on the window, shout, break it with an elbow. Maybe pull a gun and shoot me dead. It makes as much sense as everything else. Instead, as the engine catches he takes a step back, puts his hands up in surrender, and grins.

What the hell?

I throw it in reverse and spin backward, squeal to a stop, then into first. We jolt past him out of the lot. He strolls back to his car, drops into the seat. He doesn't seem worried at all.

That worries me.

I bounce onto Eds Drive. In a few seconds I see the Durango in the rearview mirror pulling out behind me. I also see Myka's face—confused with a sheen of scared. She saw the guy come to the window. She knows something's really wrong. But right now I have to lose this guy. I'm in a car chase scenario with my little sister strapped in the back.

And still not a video game.

Eds Drive goes around in a big-ass circle until you get to McLearen, and there are a couple cars in front of me, so there's nothing I can do except keep driving forward and figure out what to do next.

"You want to tell me what's going on?" Myk says, almost in a whisper.

It's hard to keep my eyes off the rearview mirror, the all-black shape on my tail. I shift up, like it'll make the car in front of me go faster. "This creep has been watching me after school this whole week, and he came after me today. Can't tell you why."

Fancy bit of lying. I know why—probably—but I shouldn't tell her. God, I hate any kind of lying to my sister.

She's quiet for a few minutes, biting her lip. "Something to do with Dad? Or with you?"

I meet her eyes. Huge, scared. But her brain is working fine. "No one knows anything about me," I say, dismissive enough that I hope she drops it. I consider the possibility seriously. "It could be Dad, I guess. Something he was up to at the Pentagon. But why now? When he's been dead for two years?"

We hit McLearen and I jet left, cutting off some woman in a minivan. She honks, her horn bleating like a sad sheep. At least there's one car between us now.

I have a little plan forming in my head, a way to get away from him. Maybe.

"I don't know," Myk says slowly. "It doesn't make sense."

No, it doesn't. Dad was a major general in the U.S. Air Force, stationed at the Pentagon for five years. Pretty high level, and I know he worked on some secret shit. But he's dead, and none of his ghosts should be knocking for me.

So it probably isn't Dad. She knows it, I know it. We're back to the original theory.

I can't think about it now.

I spin around the merging traffic onto Route 28, watching the mirror more than the road. He's still there, two cars back. But it turns multilane here, and I need more space between us. I punch it, veer onto the off-ramp. If he knows the area, by now he's probably figured out where I'm going.

I breathe. Try to focus on the plan.

"Should I call Mom?" Myk asks. "The police?"

"No!" The response is straight from my gut, strong enough to make me go with it. For all I know, he *is* the police. "Not yet." I lower my voice. "You know Mom would only flip out. And there's nothing she or the police can do right now. Hang on."

I shoot into the other lane to pass a Fiesta, then keep the speed up, rumbling over the bridge. We're three cars ahead now. We start the big loop that'll take us to Dulles Airport. If I can get there with enough of a lead . . . this might work. It isn't far. But the Durango is sneaking closer. He has a better engine than I do.

"Why are we going to the airport?" she asks, like she just looked out the window.

"Quiet, okay?" I say. "Just hang on. Trust me." I sound a lot surer than I am.

There's the stop, the U-turn into the airport. Luckily everyone has to stop, and the Durango is still stuck two cars behind me.

And then my plan. Instead of turning to go into the airport, as soon as I get to the stop, I shoot forward and turn hard right into the rental car area.

We're lucky—it's busy. Friday afternoon, plenty of travel. Tons of cars, lots of them white like ours, loaded with tired, confused people driving different directions. And it'll be a couple minutes before he can follow us. Quick as I can I pull into the Enterprise lot, park in the "serve-yourself" aisle, or whatever it's called, and kill the engine.

"Duck!" I hiss. I drop down as much as I can and scrunch my legs, my head on the edge of the seat. I don't fit, and the pedals are pressing into my ankles, but I don't think you can see me unless you look in the window. It's a good thing the car is clean, newish. It blends in well enough for us to hide. I hope. I also hope no tourists choose this moment to pick a nice Civic to tool around DC in.

"And now?" Myk asks, a tremble in her voice even with it muffled. She's folded into the space behind the seat, pretty well hidden. All I can see of her is her dark hair, spread over her hunched back like a blanket.

"Now," I say, struggling to sound calm, "we wait until it's safe to go home."

I pull into our garage about six thirty, bone-tired and foggy from all the adrenaline dumping into my blood and then draining away. I was aware enough at least to make sure there weren't any black Durangos following, or on the street. We're clear. I need to eat, make sure Myk eats, and then sleep. And think. Mom has one of her State Department dinners and won't be home until late. I have time to decide what I want to tell her about this. Maybe it's finally the right moment to tell her about me, stop hiding it all. Though Dad was always clear about that. Never tell Mom.

Myk and I didn't talk during the wait, or the drive home. I can tell from her serious face that her brain is whirring around in there, though. She's worrying. I really don't want her thinking too hard about it, not until I do. I want to keep her out of it, safe. No matter what happens.

I guess the main thing is what to do on Monday. I can't run or hide in car lots forever—they already know my school and Myk's. Eventually they'll find home.

Oh, God.

Anyway. We're safe now. First: eat. We throw our coats over the rack, and I drop my keys in the bowl. "Mac and cheese," I say. "Start boiling the water, will you? I'm gonna dump my stuff in my room."

She nods absently, and already has a pot out as I go down the hall and flip on the light in my room.

There's a woman sitting on my bed, legs crossed in a gray professional skirt, gray jacket. Dark blond hair scraped back in a tight ponytail. She blinks in the light.

"Jacob Lukin," she says, in a voice like syrup. "Did you think they knew where you went to school, but they couldn't find your house?"

My arms and legs go wobbly, and I grip the doorknob hard to keep myself up.

She uncrosses her legs and leans forward, like she's going to tell me a secret. "Why don't you lock that door? We don't want your sister any more involved than she already is, do we?"

I shut the door slowly, turn the lock, and lean back against it. I can see her cleavage, right out there as she leans toward me, and it pisses me off that I notice it. "What do you want?" My voice is a shadow.

She folds her hands in her lap and smiles with white teeth. "Right to the point. I respect that. I want to talk about a little something that happened at Caitlyn Timmerman's party two weeks ago. And I'm not the only one."

This time my legs do give out, and I slide to the floor.

3

"A Little Party Never Killed Nobody"
by Fergie, Q-Tip, and GoonRock

I wasn't going to go to Caitlyn Timmerman's party.

I was supposed to be home with Myka while Mom was away in New York, but Myk had one of her friends there for a sleepover. After being around two twelve-year-old girls for two hours, it didn't take much to convince me they'd be *fine* on their own for a while (Myk's argument), and it was Friday night and I deserved to have a little fun (Chris's argument).

When Chris happened to mention Rachel would be there—and Lily wouldn't—it sealed the deal. Rachel is . . . well, she's straight-up gorgeous, to start. Curvy in all the right places, shiny brown eyes, these beautiful, round pink cheeks . . . and smart. Focused. She didn't seem to drift through school like a lot of people. She did things. I didn't know *that* much about her. I was kind of absorbed in Lily for a long time. But I knew she was in theater with

Chris, and active in political stuff and the school paper, and she was serious about wanting to go to college, like me. A poli-sci major.

And she'd smiled at me in English the day before. So I wasn't going to miss this chance.

At the party, Rachel was surprisingly willing to sit with me on the couch and talk. We talked, and talked. About the problems of the two-party system (her) and the Jeffersonians versus the Hamiltonians (me), and as we sipped on the punch and started to get drunk, more about *The Right State* and old *West Wing* episodes. About how I was dying to go to Stanford, and she wanted to get away from DC and the East for a while and go to Berkeley. Which are practically right next to each other, she said. She smiled when she said it, and I melted a little.

As we talked, we slid closer. Her eyes got bright, her gestures wild. Once, her hand even landed on my leg and she left it there for a second, face crimson, before reaching for her drink.

I admit I was dizzy with her, with possibilities. Off my head happy, for the first time since Lily. This could really happen. Anything could happen. Everything.

So the problem wasn't that I went to the party. The problem was that I had already had so much vodka punch, and I still went along with the drinking game.

Caitlyn started it. "It's a great game!" she slurred. "Chris and I saw it . . . somewhere?" She paused, her forehead wrinkled. "I don't remember where. TV."

Words to live by: Don't join a drinking game with someone who's already slurring. But the punch tasted like grape Kool-Aid, and Caitlyn was generous with it. Every time I turned around my glass was full, tempting. And Rachel, beaming next to me, wanted to join in. It seemed like a good idea.

Hell, everything seemed like a good idea.

We made a rough circle on the floor next to the couch: me, Rachel, Chris, Jeff, Caitlyn, Stacey, Kadeem, and Ashley. All theater geeks except me. I didn't mind at all.

"Chris," Caitlyn said, nodding. Too much nodding, like a bobble-head doll. "You tell them how."

"Yes, friends, I will *tell them how.*" Chris said it in a game-show voice, too loud, his cheeks washed red behind his freckles. Also drunk, of course. "So everybody has funky things they can do. *Talents.*" He wiggled his eyebrows and we all laughed. "So show us your talent. Each of you does the coolest weird thing you can think of, and then everybody else tries. And if you can't do the other person's talent, you drink. Best one wins."

An odd thrill flicked through me. I had a talent I guarantee none of them had. Maybe nobody else in the world had. I could win. But of course I couldn't show them.

Why not? I thought. *What does it really matter?*

"I'll go first." Chris stood, weaving. I knew what his talent would be. I just didn't know if he could do it, wasted as he was. He pushed his hair out of his eyes and winked at Caitlyn. "Drum roll, please." We pounded our hands on the beige carpet. "Ladies and gentlemen, watch, amazed."

He set his palms flat, tried to flip himself up to stand on his hands . . . and collapsed onto Jeff, who spilled about half his purple drink on the carpet. I nearly pissed myself laughing—we all did. No one else even tried to do it until we got to Ashley and then, surprisingly, Rachel. Seems they were both cheerleaders in grade school. Who knew?

Rachel flipped herself upside down and threw me a grin, her face full-on glowy.

All that and smart too. Did I even deserve her?

I drank, licking sticky purple off my lips. Then Jeff licked his own elbow. I thought that was impossible. All the rest of us drank.

Caitlyn put her whole fist in her mouth, which was interesting, especially to Chris. I drank. Stacey bent her pinkie back to her arm. Someone poured me more, and I drank. Kadeem raised one eyebrow, which I could do fine—couldn't anybody?—but I drank anyway. Ashley did a cheerleader flip and knocked over a side table. Nobody cared. Everything was funny.

By the time it was my turn, I was more slammed than I had been in a very long time, maybe ever. Especially around that many people. My eyelids felt heavy. My whole body felt heavy. I looked at Chris. He was flickering, but maybe that was me.

"Do it, dude," he said, his words stretched out slooooow. "Tunnel. You know you want to."

I did want to. I *really* wanted to. Chris only knew about it because I'd told him—shown him—when we were seven, before Dad said I shouldn't tell anybody. Before Dad knew. "No," I said, shaking my head, thinking of Dad. "I can't."

"Tunnel?" Caitlyn said loud. "What's that? Do it!"

"Do it, do it, do it," they chanted.

This was such a safe place. Warm, safe. Nobody but my friends. High school kids, like me. And everybody as drunk as me. They wouldn't even remember. I felt suddenly free, light. Yes. I could do it, this one time. It was the perfect time.

I could show Rachel. That might make me cool enough for her.

"Okay," I announced, palms out. "But this is a seeecret. Okay?"

Rachel leaned over, poked me in the shoulder. "Yes!"

I smiled at her, lopsided. *Damn, girl.*

"You've got to bring me something that belongs . . . belongs . . ." I frowned. I couldn't think of how to put the words together so they made sense. "Belongs to someone who's far away." I tried to focus on Caitlyn. "Do you have anything like that?"

She thought hard for a minute, her forehead crinkling again, then flipped her hair back. "Yes." She held up one finger. "Hang on."

We waited while she disappeared upstairs. And drank more, of course. It seemed like she was gone a long time, almost long enough for me to decide maybe I shouldn't do it after all. But not quite.

She almost tripped coming down the stairs. "Here." She thrust a small object into my hand. It was a tiny velvet box, like the kind they always show in movies when the guy is going to propose. "It belongs to—"

"No, don't tell me anything." I grinned. I was sharing it, finally, with my friends. It didn't have to be such a secret. It was just fun. A relief. What was I so worried about?

I cradled the box in my hands, closed my eyes, and let it come.

It sobered me instantly. First I got the warmth, the sense of energy that tells me it's happening. It's like the light from a glow stick, a shimmer that expands around the object that only I can see. Then the light, the warmth, makes its way through my fingertips, buzzing under my skin. Then come the images. Like watching a movie in my head.

A girl . . . no, young woman. Long black hair, tiny glasses, skinny. Clearly Caitlyn's sister. I feel her location, closer and closer, like zooming in on a labeled map in Google: Hanover, New Hampshire. Dartmouth College. Hitchcock Hall, Room 220. And she is seeing . . . oh. Some guy's lips, in a dark room with curtains drawn. . . . "I love you," he said. "C'mon." She is feeling pretty warm herself as she leans in, slides her hand down his pants . . .

I pulled out of it, blinking, drunk again. Seven pairs of eyes were staring at me.

When I tunnel to someone, I can do it silently or say it out loud. If I say it, there's no filter—I say what I see, hear, feel. What that person is experiencing at that moment in time, wherever they are.

Everyone looked freaked out. Even Chris. Even Rachel.

"Dude," Jeff said, swaying. "That was creepy."

I tried to laugh. "Let's see you do that! Everybody drinks!"

Everybody sipped, silent.

"But that was *true,*" Caitlyn said, thoughtful, tapping her fingers against her red plastic cup. "That was Cammie and Adam . . . it was totally true. Do another one." She gestured around the circle. "Come on, somebody else has to have something."

They all looked at each other.

"I have one," Rachel said, soft. "Just a minute." She got up and went to the corner, where all the coats and purses were piled on a chair, and dug into a brown purse.

When she came back, she slipped something into my hand. It was a piece of paper, folded in half. A letter. I closed my eyes and felt the warmth, the tingle, even faster than before.

A man, early fifties. He is big, barrel chested, with short, stumpy legs and heavy eyebrows. He is wearing purple-flowered swim trunks. His skin is a deep red, going into tan. Location: Oahu, Hawaii. Waimea Bay Beach Park. He is waxing a surfboard. He glances at the sun. Another hour at least. The waves are perfect right now—he has to get back out there. That's all that matters, the sun and the waves. He'd been so right to leave it all—them all—and come here. He is exactly where he wants to be, finally. Alone. At peace.

When I opened my eyes Rachel had tears streaking down her cheeks. She sniffed, loud, almost a hiccup. "That's my dad. He left six months ago . . . I thought . . . he might come back . . ." She got up, snatched the letter, and ran to the bathroom.

Caitlyn gave me a look like it was my fault and followed her.

I drank, letting the vodka wash out the feeling that this had been a really bad idea.

That's when I saw a flicker of movement at the top of the stairs. I met the eyes of Caitlyn's mom, sitting on the top step, watching me. On her face was the kind of look you'd give a dog who just recited Shakespeare. Stunned, sure. But *interested*.

How much did she see?

She stood smoothly, came down the stairs, and announced that it was time to go and she'd arranged a big taxi to take us all home. Now, please. She didn't mind if we drank, but the party was over, and she wasn't having any of us on the roads.

Crammed in next to Chris on the ride home, with Rachel puffy eyed in the front, all I could do was think about what a very, very stupid thing that could've been. I could've blown it all, right there. I knew better. It had just seemed so easy, so right. Safe.

But hardly anybody mentioned it the next week, or the next. Rachel turned distant—embarrassed, I guess. I tried to talk to her, but she would look away, or give me one-word answers. Massively disappointing, but about what I should have expected, I guess. I blew it.

I allowed myself to remember it like a bad dream, one of those nightmares where you do exactly what you're not supposed to do. I allowed myself to forget about it, almost.

Until now.

4

"Life Is Over" by Curbstone

"Who are you?" I whisper. I look up at the woman from the floor, and even though the party was two weeks ago I feel drunk again, blurred.

Her eyes are an odd pale green, like they'd been real green until something sucked most of the color out. I want to look away, but I can't. She tilts her head, and her ponytail swings sideways.

"I work with Mrs. Timmerman. She had a very interesting report about that party. Very interesting indeed."

I sit up straighter, grab at a shred of hope. Maybe it isn't what I think. "Mrs. Timmerman works at Georgetown, doesn't she? Some sort of scientist?"

She actually laughs. "I don't work for Georgetown University, Jacob. I work for the Department of Defense. A division called DARPA. Have you heard of it?"

Hope smears out. The Department of Defense. It's exactly what I thought. It's what Dad said would happen, if I kept tunneling, if I told anyone. I'd never really believed him—it sounded too much like he was just trying to scare me. Step on a crack, break your mother's back. Stupid shit like that. But he was right.

With the realization comes a wave of anger. At him for being right. At myself for being stupid, for fucking up so royally. And at her, sitting there on my bedspread like she owns it.

"So you read some report and you follow me around all week? You break into my house?" I get louder. "What the hell? You could have *called* if you wanted to talk to me."

"Keep your voice down," she says, sharp. "And I said I wasn't the only one interested. The man who followed you isn't from us. He's private. We're not sure yet who he's working for. Whoever it is, it's certainly not good for you."

I close my eyes. This isn't happening.

A couple of tunnels at a party, and the Department of Defense *and* some other mystery person is all over me. Who else was at that party? Who do Rachel's parents secretly work for? Chris's? The Mafia? Al-Qaeda?

I'm being paranoid again.

No, I'm not. But I am scared.

"That's only the tip of the iceberg, Jacob. We have done a great deal of research into this area, for decades." Her voice is still soft, too-sweet. "Ever heard of Stargate?"

I don't answer. Yes, I've heard of Stargate. A government project in the 1970s to use psychic phenomena—psychics—to spy long-distance. DARPA funded it. I'd read everything I could on it, a few years back, and I'm pretty good at the research now. But it was shut down a long time ago. It was most famous for being a failure.

"We have never been able to find a subject who is consistently right, who can provide us with the kind of information we need.

Mrs. Timmerman believes she witnessed something special—exactly what we've been looking for. If this ability she saw is real, you could be extremely helpful to us, Jacob. You could locate hostages, fugitives, spies, criminals. Missing persons. That's just the start. The CIA, FBI, NSA . . . and that's only in Washington. Of course, we'll have to test you first. But I believe we could be partners. I believe we could work very well together."

I shake my head, eyes still closed, her words crashing over me. They don't really know anything. They can't make me do anything. I have to remember that.

"No."

"What was that?"

I open my eyes. She hasn't moved, hands still in her lap, but she seems more intense. Like she fired herself up a notch or two.

"I don't know what you're talking about," I say, stiff. "I'm as normal as you get. I'm eighteen. I'm graduating in a few months. I'm waiting to see what colleges I got into. I'm not some freak, like you're saying. I'm *normal*."

She shakes her head lightly. "I'm going to make you an offer, Jacob Lukin. I suggest you listen."

"What's your name?" She works my name so hard, and I don't even know who she is. Maybe if I know it, it will make her human, someone I can deal with.

She purses her lips. "Liesel. Dr. Liesel Miller. Here, I'll show you my badge, if it helps."

She pulls a badge out of her coat pocket, with her picture on it. DARPA, the Defense Advanced Research Projects Agency. Dr. Liesel Miller.

It doesn't help. She feels even more dangerous with a name, a badge.

I push to my feet, so I'm not looking up at her anymore. Try not to sway. "No, Liesel Miller. I don't know anything. I can't *do* anything.

Whatever you heard, read, whatever, it's not true. I don't need to listen to your offer because I can't help you. Now it's time for you to get the fuck out of my house."

"You're forgetting about the man who followed you," she says. "Aren't you?"

There's a knock on the door behind me, and I jump. The knob rattles.

"Jake? Who're you talking to? I thought you were coming to help me with dinner."

Myka.

"Tell her you're on the phone," Liesel whispers.

I keep my eyes on her. "I'm on the phone with Chris," I say through the door. "I've got to talk to him for a couple more minutes. Can you keep going with dinner?"

There's a puzzled pause. I never talk to Chris on the phone—we just text. I should've said I was talking to a girl. That at least is true. Kind of.

"Okay," Myk says, finally, quietly. "I'll do it myself. It'll be ready in about 10 minutes."

I wait for her to go away, but she doesn't. I can still hear her breathing.

"Jake?"

"Yeah?"

"You're acting very weird. This whole thing today was weird."

The understatement of the century. I take a deep breath. "I know. Sorry."

This time I hear her thump back toward the kitchen, and Liesel relaxes a little. I don't.

"You need to *leave,*" I say again. "Now. This is insane and an invasion of privacy, and probably illegal. We're done."

Her eyebrows—perfectly plucked—arch. "You don't want me to do that."

They don't know anything. They can't make me do anything.

Whoever the other guy is—he can't either. If I pretend to be normal from now on. . . .

She sighs, dead green eyes on me, and her voice hardens. "Jacob. I'm going to be straight with you. Trust me, your other friend is out there, whoever he is. On this street somewhere, probably. He's not in here only because I am, because my people are outside. Do you think he's going to go away because you ask him to? That he's going to believe your patently false denial? You knew why I was here as soon as I mentioned the party. It was obvious. And those men out there?" She jerks a chin toward my window. "They'll take you away without a thought, without asking. If you can do what they think—what we think—they'll push through your mother and your sister and everyone you know to get to you. You'll be gone by morning. And by the time they're done with you—"

She pauses, looks me up and down, like she's judging me. Her nose is long, pinched. It makes her face look stern. "You'll be begging to do whatever they ask."

I cross my arms. "What if I don't believe you?"

"You saw him for yourself. He followed you. You want to take the risk, with your sister here? You're normal, you say. I believe you to a point. I believe you can't defend yourself and your family against hired guns like him."

I grit my teeth, but I don't answer.

"We don't have much time—your sister's expecting you. Do you want to hear my offer or not?" She pats the bed, smiles thinly. "Come. Sit by me. I'll get a crick in my neck trying to talk to you like that."

I look at the bed, at her. I lean back against the door.

Her lips twitch. "Fine. Here's what I'm offering. As I said, I work for DARPA. We're the innovation engine for the Department of Defense—we research and fund research for experimental, bleeding-edge ideas that could be used to help protect our country, and pass them on to the military if they prove useful. We invented the stealth fighter. The M-16. A small thing called the Internet."

I shift, impatient. I don't want to hear a patriotic self-promotion spiel. I want to hear this "offer"—and figure out how I can turn it down. Get her out of here.

But how *do* I deal with the other guy?

Her voice relaxes. Honey again. "I know it's overwhelming, Jacob. All we're asking for right now, honestly, is for you to come in and do some tests with us. See what you can do, prove your abilities. Do your mother or sister know?"

"I don't know what you're talking about."

Skepticism flits across her face. "I need two days, that's all. Tomorrow is Saturday—tell your mother you're going somewhere for the weekend with Chris. Tell Chris you're going away with your family. Meet me at the Starbucks on Elden at 9 a.m., and I'll take you in. You'll be back in time for Sunday dinner."

It thoroughly creeps me out that she knows so much: about Chris, my family. And there it is again: *take you in*. "I'm supposed to serve myself up to a secretive government agency for two days, without anyone knowing where I am. For *tests*? I've read books. People disappear in places like that, no matter what they can or can't do."

A chill dances down my spine, saying it aloud. I really wish I could talk to Dad about this.

She doesn't hesitate. "You have my word, Jacob. I will bring you back here personally. And in return, whether we find you valuable or not, we offer you and your family continuing protection, so you can keep living your *normal* life." She smiles, with teeth, but it doesn't reach her eyes. "I think it's a fair offer. It's only tests. The alternative is that your private friends, or someone else, gets hold of you. I'm sure they have their own tests and plans. None of us want that to happen."

She says the last bit slowly, each word distinct, her gaze steady. I understand her well enough. It means I don't have a choice. They'll *take me in* for their tests whether I agree or not, rather than let me end up somewhere else, used by someone else. Just because she doesn't say it aloud doesn't mean it isn't plain as day.

So there's really nothing to decide. I go tomorrow—or I go now, probably. And there's that protection she's offering. I've seen that stalker guy close up. Even if he was unarmed, I'd be toast.

And Myka. And Mom. I have to protect them.

But I don't have to roll over and take it either.

"I'll do your tests." *And I'll bomb them on purpose.* "In return for protection. But I'm not spending the night in a government facility. You'll have to finish in one day, or no deal."

She thinks. Nods, slightly. "Not ideal, but it'll do. Tomorrow."

"I'll meet you at Starbucks, and you'll bring me back tomorrow night." *And then this will be over, you government freak.*

She stands, stretches out one hand. "It was a pleasure meeting you, Jacob. I'm sure we'll enjoy working together. The guards will remain posted outside, hidden, so no one else will disturb you or your family. You have my word. You will be safe until tomorrow."

I let her hand hang there, untouched, until she drops it. She pushes open the window and steps out, her heels in Mom's flower bed, and disappears.

I shut it after her, lock it, like that does much good—it was locked to begin with—and go out to eat dinner with my sister. I'll have to work hard to tease her enough to distract her from noticing what's wrong.

Pretend everything is like it was this morning.

5

"Rock and a Hard Place" by Supreme Beings of Leisure

DARPA headquarters is in Arlington, half an hour from home—only a few blocks from Mom's work at the State Department. She might walk past it at lunchtime, in the sneakers she brings every day. I wonder if she knows what it is. There aren't any signs.

It looks like any other huge office building: modern, dark brown stone, a lot of glass windows. I guess I'd pictured a bleak underground lab with secret entrances, or military gates at least. I feel a little better when Liesel pulls into the normal parking structure, and when we walk into the normal lobby, with a café and a deli and everything.

This isn't bad. Actually, it's kind of cool being inside someplace secret.

My pulse bumps up when we're waved past the regular Visitor Control Center, back to the guards at the Special Security Office.

The guard is total military, six-foot-five with a crew cut, but stuffed into a shirt and tie instead of a uniform. The one behind him looks like his slightly smaller brother. Their faces are blank, polite. I figure neither one has any sense of humor at all, like most guards on military bases. I know the type well.

"Please empty your pockets and surrender your personal items," the first guard says. He holds out a tub like the ones at airports.

I hesitate.

"Everything on you, sir," he says, impassive. "Including the watch. It's for security reasons."

I look at Liesel.

"Go ahead," she says with a smile. "It's routine." She's wearing a black suit, with another white shirt, and her badge around her neck on a lanyard.

I hand over my wallet, my keys, and my phone. Even the watch, a fat silver military one that had been Dad's, that Dedushka gave me after the funeral. The guard seals everything in a big Ziploc bag with my name written on it. Then he takes it all away, behind a white door.

"Don't I get them back?"

Liesel shrugs. "When you leave. Visitors aren't allowed to bring any items past the lobby. As I said, it's routine, until you've been cleared. Security."

I feel stripped without my watch, my phone—and vulnerable. I now have no ID, money, or way of calling out if something goes wrong.

The smaller guard takes me through an X-ray machine—in case I still have something hidden in a crevice somewhere—then positions me against a white wall and takes my picture. He tapes it on a visitor badge with my name, a bar code, and a bunch of seemingly random numbers and letters. To Liesel, he says, "He's cleared for the SAPF." Then he gives me a little smirk. "Welcome to DARPA, Mr. Lukin."

Maybe he does have a sense of humor, and he's totally jacking with me. Sirens in my head blare *bad idea, bad idea*. I look back through the X-ray, past the desk, at the glass doors to outside.

Too late.

"This way." Liesel smiles again and leads me to the elevators.

On the fourteenth floor the elevators open into a tiny room with another guard station, and a guy who is clearly a cousin of the dudes downstairs. He scans our badges with a fancy price gun-type thing, checks a computer screen, and scrutinizes our faces, comparing them to whatever he sees there. Finally he nods to Liesel.

"This area is cleared for skiff, ma'am. The floor is all yours."

"Thank you. We'll need it that way until tomorrow."

Tomorrow? No, you need it that way until *tonight*. Or like an hour or two from now, when I've proven I can't do a thing, and we all go back to business as usual. Fingers crossed.

Liesel slides her badge into a reader in the door, like a hotel key, and it clicks open.

I really want to turn around and go home now.

But she gestures through the door, and I go. The hallway looks normal, if empty. She leads me past a dozen closed doors before opening one on the right. The windowless side. It's set up like a conference room, with a big real-oak table in the middle and a few plush black leather chairs around it, all on the far side. To my left, behind the door, is a video camera on a tripod. There's nothing else in the room. Beige carpet, beige blank walls.

Liesel points to the middle seat, smiles. I'm beginning to hate her teeth.

"Jacob, if you'll have a seat there, please. I'll be back in a bit."

The door closes behind her. It has a key card slot on this side too. I wonder if my temporary badge has a remote chance of working in it.

Probably not. I sit, reluctantly, and look into the lens of the camera. A red light pops on.

I'm on TV. I guess I should be glad there isn't a two-way mirror to live up to *all* the stereotypes.

I feel like making a face at the camera.

But that's probably stupid. I have no idea who's watching me or where that footage is going. I am *so* out of my element here.

The door clicks open and Liesel comes back in. A man and a woman, both in white medical coats, follow her. The man is pushing a cart loaded with a laptop and a bunch of wires and different-size Velcro bands.

"What's that?" I ask.

"Drs. Lennon and Milkovich, meet Jacob Lukin, our subject," Liesel says. "Jacob, these are the doctors who will be performing your tests this morning."

"What's that?" I repeat. But I know what it is, now that I can see it better. I've seen it on TV. "Is that a polygraph?"

They exchange looks, but don't answer. Dr. Lennon—a short, dark-skinned guy wearing a god-awful plaid shirt under his coat—sets the laptop on the end of the table and starts fiddling with the stuff on the cart.

"Why," I say sharply, "would you need a polygraph?"

"You're a smart kid," Dr. Lennon says. "I bet you can figure that out."

Dr. Milkovich glances at me sideways. She's in her twenties, short too, but pale all over: stick-straight, white-blond hair, skin so translucent the blue veins in her hands stand out. Her body is pretty stick-straight too, what I can see of it. She moves to the video camera, adjusting the height, the angle. Maybe I'm taller than they thought I was.

I can't fake this with a polygraph. They'll be able to tell.

Dr. Lennon moves toward me with a fistful of bands. Maybe

I should clock him, stop this whole thing right here. But then what? Run past layers of guards, if I even make it out the door? Run where? They know where I live.

Liesel's watching me closely. "The polygraph is to make certain what you say is what you believe to be the truth. As long as you're honest and cooperate fully, it's not a problem. It's part of the scientific process. It doesn't mean we don't trust you."

Lennon straps bands around my chest, waist, arms, and fingers, and plugs them all into his machine.

"Let's not pretend we trust each other," I say. It makes me feel a little better, that splash of honesty.

She presses her lips together. They're red today, shiny with lipstick. "Doctors, proceed with the tests as discussed. I'll contact you if I see any issues or we need to deviate." She nods to me, trussed up like a turkey. "Jacob, I'll see you later. Please do your best. Much depends upon it."

It will be a lot better for me if I *don't* do my best, thanks very much. I'll still try to play dumb and see if it gets through the polygraph tests.

I tap my feet on the floor, tap tap tap, because they're all I can move.

I'm trying to avoid the feeling that I'm in deep trouble.

It's an hour before they even bring me any objects. It takes all that time for polygraph bullshit. Calibration. Detailed, excruciating explanation from Dr. Lennon of what's going to happen and how it all works. (*I don't care, take it off.*) Test question after test question after test question, while he stares at the screen and Dr. Milkovich sits in one of the chairs and takes notes, and I tap my feet and try not to swear or sweat or squirm like a five-year-old.

Is your name Jacob Lukin? *Yes.*

Are you eighteen years old? *Yes.*

Do you live at 902 Van Buren Street, Herndon, Virginia? *Yes.*

It gets old fast.

Is your mother Abigail Lukin? *Yes.*

Is your father major general John Lukin, deceased? I hesitate. His first name isn't really John; it's Ivan. He changed it before he joined the air force, because Ivan Lukin sounded too Russian. Still—that's what's on the records. *Yes.*

Are you working for or have you worked for any agencies of foreign governments? *No.*

Even telling the truth, I feel jumpy hooked up to the thing. It's a lot worse when Dr. Milkovich gets up to bring the objects, and I know I'm going to lie. She brings in a metal box, thin and long like a safe-deposit box, and sets it on the table so it opens away from me. She takes out something in a sealed plastic bag, face dead serious, and slides the bag down.

It's a ring. Plain, gold, scuffed. A man's ring.

Here we go, problem solved. I can't do it through plastic, but they don't know that. I'll try, fail. Done. I relax.

She nods at me. "Open it. We want you to hold it in your hand."

Crap. I look at the camera—unblinking red eye—and open the bag, let the ring fall into my hand.

I close my eyes, but I don't try to tunnel. I frown, grunt. Open my eyes.

"I told you. I can't do anything. I don't even know what you want me to do."

Dr. Milkovich just looks at me.

"It was just a party trick, okay?" My voice sounds high in my ears. "A fake, to impress a girl. My friends fed me the information beforehand."

She looks at Dr. Lennon.

"He's lying," he says, matter-of-fact. "It's all over the place."

"Try again, Mr. Lukin," she says.

I grit my teeth. I pretend again, don't do anything. I look up, shrug. If I don't say anything, they can't tell I'm lying, right?

"Lying," he says.

"Jacob." Liesel's voice blasts from a speaker somewhere on the ceiling. "Do I need to come speak with you? We have an agreement."

I stare at the camera. I can't do it. Not here. If I do it here, on record, they'll have evidence. Proof. I can't. It's too dangerous. It goes against everything Dad ever said.

"Doctors, you may leave for a moment. I need to speak with Jacob alone."

The red light goes off and they leave, not looking at me. I'm still strapped to the chair, stuck. A couple minutes later Liesel comes in, holding a tablet computer. She walks calmly around the table, pulls a chair close to me, and sits. Sets down the tablet, folds her hands on the table, and looks at me. She doesn't seem surprised, or even pissed. Like she expected this.

That's not good.

"This is sooner than I wanted to have this conversation, Jacob. By not cooperating you've forced my hand, before we've even started." She tilts her head, studies me. "What do you think we're doing here, exactly?"

I don't answer.

She turns my chair, fast, so I'm facing her, knee to knee. She leans in. I try to shrink away, but there's nowhere to go.

"We're doing tests," she says, still calm. "Simply tests. But we are using a lot of government resources, on a Saturday, to accomplish these tests. And the tests must be accomplished, must be successful, before you can go home." She pauses, studies me. "You do want to go home again, don't you, Jacob?"

My breath hitches. "Yes."

Her soulless eyes, shark eyes, are close to mine. "Because it's possible—very possible, right now—that you stay here. That you never see your mother or your sister again." She sits back in her own chair. "Let me show you something."

She props the tablet in front of me, turns it on, and presses the play button.

It's a video—grainy, but recognizable—of me at the party. Waiting for Caitlyn to come back with the object.

I look awful. Wasted, slurring, hair falling into my face.

But then Caitlyn comes back, and I tunnel to her sister.

It's surreal. My face goes blank and smooth. My voice is deeper, distant, as I recite the details. Even though I know what's happening, it's freakishly impressive. She lets the video go through the tunnel to Rachel's dad. When I open my eyes on the screen, Liesel hits stop.

"So if it's proof you're worried about," she says, "I have proof. It's too late for that."

I swallow. *Too late* echoes in my head. "But it was a fake—"

"No. It wasn't. The people upstairs have seen this already. It's why you're here, why I have any funding for this project, these tests. There has already been discussion of whether it is a national security risk to let you return home, with adversaries interested in you. That it could in fact be extraordinarily valuable to the national security of this country to keep you right here—or more likely, in a secure location." She leans forward again. "I have spent considerable effort trying to convince them otherwise."

Mom. Myka. Home.

"No." I choke it out.

She pats my leg. "I understand, Jacob. I don't want that for you either. I believe, personally, that you would be far more useful to us if you are happy, if you are out in the world living your life, protected. If you help willingly, now, we'll be able to do that. To keep you all safe."

I go very still. It sounds like she's offering me a deal.

She studies me again. "I want this project to succeed. I want your skills to be an asset to this country. But I need your full cooperation—and I mean full, here and in what we will ask of you in the future. If you grant us your full, willing cooperation, with all that we ask, you can return to your life at the end of the day." She smiles, white teeth through red lips. "There is more, of course. Further details, but we'll discuss those after the tests. The . . . successful tests. Do you understand?"

It's a hell of a deal: you're here and we'll lock you up forever right now—and no one will have any idea what happened to you—or do well on our tests and maybe we'll let you out. What can I do? I can't choose Door #1, the instant padded cell.

"Yes."

"Yes, you'll cooperate?"

I nod, silent. I don't want to say it again.

"Excellent. I'll go back to the observation room, and we'll try this again." She pats my arm this time. "I'm certain we will have better results."

The doctors come back and get all set up in their positions without a single comment. I still have the ring clutched in my hand. When Dr. Milkovich gives me the signal, I hunch over it. Close my eyes and let it come, the glow, the buzzing. I speak what I see.

A man, middle aged. Medium height, beer belly, black-rimmed glasses. Dark, wispy hair, combed flat. Tan slacks and a doctor's coat. Location: Arlington, Virginia. 3701 North Fairfax Drive, twelfth floor, lab 1235. He sees a bunch of squiggly pink things, outlined in a circle of light. A microscope. Without looking up, he says, "The SD CC 1b is definitely showing signs of preferential hydrolosis . . ."

I set the ring on the bag. "This guy's two floors down."

"It's a test." Dr. Milkovich says, even. But she has the look Mrs. Timmerman had at the party, times ten—like her fantasies have come true. Dr. Lennon peers at his screen like it has the mysteries of the universe on it.

Wonderful.

I bag up the ring and pass it back to her, and answer some questions for the Machine. She slides me another bag. This one has a small slip of paper folded in quarters, so worn it's yellow and falling apart at the creases. I pluck it out carefully, with two fingers, and hold it in my hands.

Another man. He's old, tufts of gray hair like steam escaping from his ears. A gray, grizzled beard. Location: Toulouse, France. Place de Capitole. A small café on the edge of the plaza. He has a false leg—I can feel the joint aching, at the knee. He rubs it absentmindedly. He sits in the sun at a table with a bright red umbrella, a cup of coffee in front of him: white china in a plain white saucer. He lifts his chin to survey the plaza, the noise of the crowd floating past. He raises the coffee, sips. He feels calm, content.

I let the paper fall, open my eyes. Odd to do two in a row like that. The only other time I'd done that was at the party. I feel a little disoriented, jerked from one reality to another.

Dr. Milkovich scribbles like crazy.

"Was that real time? You were seeing what he is seeing right now, in France?" Dr. Lennon asks, his voice tinged with awe. *Yes.*

"Did you really feel what he was feeling? Physically and emotionally?" *Yes.*

More questions on how it felt, what I did, how I did it. The questions take longer than the tunnel. I wish there was a way to stop this.

Dr. Milkovich jumps up. "Excuse me for a minute." She thrusts her card in the door and runs out.

"She moves like a squirrel," I say.

Dr. Lennon chuckles—it's true—but doesn't respond. He's busy typing. Dr. Milkovich is probably talking to Liesel and who knows who else. Discussing me. How they're going to use me.

I wonder if I could kill a man just by telling the wrong person—by telling them—where he is.

The answer's obvious. *Yes.*

6

"Pain" by Alice Cooper

Nothing changes when Dr. Milkovich gets back. She hands me another bag—a brown comb—and I see a woman in California mowing her lawn. A gold pen shows me a man in Khartoum, Africa, sleeping. When somebody's sleeping that's all I can say: where they are, what they look like, and that they're asleep. I guess that's still useful for lots of things I don't want to think about.

Dr. Milkovich looks at her watch, which they didn't take away from *her*. "We'll do one more and then break for lunch."

That's good. I'm feeling kind of dizzy, with a smear of a headache at the edges. I need food. Caffeine. A piss.

She hands me a bag with a small, polished stone. It's a tigereye, striped in bright orange and gold. It's cool to the touch, slick. I rub it between my fingers—it feels good—and close my eyes.

Darkness. Cold. Nothingness.

I drop the stone. It clatters on the table.

My hands start trembling. I want to shove them in my lap, out of sight, but I can't. They're strapped down. "This person's dead." I swallow hard, so I won't get sick. "Don't ever give me things from dead people."

Dr. Milkovich's pen hovers over the paper. She doesn't look up. "You can tell whether a subject is dead or alive?" she asks carefully. "With certainty?"

Crap. They didn't know that. I bet that's pretty useful information in espionage and warcraft, huh? Dr. Lennon's watching me, waiting to see if his screen will light up.

I can try. "No."

He looks at his screen, shakes his head. "Again. Can you tell whether a subject is dead, with certainty, from their object?"

I sigh. "Yes."

Dr. Milkovich jumps up again and speeds out of the room without a word.

I lean my head back in the chair. I'd had, still hiding in the back of my mind, some hope that I could wriggle away from this future that's unfolding in front of me at the speed of their imaginations. Yeah, maybe it was foolish. But it was there.

It isn't there anymore.

After lunch we abandon the polygraph, thank God. Maybe now they know I'm telling "what I believe to be the truth." I already showed them enough tricks to get their panties wet.

Liesel leads Dr. Milkovich and me to another room, this one like a huge doctor's office. It has a few chairs, a hospital bed, my old friend the video camera, and a new doctor adjusting a different, bigger machine with sprouts of wires and a digital monitor. I recognize it: an EEG. To record my brain waves.

I stop, take a step back. "No."

"Jacob," Liesel says, her voice soothing. Meant to be soothing; really, kind of grating. "You agreed to do tests. This is part of the deal."

The memory is vivid, bright. I was fifteen, and Mom and Dad and I were sitting on the sofa watching *ER* reruns. It wasn't long before he died. The patient on TV had epilepsy, and they were hooking him up to an EEG. Suddenly Dad leaned over to me. *Don't ever do that, Jake,* he whispered in my ear. *Who knows what it would show.* I nodded once. We never talked about it again.

I take another step back, almost to the door. "You didn't say anything about *that*. You're not messing with my brain."

"This doesn't do anything to your brain," New Doctor says, smooth. "It's not capable of it. All it does is record what's going on. Like a blood pressure cuff, but for brain waves."

This guy doesn't look much older than I am. In fact, he reminds me of Chris, big and stocky, but with red hair. He looks like he belongs on a farm, or in *Oklahoma*. Or maybe the *Waltons*. Except he has a doctor's coat and a DARPA badge.

"I know what it does," I snap. "I won't do it."

The doctors look at Liesel, who sighs. "Full, willing cooperation," she says.

Damn.

The EEG setup isn't as bad as I thought, about the same time frame and discomfort as the polygraph. While New Doctor—his badge says Eric Proctor—sticks suction cups all over my head, I wonder what else they have planned for me, what I've agreed to. I wonder what it will show.

For now, I'm going home in a few hours—she promised—and that's going to have to get me through.

"So you're Jake, right?" New Doctor says. "With all the fuss we didn't get introduced. You can call me Eric." He sticks another suction cup in gel and plops it on my forehead.

"What, not Dr. Proctor?" I ask. I can practically see up his nose from this angle. "But it's so fun to say."

He laughs. "That's a good one. But I'm not a doctor. She is." He points at Dr. Milkovich, writing notes as usual in a corner. "But you can just call her Bunny. Everyone else does."

She gasps, and color actually comes into her cheeks. Her round blue eyes glare at him. "*Eric*. He is a *subject*."

He shrugs. "Doesn't mean he's not a person. We should treat him like one."

I actually feel a little better, for the first time since yesterday. "I like Bunny. It suits you."

She wrinkles her nose and starts writing again.

"That's it for the torture devices," Eric says, and turns a few knobs on the EEG. "Let's see what we've got."

I see a bunch of lines appear, tracking across the screen, before he turns the monitor away.

"Sorry, mate. Don't want to distract you." He nods to Bunny. "Ready."

She brings out the box, the red light on the camera goes on. Here we go.

I don't realize there's a problem until I've done three more objects, and my temples start to pulse. I don't say anything. It's a headache. I figure it's normal to get a headache after this much tunneling. It's a lot of mental effort, right? Like studying for a test, multiplied by a zillion.

I don't realize it's a serious problem until I do two more, and my head explodes with pain. At that point I don't have to tell anybody. My screaming probably alerts them just fine.

I'm going to die. Pain burrows into my head, then swells to take over every inch. It hammers from the inside of my skull, trying to break free. Throbbing, sizzling pain. I can't think, can't move. Nothing in the world but pain, and my screams, over and over.

Make it stop. Please. Make it stop.

Liesel is there, and Dr. Milkovich and Eric and some other people. I can hear them, shouting orders, running. I can't see them, because I can't open my eyes. There is only pain.

I *want* to die. It would make it stop, and that would be better.

Someone pries my mouth open, thrusts something—things—under my tongue. They taste like Froot Loops.

Within a minute or two the headache is completely gone. A sense of peace, calm, seeps into me.

I open my eyes. There are six or seven people staring at me. I breathe, slowly, staring back.

"Are you all right?" Liesel leans over the bed, her badge tapping against my arm. Tap. Tap. In rhythm. A good rhythm. I tap my fingers to it. Tap. Tap.

I smile at all of them. "Hello."

"The medicine will give him intense calm and a feeling of well-being, like incredible pot," a man in a doctor's coat says blandly. "He'll be like that for a couple hours; he will likely sleep. The pain should be gone by the time it fades."

"Hi," I say. "You have nice teeth," I say to Liesel. "White."

She sighs. "Okay, everybody but my team can go. Thank you for responding so quickly."

There is bustling, but I don't mind. It sounds good, friendly. It makes me happy. I'm floating, I think. Floating away somewhere nice. Like marshmallows.

"Oh, and Dr. Johnson?" Liesel says. "I'll need a good supply of that drug. Thanks."

Yes. A good supply of that drug. Excellent.

I smile at everybody. Then I fall asleep.

When I wake up Liesel's the only one there, sitting in a chair by the bed. "Hello," she says, fake bright. "It looks like you've had enough for the day."

I sit up, rubbing at my head. I've been de-suction-cupped, and the camera is off. "What happened?"

"Your brain did some interesting gymnastics. It's a good thing we had you on the EEG, or we would've had no idea what was going on. Are you okay now?"

I shrug. There's no pain, no calm. Normal. "My head isn't going to fall off. That was quite a high, though. What the hell did you give me?"

She smiles, proud. "It's a new experimental drug for soldiers, called T-680. It induces theta level activity, to increase calm in battle. We gave you a rather large dose, hence the significant mood-altering. Aren't you glad you're working with DARPA?"

If I weren't working with DARPA I wouldn't have had the blinding headache in the first place. So, I have mixed feelings. "That's not enough for me," I say. "Thetas, gymnastics? What did the EEG tell you?"

I see her consider whether she should tell me. She nods. "Okay, let me try. It reported abnormal readings of delta waves during the . . . activity. Delta waves at any level are usually present only in deep sleep, but we've never seen delta waves quite like this."

Dad was right. Again.

She has her scientist on now, full teaching mode. "When you finished an object, there was a period of theta wave activity followed by normal alpha and beta activity. But after the last one, your brain transitioned directly from delta to beta without theta transition. The T-680 put your brain back into theta, giving you a chance to transition." She clasps her hands together. "We don't know why it caused pain—"

"Extreme pain," I add.

"—or why it happened. But if we hadn't had the T-680 on hand, I don't know quite how we would've stopped it."

Great. As if the tunneling weren't enough, now I have my own personal side effect to watch out for.

"Have you ever had anything like that headache happen before? Did you know that could happen?"

I shake my head. "I've never tunneled more than a couple times in a row before."

"Tunneled? That's what you call it?" She's intense again.

"Yeah." I pause, not really wanting to talk to her about it, but I'm in deep enough already. "That's what it's like. Like the object makes a tunnel to the person, and I just move through it to wherever they are."

She purses her lips. "Tunneling. I like it. I think that's what we'll call this project: The Tunnel. Now. If you're up to it, it's time we discuss the details of our arrangement."

God, she has the ability to just whip me in and out of emotions. I dive straight back into *tense*. "Okay."

"I was right—you are extremely valuable. And accurate. You got every single one right, down to the room. That's incredible." She waits, like I'm going to say thank you or something. I'm silent. "Thanks to your work today, the project has been approved to be fully funded, under DARPA control. The difficult part, as I said, was getting permission to work from the field. But I got it." Her smile this time is so wide I can see her back teeth. "You can continue to live at home, finish high school. We will post a security team for you, and we will work with you through them. For the most part, you won't even have to come to our facilities. We don't want anyone noticing anything out of the ordinary, so we'll keep to your normal schedule as much as possible."

It's scary as hell. Work with them on what? I've already agreed to full, willing cooperation, so it could be anything. Anytime. But after the past two days, the pseudonormality she's dangling is a relief, something I can live with. "And the people who were following me?" I ask. "The 'private' people?"

"We'll deal with them, I promise. You'll be protected. Oh, and I do think you should be rewarded for your time, Jacob. I believe in our first talk, you mentioned colleges you applied to? We can assist with that. If you help us fully, I can guarantee you'll be accepted to whatever college you want. Full ride."

"Stanford," I say, without a second thought. "History major. Public History / Public Service."

She nods, pleased. "Stanford it is. Look for your early acceptance in the mail."

God. Stanford. Just like that. I've wanted Stanford since . . . ever.

I'm not naïve. I see it for what it is: a deal with the devil. She has the stick, the carrot, the vague description of what I'll have to do for them with "full cooperation." But the carrot—my life, family, friends, future—I can't pass up. Maybe I should want to get into Stanford only on my own, but this is like having a connection. It opens the door so I can prove I'm worthy to be there.

And the stick I can't even think about.

"Fine," I say, "You have a deal." I thrust my hand out. She shakes it, her grip dry, firm.

"Excellent." She stands, brushes off her skirt. "Now let's get you home."

7

"Home" by Marc Broussard

Liesel's true to her word: I'm home in time for dinner. A car follows me from Starbucks, but it's a silver minivan—not Liesel and not the Durango. I figure it's my new "security," courtesy of DARPA. This is going to take some getting used to.

It's such a relief to have the familiar weight of my phone in my pocket, Dad's watch on my wrist. It makes me feel almost normal again. But the best, the moment that makes it worth it, is when I open the door to the smell of Mom's spaghetti sauce, and see Myk at the table, head bent, working on her usual mound of homework.

I stand in the doorway and blink hard for a second. "Hey! I'm back."

"Hey," Myk says, without looking up from *Principles of Chemistry*. As it should be.

In the kitchen, Mom's dumping hot pasta into a strainer. "Hi, sweetie." She smiles, briefly, as steam clouds billow up around her face. For a second she looks otherworldly, like a witch over a cauldron. "How was skiing?"

I have to remember they've had a normal day. *I've* had a normal day. It's time to activate Operation Massive Lies. To protect them.

"Good," I say. "The snow was kinda icy. But good. Can I help?"

"You can get your sister to clear the table. *Myka*!" she hollers, even though the dining room is ten feet away. "Can you get your books off the table *now* please? I've asked you three times. And set it, both of you. I'm serving up."

Myk grumbles, but I help her shift the books onto a pile on the floor, ready to pick up again after dinner. Genius School homework never ends, even on Saturday. We set the table team style, like usual: me, plates and glasses, her, napkins and silverware. In the middle of laying down Mom's fork, she stops and looks up at me, serious.

I don't want that look on me for long. She might burn through my skull or something.

"We should talk later," she says, low. "You know, about yesterday. Figure out what's going on. I have a couple ideas . . ."

I've had time to consider this—all those hours in the chair—and thought of a way to explain it that makes sense, as far as I can see. Operation Massive Lies part 2.

"Oh, yeah. I found out what that was." I straighten the napkin she set out for me, line up the fork with the edge. Look up. "Some of Chris's idiot drama geek friends were playing a trick on me. That creepy guy's a theater major at Georgetown. Pretended to be a hit man and freak me out, see what I'd do. Nice, huh?"

She blinks, narrows her eyes. "Really?"

"Yeah." I shrug and pick up a couple of glasses to go get ice, escape. "I'm sorry it scared you. Don't tell Mom, though, okay? She'd be mad you got tangled up in it. I'm gonna kick that guy's ass, if I see him again."

I sure as hell want to. I probably couldn't—okay, I couldn't. But I want to.

Her face lightens, and I let out my breath. "Good," she says. "You should. That was a douchy thing to do."

When did *douchy* become part of her vocabulary?

Mom comes in with the bowl of spaghetti, and we finish our jobs, and it all snaps back to normal.

It isn't till we're almost done eating that I'm reminded of my new reality.

Mom's drinking a glass of red wine, a sure sign that she's missing Dad. She does on weekends. Being alone, having to do all the things he used to do—I guess it's still hard on her. She seems relieved when it's time to go back to work on Monday. She fills her glass again and strokes the stem with her fingers, absently.

"So," she says. She clears her throat. "I have a family situation we need to discuss."

I put down my fork. Myk was ripping apart a fourth piece of bread—the girl eats like a ravenous beast—but she sets it down, with a glance at me. The last time we heard that phrase, it was followed by "your father's been in an accident."

Mom circles one finger around the rim of the wineglass. "I'm getting more responsibility at work. It looks like I'm going to have a lot of travel coming up, some of it extended. That's great, for the job. It's more money, and we could use it. But I'm already having a hard time keeping up with the house, and meals . . ." She meets my eyes. "And I know you're both plenty old enough, but I don't like leaving you alone all the time. I could use some help around here."

"Mooooooomm," Myk says, long, drawn out. "We're *fine*." She nudges me with her foot, under the table. "Jake, say we're fine."

I don't say anything. I wait. That's just the lead-in.

"I know we're fine." Mom sighs. "But we could be better. And this opportunity dropped in my lap. My boss's sister is moving, and they have this fabulous housekeeper they can't take with them. A live-in housekeeper, the finest references you've ever seen. She needs a place right away, and I really think we could use the help." She looks at us, one after the other. "And we have the spare room. It's perfect."

Myk and I are silent, for different reasons. Then Myk breaks it.

"A housekeeper? *Living* here with us? Like a *babysitter*?" There she goes, the first steps on the road to a major freak out. It's been happening more often lately.

I focus on Mom. Trying to be rational, make sure I have this straight. "Your boss recommended you take a live-in housekeeper?" Her boss, the deputy secretary of state. I smell DARPA. "When?"

I try to say it casually, but it comes out too loud.

She raises her eyebrows. "He called this morning." She sips her wine. "And really, I wasn't interested, and I said so, but he e-mailed me her résumé, her references. Jake, she sounds *perfect*. And he said since they were giving me the extra travel assignments, work would pay for it." She smiles at both of us hesitantly. "It's a no-brainer, really. As long as you kids are okay with it. I know it's unexpected, but . . ."

I set my hands flat on the table, for balance. It is DARPA. Planting security in my *house*. Through my *mother*. The same damn day I made the deal.

Myk plows ahead into full-on outrage, how this is a strike against her independence and she isn't a child and she doesn't need a babysitter, thank you.

I don't really listen. It isn't Myk who's getting a babysitter. It's me. There's going to be an agent with my family, living in my house, watching me. All the time. Right there to *take me in* if they ever choose to. I knew there'd be security, but I didn't think it would be like this.

Liesel is fast. And more powerful than I realized. Somehow it all feels a lot more real. I want to tell Mom no way in hell, not let this anywhere near them.

And yet I know what Liesel would say. It's for my protection, and theirs. I also *just* agreed to cooperate with everything.

Damn it.

"Jake? What do you think?"

Mom and Myk are both looking at me. Myk has tears running down her cheeks, which seems a bit over the top, but she is twelve. I meet her eyes. I wish I could back her up.

"I think it's fine," I say, dragging the words out of my mouth. "I think it's a great idea."

Mom's face eases sharply, and I have a flash of irrational panic. Is she pushing this because she *knows*? Because she's in on it all?

I shake myself. She doesn't know a thing. She's just being used, wants to please her boss, probably really does want the help. She worries about us. Even her boss probably doesn't know anything, really.

"I thought you'd agree with me," Myk says, low. "No one listens to what I say." She shoves her chair back and runs down the hall to her room, crying.

Mom drains her glass, lets out a long, slow breath. "Thanks for the backup. I think the housekeeper will be ready to start on Monday. I'll need you to help smooth it with Myk." She stands. "But I'll start now. By the way, I forgot to tell you. Grandpa Lukin called for you this morning."

"Grandpa Lukin?" I frown. "Why?"

She shrugs. "Said to call him back as soon as you got in. Oh, and he reminded you to call him on the landline."

I sigh. Not only is Grandpa Lukin—Dedushka—Russian and a little bit crazy, but he doesn't believe in electronics. No computers, TVs, video games, or God forbid cell phones. Landlines only, and that not often. I wonder if he even approves of movies, or if those are too modern.

Whatever it is, it's going to have to wait until tomorrow. I have a lot of catch-up texting and Internet stuff to do with Chris and everyone. And once Mom is done, I'll go talk to Myka. And then I figure I deserve about fifteen hours of sleep after last night, after today. I'm wiped. Yeah, about noon tomorrow will be a good time to face the world again.

At 6:00 a.m. the phone rings, and I ignore it. Someone else answers.

At 8:00 a.m. it rings again. I ignore it.

At 9:00 a.m. again, over and over, shrill, like someone screaming. I slam the pillow over my head. A few minutes later there's a bang on my door.

"Jacob!" Mom's voice. "You need to get up. Grandpa Lukin is on the phone, and he says he needs to talk to you *now*."

Oh, come on. I don't even have a landline in my room, and we have an old-style one. I'd have to get up, get dressed, and go out to the kitchen to get it. I groan.

"Jacob. Get your butt out here."

"Okay, okay. I'm coming."

Three minutes later, I pick up the phone. "Hello?" Even my voice feels rumpled.

"Yakob. You are all right?"

I stifle a yawn. "Of course I'm all right, Grandpa."

"Do not use that tedious word." I can practically see him scowling over the phone. It's a specialty of his.

"Sorry. Dedushka."

Mom walks by in her pink robe, a cup of steaming coffee in her hands. I wave at her. *Coffee,* I mouth. *Please?* She throws me an I-am-not-your-servant look, but heads back to the kitchen.

"Why did you think something was wrong?"

"It is no reason. I was poking at your father's things, and it made me to thinking . . . and I was suddenly worried for you, Yakob."

Ah. After Dad died Dedushka had gone through a period of being really attentive to me and Myka. He'd called all the time, dropped by every other week—which wasn't easy, from upstate New York. He's also extremely paranoid, with all these Russian superstitions I've never heard of before. Spitting over your shoulder three times for luck. You shouldn't hand a knife to someone, or it will bring conflict. But the attention had tapered off. We hadn't heard from him at all since Christmas.

"I'm fine, Dedushka. I promise." If you don't count secret government agencies. But I can't talk about that. I can't even think about it before coffee. Mom hands me a cup, black with a touch of sugar, and I slurp gratefully. She sits on the stool next to me, listening. Curious.

"Your mother said you went on a ski yesterday?" he asks, gruff.

"Yeah—yes, with a friend of mine. To Bryce."

Pause. "Very good. You must come here and visit me next weekend. We have the wonderful skiing here, and I wish to see you."

I blink. I haven't been to his house for years. "Okay."

"Good. It is set—you come see me next weekend. We have a good visit."

I guess I could do that. Even with a DARPA deal and babysitters, I can still go on a road trip. I still have a life. "Okay, Dedushka. I'll check with Mom and Myk to make sure they can—"

Mom raises her eyebrows.

"No. Just you, *malchik*."

I shrug at her. "Just me. Yeah, okay."

"Oh, and Yakob. When I was going through your father's things, I found a jacket I think you should have. Nice leather jacket. Yes? You can try it on when you are here."

I'm still not sure why I had to get up right away for this, but if he's worrying I guess it's all right. I don't want him to worry. "Sure, Dedushka. Thanks."

"Also, I could not find a watch that I knew he had. I meant to give it to you, but I do not remember . . . did I, or did I not?"

I rub the watch. It's stupid, maybe, but I sleep with it on—I have since I got it. It makes me feel close to Dad. "Yeah, you gave it to me. I'm wearing it right now."

"Ah." Pause. "Thank you, Yakob. I will see you soon, then."

He clicks off, and I set the phone down, take a big swill of coffee.

"What did he want so badly?" Mom asks. "So . . . ridiculously early and often?" Her hair's all wild, in dark swirls around her head—like mine, only a tiny bit longer—and she has makeup smudges under her eyes. She yawns. She must have been sleeping in too. Except for the phone calls.

"It's weird. He wants me to go see him next weekend in Standish. To go skiing, he says. And visit. Just me."

She purses her lips up. "Well, he's always been an odd bird, but it sounds like fun. It looks like I might be in Chicago next weekend, but I suppose you can go, if you don't have anything else on. If we like her okay, Mrs. Delgado will be here to stay with Myka." She perks up, gives me a wide smile. "See? It's working out already."

Mrs. Delgado, huh? I'm reserving judgment on how well *that's* going to work out until I see her for myself on Monday.

Crud. That's tomorrow. Plus school. Plus whatever else DARPA may bring.

Maybe it isn't too late to go back to bed.

8

"Eye on You" by Rocket from the Crypt and Holly Golightly

I'm late. Even after crashing most of Sunday, I still slept through my alarm. Almost twenty-four hours of sleep is apparently not enough after a marathon tunneling session plus headache plus experimental drug plus stress. The morning is a blur of shouting and throwing things: throwing clothes on, throwing my books in my backpack, throwing some food in my mouth. Nice and relaxing.

I manage to get Myk to her school on time, barely, but then I still have to make it back across town to VHS in Monday morning traffic. It's ugly.

It's fifteen minutes past the bell when I push into Mr. Vargas's class and stumble to my seat, muttering an apology. Then I pull out my calculus books, notebook, and figure out what the hell we're working on today.

So it's a few minutes before I realize that Eric Proctor is sitting next to me, head down, writing the problem from the board.

There's no doubt. It's him, red hair and freckles and all, wearing a black sweatshirt and jeans instead of his DARPA white coat and badge. My first thought is that I'm right: he does look my age. He fits right in here.

All the next thoughts are four-letter words.

I lean over, pretending to dig in my backpack, and whisper to him. "What are you doing here?"

He glances at me. "I'm sorry?" His lips hardly move.

"What the hell are you doing here, Eric?"

He shrugs, shakes his head, and drops right back into working on the problems, paying attention to Mr. Vargas.

It *is* Eric, isn't it?

I sit up, bang my knee on the desk, and swear under my breath. A few people laugh. Mr. Vargas shoots me a look, but I look straight back at him until he goes back to his talk.

It's him. He's pretending he doesn't know me, but it has to be him. I can't believe it. My house *and* my school. They're invading every part of my life. What am I supposed to do? Play along? Pretend like I don't know him either?

I did make the deal. But somehow I thought "we'll post security for you" meant there'd be . . . oh, security guards following me around at a good distance. Cars tailing me. Not strangers intertwining themselves into my school and my home.

They really are going to follow me everywhere. I can't hide from them, escape them. I am completely and utterly screwed.

When the bell rings Eric goes to talk to Mr. Vargas, not acknowledging me at all. I wait for a couple minutes, but it gets too stalkery and awkward and I have to leave for world history.

I'm sitting by Chris, trying to straighten my brain out enough for a halfway normal conversation about Operation Massive Lies part

3, the imaginary ski trip I had with my family on Saturday, when Eric comes in and heads straight for Mrs. Skinner, a slip of paper in his hand. He's in this class too.

She nods, white curls bouncing, eyes crinkling. Mrs. Skinner is ancient—the joke is that she teaches history because she's lived through it all. It's not a very good joke. It's still my favorite class, favorite subject.

My major when I get to Stanford. *Remember that too, Jake. This deal's not all bad.*

"Class," she croaks. "Please welcome a new transfer student, Ed Hanson. Ed, I believe there's a seat there at the back."

Eric nods to the room and threads his way through legs to the back. I watch him all the way, eyes slitted. Ed Hanson, huh?

"Have you met him yet?" Chris asks. "He looks fairly normal, for a midyear."

"No." I'm still watching. Eric/Ed looks at me and jerks his chin. A stranger's greeting. "I haven't met him yet."

But I have a thing or two to talk to him about.

After history I manage to hang back long enough to stop him on his way out. I lean in, so only he will hear. "Okay. Tell me. What the flying *fuck* are you doing at my school?"

He doesn't take the bait. He steps back, sticks his hand out. "Ed Hanson. Good to meet you. Jake, was it?"

I take his hand and squeeze it, a little harder than I need to. "Really, *Ed*? This is overkill, don't you think?"

He tugs his hand away, discreetly flexes it. "I hear you're a big shot on the tennis team," he says, loudly. "Maybe you can tell me when tryouts are?"

Tryouts? He's going to take over tennis too?

"Oh God no. Not another tennis freak." Chris is at my shoulder, though I don't know where he came from. "I was hoping for a little variety. Theater, maybe? Music? A rock band?" He puts out his hand, and Eric shakes it. "Chris Sawyer. Nice to meet you, man."

"Ed Hanson. Just transferred from DC." He meets my eyes. He's totally laughing.

He thinks this is *funny*? I'm freaking out. A government agent—is that even what he is? I don't know. A government person is talking to *Chris* right now.

"Oh, yeah?" Chris says, oblivious. "DC to Herndon. You're moving up in the world. That's like Hell to Hell's Kitchen." Chris is one of those people who gets along with anyone instantly. He could insult you five minutes after he met you, and you'd still like him.

Eric laughs. "As long as the girls wear those short little devil costumes? I am *in*."

They start walking down the hall together, and I trail behind, disbelieving. They really do look similar: same height, same basic build. Just one with red hair and one straw colored. My best friend, and my . . . bodyguard?

Twenty-four-hour bodyguards. Plus twenty-four-hour lying to everyone I know. Involving everyone I know. Shit.

"Hey, what lunch do you have, Ed?" Chris asks.

"C," I mouth silently. He'll have my lunch, for maximum bodyguard time.

Eric checks his paper. "C. What do you have?"

"We both have C too," Chris says. "You want to hang with us today?"

I wonder if it's always this easy. The deeper question is, does he do this often?

"Yeah, sure," Eric says. "Let me see what I have next . . ."

"English," I mouth.

He turns in time to see me, and bites his lip. "English, with Fowler."

"Jake has that too," Chris says. "You're both tennis freaks and

AP. You're like twinsies." He checks his phone, taps the screen. "Caitlyn's saving my seat in Econ. See you at lunch."

He takes off down the hall as we arrive at English. I stop Eric again outside the door. "I guess I don't know what to do here. What I'm supposed to do."

His face goes serious. "We'll talk later. Just keep cool, pretend you just met me. It's a piece of cake. Really." He grins again and pushes open the door, and I follow him.

Rachel is there, three seats back, wearing perfectly fitted jeans and a pink shirt that makes her cheeks look pinker than ever. She's writing something in her notebook, concentrating, her bottom lip in her teeth.

"Hey, Rachel." I smile at her hesitantly, remember her sitting with me at the party. That whole nightlong conversation. That couldn't have meant nothing, right? She gives me a tight half smile and looks back down. "Hey," she says, low.

Yeah. It's been just like that ever since the party. Ugh. But I haven't given up. Every day I say hi, every day I smile. A thousand ways to mess up your life in one stupid night, and counting.

Lily's in this class too, which adds to the torture. I steal a look at her, on the other side of the room, talking to Mike Weber. Her hair's curled today, blond waves down her back. Of course she doesn't even look at me.

But then I don't want her to. That's so over, and I'm glad. I'm way more interested in Rachel . . . if she'll ever talk to me again.

I drop into a seat in front of Eric, so I won't have to look at *him* and pretend more.

There's so much going on, in all parts of my life, that it feels like my brain might spontaneously explode. I have to not freak out.

The next period is study hall. It's my self-study research period for my senior project—Dr. Mathis, the vice principal, approved it special, so I could have a shot at Stanford. Time to go hang at the cemetery and work on my research.

I can't think of a justification for Eric to follow me there.

I zip up my coat and trek outside, down the street, and through the familiar gates. It's different today. It's still bare, the grass still brown. But the snow melted over the weekend, and it doesn't feel sad anymore, or creepy, like it did with that guy chasing me through it. Today I have it to myself again, and it's comforting. Like all these people—friends, almost, I've read so many of their stories, sat at their gravestones—went through worse than I have going, and they're past it now. This is my place.

"Hi, Jake."

My shoulders sag. I turn, slowly. Eric stands inside the gate, hands in his pockets.

"Hey there, Eric."

"Ed. You're going to have to watch that. I'm Ed now."

I sigh, rub at my chin wearily. "How did you even get permission to be out here?"

"Does it matter? We need to talk. It's a good time, great place. Is the caretaker here?"

I shake my head, not even bothering to wonder how he knows about Pete. "He's here Tuesday/Thursday/Saturday in the winter. Sometimes Fridays."

Like last Friday, when he saved me from that goon. I wish Pete were here now. But this one I have to deal with myself.

"Good," Eric says. "Then we'll have the other days to work. Lesson one: be aware of surveillance. A place this open, you have to watch out for satellites."

I look up instinctively, as if I'll see a red-lit camera trained on us from the sky, like a UFO. There's nothing but gray heavy clouds. Looks like snow later. "You're kidding, right?"

"Not kidding, mate. We don't want to attract some analyst's attention that something's changed. We need to either do exactly what you normally do, or find a good cover somewhere. I prefer the latter, especially today."

I want answers anyway. "I have someplace. Follow me."

I take him up the main drive, past Pete's little office building, around a couple corners. There it is: the Barker mausoleum. Huge, gray stone, with an iron gate across the front with a big padlock. The place reminds me of *Buffy*—like a Big Bad vampire is going to crawl out sometime, and I'll get to witness a major ass kicking. Unfortunately it's just a stone room with slabs and inscriptions. But I do have a key.

Eric—Ed—is thrilled. It's private, well covered from satellites, and apparently hard to bug because of the thickness of the walls. But he doesn't have too much time for his spy giddiness before I round on him.

"So. You want to tell me who you really are, *Ed*? I thought you were an EEG tech. Why are you in my school?"

He grins. "I said I wasn't a doctor. I didn't say what I was. As of now, I'm Ed Hanson. Fellow student, to them. Your primary DARPA handler, along with Ana Delgado, who will be stationed in your home. But you probably knew that."

Handler. Great. Good to know the terminology.

"And what's your job as my handler? To follow me around 24/7?" The thick walls trap the cold in, forcing it into my bones. I shiver and lean against the wall. It's even colder.

"To route work to you, for one. You'll work directly through the two of us. But primarily my job is to keep you safe."

I snort. "I'm sorry. You're not much bigger or older than I am. I don't see how you and a housekeeper are going to keep me sa—"

Before I can finish the sentence he whips a gun from his back, cocks it, and trains it on me. It's dull black, long, with a silencer attached. A foot away. Pointed at my chest.

I gulp, loud. It echoes in the small space.

I've never had a gun pointed at me before. In video games, yeah.

Lots. In games I've shot one a hundred times. It's different when it's real.

His expression doesn't change at all: still, relaxed. He clicks off the gun, and settles it in his back again. "Oh, I think we'll do fine. You all right, mate? You look a bit pale."

I press my palm against the wall. That fast . . . it could happen that fast . . . Jesus.

I can't believe he has a gun. At school, even. But he has it to point at *other* people. Other people with access to satellite pictures, who want to get at me. That guy with the pig eyes who followed me last week, maybe with a gun in his pocket. On second thought, that isn't really better. I swallow. Drop some of the attitude. "Yeah. Okay."

"Good. Now, if that's all the questions you have, I have some work for you to do. All right?"

"Work?" My voice sounds faint. I clear my throat. "But . . . I have to do my research. If I really want to go to Stanford, my project has to be perfect."

He raises his eyebrows. "I think you have Stanford taken care of, if I understand it right. Plus there's that full, willing cooperation?" It's funny how he can sound so easygoing, look like a farm boy, but now I can hear the steel underneath. Like I can sense the gun there, waiting.

"You can do your research Tuesdays and Thursdays, when Pete's here," he continues. "When he's not here, you're ours. Plus whatever Ana has for you in the evenings. If we have an object for you, you have to assume it's a priority. Work comes before everything else. You got it, Jake?"

I nod, slowly. That phrase—*full, willing cooperation*—is going to haunt me.

"Good. We only have one today, to start nice and easy. Tell me about this." He pulls a Ziploc bag out of his sweatshirt pocket and tosses it to me. This one holds a small silver key. I drop it into my palm, close my eyes.

Open them again. He has a minicamera out, trained on me. "Wait. What if I get the headache, like before?"

"Ana and I both have your medicine handy. We know what to do."

I guess that'll have to do. If all goes well, I won't need it anyway. I'd done a ton of tunnels before it happened last time. I settle my back against the wall, take a deep breath. Let it come, filling me with warmth.

A man. Fiftyish, small, but powerful. Leathery brown skin, dark hair to his shoulders. Location: Colombia, near the border with Venezuela. Puerto Carreño, in Vichada. An area called Caño Narizón. He's in a tent, on a patch of high ground in the middle of a vividly green tropical swamp. He sits on a camp chair, reading a report. The bug clicks and bird calls are constant, almost deafening.

"What does the report say?"

I open my eyes, snapped out of it. "What?"

Eric watches me intently. "I need you to read the report he's looking at. Read it aloud."

"It's in Spanish. And you can't interrupt me in the middle like that. I may not be able to get back."

"Try," he says dryly.

I close my eyes. See the guy again, his location.

He's reading a report. He turns a page and grunts to himself, pleased. Things are going well.

Usually I have only a general description of the person, a sense of their surroundings, and what they're feeling. I try to focus on the page in his hand. It swims, blurred, the words jumping. Then it starts to come clear. The weird thing, though, is I don't actually read the Spanish words in front of me. I understand what *he's* reading.

Semisubmersible run up the Orinoco River a success. Have successfully run four times to Barrancas, each time carrying 1.1 tons of product. Recommend building another submersible ASAP. Best place to build in forests near Puerto Ayacucho.

He closes the report, sips at a strong, sweet drink, and laughs.

I come back. Eric is happy, no steel underneath at all. He turns the camera off, tucks it in his pocket, and reaches for the key. "That's your first real work. Well done, Jake. We've got the location of a major drug runner, and know where to get proof, where he's going next."

I rub my head. I don't have a headache, but I do feel a little off, woozy. My watch beeps: the alarm that it's time to start packing up. That seemed short. "We've got to get back."

He nods. "You're right. We have lunch with Chris."

Ugh. The lying and pretending part—especially to Chris and my family—is harder than tunneling on demand. At least *that* I'm good at.

I'm the only one who's good at it. And I just identified the location of a Colombian drug runner. Huh.

Definitely something to get used to.

9

"Sister" by Dave Matthews and Tim Reynolds

I was right about the snow. It's wet, with heavy, fat flakes piling up fast. I have to drive slowly, peering through the windshield. My tail is slogging through it too, a blue sedan trailing thirty feet behind like a loyal dog.

Myk is quiet in the back, chin on her fist, watching the snow. When we pull into the driveway, Mom's car is in the garage and there's another car—a white, unmarked van—in the second space. Dad's old space. I meet Myk's eyes in the rearview mirror.

"She is *here*." I make my voice all menacing, and do a vampire laugh. "You ready?"

I'm not ready, after a day spent with ~~Eric~~ Ed at my side every bleeding second. I could use a little breathing space between handlers. But I can deal—it's my bed to lie in. I have to help Myka with this one.

She takes a deep breath, thinks, then shakes her head. "I don't think so."

I pull behind the van, kill the engine. In the sudden silence I turn, so I can look at her square. "You know this has nothing to do with you, dorkus. Right?"

She looks at me sideways, her eyes wet. "No."

"I'm serious. Mom doesn't think you need watching, or that you're not helping enough. She just had this offer, and it was too good to refuse."

She shrugs. "It feels wrong, having a stranger here. Why is she doing it? I don't get it."

She feels it, somehow: that this isn't as simple as it seems, a housekeeper who just happened to fall in our laps. She just doesn't know what it *is*. And she won't. Ever.

"It'll be all right," I say, gentler. "I swear. I'll make sure it's all right for you, one way or the other. Okay? Trust me?"

She tucks her hair behind one ear, eyes on me, and nods. If I ever let her down on something I really promised, I think it'd break both of us.

"All right," I say. "Let's go face the dragon."

That probably isn't a good thing to say. Not positive. But it does make her laugh, and that's all that matters right then.

"Hello," I call when we come in and drop my keys in the bowl. I set a hand on Myk's skinny shoulder.

There she is, sitting at the table with Mom, drinking coffee.

Christ, she looks like Salma Hayek. Midthirties, Latina, gorgeous smooth skin. She's wearing a black sweater, her hair pulled back in a low bun. I cough with the surprise of it. Her mouth curves up, dark eyes on me.

"You must be Jacob and Myka." She stands and stretches out a slim hand, a silver bracelet dangling from her wrist. "I am Ana Delgado. So nice to meet you."

The accent is faint, but there. She really is Spanish, or Spanish-speaking, not just as a cover. Or she's really good at accents. I wonder if she has a gun hidden in a back holster too.

She takes Myka's hand first, then mine. Her handshake is firm, strong. She smiles again, this time at Myka. "I hope you do not mind so very much my coming to help here. I believe this situation will work out well for all of us. Perhaps we can be friends, in time?"

Her eyes flick to me, and reality floods in. I have to remember who she is, and why she's here. She may be here to protect me, but she's not my friend.

Myk visibly brightens, though. "Nice to meet you," she says, polite, if quiet.

Mom relaxes. She must've been expecting fireworks. Then she frowns at me. "Jake?"

I realize I haven't said anything. "Oh. Welcome, Mrs. Delgado." I stop. Then I add, "So nice that you could come at such short notice."

She laughs, a round, full laugh. "Oh, that. That is no trouble at all. I am so happy to have found you."

I bet.

She gestures to the empty seats at the table. "Shall we sit and get to know each other before dinner? I brought enchiladas, to show your mother I can cook. I will make salad. I thought we could eat in an hour or so?"

Myk shifts, uncomfortable again. "Oh . . . I have too much homework to do. Sorry."

"Me too," I say, quick. "Got to get on that homework. But we'll see you at dinner."

And whatever comes after that.

She waves us off. "Of course. We will continue our chat, your mother and I." Her eyes narrow, a touch, at me. "She has so many good things to say about you."

Spy translation: She's pumping my mother for information before she moves on to me. Excellent.

Once in my room I take out my phone and text Chris, just because it makes me feel normal.

Housekeeper is def a dragon. But damn she is hot. Salma Hayek, anyone?

He comes back right away.

I need me some housekeeping. Can I come over and play?

Yeah, definitely more normal.

Come have dinner tomorrow and see for yourself.

I know he has *Oklahoma* tech rehearsal tonight. But tomorrow will be perfect. I drop into my desk chair and spin, already looking forward to the buffer. If Chris is here, she can't do anything wonky, can she?

Maybe I should just have Chris around all the time.

Can't. Tech rehearsal tomorrow too. After show is over will come dragonate.

Damn. I really am on my own for a while. Me, my family, and my handlers.

But expect a surprise in a minute . . .

A surprise? Like I need more surprises in my life right now. My phone buzzes again. A message from an unknown number.

Jake? Hi. It's Rachel.

I draw in a sharp breath. No way.

Chris gave me your number. Hope that's okay.

YES, I want to say. YES. But I count . . . one, two, three . . . before typing.

Yeah. That's cool. What's up?

Through the walls I can hear Ana's voice, musical, talking to my mother. I try to ignore it and what it means, stare at the phone. At what normal looks like. A normal girl.

Just hi. Sorry I've been weird. Oh, gotta go. Our scene. Talk tomorrow?

I type fast, so she can read it before she has to leave.

Sure. See you tomorrow.

I add her number to my contacts, grinning to myself, then give

Chris a virtual high five. He said he'd talk to her about me, if he had a chance. Thank God for best friends. I allow myself a minute of imagining Rachel . . . kissing her . . .

Then I dig out my calculus stuff, because I really do have work to do, especially to make up for this morning.

I don't care if I do have a Stanford acceptance from DARPA. I still want to earn it.

I don't remember the first time I tunneled. When I was little it used to happen all the time, accidentally. Random images, sounds, emotions would flick through me when I touched things. I thought it was normal. I learned quickly which things not to touch, what I didn't want to feel. Things from dead people, mostly.

I do remember the first time I did it on purpose.

I was six and a half, and Myk was a baby, about four months old. I thought she was a tiny monster. She was always fussy, bawling her lungs out day and night. Sucking up every second of my parents' time and attention. I wanted nothing more than to send her back.

We were alone for a few minutes, which was rare. I don't remember where we were living. Military housing somewhere. Dad was out mowing the lawn—I remember hearing the comforting buzz of the mower, smelling the fresh grass through the open windows—and Mom was in the kitchen. Myka was sleeping in her car seat on the floor while I played with plastic dinosaurs.

I must have *rawwrred* a little too loud, because she woke up and started screaming.

"Jakey?" Mom called, frazzled. "Can you just watch her for a couple minutes? I can't come right this second."

"Okay," I called back, and Myka screamed harder.

I stared at her, her little face scrunching, washing completely purple in seconds. Why was she *doing* that? What was worth getting that upset about?

I guess a normal kid would have picked up her binky and put it in her mouth, to make her stop. I picked up her binky, cradled it, and closed my eyes.

I could see her, just as she was—that wasn't a surprise. I could hear the same things I could before. But everything seemed magnified, distorted. The mower was obscenely loud, terrifying. Mom's clanks in the kitchen, the water running, added to it, so the noise was almost unbearable. The breeze through the window was cold, a shock on her skin. She opened her eyes and I saw myself, sitting cross-legged in front of her, eyes closed. I looked huge. The room was all huge, too bright, too many colors and shapes, all unknown, without meaning. All scary.

Shhhhhh, I thought. *It's okay, little one. Nothing's going to get you.*

Her eyes moved back to me.

That's me. I'm Jake, I thought. *Your big brother. I'll protect you.*

She stopped crying, like a tap turned off. Watched me, flailing her fists in the air.

I'll teach you about all these things. Don't worry. I'll keep you safe. I promise.

I opened my eyes, and I swear she smiled at me.

She wasn't overly fussy after that if I was around. If she started that awful crying, I'd find a quiet place somewhere, hold her binky or her blanket or whatever, and tunnel to her. With her I could actually communicate—in feelings then, if not words—not just see. She also knew I was there in her mind, which nobody else ever seemed to. I figured it was because we were blood—or maybe she had a tiny bit of what I had. We didn't talk about it. But tunneling calmed her, always. Even as we got older I did it every once in a while, when I wanted to check on her, or when I knew she was having a rough day.

Like now.

I close the calc book—assignment done—and pull a folded note out of my wallet. *I love you Jake,* it says, with a heart, in shaky red crayon letters. She'd given it to me when she was six. I hold it in my hand, let my head drop forward.

She isn't studying, for once. She's lying on her back on top of her blue comforter, hair fanned out around her, staring at the white popcorn ceiling. Her old stuffed animal, Horse, is next to her on the pillow, its worn-down brown fur soft against her cheek. She's worrying. But not about Ana. About me.

I'm fine, I think. *You don't have to worry. It's all going to be okay.*

I see the ceiling, feel Horse against her cheek. Feel her awareness of me. She relaxes, a little.

No more worrying, I think. *Just do what you usually—*

"I'm not sure I like the idea of you doing that on your own."

I turn, the note clenched in my hand. Ana stands in the doorway, arms crossed. Despite the warning in the words, her expression is friendly.

I don't feel friendly. I feel invaded. "The door was shut. Doesn't that mean it's my private space?"

Her lips pinch. "I do not think you understand this situation yet, Mr. Lukin. You no longer have private space. Not from us. Not if we're to protect you."

I meet her eyes straight on. "It's been three days since I made this deal. Since any of this happened. Maybe you guys could give me a little time to adjust to the complete loss of my privacy?"

She smooths her hair, considering. "Yes. That is true. I will keep that in mind." She drops her arm, the bracelet jingling. "I came to call you to dinner. But I think we should establish a rule of no private . . . tunneling . . . until we can discuss the implications. Yes?"

I lift my chin but don't reply. I'm not agreeing to that. Tunneling is mine, like always. I'm just letting them use it.

She nods as though I agreed. "Dinner in five minutes, please. I will go and fetch your sister."

I carefully replace the folded note in my wallet, check Dad's watch. Five minutes will give me plenty of time to bang my head on the desk a few times before going to face dinner.

Dinner is polite, awkward. Lots of silences. The most exciting thing we discuss is that Mom is going to Chicago on Thursday for four days, leaving us in the capable hands of Ana.

I can't believe this happened so fast. Myk actually seems to like her, so I do my best to cooperate and act as normal as I can. Though I'm awkwardly aware of her, of what she is.

When we're done with the (tasty) enchiladas, there's a moment when none of us know what to do. Ana pushes back her chair, stands. "Jacob, will you please help me clear the table?"

I shoot a look at Mom—*am I supposed to help the housekeeper clean?*—but she shrugs.

"Sure."

Mom and Myk head off to the living room to watch *Mythbusters*—Myk's favorite show, where something always gets blown up and mysteries of the science world are revealed—while I help Ana bring plates to the kitchen.

She doesn't say anything at first. She fills up one side of the sink with hot, soapy water, lays a towel out next to it, and stacks the dirty dishes on the counter.

"You know we have a dishwasher," I say.

She glances at me, and pushes her sleeves to her elbows. She carefully unclasps her bracelet and drops it in her pocket with another jingle. "Some things are best done the old way."

I can't help myself. "Like interrogations? Firefights?"

"I am here to help you, Jacob," she says quietly. "To protect you and your family. Just like Ed is. You do not have to like the situation, or me. But please do remember why I'm here."

"Sure." I lean on the counter, twisting a dish towel in my hand. "Completely altruistic on DARPA's part."

"No one said that." She plunges her hands into the water, wiping a plate with one of Mom's blue-striped woven cloths. Myk made that in third grade. "It is of mutual benefit. And I will assist your mother as well. It is good for everyone."

Her sweater rides up at the back as she leans forward, and I peek. No gun that I can see.

I lower my voice further. "Are you carrying a gun? Like Ed?"

"A gun?" She laughs a little. "No." She rinses the plate, sets it on the towel, and moves on to the next. Then she winks at me with mile-long eyelashes. "I carry guns when I need to, but I much prefer knives."

Of course.

She picks up a dirty kitchen knife—a big one—from the counter, dips it carefully in the soap, then the water. She turns it slowly, examining the blade, running her finger along the edge. Without looking, she holds out a hand to me. I stare.

"Towel?" she asks.

Right. I hand it to her and she wipes the knife clean, slides it back into the rack. Then she smiles disarmingly. A genuine smile, unlike Liesel's. "Thank you, Jacob. I don't need you any more right now."

I swallow hard, and leave. I know it was a show, that she was displaying her power just like Eric had. But she did it well.

This is going to be interesting.

When *Mythbusters* is over Mom surreptitiously herds us to her bedroom, checks over her shoulder, and shuts the door.

"So? What do you guys think?" she asks. "Will she work? Do you feel comfortable with her?"

She flops onto the bed. Myk does too, tucking her legs up Indian-style. I move a pile of Mom's clothes and sit on her chair. They look at me, two pairs of identical green eyes.

What can I say? If I say I hate her, DARPA will just figure out another way, another person. And she isn't awful.

I shrug. "She seems fine. As long as you're sure of her references, and she's not a crazy drug addict or anything. I'm good with it."

Mom laughs. She looks content, like some stress has been lifted already. "I'm sure of that. Myk?" She leans over and runs her hand down Myk's hair, flipping the ends up with her fingers. "What do you think?"

Myk shrugs too. "I guess. She's better than I thought she'd be. Can you ask her to leave my room alone if I promise to keep it clean myself?"

"Absolutely," Mom says. "I think that's an excellent deal."

At least they're happy. As long as Ana doesn't fuck that up, we'll be cool. Well, as long as she doesn't fuck that up or knife me. Guns by day, knives by night.

"I have something else to bring up," Myk says, eyes on Mom, then me. "I think we should do Glue."

"Glue?" Mom says, soft. "We haven't done that since . . ."

"The funeral," I finish. Tears spring into Mom's eyes, and I wish I hadn't said it.

Myk nods, solemn. She looks like an owl. "It feels like we should. With everything changing . . ."

Mom sniffs, then nods too, jerkily. "I think you're right. Your dad would like that." She touches Myk's hair again. "Good idea, sweetheart. Jake?" She stretches out a hand to me.

To keep them happy, I'd do an awful lot more than that.

I come and sit on the bed too, so we're in a tight circle. Mom rests one hand in the middle, palm flat on the bedspread.

"We Lukins stick together like glue," she says.

I lay mine on top of hers. It's weird, but my hand is actually bigger than hers now. I don't think it was last time. When I was sixteen. "Together we can make it through."

Myk's hand is cool over mine. "Anywhere we choose to roam," she says, her voice wobbly.

There's a short silence. The last line was Dad's.

Mom sets her other hand on top of ours. "Together we will make it home."

We all bow our heads, hands linked.

Dad made us do that rhyme every time we moved—in the early years, when we moved a lot with the air force, before he was stationed at the Pentagon—and every time somebody was having a major problem. It's cheesy, yeah, and it would be really easy to mock. But I wouldn't dare. It was Dad's. And it always seemed to help.

After a bit we let go, and Myk throws herself into Mom's arms. Then mine, in a bear hug. I squeeze her back as hard as I dare. She seems small, breakable.

"Together we can make it through," she whispers in my ear. "Don't do it alone, Jake."

I let go and meet her eyes an inch away. They're powerful, pleading.

I wonder exactly how much my sister sees after all.

10

"Hostage" by Marking Twain

Rachel's not in class the next morning. Someone says she had a doctor's appointment or something, but I take it as a bad sign. I didn't sleep last night, thinking too much, so today everything's getting under my skin. Maybe it's good she wasn't here. I wouldn't want to blow it *again*.

Eric walks with me across to the cemetery at fourth period, schlepping through the ankle-deep snow. I'm glad Pete's there and I don't have to do any tunneling today. I just want to be left alone. Which, of course, I can't be. For a single freaking second.

My mood must be obvious. "You all right, mate?" Eric asks.

"I'm not your mate," I snap. "What are you, British?"

He stops on the sidewalk, looks at me.

I shake my head, keep walking. "I'm just tired." And lonely, lying to everyone. And . . . I don't want to think about it.

"Okay, then." We're quiet for a while, walking. "You know," he says, "if the stress of this is too much for you—it is for some assets, there's no shame in it—we can drop it all."

I glance at him.

"We could take you to a nice, quiet room of your own . . ."

"Skip the threats today, okay?" I walk faster, pushing ahead of him. We pass through the gate, down the main drive. I have work to do in the northwest section. "I get it already. Can you just let me do my own work for once?"

He grabs my elbow, stops me cold. "Look. Jake. I don't mean it as a threat, not really. It's an option you should honestly consider." He lets go of my elbow. "This double life is tough, especially if you're not trained for it. Sometimes it's truly better for everybody if you just—"

"Fuck you," I say. "Just do your job."

Eric's gaze sharpens on something behind me, and I turn. Pete's marching purposefully toward us from his office—you can practically hear the ground thumping. When he reaches us, he stops, folds his arms.

"Hey, Pete," I say, casual.

Pete looks even more wild today, in a beat-up brown jacket down to his knees. Like a dirty bear. "What you boys up to?" he growls. "You know it's only supposed to be you, Jake. This place ain't for loitering. Or messing around. Stupid kids were drinking in here last night again . . ." He wrinkles his nose. "Don't need more trouble."

I nod. "No worries, Pete. This is my—" I pause. "My mate, Ed."

Eric sticks his hand out. "Hey. I'm going to help with his research. I swear I won't make trouble."

Pete ignores his hand. "Where you workin' today?" he asks. "I've got to shovel all the paths, so if you could stay out of my way—"

"Barker Hill," I say. "I'm doing the 890s."

Pete nods, satisfied. "Already cleared that bit." He glares at Eric again. "See you later, Jake."

He turns and stomps off.

Eric half smiles at me. "Character, huh?"

"Don't."

I head up the hill to the left, to the very far corner, Eric on my heels. It's one of my favorite places to sit in spring and summer—the graves there are up at the top of a nice slope, with a view all around. There are scrubby oaks and a small patch of aspens along the fence. When the leaves are on they make a soothing, peaceful sound, rattling in the breeze. In winter they're still stunning, tall and straight, with eye patterns on the white trunks. But they're silent.

I want silent, so it suits me.

I drop my backpack on the ground and pull out my tools: notebook, pen, camera. A copy of *Fairfax County, Virginia Gravestones, Volume IV,* for reference. The first grave today is an oldie, the white marble mottled with lichen and dirt. I take a picture, then write the text in my book. Alda Thomas. Daughter of P. T. and B. P. Springer. 1831–1891. Sixty years.

"What are you doing with these, anyway?" Eric asks.

I look at him—squatting a couple feet back, watching me—then turn back to my notes.

He laughs. "You're acting like a surly old woman. Just answer the bloody question and then I'll leave you be for a bit, all right?"

I grunt. "I'm doing an analysis of the burials, and what you can tell about the families and social dynamics of the community by how they buried and recorded their dead." I challenge him to make fun of it with a look.

He doesn't. He seems mildly interested. "And do you touch the stones to get information about the people?"

"God, no. They're *dead*."

His eyebrows fly up. "I thought you could—"

"I can tell if someone's dead. But that's all. Weren't you there when . . . ?" I remember—when I tunneled with the tigereye, that was before he came. I shake my head. "It's horrible, like tunneling to a black hole. It makes me physically ill. I asked them not to give me any of those."

I turn back to the next gravestone. We're both quiet. They'll give them to me anyway. He will. We both know that. And lots of other objects I can't even imagine.

"I'm sorry," he says. I think I hear him say, at least.

He keeps his word after that and leaves me alone, and I manage to finish the row before my watch beeps, and we head back across the street.

We're at lunch—me, Jeff, Chris, Eric, and Kadeem, all with pizza. We sit at our usual table. The girls—Caitlyn, Lily, and the rest, including Rachel—sit together four tables down.

It's the moment of truth, isn't it? Did she really want to talk to me? Will she acknowledge me with Lily right there?

I don't know how I liked Lily for so long. I mean, she's ridiculously hot and all. But . . . okay, I was distracted by the hot. But now that I'm away from her pull, I can see there's more than that. Like smart girls. Girls who can talk about politics and graphic novels.

I glance their way, trying not to be too obvious. Rachel meets my eyes, smiles, and waves, small. But a wave.

I grin back, not hiding anything.

When I look away, I catch Eric watching me.

Eric's cell buzzes. He gives it one look, then jumps up and takes it outside.

"Girlfriend?" Kadeem guesses.

I shrug. But I doubt it. I look over at Rachel again. She's laughing. She looks so . . . carefree.

A minute later my phone buzzes. Text message, unknown ID.

Make an excuse, come meet me in the band room. Now.-E

I don't even question. I say I've got to go see Coach Brammer and head out to the band room. It's a small soundproof building off by itself behind the gym. It's always locked during the day so nobody will skip off with the instruments. But the door's open. Eric's standing inside.

"How did you get keys to the band room?" I ask, incredulous.

He shakes his head. "You underestimate us. Close the door. I've got work—and this one's an emergency. They just messengered it over."

I sit at a desk, and he hands me a Ziploc bag. It holds a long silver chain with a pendant of two fish twined together. An emergency? Like somebody's going to commit a crime right now and I have to witness it or something? I drop it into my hand, close my eyes.

It's a woman. She's medium height, skinny, hair in a dark bob at her chin, wearing business clothes. Her eyes are bright blue. Location: an empty, rundown office building, the west side of Detroit, along the river. 1800 West Jefferson Avenue. She sits in a chair, her feet bound, her wrists tied behind her back. There's something in her mouth: hot, dry, sawing at her lips. A gag. She's crying behind the gag, little panting sobs. A man stands in front of her, watching. A normal looking man, except for the very large knife in his hand. He presses the point of it against her cheek, slicing the skin, filleting her, as she screams—

"That's enough, Jake."

I open my eyes. My hand is pressed to my right cheek, still holding the pendant. My throat is raw. I must have screamed myself. I'd felt the pain of the knife. The panic of that woman. The helplessness.

That is happening to her right now. For real.

Eric paces on the other side of the room, talking intently into his phone. After a couple minutes he puts it away and sits at the desk next to mine. We both stare forward at the wiped blackboard, the music stands jumbled in the corner, the collection of drums. It all seems farther away than that woman. I pinch the back of my hand, hard, to bring myself out of it.

"Is she gonna be okay?" I know better already than to ask who she is, what's going on.

"If we get to her in time. We'd have had no chance without you."

He turns to me, his voice marked with respect. "She'd have been long dead by the time we found her, without you. You okay?"

I nod slowly, feel my unmarked cheek with my thumb. In slow motion I put the necklace back into the bag, seal it, hand it to him. "Maybe you can give this back to her."

"Maybe." He's silent a bit longer. "That one might help you understand, Jake. Why we push you. What you're doing—what you're going to do—is critical. People's lives will depend on it. If you can do that every time, a lot of people."

I'd never thought of a situation like that one, where I could actually, tangibly save someone. I hadn't thought DARPA, a research agency, would have people in situations like that.

Wait. I frown. "That necklace wasn't from DARPA, was it?"

He looks at me, steady.

"They messengered it . . . but it was from someone else. Like the CIA or the FBI. Other agencies do know about me, don't they? I thought Liesel was hiding me from them? That you guys were the only ones who knew?"

He shrugs, back to the freckle-faced innocent. "That answer's above my pay grade. You'll have to talk to Dr. Miller."

Crap. If the CIA or somebody else already knows what I can do, I'm in even deeper than I thought. No wonder I have all the security. But if Liesel lied to me about that, what else did she lie about?

"You ready to go back?"

I do go back: to lunch, class, tennis practice. But all of it—lectures, problems, serves, even Rachel and Chris—seems flat. Unreal. I can't get my head out of the woman, the knife slicing her cheek open. All the surreal complexities of my life since last week. I can't just go back to normal after that. After her.

As I turn out of school that night, a blue sedan that had been parked on the street falls in behind me. I'm tempted to wave.

But if I'm right, there's a black car following *them*.

11

"Living a Lie!" by Daniel Zott

The last couple of days have been crazy, nonstop. This morning, I have to make time for Myka. It feels like I've been dropping that ball, and that's the one I can't drop.

We're in the car, out of Ana's hearing. Our safe zone. "So," I ask. "What were you talking about last night, after Glue? What are you worrying about?"

It's scary to ask. It's not like I want Her Geniusness to figure out what's going on. But ignoring won't work with Myka.

She's quiet for a bit. She braids her hair as we drive, with small flips of her wrists. "You," she says finally.

"What about me?"

Quiet again, while she thinks how to say it. That's how she works: everything deeply considered. I've seen her take half an hour to decide what kind of sandwich to have. You have to be patient, wait for her. I watch the road unfold, dingy snow piled on the sides.

"I know something's going on with you, Jake."

I go from zero to sixty on the adrenaline scale, gripping the steering wheel.

"I just don't know what it is yet," she says.

I relax my grip. Breathe. Listen for what she actually does know, so I can do damage control.

"You've been acting strange since last Friday. Since that guy chased us. You're jumpy, distracted. And you just act *weird*." She finishes the braid, wraps a clear plastic band around the end, lets it swing behind her back, and finds my eyes, challenging. Adding up the evidence in her mind. "Are you doing drugs?"

I laugh in surprise. Everybody with the drugs. "Since Friday? No. I swear, Myk, I'm not doing drugs."

"Then what is it? You can tell me." She lifts her chin. "I can deal with it."

I shake my head. "I can't."

"So there *is* something. I knew it. Now you have to tell me."

I swallow. She's too persistent to lie to outright. Once she starts something, she's like an ant on a scent trail. She'll go over or around anything to get to what she's after. She'll never believe everything is normal. But above all else I have to protect her. She can't know anything about me and the government, the deal.

I have to confess a problem, but not the real one. Something she can relate to. What does Myka understand best?

Duh.

"Okay," I say, like it's a tough decision. "I'll tell you. But don't tell Mom yet, okay?"

Her eyes get big, and her lips press tight together like she's already keeping it in.

We come to a red and I have to stop, shift. I look at her in the mirror. "I know you're the smart one and all. But my advisor talked to me last Friday. There's a chance—a really good chance—that if I kick ass on my project, I'll get into Stanford. He knows the assistant dean of the history department, and he ran into him last week and talked about me. They're interested, Myk." I pause. "Stanford."

"Really?" Her breath gets fast, she's so excited. "But Stanford rejects ninety-four percent of their applicants."

"I *know*. That's why it's such a big deal, dorkus."

I drive for a while, tap on the wheel, and let her think about it. I even let myself think about it. With a Stanford degree in the public history track, I can get a job at a heritage site, or a museum. Ever since I first toured the Smithsonian on a second-grade field trip, I've wanted to work there. Work with real, significant artifacts like the Declaration of Independence. The original flag that flew over Fort McHenry. Silver-print photographs of the Civil War. Maybe I could do research and discover something important. Maybe even do tours for school kids like Myk.

"Stanford," she echoes. "That's awesome."

"Sorry I've been weird," I say, pressing it home. "I'll probably have to put in a lot of extra hours and stuff, making sure the project's perfect, keeping all my grades up. But I'm so close. It just kind of made me crazy."

She sits back in the seat, eyes shining. "Promise I won't tell Mom and ruin the surprise."

Something shifts, and I realize what I'm doing. Cold, hard lying. To *Myka*. It actually hurts, like a fist clenched in the pit of my stomach. She's the one I didn't have to hide around, ever. Didn't lie to. The only one who knew the real me.

But I have to do it to protect her. Don't I?

And they did promise me Stanford. So maybe it will come true, Stanford and the Smithsonian and all that goes with it, just like I said. And then she'll never know I lied.

When I walk into English, Rachel's there, looking up at me. "Hey, Jake." She smiles, her lips red today. Her dark hair's pulled into a low ponytail, but there's one strand loose, touching her cheek. I want to tuck it back behind her ear. At the same time I like it just like that.

I drop into the seat next to her, thankful Ms. Gieck (yeah, that's her real name) doesn't assign seats. Eric sits in front of me.

"Hey," I manage. "What's going on?"

I am. So smooth.

She looks down, rubs one finger across a dent in her desk. "I'm sorry I freaked out after the party." She shifts in her chair, still focusing on the desk. "That was . . . weird." She looks up, her eyes meeting mine. "Was that real? Or a trick?"

To my relief she doesn't look disgusted or put off, like everyone did at the party. Just curious. Still, I don't know what to say. If I say it was a trick, that makes me less of a freak. Look how much trouble I got into already by sharing. But if it was a trick then she'd think I lied, made up that part about her dad.

I can't lie to her.

"Real," I say, like it's no big deal.

She nods slowly. "I thought so. That part about my dad—" She sighs. "I didn't want to admit it, but it seemed right."

"Sorry," I say, quiet.

She shrugs. "Yeah. It's pretty crap."

Lily laughs, across the room, and I can't help but look. She's flirting with Mike again, leaning in close.

Rachel follows my gaze. "She doesn't say nice things about you. But—" She lowers her voice to a whisper. "She's not very nice."

"You," I say, "are very perceptive."

Ms. Gieck starts writing something on the board about the *Merchant of Venice,* and everybody quiets down.

Rachel leans over. She smells like vanilla, and suddenly I want cookies. "Caitlyn's having another party on Saturday, after dress rehearsal," she whispers. "I thought maybe you could come? You . . . don't have to do the thing again. Unless you want to. But we could hang out?"

Her eyes are a very deep brown. Sparkly. It's hard not to stare at them. At her. I want to go and hang out more than life itself.

But I have plans on Saturday. "Damn," I say. "I promised my grandpa I'd go see him this weekend. He's in upstate New York."

"Oh," she says, frowning. "That sucks." She realizes what she said. "I mean, not about your grandpa—"

Ms. Gieck starts talking about Shylock, and I have to turn to the front. "I wish I could come," I whisper sideways.

"I'm sure I'll see you around at something else," she whispers back. "Soon."

I grin, tap my pen on the desk. I totally didn't expect that. Today is looking up, in a big way.

Eric raises his hand and asks to go to the nurse's office. He grabs up his stuff, snatches a permission slip from Ms. Gieck, and stalks out the door without looking back.

I stare after him. Whatever that was about, it can't be good.

He's waiting for me outside the cemetery, leaning against the wall. Face as blank and serious as I've seen it.

"What's the matter?" I say, as soon as I get close enough. "I didn't need supervision in English today? Or are you really sick?"

He slings his backpack over his shoulder. "Let's go to the crypt. We need to talk."

"It's a mausoleum," I say. "A crypt is underground."

He ignores me, strides up the path.

The fist is back in my gut. I follow.

Once the gate's shut behind us he drops his pack on the stone floor and plops down. "Sit."

Okay. I sit. "What's up? National emergency?"

He sets his hands in his lap, carefully, like he'd rather be doing something else with them. "Were you serious that you were going to go to your grandfather's this weekend? Or was that just an excuse for the girl?"

I frown. "Why would I make an excuse to avoid Rachel? Yeah, I was serious. He asked me to come."

"To upstate New York," he says, flat. "This weekend. And you didn't think to tell us?"

Oh.

"He's my *grandfather.* How threatening is that?" The truth is, I hadn't thought much about it at all, with everything else.

"I spoke to Dr. Miller," Eric says. "You're not going."

"What?" I cross my arms, sit up straight against the wall.

"You're not going. You haven't been cleared for a trip like that. We don't know where this place is. We'd need time to check it out, assess the threats. Our covers are just getting settled—it hasn't been long enough for me to reasonably accompany you. And you're *not* going on your own. Out of the question."

The anger rises up my chest, acid in my throat. I rein it in, barely, remembering the gun. "You've got to be fucking kidding me."

His eyes narrow. He looks completely different like that—like this. Not my age at all.

"Jake. I know it's very new," he says, over-patient, like I'm a kindergartner. "But in the end, you have agreed to work as a high-level asset of the U.S. government. You are under twenty-four-hour security detail. You do *not*—" Red is seeping into his cheeks. He stops himself, lowers his voice. "You do not go waltzing off on out-of-state trips unprotected, not without giving us time to properly prepare. I'm sorry. No."

I get up and walk out into the graves, the mausoleum gate clanging behind me. My breath pumps clouds of steam. My hands clench tight inside my coat.

I feel like a toddler straining against one of those asinine leashes.

I've worked to gain independence: my own bike, my own car. Trust. Responsibility. I'm eighteen, an adult. I'm almost out of high school, on to the rest of my life. My choices, on my own merits. My plans.

But now all of a sudden I'm back at square one. *Don't do that, Jakey. Stay here, Jakey. Do only what we tell you.*

I get it: I can help people. I've agreed. Plus, they're protecting me. But everything in me strains to run away, to start over. I can't. I'm trapped.

"You could go in a couple of weeks," Eric says, behind me. "If you give us the address. We'll get everything sorted, and then you and I can go."

I clench my jaw, turn. I have to be an equal partner in this deal. "I want to talk to Liesel. Now."

He eyes me. Then he takes out his phone. "Let me see what I can do."

Five minutes later my cell buzzes. Unknown caller.

"Hello."

"Hello, Jacob." Her lilting syrup voice gives me shivers, not in a good way. "I understand you wanted to speak with me."

Eric stands by the mausoleum, hands in his pockets, watching. I press the phone to my ear and walk away along the path to my corner.

"Yes." I try to sound firm. "I know it's late notice, but I want to make this trip to my grandfather's this weekend."

"I'm sure Ed explained to you why that can't happen." She pauses. "Perhaps if you'd notified us as soon as he contacted you . . ."

So that's part of it. A punishment for not telling them everything. "I'm sure with all your resources you can manage it. It's not for another three days. Can't you just send a car behind me, post guards?"

"It doesn't work that way, Jacob. You're far more valuable to me than that."

Valuable to *her*. That reminds me. "I'm not dropping this. But I wanted to speak to you about something else too."

There's silence on the other end as she waits. Oh, yeah, she's good at power plays.

"Those objects you're giving me? Those aren't from DARPA. Someone else knows about me."

She sighs. "Jacob. I told you I would keep your secret safe, only those who needed to know. Didn't I?"

I don't answer. I'm learning. I walk slowly, kicking at pebbles on the ground. They scatter, clanking into headstones. Eric still watches, behind me.

"Yes, of course the objects are from another agency," she says, almost irritably. "The CIA. They, and the FBI, often have the most need for urgent information like this. But they have no idea of your identity, where you are, or even how you're getting the information. They give me the objects, I give them the answers they want. That's all. I told you, it's a DARPA project. Very few people know anything."

I sit at the base of an oak in my corner, looking over the cemetery.

"Jacob?"

I wait a beat. Then: "I'm here."

"You're safe. I promised you that. As long as you cooperate with us, and don't spring any more surprises or act on your own, like with this trip."

Don't touch that, Jakey.

"I want to go," I say stubbornly. "He's never asked me alone before."

There's another, longer pause. I can hear her shuffling papers. "Give us the address, and we'll see if you can go next weekend, or the weekend after. With Ed. That's the best I can do."

I consider. It's something, I guess. Not that there's any threat at Dedushka's house, but I see that they need to make sure. To keep him safe too.

"I'm waiting, Jacob."

"Don't you have his address?" I ask. "Don't you have everyone's address?"

"Not handy. What is it?"

"All right." I sigh. "3430 Wolf Point Road, in Standish, New York. It's a cabin. A long way in on a dirt road."

"Got it." I hear the smile in her voice. "I'll get right on this, and we'll set it up. A pleasure speaking with you, Jacob. I'm glad you called."

She hangs up.

"*You* called," I mutter at the phone.

Eric's still waiting at the mausoleum. When I come back he looks normal. Easy again. "At least you can go to your party now." He hands me three Ziploc bags bundled together. "We won't have time for these today. You'll need to do them with Ana tonight."

I glance at them, stuff them in a zipper pocket of my backpack. Homework.

"And don't forget—" He pokes me in the shoulder, and I stiffen, expecting more warnings, demands. "We've got tennis practice this afternoon. I'm gonna take you down."

I smile. "Don't count on it."

12

"Tunneling Through" by Tweak Bird

I figured it would be hard to tunnel in the evening with Myka and Mom both there. What's the explanation for the housekeeper to come and hang out with me in my room for an hour or two?

Other than the obvious. Which I don't think the government probably wants my mom and little sister thinking.

But Mom goes into her room right after dinner to pack for her trip, and Myk disappears with her usual homework. We're clear.

Ana turns on the TV loud, and sits next to me on the sofa. It feels risky, open. But it's not like I go into a coma or anything when I tunnel. I guess she's pretty confident she could stop me if they come out.

It's still awkward with Ana. I'm with Eric all day—literally right next to him most of the time—but I've only seen her for a couple hours the last two nights. And so far only a few minutes alone.

I don't have a good grasp of what she's like, other than making decent food and cleaning our house.

She gives me an encouraging smile. Her dark hair is pulled up into a knot, exposing the curve of her neck. She's wearing jeans, a green long-sleeved shirt, and her silver bracelet. No other jewelry. No makeup. "I understand you spoke with Dr. Miller today."

I press my lips together. "Yeah. I know I'm not supposed to—"

She waves a hand, stopping me. "I do not wish to be involved with any of that. I do not wish to know the details of any arrangements you make with Dr. Miller, other than what I need to do my job." She holds my gaze. "I am a professional in this situation, and that is all. Not a confidante, a friend, an enemy. I am your handler. You have an important job, and I help you do it, and protect you. Yes?"

Blunt. Kind of cold. But also refreshingly honest, and simple. I appreciate that. "Yes."

"Good. Now let us get to work." She turns on a camera, a twin to Eric's, and focuses it on me. "Open the first."

It's a small set of pliers. Simple steel, no grips, nothing fancy except a symbol engraved in the handle: an open, many-pointed star.

I rub my thumb over the star, close my eyes.

A man. Middle aged, pale brown skin mottled with scars, deep lines from his nose to the corners of his mouth. Full, dark beard. He wears a gray-green cap with a fold in it, so it poufs up on his head. Location: Afghanistan. A long Quonset hut on the western edge of Lake Puzak, draped with camouflage netting. It's dark outside, but there are rows of bright, fluorescent lights in the hut. He's working closely on something, stripping red wires attached to something that looks like a hubcap. He looks up, and I see the rest of the building: table after table lined with men and women, even children, all doing the same thing, quietly working. Attaching wires, loading ammunition into canisters shaped like bullets. Setting detonators. Thousands of them. He's proud, satisfied with the work they're doing here. Expectant.

"Bombs," I say to Ana. I open my eyes. "They're making bombs."

She takes a deep breath, then gives a single nod. "IEDs. Just a moment—let me make a call." She heads into the kitchen.

I drop my forehead into my hand, rubbing like I can wipe the knowledge away. They're going to kill people with those bombs. American soldiers like my dad. Afghani soldiers. Innocent people. And he's proud. Sometimes I don't understand the world at all.

"Jake? What are you doing?"

My head snaps up. Myka stands in the doorway.

"I'm . . . watching TV." I point at the TV blaring *Cops*.

Like I ever watch *Cops*. She glances over her shoulder, to make sure Mom's not there. "I thought you were buckling down for Stanford?"

"Yeah. Um. I just needed a break for a few minutes." I hide the pliers behind me in the cushion, stand. Stretch. Turn off the TV. "Guess I'll get back to it. Everything okay with you?"

"Sure." She stares at me for another minute, like she's scanning my brain. "Just getting a drink."

When we get to the kitchen Ana's wiping down the counters, like a housekeeper should be. She has good ears. Of course.

I set up my books on the table while Myk gets some spicy hot V8—her addiction—chats with Ana for a minute, and then leaves. I get the pliers before I forget.

"We've got to do it in the kitchen," I say. "It's too out of character otherwise."

"Even better," she says placidly, with a last swipe of the dishrag. "The other is taken care of. Are you ready for the next?"

"What are you going to do to them?"

She pauses, rag in hand. "Them?"

"You know. The bombers."

She drops her chin. "I cannot tell you outcomes, Jake. Most of the time I do not know myself." She hangs the rag neatly over the sink, sits across from me, and spreads her hands on the table, examining her fingers. "It is best not to think of it."

I know, though. We both know. I picture that hut blowing sky-high, fire billowing to the clouds with all the explosives in there. Bombs for bombs. I picture it being gone within an hour, all those people, children, *gone*.

Does it make it okay if they were going to bomb people? Does it make it right?

Ana hands me another bag. This one has a small oval rock. Not really smooth, not special in any way. Except when I turn it over, I see it has a smiley face painted on it in blue paint.

It's a kid's object. I look at her, suddenly afraid of this one.

"Go ahead," she says, soft.

It's a little girl. Maybe five or six years old. She has yellow hair and plump, round cheeks like Rachel's, streaked with dirt and tears. Location: Louisiana. Broussard. A white trailer, parked at the end of St. Cabrini Street. She's in a dark, confined space, hunched on the floor, her head in her folded arms. She's crying, quietly, so they won't come back. The people who took her, pushed her into the car. Locked her in here. All she wants is her mother, for that door to open and her mother to be there, arms wide, all of it over . . .

I stop. Ana and I exchange a long, tired look. A little girl. I could've saved her this afternoon if I hadn't gotten on the phone with Liesel instead. Hours ago.

"We'll get her," she says, low. "We'll go get her right now."

She picks up her phone, pushes a button.

And then my head bursts open with pain.

I come to on the floor, the taste of Froot Loops in my mouth. Ana is bent over me, her hand cool on my face.

"You are all right," she says. "It is over."

Peaceful. Calm. No worries.

"What's going on? I heard—" I see my mom's feet pad around the corner. "Jake!" she gasps. "Oh my God." She's on her knees next to me. "Are you all right?"

"He's fine." Ana's quiet, measured. "He slipped and fell. But I don't feel a bump, and there's no sign of concussion. I think he just needs to go lie down."

I smile at Mom. It's a funky view, her chin looming over me. "Hi."

She frowns down at me, pushes my hair off my forehead. "You sure you're okay, baby?"

I have just enough sense to know that I have to push through the high I'm floating on, or Mom will drag me to the doctor. Wonder how T-680 would show up on a blood test. Red flags.

Flags, flapping in the breeze. That's relaxing, isn't it? The sound of flapping . . . my eyes start to roll back.

Get it together, Jake.

"Fine," I manage. I push myself up, so I'm propped on my arms. They give me room. I barely resist collapsing back. "I should lie down." *Don't slur, don't slur.*

Together they help me up and walk me down the hallway to my room, one on each arm. I'm shaky, but I make it, flop onto the bed.

Let the peace wash over me again. Stifle a giggle as Ana ushers Mom out the door.

"I don't think I should go tomorrow," Mom says, as the door shuts behind her.

I don't worry, though. Ana will take care of it.

I don't have to worry about anything. Flags, flapping. A nice easy breeze over my face, with the sound of the aspens. And there's music somewhere, a drum.

Damn, that's a good drug.

I have to stop doing that. Whatever's triggering the transition problem, we have to figure it out fast. It's freaking me out. Besides the small issue of excruciating pain, I can't pass out and then get high for hours at a time. Someone just might notice.

When I get up the next morning Mom's gone, off to catch her

flight to Chicago. Ana pulls me into the kitchen. She had to do some convincing, she says, and Mom checked on me three times in the night. But since I seemed okay, she decided to go. If Ana promised to watch me carefully.

I snort so loud Myka, at the table, looks up from her cereal. "No worries there," I say.

Ana's expression doesn't change. "How are you feeling this morning?"

"Normal." I shrug. "As normal as I get, lately."

Ana tilts closer, lowers her voice more. "I'm sorry, but orders came in—"

Myka gets up to take her bowl to the kitchen, and I dive into the refrigerator, pull out a carton of milk. Ana goes back to trying to yank out the bottom tray of the toaster, which probably hasn't been emptied for years.

"Morning, Myk," I say. But I'm thinking of what Ana said in a loop. Orders? Sorry? Why is she sorry?

Myk gives me a look stolen directly from Mom. "You okay? I heard you fell."

"Yeah." I laugh, pour a glass of milk. "Pure grace, that's me. I'm fine."

It seems to satisfy her. She makes a circle with her sneaker, on the floor. She wants something.

"Since Mom's gone, you wanna take me to the movies tonight? There are like four things I want to see."

I start to reply, but she keeps going.

"I know, I know, it's a school night. But every once in a while I have to be a kid. Play hooky from homework."

I glance at Ana. Do "orders" mean I won't be here tonight?

She nods subtly. It's okay.

I fake-punch Myk in the arm. "You're *on*."

"Yes!" She dances away from me, out of range. "And you didn't say what movie, so I get to pick . . . ha ha ha . . ."

I don't even mind. I'd sit through two hours of some dancing princesses tonight if it'd make her happy. Though she'll probably choose a twisty mind-bending thriller and figure it out before the end. I chase her out of the room, down the hall, until I catch her and tickle her mercilessly. Under the armpits, where she can't stand it.

Then I leave her, wheezing with laughter, hair all tangled up around her, and go back to hear my orders.

I swear, I can't read Ana at all. I think her face would be the same if she was telling me I have to disappear tonight, or that I have a bunch of objects to read and damn the headache.

"They want you to go see a DARPA doctor on Saturday." She finishes scraping bits out of the toaster, and turns to me. "There is concern about the headaches, and they want to check on your health, do some more tests." She sighs. "I am sorry. It will take most of the day."

I almost hug her from pure relief. Yeah, an all-day doctor visit sounds nasty. Nothing makes me feel more helpless, more like a *thing,* than sitting in a paper gown on a metal table, people poking at me. But I want the headaches to stop. I'm glad they do too. And it's a lot better than it could've been.

There's one more thing I have to do before school. I'd been putting it off, but I have to call Dedushka, tell him I'm not coming. I know he'll be disappointed. I feel like a chickenshit for giving in to Liesel, for agreeing not to go. Even worse for being relieved when it's just a voice mail that picks up, with a generic voice saying I can leave a message. I do. I'm so sorry, but I can't make it this weekend after all. It will have to be another weekend soon.

I hope it will be, and that nothing else comes up to stop it from happening.

13

"Little Truth" by the Delta Routine

The next day I'm heading into lunch, Eric ahead of me, when someone grabs my arm and yanks me back into the hallway. I have a mini heart attack—in that split second imagining all sorts of people who could be abducting me, none of them good—before I realize it's Rachel. She pulls me around the corner and up against a wall next to the drinking fountain, her hand still on my arm, her body only a step away from mine.

My heart jackhammers for an entirely different reason.

"Hey," she says, her eyes darting over my face like she's searching for something, trying to figure something out.

I frown a little, just because I'm not sure what's going on. "Hey. Is everything—"

She lunges forward, up, her arms around my neck, and covers

my mouth with hers. Her lips are soft, and so warm, and soft, and insistent, and . . .

I lose all thought except her, the velvety skin of her cheek against my thumb, her vanilla scent, her lips, *her.* Rachel. Kissing me.

Like I wanted. And yet so much better. The best surprise ever.

When she pulls away I'm dizzy and drunk—like I took T-680—and lost. I just want to be there again, back where I was. I take a step forward, my hand still on her face, but she smiles, her eyes shining like I've never seen them, and shakes her head.

"I wanted to get that out of the way," she says, her voice wobbly, "before the party, since you're coming now. So we wouldn't have to worry about it."

"I'm not worried," I say, low.

If I could stay here, like this, forever, I wouldn't worry about anything else.

"No. Me either, not anymore." She laughs, and looks over my shoulder. "But your friend looks a little concerned."

I spin. Eric's *right* there, standing at the corner watching us. He has an expression like a dad would give his fourteen-year-old daughter if he caught her kissing a boy. Then he remembers himself and the expression vanishes, like it never existed at all. "Sorry," he says, almost smirking. "Didn't mean to interrupt."

Rachel presses herself against my back and stands up on tiptoe, her mouth near my ear. "We'll *talk* more at the party," she whispers. She squeezes my arm and strolls off around Eric, without a word, without a backward look, into the cafeteria.

Damn, girl.

Eric raises his eyebrows.

"What?" I ask mildly, because I'm in too good a mood to even care much what he thinks. "Am I not allowed to have a girlfriend?"

He shrugs, answers like it was a real question. "Be careful. Your situation is . . . complicated."

He gives me another look, then heads back into the cafeteria. I stay behind for a minute. To show I can, I guess. But mostly to steal one more minute to think about what just happened. About Rachel, and her soft, warm lips. How very much I like her. And how much I'm dying to get to that party on Saturday. If I could time travel there, right now, I would.

Nothing else happens for a day and a half.

That's not totally true. I go to classes, flirt hard with Rachel, and hang out and joke around with the usual gang, who are all getting ramped up for *Oklahoma* opening night next week. I go to the movies with Myka. Eric's around all day—I beat him at tennis twice—and Ana's there at night. They give me a couple objects to do, yeah. But other than that I can almost pretend everything is back to the way it used to be, but better. Normal. Handle-able.

Until Saturday.

I wake up dreading the doctor visit: probing, blood taking, whatever else they can think of. But it's necessary, to stop the headaches. I tell Myk I'm going out with friends, grab my coat and keys, and head outside. The place is some private clinic in Reston I've never heard of, but I'm pretty sure I can find it okay. I can always stop and ask my tail for directions.

I only get as far as the driveway when a car screeches to a halt in front of me. A black Jeep Cherokee, an old one. The passenger door flies open. Dedushka leans across the front seat.

"Get in!"

I hesitate.

"Yakob!" he yells. "Get in the car *now*!"

I glance over my shoulder at the house—wondering if Ana's watching—then jump in, slam the door behind me. He takes off, jetting down the street like a bat out of hell.

"Dedushka, what are you—"

"Turn off the phone. Put it and your watch in here." He points to a thick metal container between the seats, about the size of a cigar box, propped with the lid open. "Quickly. I will explain." He flies around the corner, well above the speed limit, eyes on the rear-view mirror.

Okay then.

I unbuckle the watch, tug my phone out of my pocket, and drop them both into the box. He slams it shut with one hand, turns a knob, then jerks a thumb toward the backseat. "A bag is back there. Put box into bag, seal it. Now."

I've never seen a bag like this. It's like Tyvek, but threaded with some kind of metal fibers, silver glinting through the white. I shove the box in, tear off a strip, and seal the flap.

He breathes out a sigh of relief that ruffles his beard. The beard is longer than when I saw him last, almost to his chest, and whiter. Like Santa Claus. "Good. I must only outrun them now, and then we talk."

I swing around to look through the back window. Sure enough, there's my tail, frantically weaving in and out of traffic, trying to keep up with Dedushka's maneuvers. I imagine Ana probably isn't far behind. Though she'll have to get around my car, which is blocking hers.

What the *hell* is going on? He's kidnapping me? How does he know about *them*?

"Patience, Yakob." He sets a wrinkled, spotted hand on my knee before shifting down to flip a sudden U-turn and head back the other way. We're deep in Herndon already, near the 606. "I will explain." He throws me a searching look under snarled white eyebrows. "And you will explain. But wait until we are safe."

He zooms onto the 606, passing cars left and right, until it merges onto the 7, and heads northwest toward Leesburg. I watch the trees fly by, my brain spinning in the same circles without getting anywhere. When we're almost to Leesburg, he looks back again, and slows down. "We are clear. Now we shall see how well my protection works."

He gets off the freeway, turns sharply into a Walmart parking lot, and parks out in the far corner, where there are plenty of other cars but not much foot traffic. Only then does he turn and look at me full on.

"Yakob," he says gruffly. "What have you gotten into?"

My mouth falls open. "I don't . . . I don't know . . ."

"Laduo." He sighs. "I go first." He combs his beard with one hand, over and over, staring out the window. Then he turns back to me.

"I will start here: I do not know very much. I know you can do . . ." He flaps a hand in the air like a bird. "Something valuable, dangerous. Your father told me this. He would not tell me what it is, for my own safety, for yours." He sinks back in the seat. "He asked me to protect you, if something goes wrong. He gave me a way to know it has gone wrong."

His eyes find mine. They're gray-blue like mine, like Dad's. "That watch of his had a tracker in it, Yakob. It was my job, these two years, to watch the tracker, to make sure it was normal for you. And then a week ago it was not. You are in Arlington on Saturday morning—which is not normal. And then the signal vanishes . . . poof." He makes the shape of an explosion with his fingers. "And I call you. Your mother says you are skiing, which you are not. When I reach you the next day, you lie to me . . . yes, Dedushka, I was skiing. And you still have your watch, but nothing. Someone took the tracker out, and you did not know it. So what did you do, in Arlington?"

I stare down at my hands, at the patch of bare white skin on my wrist. I don't know what to say. It feels, oddly, like I let him down. Let Dad down.

"I look at the address, where you were when you vanish, Yakob," he says, as soft as I've ever heard him speak. "They found you, did they not? The government."

I nod, slow, still not looking at him.

"You are working for them. You have security around you,

everywhere. And they would not let you come visit me." He sighs again. "Yet they come to visit me, two days ago."

My head flies up. "They *what*? They talked to you?"

He grins, teeth yellow through his beard. "Not for a second. I smelled them coming and left. But they get the address from you, yes?"

Again, I have to nod. "But—they said they were just checking for security reasons, to make sure I could come—"

"They lie." He spits it. "They lie about everything. And they spy on you, everywhere. I am certain the watch has a new tracker, from them. Probably a bug. The phone will be bugged. I am blocking them, for the moment, with the box, the bag. But your room, your house, even your school—all of it. Video. Audio. Everywhere. Easy for them. The *durnoy glaz*." He knocks on his head three times, and makes a spitting motion three times over his shoulder.

The evil eye. He's always said things like that, always been suspicious of everything. Before it sounded like paranoia, superstition, like somebody who'd read too many spy books. This time not so much.

"Bugs?" I say. "Really? I never thought of bugs."

He reaches over and takes my hand, crushes it between his. "Do not trust them for a second." He lowers his voice. "I have experience. And so did your father."

This I've never heard before. "Tell me."

He shakes his head. "It is not the time. Now you need to decide what to do. Do you run, *radost moya*? I will help you. We will go together. But it must be now."

I gape at him. "You mean . . . leave? Right now? Leave Mom and Myka and everything?"

His head bobs, solemn. "You could not go back. We would go far away. I have a place that might last for a while, before they find us."

I feel cold, all over. How can I just leave? Never see Mom or Myk again. Or Chris, or school, or Stanford. Or Rachel. God. After that kiss . . . to never see her again? Live my life in a cabin somewhere, hiding from satellites?

"I don't know," I say slowly. I don't think I could leave like that. Especially Myk and Mom. With Dad gone, it doesn't seem right to leave them alone.

Besides, I'm doing good work. Yeah, none of this was my choice. But that little girl, that woman and the knife—they might not have been saved in time if I hadn't helped. All those bombs would have killed people. And that's just in the first week.

"I'm helping people," I say finally. "I don't know if I should stop."

"At the expense of yourself?" he asks, harsh. "They will take everything from you, these people. They will suck you up until you are dry and then toss you away."

My eyes burn. "But I don't think I can go, Dedushka. Not now. If I do this, for a while . . ."

I don't say it aloud. But if I do this, I'll have a hope of that future I want. Stanford, the Smithsonian. Rachel, even, maybe. A normal, happy life. It's a good hope. I won't have anything if I lock myself away now.

He lets his head fall forward, staring at his knees. "You may not have another chance, Yakob. They will be more suspicious, more watchful, after this. They know you know more about them. Are less gullible."

I guess I have been gullible. I never even thought of bugs. If there *are* bugs, and he's not imagining that part.

"And one more thing. I want you to think on this very hard." His eyes are like needles boring into me. "They always do what is best for them. Always. And what is best for them, if I am right, if your Papa was right, is to have you secure somewhere, in their control, making you do work for them. So why do they have you out here, in the world? What else do they want from you, that they get from you being out here?"

I swallow. "I don't know."

"Think on it. And be wary. Here." He flips open the glove compartment in front of me, takes out a man's ring. An air force ring, silver, stamped with an eagle, worn down from use. "Keep this in your pocket. It also has a tracker hidden, better than in the watch. If you wear it, they will take it from you. But if you keep it hidden away, maybe they will not find it. If you can, keep it always with you. I will watch for you."

He kisses my right cheek, then my left, then right again. He smells musty, like old smoke, like fish. It smells like childhood.

"I love you, *malchik*. I would rather have you with me, safe. But if you go back, take care of your mother and sister. Do not let this ruin them. Promise me?"

"I swear, Dedushka. I won't."

He takes a deep breath. "I must go. I will find a way to contact you. You tell them what you like—they already know about me. It is the truth that you will not know where I am, or where I will be." He reaches into the back, hands me the bag. "Take this. Wait half of an hour after I have left, then open it and throw away the box and the bag, away from you. As a test, do not call them. See how long it takes for them to track you." He smiles sadly. "I do not think it will be long."

I hug him, and he hugs me back fiercely. It's like holding a lion.

I step out of the car, bag in hand, and watch him drive away.

Half an hour later, I open the bag and the box and bury them in a Dumpster. I drop the phone into my pocket and clasp the watch on my wrist, walk across the lot to a curb, and sit down to wait, to see if he was right.

It's only fifteen minutes before two cars come tearing down the road. One is an unmarked white van, the other a gray sedan. They bounce into the parking lot and come to a stop in front of me, angled in a V like they're blocking my escape.

I sit there and watch, unmoving, arms resting on my knees. He was right.

Ana jumps out of the van, and Eric and another guy out of the car, all of them with their hands at their backs, ready.

I hold up my own hands like I'm surrendering. Then I rub my watch, with one finger. "Works pretty well, doesn't it?"

"Are you all right?" Ana is slightly out of breath, eyes darting every which way, searching for a threat.

"He's fine," Eric says tightly. "He's going to get in the van now." He nods to the other guy. "We're all clear. George, you take the Vic back. We'll see you later."

Without question George hops in the car, backs it up, and is gone.

Leaving me with two very pissed off handlers. Well, one very pissed off—Eric—and one at least a little. Both of them stand with their feet wide, arms at their sides, staring me down.

"Get in the van," Eric snaps. "You're late for a doctor's appointment, if you remember. We'll talk on the way."

I grimace, but I go. I start for the passenger side, but Eric points to the back.

"Are you going to tie me up back here?" I ask, joking, as he opens the doors.

"Do I need to?" He scowls, no humor at all.

No more jokes. "No."

The back of the van has cleaning supplies in it, instead of the surveillance equipment I'd been half-expecting, but also two seats on either side, facing each other. I sit in one, Eric in the other. Ana gets back in the driver's seat.

"Where's Myka?" I ask suddenly. "Aren't you supposed to be with Myka?"

She tosses me a hard look over her shoulder. "She is fine. She's under surveillance."

I bet she is, I think. But I don't say it.

"You want to tell me what the fuck happened?" Eric asks, before we even get on the road. "I get a call that you jumped into a car with an unidentified male, drove away, and then went off grid? What were you thinking?"

I shift in the hard seat. I hadn't really figured out what to say.

"It was your grandfather, was it not?" Ana asks, from the front.

I look at them, one after the other. Eric would as soon punch me as ask again; I can see it. "Yes. It was my grandfather."

His eyes don't change—he knew that already. They'd figured it out. They're not stupid.

"And what?" Eric continues. "You told him to meet you here, so you could run? Was that what this trip was about all along?"

"No." I take a deep breath, meet his eyes so he'll know I'm telling the truth. "I didn't know he knew anything about this. But he gave me a chance to run . . . and I chose to come back."

That surprises him. Both of them are quiet.

"Why?" Ana asks.

"The work. I'm making a difference." I pause. "And I couldn't leave my family."

"That was a smart choice," Ana says. "A brave choice, even."

"Smart, anyway," Eric says, grudging. "We would've tracked you down. And then it would have been a whole different ball game, believe me."

Ana clears her throat.

He catches her look. "We appreciate your service. Of course." Then he adds hotly, "But I damn well don't appreciate chasing after you. Having to report to my superiors that I don't know where you are. It doesn't make anyone happy."

We ride for a while in silence. His reaction is a reminder that he's not my friend, not really. That they're my security, but also my guards. Did I make the right choice? Where is Dedushka now? Why aren't they asking that?

On impulse, I ask. "Aren't you going to ask me about my grandfather?"

Eric smiles small, with a taste of bitter. "Nah. We'll leave that to Dr. Miller. She's waiting for you at the doctor's. I wouldn't count on getting to that party."

Oh. *Crap.*

14

"I Don't Need No Doctor" by Ray Charles

The first part of the doctor visit is routine. The clinic is ritzy—dark wood furniture and marble in the waiting room—but otherwise normal. The exam room isn't any more menacing than any doctor's, which is plenty enough for me: an examining table, sink, chair, instruments set out. The only thing that feels odd is that there are no other patients here.

A nurse in flowered scrubs weighs me, takes my blood pressure and pulse, and asks me to sit on the table. At least she lets me keep all my clothes on. Another woman comes in and draws three vials of blood, labels them, and goes away. I sit, wait. I read the pamphlets about high blood pressure and diabetes, but I don't learn much. That's not going to help with the high blood pressure I have right now.

The door opens. Liesel. Same as the first time I saw her: gray suit, white shirt, ponytail. It's like her uniform.

"Hi," I say, nervous.

She tilts her head. "We have a problem, Jacob. To be precise, two problems."

My hands clench involuntarily.

"One: these headaches of yours. That is why you were *supposed* to be here today. We need to do some more testing, with the EEG, to try to figure that out."

I'm silent.

She sits in the chair, crosses her legs. Pins me with her freaky pale eyes. Grass that's been bleached out by the sun. That's what color they are.

"Two, and more concerning to me: this escapade of yours this morning. You know," she says casually, "at first we thought you had been abducted by an enemy. That you might be lost. I was very upset." She frowns, and my heart picks up the pace. "Then I find it was your grandfather in that car, and you went with him freely. What does that say to me, Jacob? Does that say 'full, willing cooperation' to me?"

I clear my throat. Here we go.

"I didn't know what he wanted," I say. "He just turned up and told me to get in, so I did. I had no idea he knew anything. And I chose to come back and work with you, instead of run. For the first time, I'm here because I actually chose to be. I think that's full cooperation."

It's a dangerous game. She has to believe I'm loyal to her and her project, and willing to work, or I'll have traded a cabin in the woods for a cell. The goal has always been to stay with my family, to protect them. This is my only shot at it now. But if I've really chosen Liesel—this weird, new life—it's time for me to take some control of it.

She purses her lips. "That is something."

"I believe the work is important," I say. "In spite of the trackers, which I'm not happy about . . ."

She lifts her eyebrows.

"I'm willing to be your guinea pig, if it makes a difference. I'm willing to do—" I spread my arms. "This."

Wow. I really am. I turned Dedushka down and chose this. I'm telling the truth.

Plus there's the whole Stanford/future thing. I'm in, whole hog.

She sits back, arms crossed, and regards me carefully. "Fine. You stay in the field, under protection. If you tell me about your grandfather, and what he knows, and I'm satisfied with the answers."

I'm suddenly very, very glad he didn't tell me where he was going. And that they don't have anything of his to try to make me tunnel to him. That would be a test of my loyalty I'd have a hard time with. I have the ring, of course, still in my pocket. But she doesn't know about that. They didn't search me.

Offense first.

"He knows you went to his house on Thursday. After I gave you the address. He thinks you were trying to take him in. Why would you be trying to take him in?"

There's no reaction, nothing but blankness. "We weren't, of course. We were checking for security, as I told you we would. Why didn't he stay there?"

I shrug one shoulder. "He's cautious. A little paranoid."

"Why did he pick you up, Jacob? Why did he take you off grid? *How does he know about us?*"

We're in a doctor's office with fluorescent lights and pastel colors. But I feel like I'm in an interrogation room under a spotlight. A drip of sweat rolls down the middle of my back.

I can't say I don't know. But I don't want to say anything about Dad, either. I don't want to involve his memory in this.

I stare her down, but there's no give.

"He had a tracker on my watch," I say finally. "I told you—paranoid. I didn't know anything about it. But then . . . someone . . . removed it when I was at DARPA, and he got suspicious."

Offense again. "But you knew about the watch already. You removed the tracker." I tap it. "And replaced it with your own."

Blank. "Of course we did. But we *were* very curious to know who had been tracking you. And now we have our answer." She stands, walks to the window. It's snowing again, the sky white with it. It casts an odd light over her face. "Why was your grandfather tracking you? That's the most interesting question."

Dangerous territory. Keep Dad out of it. "He thought something like this might happen."

Her lips pucker. "So he knows about your abilities. And he knows you're working with us. And he has the ability to fool our tracking devices—which you'll tell me about, later." She turns, leans back against the sill. "I must speak with him, Jacob. Where is he now?"

I meet her gaze, hoping she can read the honesty in my face. "He wouldn't tell me, so I wouldn't be able to tell you. I have no idea."

There's a long pause. Long enough for me to sweat more. But I keep my eyes on her face.

"Very well," she says. "We'll find him on our own. And we'll talk more later, you and I. But right now we have the doctor waiting. I want to get on with that testing."

They hook me up to the EEG again, testing my brain waves in all sorts of conditions. Pre-tunnel, during tunnel, after tunnel. The objects they give me are purely tests—all staff, in a couple different locations. I figure the doctor and nurses aren't cleared for the spy stuff.

In all the downtime between objects, I imagine what Mom and Myk are doing today. Mom's probably running around putting the final touches on a State Department reception, or meeting: laying out the seating chart, making sure the food is right, arranging for the flowers. Myk's probably hiding in her room reading. Or maybe taking over the kitchen with a chemistry experiment, if Ana lets her.

The important thing is they're safe, and happy. I'm keeping them safe and happy by cooperating here.

When they pull the EEG wires off I breathe easy: they're done. At last. It's late—8:15, by the big old-style clock in the room—but I can still make it to the party. I can wipe out all the confusion of today with a round of foosball with Chris . . . or another kiss with Rachel. Yes, that.

But they aren't done. The next part is way worse than an EEG.

It's a psychologist.

His name is Dr. Tenney. He's small and neat, with round glasses and a warm, damp handshake. He's mostly bald. The fluorescent lights in the borrowed office reflect off his head and his glasses. I sit in the chair across from him—identical chairs, across a plain wood desk—and watch the reflections change as he moves. He talks, reassuring me about his background, and confidentiality, and how I can talk about anything with him. That it won't go to Liesel or anyone else. That he's here for me.

"For two purposes, Jake—can I call you Jake? Or do you prefer Jacob?" He's from somewhere in the South; he has a slow, deep drawl. Alabama, I guess. Maybe Georgia. We lived in Georgia for a year, but I was too small to remember it.

"Jake."

"Very good." He smiles, with his lips closed. "Two purposes. One, to deal with any issues you might be having with all this. It's possible stress could be causing your headaches, and I may be able to help with all that stress."

The way he says "stress" it's like a four-syllable word.

"Two—" He holds up two fingers. "To see if I can help you explore and develop your gift further." He flips through a fat folder in front of him. "I have read the reports of your work. They are extremely impressive. But I have done a great deal of research on this area, and I have a theory." Again, with the smile, proud. The glasses glint, obscuring his eyes. "I believe you can go even further. I noticed you pull out of the . . . ah, tunnel . . . just when you could—" He stops.

There's an odd, stretched silence, while we judge each other.

"But I'm getting ahead of myself. Tonight, I just want to talk."

I look at my watch. 8:40.

Dr. Tenney takes out a fresh notepad, uncaps his pen, and looks up. "Now then, Jake. Tell me about your father."

They drop me off at my house at 12:30 a.m. Ana's waiting up for me, but she doesn't say much. She offers me some maté tea, but I don't want anything.

I made it through, telling him as little as I could. All of it general, what they'd expect me to say. But I'm utterly wiped. Questions and tunneling and testing—and lying up the wazoo, plus the adventure with Dedushka this morning—have flattened me. Lying takes more energy than you'd think.

Too late, and way too tired, to try to go to the party now. Too late to do anything but check on Myka—sound asleep—and go to bed.

Bed. Sleep. Forgetting. Pretending everything is normal for a few blessed hours.

I think the hardest part was talking about Dad at all.

15

"The Good Soldier" by Nine Inch Nails

The first time Dad saw me tunnel was two days before my eighth birthday.

It's kind of crazy, looking back, that neither of my parents noticed before that. I figure they were both incredibly busy—Dad was always away at work, and Mom had her hands full with Myka. I was an easy kid, always did what I was told, so I didn't need the attention.

Plus after Chris's reaction six months earlier at a sleepover? I finally realized it was kind of a freakish thing to do, and started to actively hide it.

But this day, I was bored. We'd just moved from DC to North Carolina, on Pope Air Force Base near Fort Bragg. It was January, so it was cold and raining. It had been raining for a week. I missed Chris, and all my other friends in DC. Myk was teething—when I tunneled to her, the pain was too intense for me to take for long—so none of us were sleeping well. Mom was with her, trying to get her to take a nap, and Dad was at work.

I'd explored everything else in our little house, so I decided for once to do something forbidden, and explore Dad's office.

It was neat, precise. One gray metal bookcase that came with the house, books arranged by author's last name within subject. Books on military history, tactical specs on planes, Russian history, military projects. Nothing I wanted to read. I spun in Dad's chair a few times, but it wasn't fun with no one to push me. There was a gray metal desk with tan folders in a stack, and a pad of lined paper: all pencils and pens were in the drawer where they belonged. I knew better than to use his paper to write or doodle. There was a phone I didn't dare touch.

Drat. For all the secrecy there wasn't anything to *do* in here.

On a whim I decided to take one of the papers and tunnel to Dad, check out what he was doing right now. I had only a vague idea of what he did at work. I'd pop in, pop out. At least I'd see him.

The papers in the top folder were reports and letters, all with air force insignia on them. I took one that had Dad's name on it in the *to* field, laid my hands flat on it, and closed my eyes.

It isn't Dad. It's a man, older than Dad, in a blue air force uniform, four silver stars on each shoulder. A general. His hair is gray, starting far back on his head and combed to the side. He has a sharp nose, curved, like a hawk. Sharp eyes. Location: Washington, DC. The Pentagon. The southwest side of the five-sided building, conference room 212. The room is small, and he sits at a large table crammed with people down each side. Most in uniform, some in suits, all turned to him. He's worried. "We have to take these threats seriously," he says. "Yes, the intelligence is uncertain. But if one of these terrorist groups does successfully launch an attack on U.S. soil, and we did not act—" He bangs a fist on the table. "I do not want to be the one to answer to that."

"Jacob."

I opened my eyes. Dad was there, sitting in front of me in the guest chair, hands in his lap.

Oh my God, he was going to kill me. I'd come into his office, riffled through his papers, spied on someone in the Pentagon. I was dead.

"I'm sorry," I said, the words tumbling over themselves. "I'm sorry. I didn't mean—"

He waved the apology away, scooted forward. He was just starting to get lines in his face then, wrinkles in his forehead, around his mouth. They seemed deep that day, carved. "What were you doing?" His voice was strained, but calm. "Explain it to me."

I told him everything. He asked questions, mild, smart questions, and I answered all of them. How it worked. How I helped Myka. The things I'd figured out: it had to be an object that meant something to the person, or was significant.

I guess the report had been more significant to the general than to Dad.

I could go anywhere in the world, see what the person was seeing, hear what they heard, feel at least the surface of what they were feeling. But I never stayed too long. I hadn't told anyone before that—no one to tell—but I was always a little afraid that I'd go too far, lose myself in someone else, and not be able to get back.

I told him about objects of dead people, and how I avoided them because of that dark, sick coldness.

He listened. He never did get mad. Then he talked, for a long time, about consequences, and caution. Never telling Mom. Never doing it in front of anyone else. He'd help me learn to control it, and I could always come to him, he said. Never anyone else. *Ever.* This was power. With power there was responsibility, and consequences.

And now look where I am. If I could only go to him now.

On Sunday morning I go on a bug hunt in my room. If Dedushka was right about the tracker, he's probably right about the bugs too.

I find *five*.

Behind my headboard. On the side of my desk. Under my chair. Hidden in my books. There's another one at the bottom of my backpack. I also find two cameras, dime sized, one on the bookcase and one on my nightstand. Pointed at my bed and my desk. Twenty-four-hour Jake viewing.

I am completely creeped out.

I make a pile of them, wrap them up in one of my T-shirts, and bring them to Ana.

She's in Mom's room vacuuming. I close the door, set the T-shirt on the bed, and unroll it. "You can take all these back."

She turns off the vacuum and pushes her hair out of her face impatiently. "What is this? What are you doing?"

"I don't need surveillance in my room. I've agreed voluntarily to help you. I'm not going to run away." I gesture at the pile of bugs, cameras. "I don't want this stuff in my room anymore. I don't want to be on camera all the time. Get rid of the rest of them, too, if I missed any. And any others you have in my house."

She regards me steadily, eyes dark. "It is not just to watch you. It is for your safety, to warn us of intruders—"

"If we have intruders in my room and this"—I point to the pile—"is the first indication you have of it, I think we have more serious problems. Yeah?"

She sighs. "Jake, I can't just—"

"You can. I don't want this stuff watching me, or my family. Get rid of it."

I turn on my heel and leave.

When I get back to my room, Myk's in the doorway, staring in. "God. What did you *do* in here?"

I laugh. I feel giddy, getting those things out of here. "Spring cleaning."

"In February? And it doesn't look like you cleaned anything. It looks like you took a blender to it."

"You want me to come clean yours? I'd be happy to do the same treatment . . ."

"No, thank you." She sticks her head in again, eyes wide. "I'm getting out of here before you ask me to help you pick this up."

I frown. "Where are you going?"

"I do have friends, Jake."

I look at her.

"Fine. I'm going to Stephanie's house, okay? Her mom is coming to pick me up, so you don't have to do anything. I'll be back after dinner."

Myk's got the Lukin independent streak. Well, we all do.

"Take your cell phone," I say. "Call me if you need me. Answer if I call."

She salutes—smart-ass, also classic Lukin—and takes off down the hall.

And I realize that I have an afternoon and evening here alone with Ana before Mom gets home.

I take out my phone to text Chris, and see it's still off. I turned it off when Dedushka told me to, and never turned it on again. I fire it up and find two missed calls, six messages. Two from Chris, and the rest from Rachel.

Hey, when are you coming?

Where are u?

You did say you were coming, right? Chris tried to call you.

And last, looking out of place in its happy green bubble:

I guess you think this is all a big joke.

Crap. Crap, crap, and more crap.

Once again the whole spy thing is getting in the way of real life. How do I fix this?

I need to talk to Chris. I send him a quick message:

Sorry about the party. Will explain. Want to come over and play COD Black Ops?

Two minutes later:

Hell yes. Perfect for hangover. Also can get my dragon on. See you in half an hour.

I relax. He'll help. *That* is exactly what I need.

We're doing split screen on the stadium map in *Call of Duty,* running and gunning through a deserted hockey rink. At first it felt strange—with the guns and threats and bomb tunnels lately in real life—but after a few minutes it's just me and Chris playing, like always. We don't even talk about anything but the game for a while.

Then Chris camps behind a Zamboni for a minute, and glances at me. "What the hell happened to you last night, anyway? You didn't answer any texts."

I thought of what to say. I dive around a corner and take out a sniper. "Couldn't. Was in the emergency room."

Perfect excuse. I am getting way better at this.

"*What*? What happened?" He comes out from his camp and runs through the empty seats, checking for snipers.

I shrug. Pull myself up a ledge, duck down again when somebody shoots at me. "Shit! Um . . . Myk was puking. A lot. She's fine now, though. Off at a friend's, even. But I couldn't use the cell in the hospital."

It feels *wrong* to use Myk as an excuse like that. But it works: why I wasn't there, why I couldn't call. And puking—nobody wants to know more about puking.

Chris makes a face. "Jesus." He leans away from me. "It better not be catching. You know the show opens on Thursday."

"I won't touch you, I swear. But I think we're all gonna be fine." Liar, liar, pants . . .

"Glad she's okay. Maybe Rachel will forgive you too, if you call and tell her about it."

Somebody I didn't see jumps up and shoots me from behind. Killed. Damn.

I set down the controller and watch Chris play. "Was she really upset?"

He snorts. He finds a window and takes a couple people out. "You could say that. She thought you blew her off. Like it was all a big ruse, that you weren't interested in her after all."

I shake my head. After her ambush kiss? Um, yeah. I'm interested. "I'll call her later."

I hope my lie is just as convincing then. The truth keeps getting weirder and weirder anyway. No one would even believe it if I told them.

There's a knock on the door, but Ana doesn't even wait. She barges right in. "Jake, I have a—" She stops short. "Oh. I . . . did not know you had a friend here." She gives me a quick glare. I guess it is my fault, since I took out all her surveillance. Ha.

"Yep," I say. "Did you need something?" *Go away,* I think. *Leave me alone.*

But Chris pauses the game and stands up. "The beauteous housekeeper." He crosses the room, shoves his hand out. "Great to meet you. I'm Chris Sawyer."

She shakes his hand. It lasts too long—Chris doesn't let go—and she finally tugs it away. "Nice to meet you, Chris. I have heard so much about you."

"That's . . . probably not good." He laughs, she laughs. It's awkward. They both look at me.

"Can I see you for a moment, Jake?" Ana asks. Her expression shifts: all business.

I sigh. "Sure."

She goes out, and Chris does the eyebrow dance. "Da-yam."

"I *know*. I told you. Salma Hayek to a T." I wave at the screen. "Keep playing. I'll be back."

Ana's waiting in the hall. I shut the door behind me. "Look, I'm sorry if I broke some rule by asking him over, but I do have a life—" I sound like Myka.

"It's fine," she says. "Once the cameras and bugs are back in place it won't happen again anyway."

We do a little standoff, her stone face to mine.

She breaks first, for now. "The messenger service has dropped off a batch of objects, but one is an emergency. We can use my room."

An emergency. That's why I agreed to keep doing this, for the emergencies. "Lead on."

Her room used to be the spare room, always ready in case we had an unexpected overnight guest. That's one of Mom's hospitality rules. Ana hasn't changed a thing. The bed's made perfectly, closet shut, nothing on the nightstand. It smells like her—some kind of clean, sharp soapy smell—but otherwise you'd never know anyone was living there. I wonder what's in the drawers. Knives? Devices for tracking me? Underwear? I hesitate at the door.

"You may sit on the bed."

I glance back at her, and sit. She closes the door, takes out a bag, no fanfare, and hands it to me.

It's dog tags.

I twist them in my fingers, take a deep breath, and close my eyes.

It's a man. Not much older than me. Cropped pale hair, snub nose, desert fatigues. Location: Waziristan. Just west of the village of Tatai. He's in a cave, dark but dry, sand whipping past his face in a wind from the entrance. He's surrounded, held by a group of turbaned young men in white robes. They are furious, yelling, one of them pointing a gun at him. The others have machetes, knives. One of them spreads the soldier's right hand on a flat rock before him, and holds it at the forearm, pinning it. He cries. Begs. Another raises his machete high. He brings it down across the soldier's wrist.

"Jake. Jake, stop!"

I open my eyes. Ana's beside me, hands on my shoulders. My face is wet. I spread my own hands, panicked, but they're both still there. The dog tags slip from my fingers.

"They cut off his hand," I say, numb.

"Yes." She squeezes my shoulder. "But he is still alive. I must report it, this instant. But you will have to go and see Chris. You screamed. You will have to explain."

She dials, talks into the phone in a low voice. I stare at the dog tags, a puddle of metal beads on the floor, and grasp my wrist. I can still feel it, that shock of pain, the knife severing through muscle, bone. Worse than the headaches. Worse than anything I've ever experienced. Real.

"You must *go,*" Ana says, hand over the phone. "You must protect your cover."

Cover. That's what Chris is now, what home is. Cover.

How can I explain? I can't even think.

I stand, open the door. I see Chris's back at the end of the hall, by the kitchen. He's calling my name. What can I say?

I close Ana's door loudly, and he spins.

"Jake. Fuck. What happened? I heard you over the game. You all right?"

"Me?" I laugh. It sounds hollow, but not bad. Not as bad as my fake laughs a few days ago. "That wasn't me. That was a YouTube video Ana was showing me. Sorry, man. It was too loud."

He stops across from me, eyebrows pinched together. "A . . . video?"

"Yeah. Sounded real, right?"

The frown deepens, wavers, then clears, a cloud blowing away. "What the hell were you doing in her room, dude? She's calling you into her *room* to show you videos?"

I pull him into my room. "I know, right? How'd you do with the game?"

I play—we play, for another hour or so—but my heart isn't in it anymore.

We do three more tunnels that night after he leaves, before Myka comes home. My heart isn't in those either—I don't know who I'm helping, hurting. Whose lives I'm affecting. But I do them anyway. I never know when I may be able to prevent something like that from happening again.

Then Myk comes home, all bubbly from her afternoon, and dares me into a cutthroat game of Monopoly. Which she wins.

I totally forget to call Rachel.

16

"Tension" by the Blue Man Group

On Monday, I go early and wait for Rachel before her homeroom class. A little stalkery, maybe—but I need to clear this up with her. When I finally (finally) have a chance with an actual cool girl, I can't let her think I'm a jerk just because DARPA wouldn't let me leave.

For any longer than she already has, anyway.

She comes five minutes before the bell, charging through the crowded hall like a bull, head down. She doesn't see me until she's right there in front of the door, and I see her double take. First pleased, then . . . remembering . . . mad. Her cheeks go all red, instant.

"I'm sorry," I say, holding my hands up in innocence. "I had to take my little sister to the emergency room Saturday night. And they made me turn off my cell—I'm so sorry."

She looks at me steadily, tilts her head. "Is that bullshit? Or true?"

For a second I'm sure she can tell I'm lying. Like of everyone, even Myka, she's the only one who sees it. I wish so hard I could tell her the truth. It would be such a relief.

"True," I say, I hope convincingly.

She's still studying me. I don't add any detail, because I read somewhere that's how people can tell you're lying, if you talk too much.

She runs a hand over her ponytail, flicks it. "And yesterday? Chris said you were going to call me?"

Ugh. "Yesterday was just a mess," I say honestly. "All this stuff came up, and I couldn't. I promise I won't bail on you again."

I realize, too late, that was a dumb thing to say. How can I promise that?

But she relaxes, and rewards me with one of those bright smiles. "Okay. It's just . . . with my dad leaving and all, I'm . . . careful. You know? Cautious."

The bell rings, and she points into the classroom. "Gotta go. See you later?"

I think of reaching out, touching her hand, her cheek, something—God, I want to—but I nod, and let her go.

Then I sprint to the other end of the hall, where my homeroom is.

The rest of the day is surreal. I listen to all the talk about the usual school stuff: classes, homework, tennis politics, *Oklahoma* politics, who's doing who and who's not. But after the incident with Dedushka, the doctor, the tunnel to the soldier yesterday . . . I feel like a water strider, my feet spread on the surface of the chatter. None of it touches me like it should. I can't tell any of my friends a thing of what I'm thinking about, what I'm involved in.

I guess it's all part of Operation Massive Lies, and there'll be plenty more lies and secrets where that came from. I'd better get used to it. But every time I lie to someone—Chris, Myka, Rachel, Mom—I feel a little more uncomfortable around them. I have to be more aware of what I say. I wonder if it will ever settle down and get less complicated, or if it'll just keep piling up, lie after lie after lie, until I don't know what I'm saying anymore.

It's almost a reprieve to head out to the cemetery with Eric. It's simple. He knows who I am, what I do. And we have work that means something.

We settle into the mausoleum, sitting on our packs so the stone floor doesn't freeze our asses off. It's cold—thirty degrees—and clear, the sun low on the horizon. Winter in Virginia. At least we're not sitting in snow.

He hands me the first object without comment. It's a green plastic keychain with a picture of a beaker and three test tubes on it. I go, without comment. Simple.

It's a woman, young, black hair cut close to her head. She's wearing a brown, bulky sweater and dark pants, but no coat—she shivers against the cold. Location: Indiana. Indianapolis. The campus of Indiana University—Purdue. She walks down a wide path lined with trees. The air is brisk, icy. A pair of students pass by her the other way—she watches them. They might be looking at her. She passes a School of Nursing sign, keeps going straight, and walks over a star set in the concrete, into the Department of Pathology. She's jumpy. She doesn't know if this will work, if it's a good idea. Maybe she shouldn't have listened.

I open my eyes. "What was that? A college student going to class?"

He lifts his shoulders slightly, lets them drop. "I can guarantee she's not just a college student, if we're asking you to find her. I can also bet that whatever she's nervous about isn't a good idea."

He finishes making notes and pushes some buttons on the camera while I put the keychain back in its bag.

"I hear you pulled some bugs from your room and gave them to Ana."

"You guys talk about everything?" I say.

"Yes." He gives me a look, punches more buttons. "We talk about *everything*. Why did you do that?"

"C'mon, Eric. I'm working with you, great. It's working out fine. I don't need to be spied on constantly. Ever heard of invasion of privacy?"

"Ed, not Eric. And it's for your protection. You know that."

Enough. I stand up. "That's bullshit. You have them too, don't you? Set up around school or something?" I point to the ceiling, the stone walls. "Here? Do you have a Jake-cam on your head?"

He laughs. "Wouldn't tell you if I did, mate. You'd just take them down and I'd have to put them up again."

"Put them—? Why would you put them up again? Christ." I shake my head. "At least you're honest."

He flicks the camera closed with his thumb. "You think so?"

"What does that mean?"

His jaw clenches twice. "Just don't get too comfortable around any of us, Jake. Around anyone. Okay? It's a complicated situation."

That's the second time he's said that. I frown. He closes his hands around the camera, snaps a look up at me, then away. Is he *telling* me he's lying? That there's something I don't know?

"Here's your next one."

He slides across a box about the size of a baseball, instead of a Ziploc bag. I open the lid, see a small teacup resting inside. Fine white china, thinner than my fingernail, with a painted blue pattern of ladies dancing. I lift it into my hands, focus.

Cold. Dark. Emptiness. Sucking darkness. It reaches for me, dragging me in . . .

I drop the cup. It shatters on the stone floor into tiny slivers of white all around my feet.

"They're dead." I clench my hands into fists. "Why do you *do* that?"

"Because we need to know if they're dead," he says mildly. He writes a single line, then comes over to pick up the china. He piles bits in the box while I swallow, over and over, trying to keep my stomach down.

He gives me a glance. "I think that's good for today. You can go outside if you want. I'll be out in a couple minutes."

I don't need to be asked twice.

The freezing air helps settle my stomach, calm me. It's just an object, I tell myself. Just another dead object. You're in a cemetery, for Christ's sake. You're surrounded by reminders of dead people. The darkness isn't going to reach out and get you.

I walk down the aisle, touching my fingers to the granite markers, people I know from my research. The Cliffords, a family of five who came here from England. The father died in World War I, and the rest struggled on until they were all here, together. The Beckers, a father and forty-five-year-old daughter. The Millers, who lost too many children young. I rest my hand on the foot of the Miller angel—tall, steady, watching over them all.

And I see him.

The man from that first week. He creeps through the gate of the graveyard, hand in the pocket of his black coat. Looking for me.

I freeze, deer in the headlights, staring.

But I can't freeze. I have to *move*. I bolt back up the path to the mausoleum, the cold air stabbing at my lungs.

"Eric!" I gasp, as soon as I see the gate. "Help!"

He's outside instantly, hand at his back. "What is it? Where?"

I lean over my knees, panting. "The man. Who was following me before. Here. At the entrance."

He nods once. Draws his gun. "Get in the crypt, out of sight. Stay there until I come back for you. Don't come out, no matter what you hear."

He moves in that sideways-crab walk, gun sweeping back and forth, that people do on TV.

Part of me wants to stay and watch. But this is not TV. I do what I'm told, shut myself in the mausoleum, and sit down to wait.

My hands clasp together with nothing to do. I wish I was the one out there facing the danger, like in *Call of Duty*. But much as I hate to admit it, probably not a good idea with real guns, a real bad guy.

He's back in about ten minutes. "No one there."

"He *was*. I didn't imagine it, I swear."

"Oh, I believe you. I'll check surveillance too, and we'll get an ID from that." He tucks his gun away, half-smiles. "Since I still have cameras up."

All right. I suppose the surveillance could actually be useful.

"Now. Let's get you back to school—you'll be fine in the cafeteria with all those kids—and then I've got some phone calls to make."

To Liesel. She isn't going to like this at all. And if she decides it's too much of a threat, and I'm not safe out here . . . she could pull the plug.

Jesus.

Eric sets a hand on my shoulder. "Don't worry. We're not going to give up that easily. Yes, they were supposed to be long gone. We fed them misinformation, that your tests were useless, and supposedly they lost interest. I don't know why he's here now. But we'll find out what we're dealing with, and we'll handle it."

God, I hope so. Just seeing that man's face—I haven't felt like that much of a bull's-eye since that first day. We walk down the path and out the gate, down the street. Eric stays a step ahead of me, keeping an eye in all directions. I look over my shoulder, just in case he's behind us, following. Watching. No one there.

But he was. And it's worse when I know why.

17

"Is it Over?" by Thievery Corporation

I lunge for the ball, but it bounces past the end of my racket and slams into the wall behind me.

"Lukin!" Coach Brammer bellows. "Get your head in the game."

"Yes, Coach," I mumble. I pull another ball out of my pocket, serve it to Diego, and rock back and forth on my toes.

Be ready. Be focused.

Tryouts are *sucking*.

It probably would help if I'd slept last night, instead of staring at the ceiling imagining (a) strange people abducting me or (b) Liesel's people *taking me in* for my safety. About 3:00 a.m. I thought I heard someone outside my window. I jumped up, grabbed one of my rackets as a weapon, and stood there for twenty minutes, listening. My heart beating like a fucking rabbit's. There was no sleep after that.

Diego's slice is easy, and I hit it back, aiming for the left corner. "Out!" Diego yells. Coach shakes his head and moves on to the next court. Damn it.

Diego's serve. We move to our places. I watch the ball fly toward me in a perfect curve. I return it neatly, making him run the other way. My body *knows* how to do this, where the ball will land, where I need to be. If I can just shut off my brain.

"Well done, Ed," Coach says, two courts down. "Impressive."

I sneak a look: Eric is flying all over the court like a streak, hitting balls back with ease. I hate him. How can he do that, with everything else going on?

I miss another shot, and growl to myself.

This is your real life, Jake. Focus.

But is it? I'm not sure anymore.

When I get home Myk is setting the table, and Mom and Ana are talking in the kitchen. They sound like friends, laughing. The whole place smells like beef stew. It's one of my favorites.

I wonder if I can just skip it and go straight to bed, catch up on that sleep.

Probably not. At the very least, I have to find out if there's word from Liesel, any news, decisions. I drop my keys in the bowl.

"Hey," Mom says, poking her head out of the kitchen. "How'd tryouts go?"

I grunt. "I still have two days to do better."

"Oh." She frowns. "You okay? You look . . . tired."

Ana appears behind Mom, antennae up. Mom *and* handler once-overs. I don't know which is worse.

I shrug at both of them. "Couldn't sleep last night."

Mom gets the little line in her forehead. "Go wash your hands, please. Dinner in five."

Dinner. I can eat, after all. I stuff myself with stew and homemade bread, and stay quiet. Surprisingly, Ana starts in with the talking.

"Tell me," she says, her accent thicker than usual. "Where does the name Lukin come from?"

I stop chewing. She knows perfectly well where Lukin comes from. She probably knows more about Dedushka than Mom does, after this past weekend.

"Oh," Mom says. "It's Russian. My husband's father and mother came here from the Soviet Union, before he was born."

"From Moscow," Myk chips in shyly. "I'd like to go there sometime."

I imagine trying to protect Myk in Moscow.

"Really," Ana says. "Russian. So exotic! I thought it was hard to leave Russia then. Did they . . . what is the word. Defect?"

What is the word? What is she doing?

"You know, I'm not sure," Mom says. "We never talked about it. Grigory's a bit of an odd one, and Milena died before I met John."

There's a silence. Everybody digs in again, and I unwind a little. I guess she's pumping for more info about Dedushka. Can't blame her too much. But it's okay. Mom hasn't said anything they don't know. She probably doesn't *know* anything they don't know.

"John," Ana says. "I'm sorry, but that was your husband?"

Mom swallows, then nods. "Yes. He died two years ago. But it's okay to talk about him." She glances at Myk and me tentatively, like she's telling us instead of Ana. "It's been a long time."

I pick up my spoon and keep my eyes down, focused on the stew.

"That is good, yes. It helps to talk of the person, sometimes." Ana pauses. "How did he die?"

"*Enough,*" I say, an edge in my voice. They all turn to me, startled.

"No, Jake, it's okay," Mom says. "In a plane crash," she says to Ana. I can hear her trying to keep it even, and I want to step in and stop her. She doesn't have to say this. She doesn't have to tell them this. It's on the record, anyway. They know it. "In the mountains, in

Colorado. The plane crashed into a mountain, in a storm." Her voice cracks. "It was terrible."

I'm there again. High up in the mountains, the small group huddled around the memorial marker they'd put up against the cliff. Everyone except us and Dedushka dressed in air force blue. The cold, bitter tang of the air, the taste of salt on my lips. Myk pressed up close against me, dry eyed, still. And then afterward, the three of us doing Glue against the marker, our hands shaking.

The sense of emptiness. Betrayal. How could he do this to us?

Ana's eyes are on me. I meet them, unflinching. *Enough*.

"Ah," she says quietly. It's another moment before she turns to Mom. "I am so sorry."

Mom waves it away. She clears her throat, excuses herself, and comes back with a glass of red wine. Myk's hair falls across her face, a curtain of black.

We eat. Nobody says anything for a long time.

Then Mom pushes aside her plate, pulls her wine glass to her. Her fingers curl around it, like she's hugging it. "I have a peculiar story to tell. Guess what happened to me today?"

"What?" Myk asks.

"I thought I saw some men following me."

My gaze shoots straight to Ana's.

"What do you mean?" I ask. "Who was following you?"

"Well. It's probably silly. But I was on my walk at lunch—and suddenly I just felt . . . watched." She laughs a little. "You know what I mean? Like eyes on your back?"

I don't answer. I know what she means.

"So I got tricky and I hid around a corner, then turned back to look. And there *was* someone there. Two men, in navy suits. They went right past me, but they did look like they were searching for someone." She gulps the last of her wine and looks around the table, like she wants us to laugh it off. "I went back to work another way.

I know, it sounds ridiculous. I sound like your Grandpa. But it was just one of those feelings. I felt so *sure*."

"That is weird, Mom." My face feels as heavy as concrete. I strain to smile. "But I'm sure it's fine. It's probably nothing."

I toss a glance at Ana. *Help me.*

"I agree," she says carefully. "Probably just Washington suits, yes? There are men everywhere in Washington in suits. Maybe lost, looking for the right building."

Mom sighs, taps at her glass. It rings, a high musical note. "You're probably right."

Myk doesn't say anything, her gaze on Mom. Evaluating.

"I . . . I think I'm done," I say. "Ana, can I help you clear?"

We both stand. I grab some silverware and plates and walk, as deliberately as I can, to the kitchen. Ana's behind me.

"Stay calm," she says in my ear, as soon as we're out of sight. "We do not know yet what it is."

I spin. "Stay calm?" I repeat, hoarse. "It's my mother. Someone's after my mother. What is going *on*?"

She brings her face close to mine, her voice lower. "They could have been ours. It could have been nothing. It could be her imagination."

"But it wasn't, was it?" My throat feels raw. "She's in danger. And the man today . . ." I clench my jaw. "I have to talk to Liesel. This wasn't supposed to happen."

"Jake." She squeezes my shoulders hard. "I need you to go to your room and try to calm down. I will speak with Dr. Miller and we will work this out. If there is a threat, we *will* protect them. And you. I promise you."

I suck in, out, through my mouth, nod. Go down the hall to my room and sit in my chair, trying not to panic.

We have to keep the two of them safe. No matter what else happens. That's the *only* thing that's important.

Out of the corner of my eye I see the tiny shape of a surveillance camera, back in place in my bookcase, pointed at me.

I leave it there.

Ana slips into my room about ten. Liesel didn't know anything, but they're investigating. Hopefully they'll have answers soon. In the meantime, she promises me twice the security on all three of us. Until we figure out what's going on, if there really is a credible threat and why it's popped up again, Mom and Myk will have bodyguards too. Though they won't know about it.

It makes me feel a little better. Not better enough to sleep more than a few minutes at a time, though. I lie there, useless, the thoughts whipping through my head.

I promised Dedushka I wouldn't let this ruin their lives. I promised Dad, a long time ago, that I'd take care of them, if anything happened to him. That I'd never tell Mom about any of this.

I promised myself I'd keep them safe, no matter what.

I'm not keeping them safe. I'm endangering them. If they're threatened, it's because of me. Because of who I am. Because of the choices I've made.

At 4:00 a.m. I go to Mom's room, to check. She's sound asleep, tucked on her side. I look at her for a long time, her curls all wild, mouth open. At the picture of Dad on the nightstand, frozen in time in his uniform. Then I go to Myka. She has one arm over Horse tonight, her hair in a thick braid down her back. She looks soft, small. Vulnerable.

Damn it. I curl up a fist and bang it silently on the doorframe.

"Go to bed, Jake," Ana whispers. She stands behind me in the hall, in shorts and a T-shirt, hair loose around her shoulders. "You must get some sleep."

I meet her eyes, glinting in the faint light. "Would you?"

She's silent. Then she sets a warm hand on my arm, and nudges me down the hall. "No. I was up also. Shall I make some coffee? We can sit and talk."

I consider it. But I don't want to be inside right now. "I want to go for a walk."

Her forehead pinches. "Now? It is dark, and freezing. It must be ten degrees out there."

"I don't care."

She shakes her head. "We need to be more cautious now. It is not secure—"

"Ana. *Please*." I whisper it loud, urgent. "I want to be outside. Just for a while."

She thinks it over, sighs. "Dress warm. I will meet you in the kitchen."

We amble down my street side by side. Another man, in a thick jacket, walks ahead of us, another a ways behind. Plenty secure, for 4:00 A.M.

I let the air fill my lungs, tingle in my nose. I've walked this street so many times. Dad and I used to do it, just the two of us, to talk. The past two years Myk and I would walk it sometimes, to talk about Dad or life without upsetting Mom. In the day, though, or maybe the evening. At this hour it's so quiet, dark. We move from streetlight to streetlight, the spaces between—only pockets of shadow.

Ana doesn't speak, gloved hands in her coat, respecting my silence.

When we get to the end of the street where we usually turn, I stop. Stare at my feet.

"I don't know what to do," I say, low.

"Do?"

I look at her, so composed. Reassuring. "If there's a threat you can't control. Do I stop? Do I give in and go somewhere secure, to keep them safe, like Liesel wanted me to before?"

I'm shaky with cold. With fear.

It's giving up . . . everything. I don't know if I could do it, even if I decide I should.

"I'm eighteen . . ." I swallow. "How can I—"

Ana folds me in her arms, squeezes. I didn't expect it, but I hug her back. She's warm.

Girls, too. I'd be giving up girls, wouldn't I? Rachel . . . just when it was starting. . . . Oh, God.

Ana pulls back. "Do not decide anything yet. There is still a chance it will be okay. That it is nothing, or we can contain it."

I nod slowly. I wish I knew what kind of chance we're talking about. On a Magic 8 ball, would it be *Outlook good* or *Better not tell you now*?

"But if it's bad. I will have to decide, won't I? It'll come to that."

She runs a hand down my arm lightly. "It may come to that, Jake. It may not even be a decision you get to make."

That does not make it better.

We turn and walk back in the hard, vicious cold, and she makes a pot of coffee.

We don't speak. There's nothing to say, the thoughts whirling in endless loops. We sit at the table across from each other and drink coffee until we hear Mom start moving around. Then we split up. Ana starts breakfast, and I go into my room, sit on my bed, prepare myself.

To see what the day will bring.

18

"Gone" by Black Lab

Liesel calls Ana before breakfast: they're still gathering intelligence on the threat. With the extra security, we'll be safe. We're all supposed to go about our usual routines as though nothing has happened, until she knows more.

Ana suggested I call in sick from school—after two nights of no sleep, I must look pretty pitiful. I barely even managed to shave. Liesel overruled her. We can't get anyone suspicious that we realize anything is wrong.

So I trudge off. Even driving Myk to school I feel odd, like there's a fogged-up bubble between me and everything else.

"You okay?" Myk asks, when I drop her off.

I scrape together a smile. "Fine, dorkus. Just tired. You take care today, all right?"

She nods, still frowning, pulls on her Little Einsteins backpack, and takes off.

"Love you, munchkin," I say, under my breath. I watch her go all the way into her building before I leave.

The rest of the morning is a blur. I do calc problems badly, take illegible notes in world history and English, and do a piss-poor job of listening to Chris freak out about final rehearsal tonight and opening night tomorrow.

I don't even know if I'll *be* here for opening night. That's all I can think about. Not how the choreography is falling apart and they had to re-do the blocking, or how the costumes aren't ready. But I try to listen. It's important to him.

I talk to Rachel a little before class, but I don't know what I'm saying. She keeps looking at me strangely. Again I get the feeling she's the only one who notices that everything is *wrong*.

I ache to tell her, to talk openly about all this. But I can't endanger her too.

Eric gives me space, but keeps an eye on me. He seems tense. Maybe that's just me projecting my own tenseness. It's like there are bees humming under my skin.

At study hall Eric decides that going across to the graveyard today wouldn't be "productive enough to mitigate the security risk." We stay in the library and I actually crack the books and work on my project. It's the one thing I'm able to focus on all day. Diving into family histories, names and dates and stories. Other realities.

At lunch, Eric and I sit with the usual group—all losing their freaking minds about *Oklahoma*—and eat pizza. Midway through a story of Kadeem's, Eric's phone buzzes.

He glances at the number, gets up, and takes it outside. I try not to freak out.

I fail.

When he comes back, he heads straight for me. "Jake." His voice sounds odd, thick. "I've got to go pick up something for my dad, and I could use a hand. You want to come with?"

I look at him, the rest of them: Chris, Kadeem, Jeff. They're mildly curious. I want to say something. Do something, in case the news is bad.

I look over at Rachel, at the other table. She's watching me too, eyebrows down. She doesn't smile this time. But neither do I. I can't manage it.

I stand up. "Sure. See you guys later." I hold up a hand, and they all say good-bye. Go back to their pizza, their jokes. I look at Rachel again . . . then go.

When we get outside, Eric strides ahead, jerky, all the way to his car at the far end of the lot, and unlocks the doors without a word. We get in. He turns to face me, the freckles standing out on his cheeks.

"Tell me," I say.

"There was an attempt to kidnap Myka. She's okay, I want you to know that first. But it was a serious attempt. They were armed. We think they were trying to take her as leverage to get you."

Fear surges up, clawing at me. Myka. "She's okay," I repeat, like a robot.

"We stopped them without her knowing anything had happened. She's completely fine. I just checked, and your mom's fine, safe in her office."

I give him a long, searching look. "I'm checking myself."

"Jake," he says, sharp. "No." I ignore him. I find the note in my wallet, pinch it between my fingers. Go to Myka.

She's sitting in class at Nysmith, in a circle of chairs. There's a teacher—a tall man with a dark ponytail—in the center chair, talking about physics. Vectors, describing projectiles with numbers. Myka stops, pauses when she senses me. Love you, I think, as hard as I can. Everything's okay. Everything will be okay. She calms, as she always has.

I come out of it. Eric's watching me, his expression like a rumble of thunder. Ominous.

I don't know what to do with my hands. They feel huge, awkward. "She's okay. Now tell me the rest."

He sighs, life hissing out of him. He looks old.

"Dr. Miller confirmed that the men following your mother weren't ours. These obviously weren't ours. They're targeting your family, and we still don't know who they are." He pauses. "We can't contain it, not fast enough to guarantee your safety, or theirs."

I stare through the glass at the huddle of brick buildings I know so well, where I've spent most of my days for four years.

"It's over. Isn't it? Liesel said that's it?" I look at him. If I didn't know already, it's there, in his eyes.

"Dr. Miller has determined it's become too difficult to control. It's dangerous, for all of you. With you gone, with no doubts about that, they will leave your family alone. It's the only way now."

With me gone.

No, screams a thousand parts of my brain. *No no no no.*

Gone.

I knew this could happen, since last night. Since before that, if I admit it to myself. I knew it might come to this if I wanted them to be safe, if I wanted to fulfill all my promises. I didn't think it would be so soon. It's over. Last night was my last with my family. My last night out here.

My God.

"Swear to me," I say, fierce. "If I go away, go where you want, you'll keep them safe. Nothing will happen to them."

He extends his hand, and I shake it. Both our palms are damp. "I swear. Absolutely."

I breathe in, out. "Okay."

It's done. That simple. And that excruciatingly hard.

We don't speak for a while. I don't want to step past this moment. I don't want to go any further. But I have to.

"What happens now?"

Eric's under control again, professional. His voice is perfectly even. "Ana is on her way, with the van. She'll give you something to put you out. Then you'll be transported to a secure facility."

"*Unconscious?*"

He makes a face. "It's protocol, and necessary. I don't even know where you're going, Jake. That's why it's secure."

I can't wrap my head around it. Any of it. Except one thing. "My family? What will they think happened to me? Do I just disappear?"

He shifts. Looks down.

"Eric."

He meets my eyes head-on. "The story is we went for a drive, you and me. And I was reckless, or drunk, or distracted. They'll have a reason. I drove the car into a tree, and it exploded. We'll both be dead, burned beyond recognition. But we'll be identified. There won't be any doubt."

"They'll think I'm *dead*?" The word scrapes out of my mouth. *Dead*. "I didn't think . . . but you can't tell them that. It will kill them."

"No, it won't." He's firm now. "That's the point, Jake. It'll be awful, but clean. Far better than you being missing, the uncertainty, searches. They'll live through it. Keep living. They'll get past it. But most important, your enemies will believe you're dead. And your family will be safe."

I think of how hard it had been to lose Dad. How goddamned hard it will be for the two of them, alone. I won't even be able to tunnel to Myka again, or she'll know I'm there, still alive.

But we *had* gone on, after Dad was gone. They would too. Jesus Jesus Jesus.

"Can I see them again?" I ask. Plead. "One more time? Can we drive by or something, just to see?"

"I'm sorry. No. But you're doing the right thing. It will be best for everyone, in the end. Now." He clears his throat. "It's time. I need you to give me your personal effects, for the cover. Phone, keys, watch."

"Not the watch. The watch goes with me."

He sighs. "But you always wear it. If they don't find it . . ." He sees my face, stops. "Okay. We'll think of something for the watch. But give me the rest."

I give him my phone, keys, backpack. I don't give him Dedushka's ring, a solid lump in my pocket. I consider it, letting Dedushka believe I'm dead too. But some small part of me wants him to know. Wants someone to know I didn't die in a meaningless car crash today. That I'd done this voluntarily, for them. He'll know, when he sees wherever I go. He won't be able to get me, but he'll know.

Suddenly Rachel comes out the front doors. She doesn't have a coat on, and her arms are crossed over her chest, like she's protecting herself from the cold. She stops there on the sidewalk, searching around the parking lot.

She's looking for me.

"She knows," I whisper.

Eric was watching her too, but that makes him whip toward me. "She knows? You told her about us? My god, Jake—"

"No." I stare at her hard, like I can beam thoughts into her head from here. *I'm here. Come save me.* "I didn't say anything. She knows something's wrong. She senses it." She bites her lip, and she looks so cold. Alone.

I'm going to be alone.

"I'm going to go talk to her," I say, reaching for the door handle. *Kiss her good-bye. One last kiss before—*

"Jake, *no*."

Rachel turns and hurries back in, and the moment is lost. I can't go now.

By the end of today, she'll think I'm dead.

Ana's van swings into the parking lot and pulls up behind us. Eric gets out and speaks to her for a while, heads close, and then she opens the back of the van. He opens my door.

I get out and walk the few steps, breathe the air, feel the winter sun thin on my head. I look back once at Virginia High, then at Ana's face, solemn next to Eric's.

I wonder if I should run, now. If I should go back to the cafeteria and tell everyone what's going on here. If I should get in my car and drive away.

I wouldn't get anywhere. I know that. They wouldn't let me. The choice is past.

"Quickly," she says.

I climb up into the van. Eric reaches up to shake my hand again. "It's been a pleasure working with you, Jacob Lukin. I'm sorry it had to end this way."

I shake it, let go. Then Ana gets in and shuts the doors with a click. She opens a metal cabinet and takes out a small hypodermic needle, loads it carefully from a bottle.

"I said before you were brave," she says quietly. "You are. You are doing a very brave thing for your family."

I can't answer.

"I will stay with your family, for a while. I will help them. I promise you that."

I nod, breathe. In, out. In, out. Life is breath, heartbeat, my clenched fists. *I can't do this. I can't.*

She presses her hands, cool, on my cheeks. Then she pulls her hands away, studies me. "Ready?"

In, out. In, out. I close my eyes. "Ready."

The needle pricks, then stings as she pushes it into my arm. A cold tingle rushes through my veins. Then there's nothing.

19

"Underground" by Redlight King

When I wake up I'm alone, lying on a bed in a dim room. I listen: no sound but a low electric hum. No movement.

I push myself up on my elbows and lights come on. I squint against the god-awful glare of fluorescents.

The room is stark white, the size of an average hotel room. No windows. There's the bed, attached to the wall, and a short dresser. A single black armchair in the opposite corner pointed at a flat-screen TV on the wall. White tile floor. A white door that might lead to a closet or a bathroom. A table with two chairs in the front corner. Next to that, a floor-to-ceiling panel of smoky glass I can't see through. A door, I guess. There's no knob, no handle for opening it from the inside, though there's a card reader like before, and something that looks like an intercom box. No switches for lights.

There are two cameras mounted near the ceiling on opposite corners, red lights on.

Welcome home, Jake.

I want to throw up. But that might be the effects of the tranquilizer.

At least I'm still wearing my own clothes and Dad's watch. I stick my hand into my pocket. Dedushka's ring is gone, replaced by an odd, bumpy shape. I pull it out with a jingle, cupped in my hand. Ana's bracelet. She must have taken the ring after I was out, slipped this into my pocket instead.

I can't figure it out at first, still groggy. Then I realize: it's an object. With the bracelet I can tunnel to her, make sure Mom and Myk are okay.

I don't know if I'll be able to handle seeing them, what I'm putting them through. But she gave me the option. It was a generous, thoughtful gesture. And probably will get her in deep trouble if Liesel finds out about it.

I stuff it back in my pocket as the door slides open.

"Jacob." Liesel holds out her hands, palms down, as she walks toward me, like she expects me to take them.

I don't. In the end I agreed to this. I'm here. But I don't have to be happy about it. I sit up, prop my back against the wall. The room dips, swims.

Liesel drops her hands and settles herself on the bed next to me, ponytail swinging. Just like that first night at home.

I look for signs of satisfaction—that she's pleased she got what she wanted all along—but to her credit, I don't see any. She sets a hand on top of mine. "I am sorry it had to be this way. We'll do our best to make you comfortable here. And safe, of course."

"My family?" My voice cracks, and I hate it. "Do they already think—?"

She lets go of my hand, folds hers together. There are tight lines around her mouth. "It is done, yes."

I press my tongue against the roof of my mouth, breathe through my nose. *Keep it together.*

Done. Far past fixing. Mom, Myka, Rachel . . .

I breathe. That's all I can do.

"Now." She waves around the room. "I have to apologize for the accommodations. This was unexpected, and DARPA doesn't routinely use secure facilities. I've had to borrow some space from the CIA. It's a bit . . . sparse, but we've done our best to give you what you need, at least to start. You have your own bathroom, there. Clothes will be coming today. Meals will be brought to you here. There are facilities you can use, accompanied, if you request a time. A gym, a chapel. There are doctors on site for medical needs." She smiles, a little hesitant. Her lipstick is smeared at the corner. "And the TV. We can get you video games, movies, books. Whatever you like. A mini-fridge, maybe. Let me know if there are other necessities, and I'll see if we can accommodate them."

I sigh. "Music. And a computer. I need a computer."

"No, Jacob. No computer, no Internet. We can't risk being tracked, or you communicating with anyone from the outside. Any games, music, et cetera will be strictly offline."

I hadn't thought that far. No phone, no Internet. No contact with anyone outside of here. Ever.

Because Jacob Lukin is *dead*. Really dead, like an obituary and funeral, and counselors at school. Like I-am-not-going-back. I'm having a hard time grasping this.

"Speaking of tracking . . ." Her eyes change. "Were you aware that you were carrying a tracking device with you when we took you in?"

I frown, play dumb.

"Do you know how foolish that was? If you were tracked here, you could have compromised an entire secure facility. Not even ours. I would hate to have to explain that."

"What tracking device?"

Skepticism flashes. "The ring in your pocket. From your slippery grandfather, I would guess. A little souvenir, to keep an eye on you? Like the one he had in your watch?"

"Oh, the ring." I shrug. "I thought it was just a ring. It was too big for my finger, so I stuck it in my pocket. It had a *tracker* in it?"

She doesn't believe me. "Fortunately, it doesn't matter now. You're here, and we are secure. If you need anything, you can just press the intercom. We . . . don't have a lot of work for you yet, but I'm getting some. You'll have something starting tomorrow."

"Liesel?" I ask, low.

She raises her eyebrows.

"Where am I, anyway?"

She shakes her head. "I'm sorry. It's best if you don't know."

"Can I go outside? *See* outside?"

There's a moment when her eyes scan my face, and I hope. "Not now, Jacob. We'll see how it goes."

This is going to be my life? *This?* What the fuck have I done?

Remember Myka, Mom. The threats. I had to. I had to. *I had to.*

"Dr. Tenney is here. I'd like for you to see him this afternoon. I know this has to be tough right now, and he'll be able to help you deal with all of it."

Somehow, I don't think Liesel—or Dr. Tenney—has any idea.

This time, Dr. Tenney comes to me. Not a surprise. It sounds like it'll be a while before I see any walls but these.

He sits across the table, a small brown notebook in front of him, fluorescent glare on his head. Does he polish it? His expression is grave, understanding. I look away.

"Tell me how you're doing, Jake," he drawls.

Is he kidding? "Great, Dr. Tenney. Best day *ever*."

"I've asked that the cameras be turned off for our sessions." He points, and I realize they are. At least the lights aren't on. "Dr. Miller agreed. Anything you say is confidential, between us."

I rub my palm on the edge of the table, back and forth.

"You've gone through a lot in the past couple weeks," he pushes. "You've lost a great deal. I know you're strong, but you'll have to talk about it, work through it, or it'll break you down."

I glance at him, patient, waiting. I shake my head. I'll lose it if I talk about this—them. It's too raw.

"Jake. Please talk to me."

"No! All right? No." I look at my hand, unsteady on the table, and make a fist.

He writes a note, flips the page. "All right. I understand. Not now, but soon." He sets the pen on the table with finality and leans back in the chair, tipping it back on two legs. "Would it make you feel better to work on the tunneling? Are you up to that?"

"Hell, yes." *That* I can do. That hasn't changed.

He smiles, slow. "I so hoped you'd say that. I think we can do some excellent work together."

He reaches down to his case. I'm almost relieved to see the familiar Ziploc bag. This one holds an even smaller flip notebook, the kind old engineers carry in their shirt pockets. He pushes the bag across to me. "This is not for anyone's purpose but ours," he says, his fingers still on the bag. "It's not real work. It's just to practice, and see what you can really do. I am going to ask that when you tunnel, you let yourself go further, deeper. See how far in you can go."

I eye him. "But the headache—"

"May happen, yes. Though we understand what it is, we don't know yet what triggers it. But if we don't test, we will have no idea what your boundaries truly are. And we are ready for the headache."

He takes a small green glass bottle out of his briefcase and removes the stopper. T-680. My own special Froot Loops medicine.

I open the bag, grasp the notebook, and take a deep breath. Eager to get away from here.

A man. Small and neat, with round glasses, balding . . .

I open my eyes. "This is you."

He cracks up, like he told a good joke. I don't even smile. "Yes. I thought it easiest if we don't involve anyone else, for the time being. While we're starting."

"But . . ." There are lots of reasons it's odd. "I'll know where we are."

He nods. "True. Does it matter? Pardon my saying, but you're not going anywhere, and you're not talking to anybody. You're not exactly a security risk anymore. I know Dr. Miller thinks differently, but personally I do not think it is significant." He points at the cameras again with his chin. "And it is between us where you go, for now."

I do want to know. I close my eyes again, concentrate on the object, and speak.

He sits at a small, oblong table in a white room, notebook in front of him. Location: New York. Long Island, far out on the very point. Montauk. A facility underground, below what used to be Montauk Air Force Station. Room 323, in the east wing. He's watching a young man with dark, wild hair, his face scraggly with stubble. The young man's eyes are closed, and he's hunched over something in his hands, muttering. The man is pleased, hopeful. Encouragement flows through him.

That's as far as I've ever gone. I want to pull away, while it's safe. But he wants more. Deeper. I hesitate. Then I let my mind settle, spread into him.

There's a dull ache in his shoulder when he grips the pen. He writes anyway, with his left hand in slanted script: Tunnel successful. No awareness of presence. The pen feels cool and solid against his fingers, the ink smooth as it rolls onto the paper.

Samuel. His name is Samuel Parker Tenney.

A thought flashes through: His daughter, Annie, has a piano recital to-

night. He doesn't know if he'll make it back in time. But he can't disappoint Annie.

I feel dense, stiff. Like wax beginning to harden into a mold. I feel my fingers inside his, my legs in his legs. My heart, beating faster than my heart should. His belly, curving where mine shouldn't curve.

Any longer and I'll be stuck here.

I yank myself away, open my eyes. I'm breathing hard. My skin feels stretched. I push the heel of my hand against my forehead, trying to shove back the pain lurking there.

"That was marvelous." Dr. Tenney is practically bouncing, like a leprechaun about to break into a jig. "I had no idea you were there at all. And you read my name! And my daughter's name. I *knew* you could go further, if we just tried. And there's more, I know there is."

I don't tell him about the physical aspect, about feeling part of him. Not yet.

"It's coming," I say, strained. "I can't stop it."

And then it's there, crushing my head in.

I fall to the floor.

Dr. Tenney's hands are in my mouth, his fingers fat, rough.

There's the sweet taste of the pill, the pain flying away as quickly as it came.

He gets me to the bed. I'm so happy with the bed, with him, with my little hidden place underneath Montauk, Long Island. Liesel and DARPA and the work I'll do. It all seems right, exactly as it should be. Where I should be.

If only I could take that pill all the time, maybe I could deal with this new life.

20

"Let Me Out" by Imelda May

When I wake up this time, it's dark and I'm alone again. The cameras are back on. Dr. Tenney must have had to pack up and go—if he's going to get to Annie's concert, wherever that is.

It doesn't seem fair that he can leave and I can't. Just because I'm dead and in permanent protective custody.

I peer at my watch without triggering the lights: 9:22. The funny thing is I have no idea if that's a.m. or p.m. If someone doesn't tell me, I'll never know. At least if I had an object I could tunnel to someone, to see what was happening in the world.

But I forgot. I do have an object, still in my pocket. Ana's bracelet. I could go now, in the dark, without anyone knowing. I could go and see Mom and Myk, quick, just to make sure they're okay.

I tug the bracelet out, run my thumb over the charms. Can I stand to see what I did to them?

If they have to deal with the loss, the least I can do is witness it.

Fucking just do it, Jake.

I close my eyes.

A woman, long, dark hair pulled back in a knot, black eyes. Ana. Location: 902 Van Buren Street, Herndon, Virginia. She sits on the edge of a big bed. It's morning, light pushing in through the curtains. There's another woman slumped on the bed, arms around her knees, head down. All I can see of her is knees and the top of her head. I can hear her, though. Sobbing. Heaving. So violently it seems like there's no way she can breathe. Ana reaches out and places a hand on her back, rubs in slow circles. She feels sympathy, an ache of sympathy, and sorrow . . .

I pull away, but I don't open my eyes. I lie there, bracelet in my hand, and cry too, just like Mom.

I don't care who hears me.

After I finally sit up and trigger the lights, a youngish guy with a key card wheels in a cart with toast, eggs, and coffee. He nods, but doesn't speak, and goes away again.

I eat, drink coffee, and go into the bathroom—the only camera-free zone, as far as I can tell—to change into some of the clothes I found in the dresser. A black T-shirt, long shorts. Why not shorts, I figure. There are no seasons in here. The floor is cool on my bare feet.

I don't shave. I don't feel like it.

I wonder what Rachel's doing today. Chris. Are they falling apart too? Did I mess them up like I did Mom? Are they still going to do *Oklahoma*?

I want to take the last twenty-four hours back. No. I want to take the last two months back, listen to Dad, and everything would be fine.

When the door opens again I'm sitting in the chair watching a car show with zero interest. I turn slowly, not really up to dealing with Liesel.

It isn't Liesel. It's Bunny—Dr. Milkovich—in the doorway, a metal box in her arms. Her pale blond hair is pulled back on the sides with little clips, but hangs straight and smooth around her chin. She's not wearing the lab coat today, just pants and a sweater. She smiles tentatively. "Hello. Ready to do some work, Mr. Lukin?"

"Hey, Bunny," I say tiredly. I stand, turn off the TV. "Didn't think I'd see you again. And it's Jake."

Her nostrils flare at *Bunny,* but she doesn't comment. She sets the box down on the table with a clunk. "I've been assigned as lead investigator to your project, Mr. Lukin. You'll be seeing me most days."

"Jake," I repeat.

She's so small and thin, like a white bird. I can see her shoulder bones, sharp. "Dr. Miller is still the project head. She'll be here often."

"Yay." Like I was missing Liesel. I glance up at the cameras. "Sure, let's do some work."

We sit at the table while Bunny sorts through her box, her notes. I guess she doesn't need a video camera, since that's amply covered.

She seems even more jittery today than before, throwing glances at me rapid-fire. Maybe she's always like that. Or maybe I make her nervous. I stroke my jaw with my thumb. Scratchy, already getting out of control. I'll have a beard in a couple more days if I let it go. Why not?

She passes across the first bag. I smooth my fingers across the plastic, but don't open it yet.

"Have you heard from Eric?" I ask. "Eric Proctor?"

She slants a look at me. Her eyes—blue—are round, but they tilt up at the corners a touch. She's not like a bird. She's like a white kitten.

"I just . . . want to know if he's okay."

She shakes her head. "I'm sorry."

"Of course." My voice turns hard. "You couldn't tell me if you had, right? He's already on to something else. Some other case."

She shrugs again. There's an awkward silence. Fuck conversation anyway. I open the bag, drop the foreign coin into my hands, and focus.

It's a boy, maybe ten years old. Dusky skin, a small cap, a white caftan to his ankles. Location: Pakistan, Mingora. A large walled house down a side street off Haji Baba Road. It's late, the stars bright above. The boy stands by a gate, shivering. He's waiting for someone, a message. He's worried something will go wrong, the messenger won't come. Everyone would be angry. The boy scratches his foot, watches the full moon overhead. Not much longer. Footsteps. A man comes. It is the messenger, wrapped up so only his eyes show. He hands the boy a folded packet of news. The boy relaxes.

I open my eyes. "Is that enough?"

Bunny looks over her shoulder at the camera, goes still for a moment. "Yes," she says quietly. "That's perfect."

"Wait. Are you wearing an earpiece?"

Her mouth quirks up. She isn't going to answer. "Are you ready for another, Mr. Lukin, or do you need a break between?"

"Jake. And you know whoever is listening can just talk to me directly. I'm right here. They don't need to mediate through you."

She taps her pen on the paper, eyes on me. "This is how it's going to work, Jake. At least for now."

I rub my temples, shoving down the sudden burst of temper. For some reason out of everything, this—some faceless person watching us and giving her directions instead of just dealing with me—pisses me off. It makes me feel like a prisoner.

I'm going to have to get it through my thick skull that I *am* a prisoner. For life. And I'm making my mother sob like a baby right now.

"Jake?"

I lift my head. "Yeah. Fine. Let's do another one."

Bunny is still excited about the tunneling. I can see it in the way her small hands jump across the paper, the energy she flings out. It just makes me tired. And this is my first day.

She gives me another bag. I have the object in my hand before I realize what it is.

An air force ring. Silver. Stamped with an eagle. Dedushka's ring. Dad's.

"Oh, no." I drop it back into the bag, seal it with one swipe. "I'm not doing that one."

Bunny frowns. "But you have to do all the objects we give you."

"That's my grandfather's," I say loudly, like I'm speaking for a microphone. She flinches. "I will not help you track him."

It's silent while she listens to the voice in her ear, and I watch her.

"Very well," she says finally. She takes the bag back and hands me another one. A silver pen.

I'll work, I'll do what they ask. Terrorists, smugglers, other people on the run: yes. I'll tell DARPA where they are, spy on what they're doing. That's why I'm here.

Not Dedushka. Wherever he is, he's safe from me.

21

"Cell" by Sunday Munich

Weeks go by like that.

I work with Bunny most days. Other than that, nothing changes except the TV shows, censored so they don't have any news. Maybe they don't want me to understand what I'm tunneling to. Maybe it would complicate things if I actually had a clue what was going on in the world.

I tunnel, sleep, eat, listen to music, play offline *Halo, Call of Duty,* and *Top Spin.* I play *Death to Spies* just for the irony, but nobody notices.

They're careful never to leave anything personal in my room—everything, even utensils, is cleared out after sessions or meals. Even in the bathroom there's nothing sharp, nothing I could use to hurt myself or anyone else, unless I want to drink shampoo. Nothing I could use to tunnel to anyone.

It's controlled. Every second, every inch, is controlled, observed.

My mood flops all over the place, from anger to resentment to simply not giving a shit.

I try tunneling to Ana again, twice, but one time she's asleep and the other time she's in the kitchen, alone. But I think about Mom and Myka. All the time. Think about Stanford and tennis and Chris and skiing in the sunlight. Swimming at the pool in the summer, the bright smell of chlorine. Sitting in my corner of the graveyard, the rustle of the trees behind me, shooting the breeze with Pete. Tickling my sister. Eating spaghetti with my mom. And over and over, that moment in the hall with Rachel, her lips soft on mine, with the promise of more.

Things I will never, ever do again.

I see Dr. Tenney three times a week. We talk. It helps some. With no cameras, I trust him more than the others. I tell him how much I miss, and he acknowledges it. At the end of each session we do our tunneling practice, always to him, to try to go deeper. So far I've only managed a few seconds longer than that first time. The fear of getting stuck is too strong—I can't get past it. But I keep trying.

It doesn't click until we do something different.

"I have a treat for you today," he says. It's a Wednesday. I've been making sure I keep track. "I think you need a vacation." He hands me a bag with a key in it.

I dangle the bag in my fingers. "The key to my room? *Yes*. You do know what I want."

He smiles. "Just do it. When you go this time, I want you to keep going as deep as you can. This is a safe one that I set up just for you. I want you to *feel* what it's like, to be that person." He leans in. "As far as you can. Trust me."

I throw him a look. We've been trying this for ages. I trust him to a point. But I don't know if I can go deeper.

"You'll be able to return. Do your best. And *enjoy* it."

Enjoy it? I close my eyes. Let the glow, the buzz, come.

A man. Average height, muscled abs, bulky arms. Military haircut, black skin. He's wearing only a pair of swim shorts and sunglasses. Location: Guam. The northernmost tip, Ritidian Beach. He's lying on the sand, no one else anywhere near. The sand is white, clean. Tropical bushes and palm trees line the curve of beach behind his head. At his feet, a hundred yards away, clear, turquoise water sparkles in the sun. There are big concrete stacks, World War II bunkers, off to the right, in the water and on the beach.

I relax into him. I haven't been to a real beach since we lived in Florida. I'd forgotten how great it is. Was. I wish this was real.

His eyes are closed, the sun a red glare through his eyelids. It's warm, steady, but the breeze from the ocean keeps it cool. The only sound is the swoosh of the waves, the faint call of birds behind. The sand is soft under his shoulders, legs. He's content, utterly relaxed.

I go deeper.

His name is Lance Buckley, but he thinks of himself as Buck. He doesn't know how he scored this trip—assignment, whatever—but he owes God a big one. Best assignment he's ever had. Just lie there on the beach, Buck.

Deeper, into his toes, arms, fingers. I have that sensation of wax hardening, stiffening, and start to panic. Stop. Push myself farther. Let it happen.

I am Buck. I can feel his strength, physical, mental. His ability to put everything he experiences—dark, scary stuff—into compartments he doesn't visit again. He lives in the moment, and the moment, right now, is perfect. He stretches, flexes his toes. I suddenly want to turn his head, look down the beach. Turn his head. A simple movement. Lift, turn. Open your eyes. You want to look over there, Buck. See if anyone's coming.

He turns his head. *I* turn his head. And open his eyes.

Just like that, without knowing I could, I controlled him. Enough presence in his mind to suggest that he wanted to make the movement. Enough presence in his body to make it happen.

I don't want to leave Buck, leave the beach for my damn white cell. I am enjoying it. But I'm starting to feel lost, more caught up in him, less in me. Reluctantly I drag myself out and open my eyes.

God, I feel stiff, thin. Like Silly Putty stretched too far, cracking.

Dr. Tenney beams so hard it's like he's got a freaking flashlight inside him. "I *knew* you could do it. I knew you could move a subject, if you only went far enough. All my research pointed to it as the next step." He scribbles on his pad, blue ink streaming. "Good God," he says, almost to himself. "Think of the implications. If we refine it, strengthen it. If we have an object, you could go anywhere, to anyone."

Implications? So I moved some guy on a deserted beach. Big deal.

But I *moved* someone. Without their will. From a distance.

It takes me a minute or two, but I see it in a flash of clarity. The implications. If I can move someone from inside, without detection—I can make them do things they wouldn't. I can make them write things. Sign things. Move a gun or a knife or a bomb.

Jesus Christ. I could be far more than an intelligence source. I could be a secret weapon.

"Don't tell Liesel about this," I say, fast. "We don't know if I can do it again."

"Oh, no," Dr. Tenney says, writing, his head blaring in the lights. He sounds insanely cheerful. "I won't tell her yet. Not this early. Once we've refined it, we can present to her the results of my research. Our success."

"No," I repeat, stronger. I lean forward. "Don't tell her at all. I thought what happened in here was between us. Confidential, right?"

He glances up at me. "Until we had something to report. Don't you see, Jake? This is a tremendous development. This is what we've been working toward. Your value has multiplied a hundred times. A thousand. She will have to know, when we've proven it."

He goes back to writing.

Understanding settles deeply into my bones, at last. I feel awake, alive with it. More alert than I have been in weeks.

He isn't my friend, or even my doctor. He wasn't listening, pushing, to help me at all.

He's simply been doing a side project, to develop the Tunnel as a weapon. That was his goal all along. He'll get research bonanza. He'll be a hero with Liesel and DARPA and whoever else. He doesn't give a damn about me as a person. Just what I can do. Like all of them.

I'm not going to be their weapon. I'm never controlling someone again. Not for them.

While he's busy with his frantic writing I lean down, under the table. I dip my hand into his briefcase and fumble through all the items there, until I find something that will work: one of the small notebooks, the kind I use to tunnel to him in practice. I pull it out carefully, eyes on him, and put it in my pocket.

I don't know what kind of info I'll get out of an off-hours tunnel to Dr. Tenney—but I'm going to find out. With the truth comes determination. I am *done* being a pawn, a schmuck, without any clue or control. *I* have the ability. It's mine.

It's time to find out what's really going on around here.

The good thing about no windows is that I can make it dark whenever I want, just by lying still long enough. If I'm going to get any good info out of him, it'll probably be while he's still in the building. Before he heads back to Washington or Georgia or wherever.

So after that tunnel, it's clearly time for poor worn-out government asset Jake to take a nap.

I lie on the bed, perfectly still, hands in my pockets, until the lights go out. A few minutes longer, for buffer. Then I grip the notebook in my hand, still in the pocket, and focus.

I go through the usual description of him, my brain telling me who he is and where. Montauk, Long Island, yeah yeah.

He's walking down a hallway on the second floor. The walls are pure white. These aren't cells, but offices, with normal wooden doors that open. He stops at one, knocks. There's a muffled answer, and he goes inside. Dr. Miller sits at a desk in an office cluttered with boxes, in a black suit, her hair pulled back tightly. She gives him a full, real smile.

"Samuel," she says. "You did it. Very well done."

She knows what he did already? What I did? So he was lying about not telling her yet?

I'm starting to feel uncomfortable in him already. Too close, too much, after the long tunnel to the beach. I don't want to go that deep again right now. If I get a headache they'll know what I was doing.

I pull away, open my eyes. Take a breath, two, let myself settle. Clear.

Then I go back in. Just for a second.

He's speaking. "I did tell him you'd have to be informed, eventually. But he thinks you don't know anything yet. We should keep it that way for a while, while we develop this. He is much more free with me when he believes it is confidential."

"Yes." She taps her nails on her desk, considering. "I still want you to get more information from him about Grigory Lukin. I cannot leave that thread dangling. We have to find him and close the loop." She frowns. "The Soviet records are sealed too deep for me to access. But we know he has abilities of some kind, that he was of value to the military. We may be able to use him too. And then maybe we won't have to struggle so hard to prove ourselves."

I yank out of it, breathless, my head fuzzy. I have to stop there. But I learned a lot in a few minutes.

One: Dr. Tenney lied to me the whole damn time about the sessions being private. He's been reporting everything I said to her. There's probably a bug or something. And the two of them had always been plotting to make me go deeper, to make me into a weapon.

It's not going to happen.

Two: Dedushka has "abilities" and was "used" by the Soviet military. That odd conversation in the car makes so much more sense now. The tracker, him wanting to run. "Do not trust them for a second," he'd said. "I have experience. And so did your father."

What does Dad have to do with all this?

One thing for sure—that wasn't my last private tunnel to Dr. Tenney. And I'm going to find a way to tunnel to Liesel too. It's the only way I'm going to get any answers.

Still in the darkness, I hide the notebook between the mattresses, where I can reach it without triggering lights. After discovering all the lies so far? That every one of them is lying to me? I am going to get answers.

22

"Lies" by Billy Talent

How do you spy on professional spies when you're under twenty-four-hour surveillance, without giving them any clue you're onto them?

Very carefully.

I don't want to confront them on anything I've learned—it'd just give them more chances to mess with me, to take away my object.

But I'm not going to stay in here the rest of my life. Not anymore.

Bunny bubbles in the next morning, carrying her metal box. "Hello, Jake. We have hostage work today. From the FBI."

I go straight to the table. If I can actually save somebody? I figure it balances out all the people I . . . actively help to *not* save, every day. A little.

She opens the box and pulls out the first bag; a small, gold dangly earring.

My chest tightens. A woman hostage. *Okay. Go.*

She's too thin, hollows under her cheeks. Her hair is dark with grease and dirt, stringing over her face. Location: Alaska. Harding Lake, forty-four miles south of Fairbanks. A cabin on the east side of the lake, in the trees at the end of Friendly Road. She's on a bed in the corner of the one-room cabin, handcuffed to the metal frame. A man sits in a chair, watching her. He licks his thin lips, slow, eyes never leaving her face. She's terrified. Hopeless. No one knows where she is. No one can save her. She'll die here.

I come out of it quick. "Enough?"

Bunny pauses. "Yes. Thank you."

I go to the mini-fridge for a Coke and suck it down, eyes unfocused. The hostage ones rattle me. It's harder to be in their heads than the bad guys, the people who are wanted for their own choices. But they're still why I do this. For now.

After a while I circle back to the table, take a deep breath, and drop into the chair. Silently Bunny passes the next bag over.

It's a girl's diary, a fancy one with pink and green swirls all over the cover, and a small gold lock. Myka had one like that when she was nine or ten, pink and silver. She'd been so protective of it I hadn't even had the heart to spy, to find out who she thought was cute and which friend was fighting with who.

Deliberately I pull this one out of the bag, run a finger over the swirls. It makes me feel close to Myk somehow. Even though this isn't hers. Even though she's far away.

I squeeze my eyes shut.

Sucking, empty blackness. Painful. Frost filling up my veins.

I gasp out of it, my hand still flat on the cover, and shove it away. It slides too far, into Bunny's lap. "Dead," I manage.

That little girl, whoever she was. Too late to save her.

Bunny's eyes look big in her face. "Do you need to stop?"

I swallow, breathe, shake my head again. Not if there are some in there I *can* save. She takes her time wrapping the book in its bag, settling it in the box. Like a good umpire brushing off the plate, giving the catcher time to recover from a hit to the groin.

When I'm ready I hold up a hand, and she passes me the next one.

We do two more. One is alive, and hopefully will stay that way if responders can get there fast enough. The last—another woman, her object a mini–Big Ben—isn't.

Did she get to Big Ben before she died? I'll never know. Or her name.

Bunny sits a minute, looking at the box, her pale hair swinging around her chin. A pink blush creeps across her cheeks as I stare at her.

She's almost pretty, with the pink. And looks young, almost my age. Of course I haven't seen a girl other than her and Liesel for a couple months—and I see Bunny almost every day—so maybe I'm losing perspective. But I think she might have a little crush on me, if she'd let herself.

I miss Rachel. I wish, powerfully, that she were here right now. Just for an hour. Even if I couldn't touch her, just talk. About movies I haven't seen, comics I haven't read. I'd even take that.

But I'll never see Rachel again. Even if I do get out of here. She thinks I'm dead.

Bunny lifts her eyes to mine. "I know it's hard for you, being here. I hope you know we're doing good work. We're making a difference in this room."

Dedushka's voice echoes in my head. *"At the expense of yourself? They will take everything from you, these people. They will suck you up until you are dry and then toss you away."*

I drop my head, don't answer. There's nothing to say.

I do another tunnel that night, on my own in the dark with Ana's bracelet. After that little girl, that diary, I have to see Myk again. Even if she's hurting, I need to know she's alive, okay.

But when I go to Ana, she isn't in my house anymore. She's sitting in a car in New Jersey, watching a warehouse with binoculars.

She's off the case. That means Mom and Myk really are alone. And I can never tunnel to them again. It's just me.

Now I really have to scrounge all the information I can and find a way out of this.

On Saturday I decide to try to get an object from Bunny. I probably won't learn much from her—I doubt she's on the inside track, like Liesel—but it can't hurt.

I've only thought of one way to get an object from her, and it isn't very nice. But if it comes down to nice Jake staying in a cell forever as a pawn, or not-nice Jake taking control of his own life . . .

When she comes in I'm sitting on the bed, legs swinging. I smile, lazily. "Thought you'd never get here."

Her forehead creases. "What?" She's wearing the silver clips in her hair, on either side, just like every day.

I shrug. "You're all I have to look forward to, Bunny."

The blush spreads across her cheeks like magic. Jesus. I was right about the crush.

I feel like I'm being disloyal to Rachel even pretending this. Which is weird, maybe, since I can't see her again. But real.

She drops the box on the table too hard. "You shaved your beard."

"Yeah. I figured that was enough of the mountain man look and requested a razor." Which they took away as soon as I was done. "Mostly I thought you'd like it better. What do you think?" I sit across from her, watch her as she sets up. She's all fumbly, glancing at me sideways. I don't want to overdo the flirting—but I don't seem to be.

"Nice." She says it soft, ducking her head.

"Bunny."

"Yes?"

I clear my throat. "I want to say . . . thanks."

"Thanks?" Her mouth opens a little, her eyes wide.

"For the other day. What you said about doing good work? It's hard for me to remember sometimes." This, at least, is true. "It meant a lot."

She smiles, her whole face brightening. "You're welcome. It is important. *You* are."

I study her intently. Tilt my head. "Can I do something?"

She laughs, a tiny bubbly laugh she stops as soon as it starts. "What?"

I reach across the table slowly, like I'm approaching a small animal, until my fingers are in her hair. Her breath goes fast, her eyes fixed on me. I undo the clips, one, two, and let her hair fall.

"I wondered how it would look like that. Much better."

I draw my hand back, the clips safely tucked in my palm, and hide them in my pocket, under the table.

She beams at me.

I breathe. That wasn't so bad. Wrong, yes. Manipulating her. But not *evil* or anything. Now to do some work, and then later I can tunnel to her. And not flirt quite so hard next time.

She goes for a bag, then stops, hand in midair. Listening. Her cheeks blaze, instant, like somebody splashed red paint across them. "Yes," she whispers. "I understand."

She keeps her eyes down, holds out one hand to me, palm up. It's shaking. "I need my clips back, please."

Crap. I look at the camera. It worked on her, but not on them.

Slowly I take them out, hand them to her. Without a word she flings them into the box, picks it up, zips to the door, and slams her badge in the key reader. When the door opens she scurries out, without looking back.

I let out a long breath, stand, and go to the black chair. I sit, hands flat on the arms of the chair, and wait. If I'm right, it won't be long. About as long as it would take to get here from the second floor.

I'm right. The door opens in a few minutes.

I stay like that, back to the door.

"Jacob Lukin." It sounds like a curse.

I turn slowly in the chair. Liesel stands inside the door, her entire body rigid.

My face tries a smile, but it doesn't get very far before sinking away.

"What the *hell* did you think you were doing?"

"Flirting?" I clear my throat again. "You didn't say I couldn't—"

She paces in front of me. "Don't mess with me, Jacob. You were trying to steal objects from her. You *did* steal objects from her. What were you going to do with them?"

I haven't seen this side of her before. This seems like a good time to not answer.

"Stand up."

I stay where I am. I keep my face, my hands, perfectly still.

"Stand up, and don't make me ask you a third time. This"—she flings a hand out, pointing around the room—"may not be ideal for you. But it can be a whole lot worse, with a few words from me."

I push myself up. She crosses to me, thrusts her hands in my pants pockets, one after the other. The first is empty. The second, the right pocket, has Ana's bracelet. She tugs it out, triumphant. "What is this?"

"My girlfriend's," I mumble.

"Rachel Watkins? No, I don't think so. You forget I know everything about you. Whose is it, really? Your mothers? Your sisters? Were you tunneling to them on your own?"

Almost. I flinch, but don't answer.

She closes her fist around the bracelet. "I'll need to keep this."

"No," I say through gritted teeth. "I don't have anything else left of them."

Even though I can't use it, I want it. It's all I have, except Dad's watch.

She breathes through her nose. "You shouldn't have anything left," she says, lower. Almost gentle again. "You need to let them go, let that life go. And I *cannot* take the risk that you're tunneling privately. As to today's incident." Gentle vanishes. Her lips pinch tight. "I will not tolerate this kind of behavior. You will be told what you need to be told, and nothing else. You will not use my staff, and you will not go behind my back for more information. Got it?"

Except for Dr. Tenney, I think, thankful I hid the notebook in the mattress. *And you, when I get something of yours. And I will.*

She takes a step closer, pushing into my space. "Do you understand, Jacob?"

"Yeah." I meet her soul-sucking eyes. "I understand, Liesel."

"Good. Since you have compromised Dr. Milkovich, she is off the project. I will find someone else." She pauses, narrows her eyes. "Male, I think."

Because I need less estrogen in my life. That leaves me with Liesel representing the female sex, and she definitely does not count.

"In the meantime, if we have any urgent work for you to do, I will handle it personally."

"And today?" I ask.

"Today I'm busy," she snaps. "Consider yourself lucky I don't put you in a real cell, in cuffs, for a while. If you try any more tricks like that, I will. Be careful, Jacob. I will be watching you very closely."

She spins, thrusts her card in the reader only slightly less violently than Bunny had, and leaves.

That went really well, I think.

23

"Things Are Looking Up" by Blues Traveler

By Monday morning I'm ready to do something again, even if it's DARPA work. Even with some random new guy. When the door opens and I see the shock of red hair, the freckles, I grin.

"Thank God it's you. I figured she was going to send some tough hard ass to keep me in line."

Eric sets down his box and holds out his hand. I shake it. He smiles his easy smile. "Hello. I'm Eric, the tough hard ass sent to keep you in line."

We laugh, and sit at the table.

"Seriously," I say. "I can't believe they sent you here. I figured you were long gone, off on bigger and fantastically more exciting assignments."

He shrugs. "I am a field agent, but there are very few people who know about you—and it seems they want to keep it that way." He gives me a shrewd look. "So what happened with Bunny?"

My turn to shrug. Even though I'm glad to see him—even though I trust him far more than any of the others—his loyalty is still to them, and I know it. "Misunderstanding."

"I see." His eyes travel around the room, taking it in. "You okay here?"

I glance at the camera, then at him. "Brilliant."

"Is there anything I can get you? To make it easier?"

I smile.

"No, I can't get you a girl, or porn, or the Internet," he says.

I snort. "A card key? A field trip? A new room, with an actual window? Five minutes of sunshine?"

He gives me a wry smile. "Nice try. Look, I really am supposed to keep a close eye on you. No stealing objects from me, or other shenanigans. All right, mate? We do that crazy thing you do, and that's it."

I nod. I don't think I could steal anything from him anyway. He's too sharp. And he knows me a lot better than Bunny ever did.

It's a relief having someone here who knew my life before. He sat in Mrs. Skinner's class, ate lunch with Kadeem and Chris, met Pete. I know he left at the same time I did . . . "Ed" is dead too . . . but it's almost like having a smidgen of home. It's more than I've had in a long time.

"At least you know where the secure facility is now," I say. "You're moving up in the spy world."

He laughs. "I guess I am."

"Eric . . ." I pause, then push on. "What's it like out there? Are there wars? Earthquakes? They . . . don't tell me anything."

He opens his mouth, but the little voice in his ear clearly tells him not to answer. "The same as it always is. But we have work to do, to help it stay safe out there. You ready?"

I sigh. "Sure. Let's go."

After the second tunnel I get slammed with a headache, a bad one. It had been a couple weeks, and I'd almost forgotten how disabling they can be. In two seconds I turn into a puddle on the floor, screaming.

Way to break Eric in. The rest of the day is shot, and I miss another session with Dr. Tenney.

It will have to be Wednesday before I learn anything else.

Dr. Tenney is growing a beard. I keep staring at it. His face looks different with it, more professional, doctorlike. Like he's channeling Freud.

"And Dr. Milkovich's departure?" he asks, scribbling in his notebook of the day. "How are you adjusting to that?"

I shrug. "Fine. Who cares?"

He glances at me, makes a note. "You seem unhappy, Jake. Has something changed?"

"No." Other than that I found out you're lying to me, you two-faced bastard. "Can we be done now?"

"Oh, but I have a tunnel today, to work on moving the subject. Progress after our breakthrough last week."

I expected as much. He takes a bag from his briefcase, hands it over. It's another key, this time a smaller silver one. I close my hand around it, hoping for the beach.

"This one is set up to test your ability to move his hands, arms. Don't be afraid to go deep, like last time."

It's a man. Average in every way: height, size, looks. Hair muddy brown, cropped short. Location: Arlington, Virginia. DARPA headquarters. 3701 North Fairfax Drive, fourth floor, room 420. The room is empty except for the man, a camera, and the table where he sits, arms laid out in front of him. There are items on the table within easy reach: a pen, a pad of paper with some writing on it, a stapler, a paper clip. The man doesn't move. He simply sits, eyes open, waiting.

It's creepy. It's like the guy is a doll, a puppet, just waiting for me to take him over. All kinds of wrong. Still, I keep going.

He's a little nervous, worried about what this is for. They wouldn't tell him, except he was to sit here and not move. His fingers twitch, and he stills them.

I feel myself stretching into him, crystallizing. This is where I could probably control him, if I wanted to, if I did it right. I don't try. I ignore his limbs, dive deeper into his brain, and rattle off details.

His name is Mike Holmes. Research assistant at DARPA. Working on the AFPA project, an electro-optical imaging sensor for surveillance. Though he's just an assistant. Treated like one too. If they'd just recognize his last proposal—

Far enough. I open my eyes. "Couldn't get him to move. Sorry."

Dr. Tenney writes something, flicks a look at me. "Try again, please."

I go in again, but I still don't try. I pretend to. I grunt, crease my forehead all up. "Nothing." I rub at my head.

"Are you certain you're trying, Jake?"

"Of course," I say, innocent faced. "Why wouldn't I be trying?"

He gathers up his things, disappointment stamped all over him. "Well, it can't happen every time. We'll try again Friday. Perhaps you'll be a bit . . . cheerier then."

"Sure, doc. I'll work on my cheery, just for you."

He rolls his eyes and leaves.

I yawn big, stretch, and wait a couple minutes. Then I wander over to the bed to lie down and wait for the lights to go out. That should be long enough so I won't waste my time on him walking down the hallway.

I push my hand carefully into the fold between the mattresses, curl it around the notebook. Finally. Showtime.

He sits in Dr. Miller's office, room 205 on the second floor of the east wing. She's in a suit again, red lipstick a slash. She pages through his notebook, frowning. "That was particularly useless."

"I agree," Dr. Tenney says, his voice a rumble in his chest I can feel. "Something was wrong with him today. He is hiding something, or afraid."

"Afraid to go further? I'm not surprised." She clicks her tongue. "He's smart enough to have grasped the consequences. I suspect that's why he was trying to get an object from Dr. Milkovich—he is aware of his potential value. He wants to know what we have planned."

"He cannot be allowed to know anything," Dr. Tenney says. "He'll shut down."

She glares at him. "Of course. I handled it. I don't think he'll be doing that again. If he does try anything . . ." She raises her eyebrows. "Well. Nothing will happen to the boy if he lives up to his potential. But I need better results from you. You did not get any information on Grigory Lukin. And my sources still have not located him. We need more from Jacob."

I struggle to stay on the surface of Dr. Tenney, to not go deeper, not yet. But I'm sinking. It's been a long tunnel already. I have to come out for a minute.

I lie still, counting my breaths. Dying to go back in. But I have to pace it. Ninety-nine . . . one hundred.

I go back. Waste a few seconds on description, location.

". . . use this relationship with Proctor," she's saying. "Maybe he can extract some information you can't. I'll speak with him, and let you know what I want you to target."

"Have you thought of going to the sister for info on Grigory? He might have contacted her."

Myka? He knows how close I am with Myka. I've told him, confidentially. I want to scream at him, stop him. Instead I go deeper.

"She's under surveillance," Liesel says. "If there is contact, we should know real-time." Dr. Tenney is impatient, ready to go. She never listens to him anyway. She just wants to hear herself talk, like always.

I need an object, and I may never get a better chance. I let myself solidify into him, into his body instead of just his mind. I feel him. It's familiar, now. I've gone into him so many times.

He looks over the desk littered with stacks of papers, books, notes, sliding every which way. So messy. How does she find anything? Nice pen, though.

It's a silver pen, the kind you get in recognition of something. *Insight* is engraved on the side. Perfect.

She glances at the monitor on her desk, the feed of Jacob's room. "We're done. You can go now. Let's try for better on Friday." She turns to her computer, dismissing him.

I don't have long. You want to take the pen, I tell him, as though he's thinking it himself. Even superspy won't be able to figure out where it went. There. Pick it up, drop it into your briefcase while she's looking at her computer. I nudge his body to lean forward, his arm to swing out, sweep the pen off the desk.

He leans forward, slightly, and swipes the pen into his own briefcase. Serves her right, the monumental bitch.

I yank myself out of it, panting, sweaty. Exhausted from the effort, but hyped too.

I did it. I found the right motivation for him, and I got something of hers, something I can use. Now if he just keeps it in his briefcase until Friday, I'll have one more piece of stealing to do and I'm golden.

Whew.

I didn't learn much today. Just that Dr. Tenney doesn't like her any more than I do. They're watching Myk, and they haven't found Dedushka.

And Liesel is serious about her threats. But that doesn't surprise me. So am I.

24

"Dreaming" by Nikki & Rich

That night I dream of Dedushka.

It's Christmas, the year I was five, and we were in North Carolina. I always go back to that year when I think of Christmas. Mom was six months pregnant with Myka, so it was my last as an only child. I was old enough to understand what was going on but still utterly believed in Santa Claus. Both Dad and Dedushka were there. Plus I got my first real bike with no training wheels, a red one. It was pure magic.

In the dream I'm sitting alone in front of the Christmas tree, piles of presents and scrunched wrapping around me, playing with my new Godzilla. Mom's in the kitchen baking cinnamon rolls, the sweet, heavy scent making me hungry. But I remember I have to do something. There's somewhere I urgently need to be. Something about Dad.

I drop the Godzilla and run to the hallway, which is overgrown with bushes and vines creeping up the walls, clogging every inch. I shove my way through, branches slapping my face, my legs, scratching at me. Down to Dad's office. Something's wrong. I have to get in.

The door's stuck shut. I shove at it with my shoulder, again, again, even though I'm too small to budge it. Suddenly it opens from inside and I fall in, stumbling across the room. Dedushka—the Dedushka of 1998, with his still-mostly-black hair and short beard—catches me by the arm, wordlessly turns me toward Dad's desk.

Dad is lying across the length of the desk, in uniform, eyes closed, EEG wires stuck all over his head. They're attached to a machine in the corner that's beeping, flashing a red light.

"No!" I cry, clinging to Dedushka's arm.

He turns me back to face him, kneels down so we're face-to-face, and places one finger to his lips. "He is sleeping. Now listen close, *malchik. Sushchestvuet ne stydno ne znat, stydno ne lezhit v vyasnit.*"

I stare at him, eyes big.

He grips my shoulders and repeats it impatiently, louder. "*Sushchestvuet ne stydno ne znat, stydno ne lezhit v vyasnit.*"

"I don't understand," I whisper, in my child's voice. "I don't speak Russian."

He sighs. He stands, strides over to Dad, and tugs the air force ring right off his finger. Dad's hand flops off the table, blue, stiff, and I bite back another cry.

Dedushka carries the ring back to me and presses it into my hand. It's cold and hard. I can feel the raised mold of the eagle against my palm like it's branded there. "There is no shame in not knowing, *malchik,*" he says, blue eyes close to mine. He speaks slowly, clearly. "The shame lies in not finding out."

I jolt awake into the dark of my solitary room, his words pounding in my head.

It almost feels like he's with me, like he was talking to me. Find out all that's going on here. Yes, Dedushka. That's exactly what I intend to do.

Friday. Everything starts with me sitting in my room, waiting. This time it feels like there are jumping beans inside my belly.

I have to be careful. Maybe the cameras aren't on, but Liesel must be listening somehow. If I fail at trying to get the pen, and they realize what I really can do, what I already have done . . .

It isn't hard to imagine myself forced to make faraway people do despicable things, without any pretense of helping anyone. If they threaten Mom and Myka, I probably would do whatever they wanted. I'd have to. I don't know if Liesel and her bosses would stoop that low, if they really are desperate enough. But I can't risk it.

I can't fuck this up.

No pressure.

I play *Halo* to keep my hands busy, the volume as high as it'll go. It helps to blow things up, have the crash of explosions and gunfire and music surround me. When Dr. Tenney comes in I don't even notice for a few seconds, until he walks into my line of sight, waves.

Here we go.

I save and quit the game before I turn to him. "Hey."

"Hello, Jake. Would you prefer to sit here, while we talk? I could bring over a chair . . ."

Panic snatches at me—the plan crumbling under a simple change—but I don't show it. "Nah. The table's fine."

We get settled, and I meet his eyes. We blink at each other for a minute, waiting for the other to start.

I win. "Tell me how you are, Jake."

"I am *so good,* Dr. T. *Excellent.*"

He makes a note. "You're using sarcasm as a shield again. I thought we were past that."

"Maybe I'm regressing."

He sighs. "Very well. Let's talk about your family today."

"I *miss my family*." I say it fervently, with undeniable truth, and he lifts his eyebrows in surprise, crinkling the skin on his head.

"Let's work with that."

"What is there to say?" I ask. "I miss them. I can't ever see them again, because they think I'm dead. What does talking do?"

"I think you're progressing, actually, Jake. You're facing reality. This is good."

I sigh. "Great. Can we just skip this bullshit for once, and get to the tunneling?"

So I can get that pen.

He tries again. He wants to please Liesel. "I was thinking first we could talk about your grandfather, for a bit. We've never explored . . ."

I shake my head. "Not today."

He caps his pen—not *the* pen, unfortunately; I'll have to work harder than that—and lays it on the table. "What do *you* want to do today, Jake?"

Steal your stolen object. "Tunnel."

"Really. On Wednesday you clearly didn't want to—"

"I changed my mind." I fidget with my hands. "See, I think I figured out how to do it—the controlling thing—and I've been waiting to try it again."

His wet dream, a willing subject who can do what he most wants. His whole body language changes. He leans in, practically drooling, and his drawl deepens. "Truly?"

I nod. God help me, I'm getting good at lying, pretending, manipulating.

He pulls a bag out of his briefcase, passes it across to me.

It's the small silver key again, the poor fool sitting in an office waiting for me. I go to him for a few seconds, silently, to get a quick glimpse, then I back out without showing it. I list off the details in that deep voice, like I'm still there, narrating.

Don't fuck it up.

Mike Holmes, average in every way. Hair muddy brown, cropped short. Location: Arlington, Virginia. DARPA headquarters. 3701 North Fairfax Drive, fourth floor, room 420. The room is empty except for Mike, a camera, and the table where he sits, arms laid out in front of him.

There's a pen and a pad on the table, one near each hand. He could reach them with an easy stretch of his fingers. He waits. Pretty damn weird assignment, sit here a couple times in a week motionless for an hour.

I go quiet, stick my other hand in my pocket—I specially chose the cargo shorts today for their deep pockets—and grasp Dr. Tenney's notebook. I dive into him instead, silently. Skim past the description, location. Straight into him, as deep as I can fling myself.

He's worrying about what I'm doing, why I'm silent. He doesn't want to interrupt, in case it's part of this new process. He waits for word in his ear that the subject is moving.

But first, I tell him he needs to get that pen out. He needs it to be on the table. It's lucky. Hadn't it been lucky, how he'd taken it? It would be lucky for this tunnel too. This critical tunnel, that'll show his success to them all. But only if he can see the pen.

He needs Liesel's pen to be on the table. What is the Tunnel doing, quiet so long?

I nudge him to lean to the side, drop his hand into the briefcase, find the pen. I know he's superstitious. The tunnel won't work if it isn't there, in plain sight. It's lucky.

He finds the pen with his fingers, relaxes. It's lucky. He brings it up and puts it on the table.

I pull away, open my eyes, frowning. "Something's wrong." I press on my forehead hard with the heel of my hand.

Concern creases the wrinkles around his eyes. "Are you all right, Jake?"

"Let me try again. I almost had it . . ."

I grip the key in one hand, the notebook in the other. Dive back into him. It's faster this time.

Look away, I tell him. You hear something at the door. You don't want to be interrupted. Look, just over your shoulder, there.

Is there someone at the door? He turns, looks over his shoulder.

Thank God the cameras are off. I come out, grab the pen with the key hand, stuff it into my other pocket, and have my hand back on the table by the time he turns around.

Showtime.

I fling the key and scream, like I've heard myself scream before. Keep screaming, my throat raw with it. I fall across the table, knocking everything onto the floor. Press my hands to the sides of my head and drop, moaning. Until he scrabbles in his bag for the medicine, and I feel his fingers in my mouth, the too-sweet, strawberry taste.

Everything goes slow, distant. Even Dr. Tenney's voice, as he helps me up, sounds far away, his drawl exaggerated. "There we go," he says. "You're all right now."

It sounds like "Yoooooouwww awwwl riiiight naow."

I gape at him. Why is he talking like that?

Stay sane, Jake.

All I have to do is remember to hide the pen and the notebook when he's gone, when it's dark. The hard part's over. That's all I have to remember.

I start to drift as he gets me to the bed. I'm on a boat, swells lifting and dropping my feet. I laugh, trying to keep my balance. Up, down, up, down. I keep almost falling, because I can't judge the swells right.

But it's only a few steps, and we make it. I'm lying on the bed looking at the white ceiling, and he's gathering his things. He takes a long time to gather his things. I close my eyes.

What was I supposed to remember?

The lights are out now, so he must have been gone a while. I've been floating, happy, on the waves. But there was something I was supposed to . . .

The pen. It's still there, in my pocket. Like pushing through honey, I manage to pull it out, slide my hand down the side, between the mattresses, and stuff the pen in the gap.

I rest. Rising, falling. Like being on Grandma and Grandpa Marden's boat when I was small. I bet Grandma and I could catch some excellent trout later. Fry it up for Mom and Dad as a surprise.

Notebook. I take it out of my left pocket, pass it underneath my back . . . slow . . . and tuck it in beside the pen. Safe. Done. I smile to myself.

I can't go to her now. I'm too out of it. But I did it. And nobody's come charging in here to lock me down, so they didn't realize what I did. The beauty is even if Dr. Tenney realizes the pen is missing, he'll never think I did it, and he can't report it to Liesel. I can relax.

I close my eyes and drift off with the tide.

Myka comes to see me later.

I hear her when I'm sleeping, her voice, this annoying song she always used to sing in my ear to wake me up.

"Good morning, good *morning,* it's great to stay up late. Good morning, good *morning* to you."

I sit up, blinking, and the lights come on. I don't know how long it's been, but I'm still loopy from the pill, so for a minute I just stare at her. She smiles happily, and starts braiding her hair.

"Myka?" I manage finally, squinting. "What are you doing here? How did you get in here?"

She makes a face. "Duh. I walked in." She points. The glass door is open, the hallway empty beyond it. "Why are you hiding in here, anyway? You have to take me to school." She frowns. "And why are you so skinny?"

I shove the covers back and stand, my eyes on the open door. "Follow me. We have to leave. Right now."

"*Okay,*" she says, exasperated. She drops her arms, and her hair falls out of the braid, slowly unraveling. "I told you so. I have to get to school. I'll be late."

I grab her hand—warm, real—and launch us toward the door.

I come up hard against it, crashing my nose into the shatterproof glass. "What the—" I turn, but Myka isn't there. There's no one there. Just my empty room with the lights on.

I sit down on the bed bewildered. I'd *seen* her, talked to her. It was like a dream. A realistic, detailed dream.

Except I wasn't asleep.

25

"Games" by LaFran

Liesel's away all weekend. Monday it's finally time to do something again, to go to her at last. I just have to make it through sessions with Eric and Dr. Tenney first.

But when Eric comes in, he doesn't have a metal box. He's wearing shorts and a T-shirt, and has a black duffel bag in his hand. He bounces on his heels, clearly pleased with himself.

"I managed to swing you some R&R . . . if you're willing to leave your little den."

Oh, hell yes. "Outside?"

His smile fades. "Not that far, but out of this room. Only problem is . . . there are conditions. This isn't our facility, right? You can't know how we get there." He takes something out of the bag and holds it up for me to see. It looks like a half hood. Or a weird, ugly hat. It's black stretchy cloth, with thick patches where the eyes and ears would go. But it doesn't cover the nose or mouth. A muffling hood.

I raise my eyebrows. "DARPA technology?"

His nose scrunches. "Better than knocking you out and dragging you. Especially since I want you in good form when we get there." He holds up some handcuffs. "These are for security. I had to agree to that too."

I make a noise in the back of my throat. "I don't think—I don't think I can do that."

He meets my eyes. "Sure you can. You've done worse. It'll only be for a little while. And the reward'll be worth it, I promise. Trust me?"

I don't trust him, not really. But I want so badly to go—wherever it is, as long as it's not this cell—so I let him pull the hood over my head. Instantly there's no sound, no light at all. I can hear my own breath, my heartbeat, but that's it. My hands are pulled together behind me, and I feel the snap of metal over my wrists. Then a hand on my shoulder, steering me.

They probably use this on terrorists, don't they?

We walk, turn, go up stairs, walk more, go down stairs, walk, then up again. I wonder if he's doing the random tour to confuse me. He doesn't have to. Without any sensory input, with my hands useless, I'm completely disoriented. If he let me go I'd probably fall over, or bump into a wall. Or just stand there helpless until somebody moved me.

It's crippling, the most humiliating thing I've ever experienced. Like that, I am utterly powerless. It makes me crave to get out of this place like nothing else has.

Finally we stop. After a few more dark moments, Eric tugs the hood off. I blink, dazed, as he undoes the cuffs.

It's a tennis court.

An improvised court, in a huge warehouse-type room that obviously wasn't meant for it. But there's a regulation net, a padded floor marked off with chalk, and two cans of balls. Wilson tour rackets just like we used at school.

I look at it all, rubbing my wrists. "Thank you." My voice is scratchy. "I never—"

I never expected to play again.

Eric hands me a ball can. It's just him and me, no other guards, no cameras I can see. "You do the honors."

I rip off the silver tab and hold the can to my nose, inhaling the perfect fresh rubber scent of tennis balls. Then I pile my pockets full and take one of the rackets, spinning it in my palms.

"You're on."

It comes back, faster than I would've thought considering it's been a few months, and I'm completely out of shape. Of course maybe Eric hasn't played either and we both suck equally, or maybe he's holding back. I don't care. The first set I barely pull out, after a deuce we're stuck in forever. The second one he wins, but just as close. We're both soaked in sweat.

After the second set he takes some Subway sandwiches, Cheetos, and Coke out of the duffel bag. We sit against the wall, midcourt, and eat lunch. It's the closest I've been to normal since I came here. It's amazing.

When I finish the sandwich, I crumple the wrapper and toss it in the air. Totally fail to catch it. "Can we do this every day?"

He swallows a bite. "Sadly, no. Maybe once a week, though. If you do all right."

"Ah." Always an underlying purpose. "Meaning it's a reward I earn or don't earn, depending on what a good boy I am?"

He shrugs. "Doesn't everybody like the carrot better than the stick?"

"Everybody isn't a freaking circus donkey."

He snorts. "Point taken."

"But it is fitting you're the carrot, with your hair. And Liesel . . ." I let it hang.

"Is the stick. You ain't kidding, mate."

We're silent again for a while, eating Cheetos, coating our hands completely with orange dust. The black bag is next to me, open. I peek in, curious. Just a change of clothes. No more surprises.

I have to ask, in case we *aren't* being watched. "Listen. Is there any way you can see if my family's okay? Drive by, or make a phone call—"

"Can't." It's curt, and I know him well enough to wait for the rest. "You're right, I know where we are now, and we're nowhere near them. And I'm not allowed in that area, any more than you are. What do you think happens if somebody recognizes me?"

He pauses, lets me think. It'd blow the cover, of course. Throwing into question whether I'm really dead too. Putting Mom and Myka in danger again.

"Even if I could, no contact means no contact. No updates. You assume they're well and living their lives, and let them go."

I swig some Coke from the can, staring at the wall. On closer inspection I think thcrc is a camera, a small one, mounted up there. I should've known Liesel wouldn't leave me unsupervised.

"They're safe," he continues. "They'll still have security on them, to make sure."

I snort. Yeah. I bet they do. But I'm glad about that.

Maybe. What happens with that security if I do get out of here somehow?

He pops another Cheeto in his mouth, talks around it. "There's reason to believe your grandfather might be in danger, though. Is there anything else you could tell us about where he might have gone?"

I sigh. There it is. He *is* Liesel's stooge, at least that far. Well, he more than made up for it with the tennis, but I still wouldn't talk even if I knew. I guess we're the same that way.

"Nope. Sorry." I stand up, wipe my orange fingers on my pants, and pick up the racket. "Do we have time for another game?"

After tennis, Dr. Tenney is a letdown.

He seems strange. Subdued, cautious. He zooms straight in on what I'd tried with the tunnel last week, and how it went wrong.

I wonder how hard Liesel is twisting his arm.

While I'm laying out a bullshit theory, and he's making notes, Ana appears behind him. Just . . . appears, poof. She stands there, hair down, in shorts and a loose T-shirt like she had on that last night. She waves at me, bracelet dangling from her wrist.

I stop talking and gawk at her. Ana smiles and makes a shooing motion, like she wants me to go on. I squeeze my eyes shut, open them again. She's still there.

"Jake?" Dr. Tenney follows my gaze, looks over his shoulder. "What do you see?"

He can't see her. I still can. This is a problem.

Then I can't anymore. She's gone, like she came. I swallow, shake my head. "Um. Nothing. Just thinking."

He nods distractedly, and writes for another few seconds. Then he gathers up his things.

"We're not going to tunnel today?"

He shakes his head, glasses glinting. "Since your dramatic . . . attack and the aftermath, Dr. Miller does not want us to continue the deep tunnels without monitors on. In fact, for the time being she wants them done only with an EEG hooked up, so we can see what's going on in your brain when you control someone."

I hate that damn EEG. It's a good thing I got the pen when I did, before the brain-spying machines get involved again. And I'm *not* going to control someone under surveillance.

But I have to remember what they think I know, and react appropriately. "Wait. Liesel knows about how I controlled him? But you said—"

"I would tell her when I had to." He sounds tired. "And I did. She'll be taking charge of it now. We'll only be doing our regular therapy."

And he's lost his big research coup. No wonder he's worn down.

More tests, plans. Liesel taking over.

It's hard not to feel like there's something going on I don't understand. The net's getting tighter, leading me toward . . . something. Something bigger than this.

And what's going on with Ana—and Myk—appearing out of nowhere? I can't tell anyone about that. But it scares the crap out of me.

It's past time for me to tunnel to Liesel and find out what she's hiding.

26

"Lies" by Violent Femmes

After Dr. Tenney leaves, I go straight for my "nap," keeping up the pattern. But I don't go to Liesel right away. I lie there in the dark, rubbing the slick silver pen with my thumb.

I'm nervous.

I don't know why. The answers I've been working to get, that I've risked everything for, are right here within reach. But I'm afraid to face them. Afraid I can't deal with whatever Liesel's hiding.

In the end my thoughts circle back to Dedushka, the dream. *There is no shame in not knowing, malchik. The shame lies in not finding out.*

I can't let him down.

I close my eyes and go.

A woman, tall, with dark blond hair. Location: A facility underground, below what used to be Montauk Air Force Station. Room 205. Her legs are tucked under her desk. She's reading from a thick file. The label on the folder, in neat black script, reads The Tunnel.

Got her. I don't even have to make her read the file—my file. She's already doing it. I go in further, for a better look.

The page, a report, is typed, and stamped Top Secret. *The date at the top is February 12.*

The day of my first testing at DARPA.

It's about the EEG tests, the theta level problem. She lingers on it, reads.

Nothing I don't know. Transition problem, blah blah, result extreme pain, T-680.

She turns a page. Still February 12th, still Top Secret. *There's a paragraph labeled* Custody Deviation:

"Notified by Special Security Office that subject's watch contains a tracking device. After consultation, have concluded that it likely is not from any external threat, but possibly tied to Grigory Lukin. John Lukin deceased two years ago, but may have set up tracker. CIA has great interest in Grigory Lukin, who is believed to have intel on Project Veles, possible significant abilities. Have requested we use opportunity to observe subject's family, try to secure Grigory. Must deviate from original plan to move subject to immediate secure custody. Will establish appropriate security detail in field. Retained DARPA control of operation, right to reclaim subject at any time on my judgment of risk and usefulness of fieldwork. Retain—"

Liesel flips the pages forward, looking for something else. She wants to know more about the headaches, the T-680 effects, the pattern. There must be a way to prevent it. It seems the T-680 is not a good solution in the long run . . .

No. I need to know what the rest of that *Deviation* paragraph said. It's getting tight, difficult to keep shallow, so I let myself go deeper, melting into her. My fingers in hers.

Turn the page. You need to go back to that report. There's something there. Look again.

She turns the page back, her eye jumping to the end of the Deviation *paragraph.*

"Retain appearance of outside threat established for first contact for later use in securing subject's cooperation."

Underneath that is a handwritten note, in that same curving, neat script.

"I want this subject in custody ASAP, willing. Minimum time in the field. Too risky. Must be handled carefully. Handpick field agents."

I'm losing myself in her, all my alarm bells sounding *too far*. I jerk out of it, breathing hard. I stuff the pen away and bolt upright, not caring that the lights go on. What I want to do is smash the door to pieces, find her, and scream in her face. Maybe punch her in the gut.

I failed. I didn't find out what they're planning. But I found out what they've *done*.

I stare at the white walls, panting, trying to understand it.

She lied to me. The whole time. Maybe they all did. She'd always been planning to have me here in her little cell. She would've had me locked up the first day, as soon as the testing panned out, except someone else wanted to dangle me as bait. To get *Dedushka!* What the hell? What did he do that the *CIA* wants him? What can he do?

There never was anyone else after me, no threat to Mom or Myka. The pig-eyed man was a plant, theirs. There was no reason to give myself up to them, to be in this place. No reason for self-sacrifice. It was just them playacting. The whole damn time.

It isn't hard to believe Liesel lied. I would never have guessed how far she'd go, but I hadn't trusted her.

But Ana probably knew it. Living in our house, knowing it was all a lie and they were going to rip me away from my family no matter what happened. That last night, walking with me, consoling me. Telling me I was brave. Knowing the threat wasn't real. Knowing it'd be over the next day, and I'd be dead to them.

And Eric.

How can he look me in the eye? What kind of an asshole pretends to be your friend, your protector, when he's part of the whole threat? What kind of cold do you have to be to do that?

I want to get up, pace, hit things. But I can't draw that kind of attention. I need to think. I lie down again, barely able to control the twitching.

Now I know how badly they fucked with me. As far as I see it, I have two choices for how to respond.

One, I could stop being *willing*. I could shut down, refuse to do any more tunneling, tell them what I think of their fucked-up ways of dealing with people, and go on strike. It's straightforward, and honest.

But I'm not dealing with honest people here. Not a single damned one of them could probably tell the truth with a gun to their head. And there's still the threat to Mom and Myka, from them. DARPA, and maybe even the CIA, knows where they live, work, go to school. They already have people in place. Yeah, it's not legal. It's not ethical. But I don't think that they give a rat's ass about any of that anymore. Liesel could pull that trump card out any time and force me to do whatever she wants. And if I reveal what I know, no matter what, I'll be stuck in here. They'll know I'm hostile. They'll know I tunneled to them. They'll find and take away my objects. I'll never have a chance to escape.

Option two. Be cool. Pretend I don't know any more than I did an hour ago, days ago, before I started tunneling to Dr. Tenney. Play along. Keep dancing to their tune. And then find a way to use my unique skills, make a fucking brilliant plan, and get out of this place for good.

Outside, I'm dead to the world—except maybe to Dedushka. And if I make it out of here, I will be hunted by people used to hunting fugitives. People with access to guns, satellites, and smarts. Liesel will never give up trying to get me back in this room, and her resources are terrifying. I know it well. I've been one of them.

It isn't even a question which one I choose.

I'm going to have to be a cold motherfucker, as cold as Eric and

Ana and Liesel have been, to pull this off. And it's going to have to be a damn good plan.

Liesel busts into my room, triggering the lights.

I figure I'm done. Somehow she knew I was in her head, and here come the consequences—and any hope of an escape plan.

She stops in the middle of the room, hands on her hips. "Why are you sleeping?"

"I . . . um . . ." I rub my eyes, buying time. I hate her for tricking me to get me here, for using my family. I hate her so much I can barely restrain myself from charging across the cell at her.

She shakes her head. "I'm sick of pussyfooting around this headache thing." She drags a chair away from the table, plunks herself down in it, and stares at me, arms crossed. "We've got to figure this out. I am struggling to get work for you, to find customers who are willing to share their information on a secret project. I am continually scrambling to justify this project. But when we do get work, you get one of these headaches and you miss whole days at a time." She blows a breath. "*And* we should be exploring your abilities, really probing to see what's going on in there, how we can use it to its full potential. It's a waste, frankly, and I'm tired of it."

"A . . . waste?" I'm torn between being relieved as hell I'm not busted, and wanting to strangle her with my bare hands. I can't show either. I stay blank.

"We know what causes the headaches; we just don't know what triggers them. We'll test it until we figure it out. And then you can work as you should. As you're meant to."

Like a machine. I make a face. "Great."

"That's right. Work." She stands abruptly and comes to the bed, looming over me. Her hand shoots out and I think she's going to slap me. Instead, she strokes my cheek gently with the tips of her fingers. She leans in. "Your work is going to be *amazing,* Jacob. You are going to prove this project is a phenomenal success, unlike the failures of the past. You are going to vindicate us."

I don't know if that's a prediction or a threat. But a waste? My whole life gone, and it's a *waste* for her?

"Don't touch me." I keep the violence out of my voice, mostly.

Her eyebrows fly up, but she takes a step back, folds her arms. "I've called Eric back. We have some real work for you to do, instead of piddling your time away playing *tennis.* So get up. There is a lot of pressure to make this project work. I've gone through a great deal to get you here. Stop wasting my time."

She gives me one final look, eyes narrow, and leaves.

She's gone through a great deal to get me here. *She* has. Ha-fucking-ha.

So now I have to try playing it cool with Eric—pretending that I don't know what an absolute two-faced liar he is. The worst of all of them. Pretend nothing has changed since we hung out eating Cheetos this morning. I take a breath. I can do this.

The new Jake. Cold, hard, manipulative liar. Play by their game, their rules—none—and beat them at it. It's the only thing that will get me out.

Eric's all friendly professionalism—a look of sympathy, then straight to the contents of his new metal box—so I match him.

"You up for another set?" he asks. Like we're playing tennis again.

I nod. Make fists in my lap under the table where no one can see. Close my eyes without comment and go.

Today I don't have kidnappings, terrorists, or even criminals, as far as I can tell. These objects, all of them, feel different.

The first one is a woman working as a waitress in a bar in New Orleans. She has short, choppy black hair, brown contacts over blue eyes. She's wearing a short denim skirt and a cracked, anxious smile. She eyes every customer who comes in the door, watching to see if they have earpieces, radios, weapons. She's terrified.

The second object is a tattered brown cigarette. It belongs to an old man, bald, with a short, neat, yellow-white beard. He walks through a market in Cairo, in a white shirt and tan pants, the scent of spices thick around him, vendors calling out as he strides by. He seems confident, at home. Until I dive into his thoughts, see how he scans everyone he passes, stops to smoke and check behind him for a tail. How he twitches involuntarily at the sound of a siren.

They're all like that, six of them. All fugitives: of the CIA, the government, whatever agency or organization gave these objects to Liesel. There are attempts at disguise, attempts at blending in, sometimes very good ones. But every single one of them is jumpy, eyes over their shoulders, always watching.

I find all of them, turn them in. Just like that. They'll be caught within the hour, brought to prison, or worse.

It freaks me out like nothing else has, except controlling Buck at the beach. The power I have, without even really trying. If a personal object can be collected—not very tough with most people; just go to their past—there can be no hiding from me. From anyone who uses me. If you're alive, and I have something of yours, I can find you.

And yet if I manage to come up with a plan, make it out, I'll *be* one of those fugitives. Can I live like that, always looking behind me? Can I succeed, where they've all failed?

I have to hope there really isn't another tunnel like me out there, hidden away.

"You okay, mate?" Eric's the picture of normalcy, eyebrows creased in concern, eyes clear.

How does he lie so well?

But then there's been no change for him. He's been lying all along.

He sat there in the car with me and told me an attempt had been made on my sister. That it was best for everyone if I locked myself up and let my family believe I was dead. Did he really believe that? Or did he always know?

"Sure." I shake myself. "I just have to clear my head, that's all."

"Impressive work there. Months of work—years—you save, every time you do one." He packs everything away, closes the box. "Keep it up."

"Thanks." Like I have a choice. For now.

"Look," he says. "I know they're tough on you sometimes. She is. But it's only because of the value of the work."

I keep from rolling my eyes. I see it now, clearly, the good cop / bad cop routine they've been running. I only wonder why I didn't see it before.

"So are we done here?" I tap my watch. "Because you know, I have someplace I need to be. Hot date."

He laughs, only a touch uncomfortably. "Wouldn't want to hold you up. I'll see you tomorrow morning, yeah?"

He leaves, and I breathe out, slow. I can totally do this.

27

"Practice" by Capital Z

It takes a couple weeks to work out a rough plan. There are holes—and a big, unknown cliff at the end—but at least I know how to start.

I wonder a lot about what's happening at home, at school. I don't even know the date anymore. I lost track about six weeks in, and they won't tell me. It seems warm outside, in my tunnels. May, maybe?

It'd be graduation soon. I would've been walking, with a cap and gown in Hornet black and red. With Stanford after. I'd have my acceptance packet already, everything lined up. Mom would be so proud of me, telling everyone she knows.

Chris and Rachel and all the rest are graduating. Do they think of me much? Was there a memorial somewhere at a random tree, with teddy bears and flowers? Has it all faded, been taken down? I wonder if Rachel thinks of that one kiss as often as I do. I don't want her to go around being sad. I don't want anyone to, not really. But I figure it's normal to hope they miss me.

Most of all, I wonder how Mom and Myk are. If I could see them, just for a second or two, this all would be so much easier.

Well. I do see them, both of them, here in this room. Ana too, and Dedushka. Even Rachel and Chris and Caitlyn and Lily make appearances. Almost every day now, they pop up and talk to me. I try to ignore them. They're not real, even though they seem real. Even though they talk to me, touch me, even though I'm awake.

I don't know what's wrong with me, but I don't tell anyone.

I spend the days hooked up to machines. I am *not* a fan of tunneling while in a tiny MRI tube, but I do it. And MEGs, and EEGs. There are enough different images of my brain that they could probably build it again from scratch if they wanted to.

Actually I hope they don't have the technology to do that.

The kicker is they aren't any closer to preventing or anticipating the headaches. It's pissing Liesel off. She gets more and more cranky every time I get one, every time I take the meds.

Still I tunnel. Criminals and terrorists, but also hostages and missing people, and a good chunk of fugitives. I pretend to be pseudobuddies with Eric, compliant with Liesel and Dr. Tenney, without making any ounce of progress on controlling.

Not with them.

At night, when the machines are off, I practice on my own with Dr. Tenney. This ability is the most critical part of the plan, and I have to get good at it. Already I'm able to stay longer, deeper. Control him more easily.

It isn't that hard with him. He's pretty susceptible to suggestion. If it's something he would do already, something that seems reasonable to him, I just have to nudge him. It doesn't take much physical effort.

But I *can* make him do things he doesn't want to. I managed to force him, once, to stick a pin in his thumb—to see if I could. I made him say things.

I don't like it. It's using an advantage to compel somebody weaker than me, like bullying someone. Maybe there's a thrill for a second or two. But afterward it makes you feel crappy inside, because you *know* better. It isn't right. It's only a pinch away from being the weapon they want me to become.

But I have to practice. I have to be cold, fearless. Lie, cheat, manipulate. Just long enough to get out of here. I may be able to be normal Jake once I'm back in the world. Not here.

I've set myself two major tasks next. First: go to Liesel again, practice controlling on a harder subject—and learn more if I get her near her files. Second: steal an object from Eric, and get started on him. That one will be the toughest. If I can even do it.

It's a Thursday—I've still kept track of that. There's some meeting or holiday or something, I don't know what, and the small army of techs is away, so no machines. Liesel and Eric are both here, though. Eric and I do a set of objects from my room, like we used to. "Tennis on Saturday," he says when we're done. "If everything's smooth between now and then."

Then he takes off, the door sliding shut behind him. I dive for my bed. It's time to go visit Liesel.

She's looking at one of her screens, scrolling through a page. The banner at the top says Intelink-TS. *There, she thinks, stopping on a name. She picks up the phone, dials a short number. "Roger. What about Target 14–532? Do we have any potential objects on him?"*

The voice on the other end is calm, even. "That's Mulcahy's. You know he doesn't believe in any of that—"

She interrupts, irritation surging through her. "I don't care if he thinks I'm a certified wacko. Get me an object, and I'll find his man before Monday." She hangs up, her hand still resting on the phone. Why do they continue to doubt this project, even with all the successes? Why are they reconsidering the funding? Haven't they proven themselves by now? Fools, protecting their traditional methods. Stuck in the past, that's all. They'll all have to believe in her—in him—eventually. If she can solve this T-680 problem. He is having hallucinations. It's obvious. And they'll just keep getting worse.

Hallucinations. That's what's happening. It's a goddamn side effect of the drug.

Concentrate, Jake. That's not the mission.

My file is there on her desk, closed. Open it to the first page, I think. You want to remember how all this started.

She resists, turning back to the screen, her fingers moving across the keys.

I try again, deeper, feeling her fingers, the pressure of the keys under them. You need to look at the file. There's something there at the beginning. Remember, how you first found out? Maybe it would be useful now . . . with the T-680 problem . . .

Her fingers stop, and I take the pause to move them to the file, just a nudge. She does. Her thumb plays with the tab.

Open it, I prod again, slightly. She's too smart to push hard, to force. What was that in the file? At the beginning?

She opens the file, runs her finger down the first page. A bio of the subject. No, she knows all that. She turns a few pages, allowing herself one moment of pride. The party. A report from Dr. Timmerman: her daughter told her a rumor that John's son, Grigory's grandson, has a strange psychic ability. The daughter's boyfriend let it slip, and after all these years of waiting, watching, she jumped on it.

The Tunnel would never guess how Liesel had set up the party, the game, the drugged punch that suppressed inhibition. The encouragement, started by Dr. Timmerman's daughter, who didn't even know what she was doing. The camera to record it all.

And finally, finally she got him. Got one of them. John would never forgive her, she knew that. But he was past forgiving or not forgiving. And she'd done it.

Something's wrong. I can't pull away. I'm sticking inside her skin, like gum on a shoe. Every time I try to come out, it feels like I'm stretching, cracking. She'll feel it unless I get out now.

I yank as hard as I can and finally get free. I tuck the pen between the mattresses and lie on the bed, panting. The story gets worse and worse every time I learn something. Chris. That sleepover when we were seven. And Chris told Caitlyn. Liesel set up the party to prove it, then lied about a threat and brought me in to test me more.

It had all been a grand plan. How long had she been watching me, anyway, waiting to see if I showed something? My whole life?

Is that why she was watching Myka, too? *Got one of them.* Something to do with Dad, with Dedushka, even bigger than me?

And she knew Dad. *John would never forgive her.* How had she known Dad?

The headache crashes into me like a freight train.

I can't scream. Can't get medicine to stop it. Can't react at all, or they'll suspect. Search me. Stop me.

Jesus. Please . . . stop. My head explodes, surge after surge of pain. A volcano. I go rigid, arch. Grip the sheet. Hold on enough to not make a sound. Agony. It's ripping me apart. It will. I can't breathe. I'm not breathing. Fighting, fighting the pain—

I must've passed out.

When I come to, my head still hurts, but it's a hammer instead of a machete—a dull, constant pounding. I breathe, slow, steady, eyes closed, dealing with it. Feeling oddly victorious.

I made it through a headache without T-680. I successfully hid it.

And considering that T-680 is apparently causing fucking *hallucinations* that Liesel knows about and isn't telling me, it's probably a good thing not to pile more into my body.

I wish I could flip off the camera, and Liesel, who I know is watching. Ha. I fooled *you,* for once.

I can't, won't. I'm still collecting information, playing along.

But with every bit of info I learn, I keep seeing more pieces of the puzzle that don't quite fit.

What's going on with Dad and Dedushka and Liesel? Dedushka has some mysterious abilities, maybe like mine—I knew that from before. But what else? How is it connected with the rest of my family? And why me?

28

"Fake It" by Brad Sucks

Saturday. Tennis with Eric.

The next step.

Problem is, Eric doesn't carry any personal objects on him. No handy hair clips, no briefcase with pens and paper and things that count as *his*. He only carries in the metal box of objects, prepped for him by Liesel or some other grunt in the food chain. He wears Dockers and collared shirts every day. The only thing personal on him is his watch, and there's no way I can get that off his wrist.

Except for tennis: he always brings the black duffel bag, and I know it has his spare clothes in it. Clothes should work. It's the best shot I have.

But I come and go from tennis with the awful hood on, my hands shackled behind my back, Eric with me the whole way. So how can I steal anything from the bag?

When he comes to get me, I reluctantly let him put the hood and cuffs on. We wind our way through wherever-the-hell in the building, up down and all around. I still hate it. These are the worst moments I have.

Finally, we get to the tennis room. I can see, hear, and move my hands again. Thank God. I have a sudden image of being isolated like that for hours, days. How long would it take to go insane?

"I still can't believe she lets me do this," I say truthfully.

He shrugs with a smile. "She's not as bad as you think. Most of the time she is trying to do her best for you, y'know. My advice: don't question it. Take what you can get."

Like any of you care about anything except what you can get from me. I shove the thought away, smile back, and pick up a racket.

I play hard. Slamming the ball across the net, killing him with impossible serves. Making him trot back and forth across the court, chasing where I lead him. It feels good, powerful. Like I'm a real person again.

"What's got into you today?" he asks, using his shirt to wipe the sweat off.

I shrug, serve. I take the first set 6–4, the second 6–3.

Eric holds up one hand. "Lunch."

We sit in the same place, against the wall at the middle of the court, and he passes out lunch and drinks from the bag. I pop the Coke, take a long sip. Then I set it down carefully next to me and absently hit it with my elbow—on its side, the sticky brown liquid running under my butt. I take a bite of my sandwich, pretend not to notice.

"You're an animal today, mate." His face is bright red, blotchy. He tries to open his bag of Cheetos, fingers slipping. Finally he wipes his hands on a dry spot of the shirt. "I'm going to have to bring a towel if you keep playing like that. Taking out some aggression?"

Too damn smart.

"I've got to get it out somewhere," I say, cool. "The only other way I've got is *Halo*."

The Coke's soaking into my shorts. Just a little more.

He snorts. "I never got into those games. I guess if you use a gun in real life, it loses the appeal."

"I'd be happy to use a gun in real life." I pause, lift an eyebrow. "You want to give me one?"

He laughs. "Sure. Right after I give you the key to your room and an escort out of the building. No problem."

"Oh," I say. "*Shit*."

"What?" He jumps up, on high alert just like that.

I stand. There's a puddle where I was sitting, and the whole butt of my shorts is dripping with Coke. I lean over to right the can. "Fuck."

"Dude." His mouth twitches. He's trying not to laugh. Good. "How did you not notice that?"

I shake my head. "I thought it was just sweat. Now what am I going to do?"

I hold my breath.

"Stop the match and go back to your room with a wet ass?"

Not what I want. "C'mon. It's bad enough to be pushed around clueless with my hands cuffed. I can't go all the way back like this, parading in front of who-knows-who, generals and spies. It looks like I shit my pants."

"It looks like you spilled Coke on your pants. Relax, Grace."

I can see him wavering, thinking of options. The easiest one, Eric. Right there. But I have to let him think of it.

"All right. You can borrow my spare pants." He digs them out of the bag, tosses them to me. Tan Dockers, like always. "Leave the shorts here. I'll send somebody to get them washed."

Yes.

The plan had some variables, yeah. But even if it hadn't worked, it was a low-risk operation. Worst case was I didn't get the pants, but it was pretty doubtful they'd suspect anything.

He turns his back, starts collecting the gear. I peel off the sopping shorts, pull the Dockers up. It feels odd, since I haven't worn anything but shorts for months. They're about an inch too short, and too wide around the waist—I *am* skinny now—but they'll do perfectly for what I need.

He finishes with the trash, the gear, and mops up the rest of the puddle with the shorts, leaving them sitting there.

He eyes me, mouth twitching again. "All right. Suit up. I guess you're the winner for today."

He puts the hood and cuffs on, and we make our tortured way back to the room. When he takes off the hood, the fluorescent lights glare at me.

God, how I hate this place.

He crams the hood and cuffs in his bag, then turns to me. "I need the pants back now."

There's a beat, while his eyes search mine. Too damn smart. *Don't question, don't question, adapt the plan*. "Sure," I say, completely even. "Let me just change in the bathroom. Give me a minute."

He sighs. "You just changed—" But he stops. I never change in front of the cameras, in front of whoever might be watching. It's the principle of the thing. And what can I do in the bathroom? "Fine."

I grab a pair of shorts from the dresser and shut myself in the tiny bathroom.

Think, Jake. You've got about a minute.

I don't need the whole pants. All I need is a tiny piece from somewhere. I tug them off, try to rip a piece of fabric from the bottom cuff. Too thick: not possible. I can't take a button—he might notice it, put it together that I did all this on purpose. It has to be from somewhere he won't notice.

The tag. The thinnest piece of fabric. I try to tear off a strip, but still can't get it. I need scissors.

Damn it. Tick tick tick. I have about ten seconds before he gets suspicious.

There's nothing in the bathroom but a toilet, a sink, a shower with a clear door. Nothing sharp.

I need more time. I lift the toilet seat loud, let it clank. Turn on the faucet low to sound like pissing.

Then I look at the toilet.

Silently I lift the top off the back, peer in. There has to be something . . . there. There's a small pin hooked to the overflow pipe. Metal, like a paper clip partly straightened. I jerk it out, push it through the bottom of the tag, and rip for all I'm worth. It takes three tries, but I get it. A tiny strip off the tag, no more than a few rows. The tag just looks frayed. I hope it's enough.

I replace the pin and the lid, turn off the water, and flush the toilet. I pull up my own shorts, tucking the tiny, vital piece of fabric deep in the pocket.

When I come out Eric's leaning against the wall by the door, arms crossed. I fold the Dockers, hand them over. "Thanks. Sorry, they got a little Coke on the back."

He unfolds them and does a quick once-over, checking that all the buttons are there.

See.

"No problem. No objects today, so you've got the rest of the day off, unless Liesel comes up with something." He grins, a flash of the old Eric I trusted. "See you Monday, Jake."

I nod, fall into my chair, and fire up the X-box as he leaves, for cover.

No, Eric. If all goes well, I'll see you tonight.

I don't expect to get any intelligence from this tunnel—Eric probably doesn't have much intelligence for me to find. Handpicked or not, he's an agent and enforcer for Liesel, a worker bee like Bunny was, but not an equal. I don't figure she tells him many of her secrets.

This trip is just to see if the cloth worked, and test if I can control him.

I lie on the bed until the lights go off, close my eyes, and pinch the cloth between my fingers. Here we go.

It comes right away. I surge past my own relief into him.

A man. Stocky, red haired, freckle faced. Wearing a hooded sweatshirt and jeans. Location: New York, Brooklyn. An apartment on Flatbush Avenue—192, Apartment 8B, just north of Prospect Park. He's doing the dishes in a tiny, cramped kitchen not meant for cooking or doing dishes. This whole apartment wasn't meant for a family. Still, he's glad they can be together, for a while.

"Eric?" A woman's voice floats from a back room. "Come and say good night." He smiles to himself. He dries wet, soapy-slick hands on a rough towel, takes the few steps to the bedroom. There they are, his boys, his girl. The two boys are curled together, head to toe, in a crib stuffed into the space at the foot of the double bed. He squeezes the woman's neck, briefly, and she sighs in pleasure. He leans over, the crib rail pushing into his belly, and kisses each baby on a fat little cheek. This is happiness, he thinks. This is worth it.

I almost want to stop. For the first time it feels like real intrusion, like I'm somewhere I'm not supposed to be. But this test is too important. I go deeper, spread myself thin.

Feel his calmness, centeredness. He knows about the threats out there, the danger. He knows all about the harshness of the world. But that isn't here, in this apartment, with Joanna. He circles his arms around her in the dark bedroom. She's soft, still with the extra baby weight, her breasts bigger, swollen. He likes it, pulls her tighter against him. Stiffens. Leans in to kiss her.

Here's my chance to test. Lick her instead, I think. Lick her. You want to taste that skin next to her mouth, there. Quick, a small taste.

He leans in and licks her, a stripe across her mouth. She squirms away, frowning. "Eric! Why did you do that?" She wipes at her face. He shakes his head, laughs, low. "I don't know. I just wanted to." Then he pulls her close again, kissing her for real.

I come away. Enough. Much as I ache to have a little of that, I'm not going to do it through Eric, with Eric's wife, in front of his babies.

Who would've thought he had a wife, a family? With my assignment alone he'd been gone for weeks, undercover at school, and then here. I'd assumed he was single, available to go wherever DARPA sent him. Are field agents even allowed to have families?

What a weird life. And he *chose* it.

But in the end it doesn't really matter. I have an object, and I proved I could do it. I went to him and made him do something he wouldn't have otherwise. A grand slam for the day.

I wish I didn't feel uncomfortable about it. But it doesn't matter. I have to ignore my feelings now. All the pieces are in place. So far, the plan is working. Now it's time for the next phase.

I need to recruit some outside help.

29

"Connection" by the Rolling Stones

I try to connect to Myka, every night, for hours.

I grit my teeth, fists clenched, trying as hard as I can. I focus on her: her long, thin face hiding behind her hair, her knobby legs, her clear eyes. The way she loves numbers and chemicals, the lab smell of Lysol and Bunsen burners, or reading a thick book in her room. The way she read all the Harry Potter books three times but didn't like the movies.

I try to imagine what she might be doing now, at 9:20 p.m. It's hard to be sure, since I don't know even what month it is. Is she doing homework? Asleep already? On summer vacation, watching TV? I try to go, to feel her, to connect with her like I used to.

I can't do it. I stare at the dim, white ceiling in total failure.

I don't have an object from her, and I can't get one. But I thought . . . maybe . . . I could tunnel to Myka without one. My connection has always been stronger, deeper with her than anyone else. If I could do it with anyone, it would be her.

But no matter what I try, I slam into a brick wall of nothing. It doesn't work.

Maybe it's because so much has happened in the past few months. She thinks I'm dead—maybe our connection is cut off. Or maybe it's just a real, hard-core limitation of tunneling, and I need an object no matter who I'm tunneling to.

Damn it. I need help to get out of here. I don't know how to get out without help. I'm not sleeping, and every waking moment is spent lying, pretending to be the ignorant dunce they think I am. Plus I've had a couple more headaches, and more T-680, since they don't have any other solutions. The hallucinations are getting worse. There are multiple visits a day now, from everyone I've ever met. Chatting to me, telling me nonsensical things. Wandering around the cell singing numbers from *Oklahoma*.

I'm starting to lose it. Before long I won't need to pretend—I'll be a basket case gibbering on the bed. Useless.

I'm in the middle of a session with Dr. Tenney when Dedushka appears behind him.

His arms are crossed, eyebrows locked down. Even his beard is jutting at me.

I glance at him quick, then away. There's no point. It's kind of cruel, actually. The people I most want to see, right there, but totally in my mind.

"Is anything wrong, Jake?"

I shake my head at Dr. Tenney. "Completely normal over here."

"Okay, then." He leans in, all confidential, even though the cameras are on. "Dr. Miller has approved for us to do a tunnel today. Revisit the beach, and see if you have any luck with that subject again."

I won't, thanks. But I'll take some beach time. I can pretend I'm really in the sun, escape that way. I can stay there as long as possible.

"You do this for them?" Dedushka paces behind Dr. Tenney's chair, gesturing. "For these pigs? You do whatever they ask you to?"

I sigh. He's always pissed at me in these visits. Like all my guilt on overdrive.

"You don't want to do the tunnel? I thought you'd be pleased."

Guilt in stereo.

"No, it's good," I tell Dr. Tenney. I don't look at Dedushka.

"It's good," he mocks. "It is not *good,* Yakob. It is slavery. You are their *slave.*" He yells the last, spit flying over Dr. Tenney's head.

"Just give me the object," I say, edgy. "Please."

Dr. Tenney passes me a bag with a key in it. "Try to move him," he says. Tension creeps into his voice. "You really need to try."

It's the same beach and the same soldier: Ritidian Beach on Guam, Lance Buckley. Buck.

He lies on the sand, soaking the tropical sun into his skin. There's a new scar, still-healing, puckered against the rest, on his shoulder. He doesn't think of it beyond noticing the twinge of pain and letting it go. Only the moment. That's all that matters. Colonel Martin must be satisfied with his work, to send him here again. He stretches out on the soft sand, the waves crashing at his feet.

I don't try to control him. I let him lie there and enjoy the sand, the warmth. I enjoy it too, molding into his skin, feeling what he feels.

I could stay here, I think suddenly. I could not come back. I could become Buck, get up from here and go on with *his* life. Leave Jake Lukin back at Montauk, dead.

Like he is.

"Yakob!"

My eyes fly open. The moment's snapped. Dedushka's leaning down next to Dr. Tenney, their faces even. Both of them blaring disappointment.

My lip curls. "Just go." I mean both of them.

Dr. Tenney protests, tries to get me to try it again, but I don't respond. Finally he packs up and leaves.

Dedushka's still sitting there.

"Go *away,*" I say. But I look at the cameras. I can't do this on camera. Even if Liesel knows about the hallucinations, I don't want hard evidence of my insanity.

I turn my back on him, go to the chair. Turn on the TV. Pawnshop reality show. Good enough.

He moves between me and the TV, frown carved deep. "It is *not* 'good enough.' You must get out of this nightmare place."

I can't answer. I can't answer.

I'm trying, I think. I look straight at him—since he's in front of the TV, it won't look crazy.

He spreads his hands wide. "No trying. Do. Do you ever think of coming to me?"

My mind stills, and my vision blurs. Coming to him. Tunneling to him without an object, instead of Myka.

Because he has "abilities" of his own. Because he knows I'm alive. Because he's the one I really want to talk to. Why didn't I think of that?

I blink, and realize he's gone. It doesn't matter. Message delivered. I know what I need to do now.

I think it's time for an afternoon nap.

I imagine him the way I remember him best: out on the water, fishing. He always had gear with him. Wherever we were living, he'd find water—and then he'd bundle us all up, me, Myk, Dad, sometimes Mom—and head out. In Standish he had his own boat, and he went out on the lake every day he could.

Fishing is a good time for talking, he said. Away from the TV, computers, video games, cell phones, all the things he hates. Also conveniently away from surveillance cameras and spies. In a boat you can see and hear somebody coming a mile away.

I like that idea.

I picture him on his boat, perched on the old patchwork quilt Babushka made, fishing hat low over his eyes. Beard splayed out over his chest. He's alone, tossing out his trusty silver minnow lure, retrieving, over and over. A splatter of rain starts to fall. Then a hit, a fat rainbow pulling hard at the line, dancing. He smiles to himself as he brings it in, twists the lure off with his calloused fingers, drops the fish in a bucket of water. Dinner. It is good he can manage for himself. So much easier to stay hidden from the *durnoy glaz* when you can find your own food.

I open my eyes. Did I *imagine* him thinking that? It was so vivid, the thoughts so clear. But it wasn't a real tunnel—there wasn't a buzz, or warmth, or a location. It felt different. And he couldn't be on his boat in Standish. I gave DARPA that location.

It was Standish I was picturing, wasn't it? I can't remember the lake well enough to be sure. But I *am* sure there was a connection, something . . .

I try again. Picture the same scene, same place. This time the boat seems different. Smaller, and he isn't sitting on Babushka's quilt, just a dark blue towel. The rest is the same: the hat, the lure, the beard. But those would be the same anywhere. I try tentatively to go into him, to *feel* him.

A breeze brushes his cheeks, ruffling the beard. He checks the sun—two o'clock. Still time to catch another one or two. He must call Abby tonight on the safe line, see how they are. Abby is struggling, bednyaga. *Sometimes he wishes to tell her, give her hope. He cannot. If he is wrong, or if the boy cannot be retrieved . . .*

This is a real tunnel. I did it. May be pure luck that he's fishing, doing what I remembered. But it might be my only chance. I have to make him *know* I'm there. I hadn't felt the location. I try to sense it, see if I can tell.

Location: Canada. Quebec, not far over the border from Vermont. Lac Bromont.

He can't sense me, not like Myka can. I'll have to be more obvious. I'll have to control him, show him. I go deeper.

He casts again, the motion sore to his old arm, but familiar. Come on, little riba. *I know you are there, fish, hiding beneath the waves. Nothing. Again . . .*

I nudge him as he lifts his arm back for another cast.

No. You need to stop and open the tackle box. Right there, the top. Flip it open.

He sighs. Why does he want to get into the tackle box? The lure is fine, working. Always the same lure, silver for afternoon. He ignores the thought, casts again, reels.

Open it. You need to write it down on your notepad. You didn't record that last fish, did you? You always record your fish. Take care of it now, before you forget.

Reluctantly he props the pole against the side of the boat and leans over to the tackle box. Little voice, you are annoying to me. You grow more annoying as I get older, pushing me to do things. I can record when I want to record! Should you not let an old man alone?

Still, he opens the lid, pulls out his notepad and small pencil, and starts to write.

I concentrate. I've never tried to write through anyone. I don't know if I can. I fill his fingers, his thumb, with my own. He'd written RAI, but I stop his hand, scratch the letters out with big, dark scratches. I'm not even trying to convince him to do anything. Just doing it.

He stares at the page, puzzled. Watches as his hand moves on its own. He feels it move, part of him, but he did not do it. J-A-K-E, his hand spells. The letters are shaky, too large, like a child's. But he can read them. He lets his fingers move. A new line.

I-t i-s J-a-k-e. H-e-l-p m-e.

He looks around, quick—are the durnoy glaz *watching? Is this a trick? There is no one near. "Malchik?" he whispers. "Is that you?"*

His fingers flip the page, cramp again to write. He watches, fascinated.

Y-E-S! Alive. Locked in—Montauk.

I'm losing myself, sticking too much, too deep, like I did with Liesel. I have to pull away, and I don't know if I can get back. I have one or two more seconds.

Need HELP. Later . . .

I jerk away, as hard as I can, and make it. I'm confused by the white above me, the bright white. Brighter than it should be . . . the lights.

The lights are on.

I sit up, fast. Liesel stands by the door, hands clasped in front of her, eyes on me.

"Oh," I say, my breath coming fast. "Bad dream."

"Yes. You were making . . . noises." Her eyebrows curve. "I thought we'd talked about sleeping in the afternoon."

"If you don't have work for me to do, I assume my time is my own," I snap. I swing my legs around. "It's not like there are a lot of options."

"Yes." She clicks slowly forward, stops about a foot away. "We should talk about that too. You've stopped going to the gym altogether, and you never went to chapel. On your downtime, you sleep. You haven't made any progress with Dr. Tenney in a long time. Frankly, I am concerned. My oversight committee is concerned."

"You have an *oversight* committee? Like people who know I'm here and *allow it?*"

She frowns. "Of course. Even classified programs have oversight, Jacob. You were brought here for your safety. You agreed. There's nothing illegal about it."

Except for all the lying, and misrepresentation, and manipulation. Entrapment, I think it's called. I stand, the floor cool on my bare feet, and take a step toward the door. "So I can leave, then, whenever I want?"

She smiles, and I really want to punch her. "No. You're an intelligence asset of the U.S. government, and the subject of an ongoing study. You know far too much about us to leave, and you're very aware of that. You're here for national security now, as well as your own."

My security . . . big, fat-ass liar. I close my eyes, clench my fists to keep from saying something I shouldn't. One . . . two . . . three. Think of Dedushka fishing. That speck of hope. "Why are we talking about this again?"

She blinks. "You asked. And my oversight committee is concerned with your continuing mental health and happiness. As I am."

"You want me to be *happy*?" I ask, incredulous.

"Content. Productive. Stable. Yes, Jacob. I have always wanted that. You should be nearing that point by now, settling in. But you're not." She tilts her head. "What can we do to help?"

"Let me go outside," I answer. "Let me breathe the goddamned air."

"Possibly . . ." she says, low. She frowns. "I have resisted the idea, for security reasons. But a guarded visit to a secure, isolated area . . ." Her eyes come up to mine. "Possibly. The committee also had this on their options list." Her voice softens, the honey voice I barely remember. "It has never been my goal to make you miserable, Jacob. The happier you are here, the better your work. And that's best for all of us. Your work benefits *all* of us."

She stares at me with her bleached-grass eyes, steady, like she's going to say something else. Maybe tell me she knows about the hallucinations, instead of letting me think I'm insane?

She turns and leaves without another word.

I plop onto the bed, triumphant. I could get to Dedushka—I did. I just have to do it again.

At 5:30 a.m. I click the alarm off before it beeps, alerts anyone. I'm already awake.

I imagine Dedushka pushing out the boat, bundled in his jacket.

Using the oars, because he always uses the oars instead of the motor in the early morning, so he doesn't startle the fish. I imagine him at a good spot not too far off the shore, unhooking the gold lure, making the first cast. Reeling. Casting again.

It falls into place, and I'm there. The same place, Lac Bromont.

It's chilly, the sun starting its rise over Iron Hill to the east. No matter. The bugs are rising too, and fishing will be good. He's eaten all his trout. He needs more today.

And Yakob. Will Yakob come? He has the big notepaper ready, in case.

Put the pole down, Dedushka, I think. Go to the paper.

He sets the pole down, without question. The little voice! Yakob? The paper. There is a big yellow pad, a fresh pencil ready, laid next to him on the seat. The pencil . . . here. In his fingers.

Dedushka, I write painstakingly, slowly. *Love.*

"Yakob," he says aloud, gruff. I feel the tears well up in him, his rough hand brush at his eyes. "You are all right?"

His hand writes.

Yes. Don't have long. Must escape.

It takes so much effort to write, to focus his fingers. I'm already feeling heavy.

He nods, speaks to the air. "I have called friends, found out about this Montauk CIA base. I have a plan. It will get us together for a meet, at a place of my choosing. They cannot help but bite on it. If you can do this, with me, perhaps you can . . . ?"

He doesn't finish, but I know what's in his mind. Perhaps I can get us away, if he can get me outside, get me to him.

Yes, I write. I *will* make it work. *What do I need to do?*

"Nothing, malchik." He strokes his beard, over and over, the hair wiry under his hand. "I will do the first part. What is the name of your control? The leader."

I take his hand again, write.

Dr. Liesel Miller. Then: *Must go. Thank you.*

"My love, Yakob," he whispers. "Pray to God, but continue to row for shore. We will be together soon."

I pull away, with a lurch, back into the room.

I'd forgotten that saying. Dad used to say it all the time, even though he stopped going to temple. Now I know where he got it from. And it does fit perfectly. Hope, yes, but make it happen yourself. Put that together with the other thing that's been repeating through my head the past couple days.

We Lukins stick together like glue.

Together we can make it through.

Anywhere we choose to roam,

Together we will make it home.

Dedushka is a Lukin, and so am I. I have no idea what his plan is, how he can force Liesel to arrange a meet. I'll spy on her in the next couple of days to see. And I'll come up with my own plan for what to do once there. I already have an idea.

Whatever happens, I'm not alone anymore. Together we will make it home.

God, I hope so.

30

"Caught" by Descendents

The next morning, during our usual tunnel session, Eric stops midmovement. He sets down the bag he's holding, his expression intent. It reminds me of Bunny. He listens for a long time, eyes trained on me. I wait, silent.

"Yes, ma'am," he says quietly. "Understood."

He sets the bag in the metal box, leaves his hand there. Still staring me down.

"What's going on?" I ask.

"Stand, please," he says.

I sit back. It has to be Dedushka. Did he really work that fast? What did he do?

"Stand," Eric repeats, voice frozen. "Now. Hands behind your back."

It's the look he gave me in the parking lot after my ride with Dedushka. I swallow and stand slowly. "What *is* it, Eric?"

"Hands behind your back!" he shouts.

I snap my hands together behind my back. He takes a zip tie out of the box, strides over to me, and hauls it tight over my wrists, cuffing me. Too tight, pinching. I flinch, but don't say a word. I don't know what's going on yet. I don't want to make it worse.

He sticks his hand in each of my pockets, like Liesel did before. He leaves them turned inside out, empty. Then he unlatches my watch and tugs it off.

"No!" I say, hoarse. "Don't take that. Please."

He tugs a chair away from the table, sets it in the middle of the room. "Sit. Don't move until I come back."

I sit on the chair, facing the door, hands awkward behind my back. Bare, without Dad's watch.

"Yes, ma'am," Eric says. "On my way."

He leaves. I wait, silent, mind flipping through possibilities. Whatever Dedushka did isn't starting out well. Clearly they suspect me of secret tunneling, of collusion . . . of something. I can't tunnel to anyone to find out what, why. I'm blind. Pinned in this chair. I stare up at the camera, like it will tell me something.

But there's nothing I can do but wait.

It feels like hours before the door opens and Liesel stalks in, followed by Eric and two guards. I'm cramped, sore, and I have to piss. I don't mention any of that. I lift my chin.

"Want to tell me what's going on?"

"Be quiet," Liesel snaps. "Don't make me gag you."

I press my lips together. Okay, then. Things aren't better.

"Search it," she says, with a wave around the room. "Search all of it. Behind the drawers, in the clothes, the sheets, mattresses, inside the toilet. Inside the drain. Everything. Show me anything you find that's even slightly out of the ordinary."

Oh. *Crap.*

I keep my mouth shut, eyes on her. The guards, two twenty-something guys, one black, one pasty white, start turning everything over. They don't look at me. Eric stands behind Liesel, arms crossed.

Liesel is pure ice. "You want to know what happened, Jacob? I'll tell you what happened." She paces, in a tight oval. Her fingers tap against her skirt as she walks. "I was quite surprised to have a call this morning from a Mr. Grigory Lukin." She pauses, gauges my expression—carefully blank—then starts up again. "He knew my name. He knew I was here, in Montauk, in a secret facility. More to the point, he knew *you* were here, and alive, in our custody." Another pause. "How would he know that, Jacob?"

I don't move.

"I'll answer for you, shall I? There are two ways he could know that. One: he tracked you here after all. I don't know why he's been quiet all these months, but that's not my primary concern. Two: you told him somehow. You tunneled to him, and you told him."

Pause. I focus on my breaths, keeping them even. Stare at the table behind her.

"My guess is you used that watch we should never have let you keep. I take the blame for that. But I am going to make damn sure you don't have anything else squirreled away in here. And that you never see that watch, or anything personal, again."

I grit my teeth, meet her gaze. It slices right through me.

"But wait, there's *more,*" she says, fake cheerful. "What did Mr. Grigory Lukin want? Why, he *demanded* that he have an in-person meeting with you, off-site. To make sure you were being treated well. Not abused, or tortured, or 'made to do anything unsavory.'" She snorts. "Does this place look like you're being abused or tortured? No. It's not luxury, I'll give you that. But video games and tennis, for God's sake."

My eyes go to Eric. He's as stone faced as I am.

"If he's satisfied that you're okay, after he's talked to you, he'll deign to let you remain with us, *safe*. And if I refuse to accede to this demand? He'll tell the press about you, about this program, and this place. He'll tell your family you're alive, and they'll start a legal process to wrest you away from us. Revealing all our secrets in the process. What do you think of that, Jacob Lukin? What do you think of the *balls* of that?"

I don't answer. She clenches her fists tightly. But she doesn't hit me. Now wouldn't be a good time to start hitting me.

It is pretty ballsy. He knows they're looking for him, that they've tried to trace him. But he walks right up to them anyway, from a position of strength. Demanding a meeting.

Also, he's throwing himself in as bait. He knows if they don't give in based on the threat, they might based on the temptation. If they can take him too, they'll have both Lukins in one swoop, threat wiped out.

I just hope if they go through with the meeting, I really can get us out of there.

The pasty guard yanks off the sheets. I try to keep my gaze away from him.

"I can't believe you," Liesel hisses. "The pair of you. I've treated you well, Jacob. I've done my best for you, in difficult circumstances. I've protected you. Who the *hell* do you think you are?"

"Ma'am? You'll want to see this."

He's tugged the top mattress off, and there's my cache.

I close my eyes. I don't want to see her face, Eric's.

"My *pen*?" Her voice goes soft, dangerous. "Dr. Tenney's notebook? You *were* spying on me. Us. How did you get these?"

I stay perfectly still.

The click of a safety. The cool metal of a gun muzzle presses against my temple. "Answer her," Eric says.

There's a long silence, my heartbeat deafening in my ears.

"You're not going to shoot me." My voice is quiet, but clear with truth. They won't kill me, not now. Not for this. They have too much to lose.

The moment stretches forever.

"Put it away," Liesel says. "I can't stand to deal with him right now."

The gun is lifted away, and I open my eyes.

She picks up the pen and notebook and waggles them in front of me. "Gone." She turns to Eric. "Stay here while they finish searching. He may have more. Then take everything out—everything—and come see me in my office."

She slams her key in the door and leaves.

Eric sets the safety back on but keeps the gun in his hand. Ready.

The guard slides the mattress back in place, and I have a small flicker of satisfaction. They didn't find Eric's object.

"I would shoot you," Eric says casually. "If she told me to. Just so we have that straight. What you did, stealing? Spying? That was uncalled for."

"Oh, and you're an angel?" I retort. "You knew the whole time you were going to take me in—you *knew* I only had a few weeks. You knew there wasn't a threat to me, to my mother or sister—you made that up. You lied to me the whole time. *The whole time, damn it*. But you pretended to be on my side. My *mate*?"

He looks at me, steady, for a long minute. Then he sets the gun down on the table, and sighs. "I didn't know that until the end. The last day. And it was for the mission, for your ultimate protection. You weren't safe out—"

"Bullshit." I scoot forward on the chair. Like I can do anything with my hands cuffed. "It was for *her,* what she wants. For DARPA. Not for me. I was fine where I was, thanks very much. No one was after me. No one *knew* about me. And I did what I did to try to find some answers about myself. That's all."

He sits in the other chair, his hand curled around the edge of the table. "I see that," he says finally.

"I think we're done, sir," the other guard says. "There's not much to search."

"Nothing else?" Eric says.

"Nothing. Should we take all this stuff out?"

He sighs again. "Yes. Leave the furniture, empty. Take the clothes and sheets and anything else." He raises his eyebrows at me. "We have to check it all for bugs, or anything else you've got hidden."

"There's nothing else," I say quietly. "I don't bug people for a living. Or screw with their lives for my own purposes."

He shrugs, stands. He waits at the door while they move out all the clothes, sheets, the Xbox, books, even the mini-fridge and the TV off the wall.

My tiny strip of cloth from Eric's pants is still there, between the mattresses somewhere. I still might have my small advantage.

But not right now.

"Eric?" I say, when they're done, and he's about to leave. "Can you take this off my wrists? For one thing, I've got to piss like a racehorse, and I don't see how that's going to work."

"Sorry, ma—" He stops himself. "Jake. She was clear. You get to keep that on for a while." His mouth quirks up on one side. "But you're resourceful. You've proven that. I'm sure you'll think of something."

That was a farce. I nearly pissed the only shorts I have now. But I did manage it, even managed to get the shorts back up.

Now there's only me and the room.

It looks naked, without even the small comforts I'm used to. I sit uncomfortably in the black chair. I don't want to go near the bed, not yet. I won't be able to get the cloth with my hands like this, and I don't want them to have any reason to suspect I have anything else. They probably have somebody watching the camera full time now.

I can still escape, maybe, with Eric's object. And there might be a chance—if I'm extremely careful—to get another one from Liesel. I need Eric's to get away, but once outside I really want one from Liesel. If I get out of here, she'll hunt me. I'll need to know where she's hunting, so I can stay one step ahead.

Is it ridiculous for me to be planning for after my escape, when I'm sitting cuffed in a chair, in a guarded cell?

The good news is they still have no idea I can control people, easily, anytime I want. That would be a deal buster.

I wonder if they'll really go through with a meet, after finding my stolen objects. Or maybe I'll never hear about it again, and be stuck here with cuffs on. Will they make me do tunnels at gunpoint?

So much to think about. And I have nothing—nothing—but time.

Hallucination Ana appears while I'm sitting there. She doesn't say anything, just stands in front of me and watches, with her sad, dark eyes, her hair pulled up in a knot.

"You want to help me out with these?" I ask her, straight out. I don't care anymore if they think I'm crazy. "You got any knives handy to cut this with?"

"You have to help yourself now," she says, in her beautiful voice.

It's true. If I can get to Dedushka, he'll help. But in here I still only have myself.

31

"Answers" by Goldfinger

Eric comes by some hours later with a sandwich and some water.

"Bread and water for the prisoner?" I stand clumsily. It's tougher than you'd think to stand up with your hands cuffed in back.

He doesn't answer. He goes around behind me and cuts the zip ties.

"Thank God." I rub my wrists to get some feeling back.

"You'd best eat quickly," he says. "I don't have long."

Not a problem. I'm starving, thirsty. I tear at it like a wolf. He sits at the table and watches me, impassive.

"So," I say, between bites. "What's going on out there? Has she talked to my grandpa again?"

He shakes his head.

"Am I going to get to see him? Will they agree to it?"

"Jake," he says, tired. "I can't talk to you."

That's that, then. If he says he won't, he won't. I chew, drink in silence. He keeps his spy eyes on me. He tells me to have a bathroom break—with the door partway open. Then he takes metal cuffs out of his pocket.

"Come on," I say. "I don't need those in here. What am I going to do?"

"Orders. Here, put your hands in front. It'll be easier to sleep that way—" He listens, makes a face. "Or not. Behind your back, please."

"Damn it, Eric. I don't—"

"Just do it," he says. "You made this bed. Protesting's not going to help."

I clench my jaw, put my wrists behind my back. He turns them palms out, clasps the metal cuffs on. They aren't quite as tight as the zip tie was. Still. My arms already hurt. He jerks his chin in acknowledgment, and is gone.

Leaving me standing alone in the room, cuffed. Again.

Two days.

Two freaking days with nothing. Eric or someone else comes in with three meals a day—that's the only way I have any sense of time. They uncuff me, have me use the bathroom, let me eat and drink, put the cuffs back on. That's all my life is. No tunneling, no other interaction except with hallucinations, mostly berating me for being so stupid. Even the lights are left on all the time. I try to sleep on the bed—incredibly awkwardly—but I don't go near the cloth. I can't.

I don't dare go to Dedushka either. Not with the lights on. Not like this.

What if they arrange a meeting and I'm never uncuffed, can't ever get to the cloth? What if they don't arrange a meeting and I live like this for months, years?

I'll go insane, that's what. I'm not far off now. In the faint reflection in the door panel, I look like hell. My wrists are starting to chafe, with raw scrapes. I haven't washed or changed clothes since this started. I have a good growth of beard going, and bags under my eyes from not sleeping. If Dedushka—or Mom or Myk—saw me the way I am now, it'd be hard to say I haven't been mistreated.

I finally do manage to get to sleep in spite of the light, and the constant ache in my arms, and am having a vivid dream of Myka—we're young, and flying kites in a field of tall grass, the blades scratching our legs as we run, laughing.

The sound of the door jolts me out of it. I sit upright, blinking.

It's Liesel, in her jacket and skirt. It's odd to see her look so normal, so put together, after my past couple days. But she seems calm. She sets a chair in front of me and perches in it delicately, brushing lint off her skirt, crossing her legs.

I wait.

She clears her throat. Her voice is composed. "In spite of your betrayal, Jacob, I have decided that it is worthwhile to continue working with you."

I swallow. Is that good, or bad?

"To that end I have seen the wisdom of making an agreement with your grandfather that will allow us to continue here."

And allow you to catch him.

"Good," I say.

Her nostrils flare. "If you tell me what you know first. I want to know exactly what kind of confidential information you extracted from your illicit tunnels."

"Does it matter? Aren't I *secure* anyway?" I wiggle my fingers in the cuffs.

"It matters to me."

There's a standoff, for a few seconds. Then I shrug. I want to meet Dedushka. I want my escape route. "Okay. If I can ask you a couple questions too."

Eyebrows up. "Such as?"

I pause, study her. I wonder if I can tell if she lies, now that I'm looking for it. "I wasn't in danger. It was all a sham. Why? Why did you do this to me?"

She shifts, resettles herself. "Everything I've done is for the good of the project, Jacob. For the good of the country, the people we find, or the people we're protecting by finding fugitives. I'm looking at the big picture, always." Her voice drops, softens. "In the end, your talent and the opportunities it offers were more important than your everyday life." Something flits across her face—regret? Understanding? Just as quickly it's gone. "How did you get my pen?"

"I stole it from Dr. Tenney's briefcase," I say, honest. "I don't know where he got it." Not honest.

I wonder if *she* can tell the difference between lie and truth. I don't think so.

"So you saw my office, and apparently some of your files. What else?"

I shake my head. "Nothing else." Suddenly I'm exhausted. So exhausted I could lie down and go to sleep with her sitting there. I repeat what I said to Eric. "I only did it to find out about myself. I looked at my files through you. Listened to one conversation through Dr. Tenney, and you talked about tunneling. Nothing else. I swear."

She considers it, me. Then she nods. "Let's say I believe you . . . enough for now. We'll do this more later, with the polygraph. You're a mess. We're meeting with your grandfather in a week's time, and I can't have you looking, and smelling like . . ." She flaps a hand at me. "That."

I snort.

"Stand up," she says with a sigh. "And I'll take those cuffs off."

I stand, let her take the cuffs off, and flex my arms, which will probably take the full week to recover.

Inside, I'm dancing. *Yes*, I'm getting out. *Yes*, I'll see Dedushka. And *yes yes yes*, I'll have a chance to recover the cloth so I can use it if all goes well. I can leave this hellhole and these crazy controlling people far behind.

I can almost taste the air.

I don't say thank you, or how glad I am to have my hands free. "Can I have some fresh clothes, and soap?"

"And deodorant." Her pale lips purse up. "I'd suggest a razor too."

"Whatever you say."

Anything to make it happen.

She pauses on her way out the door. "So you know—I no longer trust you, Jacob Lukin. I probably won't trust you again. And that's a great loss to you."

I shrug again. "Whatever you say."

Her eyes narrow. But she leaves. And I'm almost free.

I don't get the cloth that night. I'm learning patience, bit by bit. I'm learning strategy, from the mistakes I've made till now. Too many of them.

Mostly I'm learning ruthlessness. I know how to do it, get both Dedushka and me out of that meeting safely. It's bold, risky, and utterly ruthless. I'm going to do it. And I'm going to succeed.

I hope. I've also learned not to be cocky. Two days in cuffs will help with that.

I wake myself in the middle of the next night, and carefully—so carefully—slip my hand under the mattress beneath me. My wrists scream as the sore flesh scrapes along, but it doesn't matter. It has to be there somewhere, unless it fell under the bed. I hope not. That would be a lot trickier to get. Or—God forbid—it fell on the floor and was swept out with all the clothes and such. My fingers bump slowly across every inch of the mattress, feeling for that minuscule strip.

Nothing. I'm sure.

I pull my arm out gradually, and stick my left arm under the other side. This is the camera side, and I didn't want to do that. The same process, feeling, feeling . . .

There. It's in my fingers. I bring my arm out, careful not to trigger the lights, the cloth curled in my hand.

Ruthless.

I can do this.

Dr. Tenney sits in the chair like he's the one forced to be here. Ever since they found my objects—his notebook, and the pen—he won't look me in the eye. "Tell me again. What are you going to say to your grandfather?"

I sigh. This is useless. I don't even know why they're putting up the pretense—they're going to try their best to take Dedushka. If they don't think I know that, even without any tunnels to Liesel, they're underestimating me. So what does it matter what I say?

And of course I have my own agenda.

"Mr. Lukin?"

Oh, yeah, and he's reverted to my last name.

"That I'm fine, that I've been well treated, that it was my choice to come here."

"Thank you." He makes a mark on his paper, glares at me over his glasses, and closes the notebook.

"Why don't you just say what you're thinking?" I scratch at my wrists—they're still sore, healing. "I'm so tired of lies."

"Really. You've become a master liar, Mr. Lukin. How can you be tired of it?"

I blink, surprised. That was uncharacteristically honest. Then I realize his lips haven't moved. And it came from behind me. I turn my head slowly. There's another Dr. Tenney sitting on the bed, legs crossed, fingers laced over his knee.

Perfect.

I turn back to the real Dr. Tenney. He's studying me, the old glint in his eye. "You're seeing someone right now, aren't you? Over there?"

He stiffens, listens. Then he deliberately puts a hand to his ear, takes out the earpiece, and sets it on the table between us. "I need to talk to you, Jake, no matter what they say. You should know."

"Here we go," says the hallucination. "This is going to be good."

"Know what?" I ask.

"Are you seeing someone right now? Here in the room with us?"

I glance at the bed. That Dr. Tenney nods, waves me on. Oddly, he pulls a cigar out of his pocket and starts to light it, puffing. "Yes." I turn back. "I should know what?"

"That the drug we've been feeding you so blithely has a significant side effect, Jake. That in tests it's been shown to cause severe auditory and visual hallucinations."

I don't react.

"That we've known for some time that you've been experiencing these hallucinations." He pauses. "Why haven't you told us about them?"

I push away, pace to the bed. Stand over the hallucination. I can smell the cigar smoke, drifting into my face. Fake Dr. Tenney grins with the cigar in his mouth. I swipe a hand through him, and he vanishes. Sometimes they do. "Would you?"

There's a long, strained silence.

Then the chair creaks, and I hear the squeak of his shoes across the floor. He stops behind me, his mouth near my ear.

"It'll get worse," he says, low. "With every dose. Liesel knows it. Eventually you will be useless to her. To anyone. You won't be able to tell visions from reality. You'll trade this cell for one with rubber walls."

I don't know if his breath smells like cigars, or if it's still the lingering scent of the hallucination. I stare straight ahead, at the wall. The solid, plaster wall.

"You have to stop," he whispers, urgent. "Stop the medicine. Stop tunneling. They won't listen to me."

The door opens, and Dr. Tenney steps away. It's not Liesel, though. It's Eric. The loyal minion.

"Time's up," he says.

I watch Dr. Tenney pick up his pen, his notebook, the earpiece, the light slanting on his head a comfort. Familiar.

"Thanks," I say. I mean it. It's been a twisted relationship. But he's trying to help, at least now. He nods once, and Eric ushers him out.

Somehow I know that's the last time I'll ever see him.

32

"Revenge" by Sean Murray

I sit on the edge of the bed, dressed in shorts, a T-shirt, and sneakers. Ready.

Not ready.

No, ready. I have to be. It's almost time. In my pocket I rub the cloth between my fingers, close my eyes. A quick dip first.

Eric stands in a small, white room with Liesel. Room 322. The gun is heavy in the back holster, but it feels right. Its weight, its bulk, are familiar. Liesel checks her own gun, an M-9. He'd expected her to carry something smaller.

"You sure you want him uncuffed during the meet?" he says. It doesn't make sense for security. She insists he be cuffed in the building, for God's sake.

"It's the appearance of the thing." She secures the strap on her shoulder holster, checks the safety is on, and tucks it away. "He wants to see the boy is well treated, not a prisoner. We'll show him."

"But we're going to take Lukin anyway," he says. "So what difference does it make?"

She pulls her jacket on, her lips drawn down. "Who knows what Lukin has planned. Media? Witnesses? We know he's not stupid. I'm preparing for all contingencies." She throws him an ugly glance. "Now stop questioning me, and let's get on with it."

One more thing, Eric.

I mold into him, use his hands to feel in his jacket. Yes, the pills are there, right pocket.

I should've known he'd be prepared, bring them. Just in case.

I come out, swing my legs against the bed. That's enough to tell me what I need to know. They're planning on taking Dedushka, and they're both armed.

Go time.

They cuff and hood me for the trip. I'm led up in an elevator—I can feel the movement—and out of the building. There's the warm touch of real air on my mouth, my arms, and legs. I stop to feel it. But I'm pushed on, up a step, settled on a seat. The motion of a car starts under me.

God, how I hate this hood. I swear I'm not going to wear it ever again, no matter what happens.

It seems like a long time in the car. I use the time to prepare. I play out what I have to do in my head, see the kinks, steel myself.

What if I can't get out again?

I can't worry about that. I have to just do it, trust that it'll be okay. This is my only chance—and Dedushka is risking his freedom on it too. I can't fail.

Finally, the car stops. I wait. I feel people moving around me. Eric pulls off the hood, and I squint in the sudden light. I'm in the back of a van, white just like Ana's, sunlight pouring in the front windows. I stare at the light, the dust motes dancing in it. He smiles at me as he takes the cuffs off, his eyes crinkling in the old way. "Ready?"

I'm ready, I think. *But you're not.*

I stretch my hands, take a deep breath. "Ready."

He opens the back, and I step outside. And stop.

We're in the parking lot of a park. There are trees everywhere: cottonwoods, aspens, oaks, all in full green leaf, the grass bright. The air is hot and still. It smells like summer.

The last time I was outside, it was the dead of winter. I breathe, deep.

This. Oh God, this. I can't go underground again.

"This way." Liesel's voice is packed with tension, her hand on her side, where I know the gun is. There are five or six other agents there, men and women, all openly holding weapons.

Two of them walk across the lot, toward a path, Liesel behind them.

Eric takes my elbow, and we follow. There's one car—a dark blue Cherokee—parked a few spots down. Dedushka really is here. There are no other cars, no other people. They must've closed it down for this.

I judge it all, the angles, the people. The strategy. Contingencies. Thinking of *Call of Duty, Halo.*

Pay attention to everything. Use everything.

Be ruthless.

We walk on into the park, halfway between the two cars. Dedushka sits at a picnic table, watching the parade of agents. When I come in sight, his face lights up, his teeth gleaming through the beard.

"Dedushka!" I try to run to him, but Eric blocks me, his arm in front of my chest.

"Not like that," he says, low. "Slowly."

Dedushka stands up, his arms in the air.

"Is he clear?" Liesel calls. "No others?"

"Clear," an agent calls back from behind Dedushka.

"Let them go forward, then." She turns to me, her expression severe, nervous. In this moment I'm amazed she's gone through with this. She must want him badly. "You have five minutes. Remember what to say."

I remember what I'm supposed to do.

I walk forward, at a snail pace, about six guns trained on me. Finally, I'm close enough. Dedushka holds his hands out, and I take them, squeeze.

The cloth is curled in my fingers.

"Yakob," he says, loud enough for them to hear it. "*Malchik*. You are all right?"

"I'm okay, Grandpa." He flinches at "Grandpa"—he knows I'd never call him that to his face. I hope he understands that means anything I say, aloud, is a lie. "They're treating me well. I'm fine."

He leans in to kiss me on each cheek. "The plan?" he whispers, his whiskers tickling my cheek. He still smells of tobacco.

"We only have a couple seconds. Go along with *whatever happens,* okay?"

"*Da,*" he whispers.

"Hug me," I say, "and hold me up. *Now.*"

I close my eyes and tunnel to Eric.

Hempstead Lake State Park, New York. Eric watches the two suspiciously. They're too close, too long. Is Jake . . . sagging? What's going on? He's ready to move.

I flood myself into him with all my strength, and move for him. I pull his gun, stride straight to me and Dedushka, and pretend to give myself a whack on the head with the butt of the pistol, holding back the hit so it's not as hard as it looks. Dedushka lets go, and my limp body rolls to the ground, fingers still tightly closed.

I feel Eric inside, stunned. But I have control now. Thank God I practiced this. All those hours with Dr. Tenney.

"No!" Dedushka cries, at the same time Liesel yells "Eric! Stop!"

I make Eric pull my body up, cock his gun, and put it to my head. The gun is a lot heavier than I expected, but Eric's hands know what to do. "Shut up, *Grandpa,*" I say, in Eric's voice. He turns to Liesel, holding my body to his chest as a shield. "And you!" he yells. She's pointing her gun at us, steady. "All of you! Stand down. I'll kill him, and none of us want that."

"Eric," Liesel says, tight. Utterly shocked. "What are you doing?"

"I got a better offer," I say in Eric's voice. "I'm taking him and the old man. Get out of my way. You can shoot me, but I'll get my shot into that valuable brain first. And the second shot will be for the old man. You'll lose them both, and you won't have any chance to get them back."

I make him start dragging me, backward, toward the Jeep. He's strong, and I'm skinny. It's not hard. He jerks his chin at Dedushka. "You too, Grandpa. We're all going."

"You got a better *offer*?" Liesel says, still firmly controlled. "From whom?" She gasps. "Is it Smith? Wait. It was you who called Grigory! You set this up, so you could take both of them!"

"Bingo," Eric says.

Why not? It's working out even better than I thought. I can feel the real Eric struggling against me, and I'm crystallizing in him badly. But I have to stay put. I have to be him for as long as it takes.

"I told you to stand down, all of you." I stop, wait.

Liesel gives the go-ahead, and they all set their guns on the ground. Even her. "Hands in the air," I say. I make Eric look at Dedushka hard. "Take her gun, put it in my holster. No funny business, now."

Dedushka nods, playing the part of the scared old man. He scurries over to Liesel, picks up her gun, and slides it in Eric's back holster.

Object acquired. I feel more stuck than I've ever felt, like I'm part of him. I don't know how I'll ever get out.

"Time to go," Eric's voice says. I make him drag me again. Only a little farther.

"You won't get away with this." Liesel's voice is spiked with fury. "We'll have you—and them—back within the hour. And then you'll be the one in the cell."

"I wouldn't be cocky like that," Eric says. "I'll have my gun to his head the whole time, until we're safe, until the exchange is made. You try anything, bye bye assets."

We reach the Jeep. Finally.

"You drive," I make Eric say to Dedushka. "Do anything crazy and I'll kill him. Now open the back."

Dedushka flings the back door open, and I make Eric heave my body in, diagonally across the seat. I have Eric jump in too, shut the door. Dedushka runs around to the front, jams the key in, and slams his door. He starts the engine.

"It is you, *malchik*?" he asks quietly.

I keep the gun up, showing it to them all. Liesel and the others watch us, their hands still high. "It's me, Dedushka. *Go*."

He floors it backward, then across the lot and onto the street, with the driving skills I saw before. Quickly I pull Liesel's gun out of the back holster, toss it onto the front seat. Then the one in my hand. Then the T-680 from Eric's jacket.

"Keep driving," I make Eric say. "Head somewhere safe, as fast as you can go. I've got to get out of him, and I don't know what he'll do, how much he'll know. Don't let him near the guns."

Dedushka nods. With one hand he opens the glove box, throws both guns and the medicine in it, and slams it shut. "Come back to yourself, boy," he says, curt. "It worked, but this I do not like."

Me either. It feels awful now, the worst kind of claustrophobia. Like I'm stuffed into a tiny box, my skin stuck to the walls. I feel Eric too, shoved into an even smaller corner.

I try to pull away. Yank. Feel myself start to tear. Yank again, with all the force I can manage.

It isn't working.

"They follow us," Dedushka says. "I see them. I will do my best." We're flying down the road as it is, swerving all over.

I look at my body, where I'm supposed to be, touch my hand, try to tunnel to myself. But that doesn't work either. I'm panting—or Eric is, I'm not sure which anymore—with the effort.

"Come on," I mutter. "Come *on*."

"Deerma!" Dedushka yells, and flings the Jeep hard to the left.

There's a crack. A spray of glass. Without warning I'm back in my own body, gasping, looking up at Eric as he slumps to the side, unconscious.

There's a bullet hole in the window, and blood streaming out over the seat.

"They shot Eric!" I yell in my own voice. I scramble across the seat and lean him forward, so I can see. There's a lot of blood. "Jesus."

"You make it back." Dedushka grins back at me. "*Slava bogu*."

"But they shot Eric!" I feel the back of his head. I can see a wound, but I can't feel a bullet or anything, and it doesn't seem deep. Maybe it glanced off when we swerved? I grab a towel from the back and press it to his head.

"This is bad thing?"

"Yes," I say, thinking of his wife, his babies. My chest aches. "This is a very bad thing."

It's my fault, of course. I used him, made him seem like a traitor. I was ruthless.

But I didn't want him killed, damn it. I figured he'd be able to clear his name after a bit of interrogation. Liesel would believe him. Probably.

We're still zooming down the road, zigzagging between other cars, ignoring stoplights, *Grand Theft Auto*–style. We seem to be out of range of the shooting car for the moment.

"We have to drop him off," I say. "Pull over long enough for me to leave him. They'll find him, take care of the wound. And maybe it'll slow them down."

I see Dedushka's eyes move to mine in the rearview mirror—he doesn't want to slow down, much less stop.

"Besides," I add, "he probably has a tracker on him."

He pulls to the side of the road, slams on the brakes.

I reach across Eric, open the door, and roll him out—as gently as I can, given the circumstances. He lies on the sidewalk, head lolling.

"Sorry," I whisper.

Then I slam the door, Dedushka hits the gas, and we fly off.

About an hour later, when we haven't seen anyone behind us for a while, Dedushka pulls into another Walmart parking lot. He parks at the very end and kills the engine. We're quiet for a long moment. Then he puts his arm over the seat and smiles at me, his eyes bright.

"Time for a new ride, as you say. This one will not last much longer." He waves a hand at the air. "Satellites."

I nod, immensely glad he has this part under control. "Don't forget the guns."

"Right! The guns!" He takes them out of the glove box and hands one to me. Liesel's. I make sure it's safe and tuck it in my pocket.

Dedushka examines the green glass bottle with curiosity. "And what is this?"

I put out a hand for it. "Something I hope I'll never need again." I don't look at the seat next to me. Hallucination Myka's been sitting there, bouncing and chattering, since I dropped Eric off. "But just in case."

We get out, leaving Hallucination Myka behind. I follow him as he strolls around the nearest aisles of the parking lot, looking for something.

"Here!" He takes a thin metal bar from his bag and jimmies the lock of a battered mint-green Ford F-150. Then he hops up, tugs out some wires, and starts it. The whole thing takes twenty seconds.

I stare at him like he's sprouted wings.

He shrugs at me. "What? It is useful. I will teach you. Now, get in. We will go to my safe house, and then we will talk." He beams again. "I am so glad to see you safe, Yakob."

"You too, Dedushka. Thanks. For—"

He shakes his head. "Not now. Get in."

I get in the truck. It's a bumpy ride, but it'll do. It'll get us farther away from them.

33

"Feeling Good" by Nina Simone

We change vehicles four times on the way to Lac Bromont. I worry about the border, but Dedushka steals a motorcycle and takes us on a track through the forest he says only the locals know about. He says Jeeps can make it through here too. Though the last Jeep is back in New York, probably crawling with agents.

I hope Eric's all right. I can't check, even if I dared tunnel again. I lost the cloth in the first car. And I don't dare tunnel to Liesel, not yet.

We arrive at Dedushka's cabin at about nine that night. He unlocks the door, and I start to follow him in. But something stops me cold in the doorway.

It's a perfectly normal, rustic cabin. Square, with a wood cot on one side and a sleeping bag rolled up on the floor at the foot of it, a woodstove, a small kitchen table and chairs. Two windows. A few things scattered around, mostly fishing tackle.

But it's inside, enclosed in walls, and even that reminds me too much of the room. I can't breathe. "I can't. I . . . can't. Can I stay . . . outside?"

His eyes are full of sympathy. "Stay wherever you most like, Yakob. You sleep in the boat, if you like. But the porch will likely be better."

I let out a slow breath. I don't have to go in. I don't have to be closed up again.

I back up onto the porch, sit on the steps. It's just getting dark, the whole sky, the lake before me, washed with orange. The night breeze is cool on my face. It smells of pine, mud, fish.

I should've run in the first place. I should've come here before, when I had the chance, the first time.

I hear Dedushka come out on the porch behind me, the hiss of a match, and the sharp, rich smell of pipe smoke.

"What's the date?" I ask.

He puffs for a while, then sits next to me. "June ninth."

"Four months," I say. Then, violently: "I'm never going underground again."

"No." He takes the pipe out of his mouth, holds it loose in his hand. "Nor me. I have kept that promise to myself, for forty years."

I look at him sideways. The beard, the gray hair, the sagging skin. But underneath, the resemblance is obvious. Lukin men look alike. Live alike.

"You were underground, Dedushka?"

He nods slow, grudging. "I will tell you that story, someday soon. Enough for you to know that it is not far off from yours, except in Russia. Also I never had the"—again his hand flutters—"level of talent you have."

I shrug. It's a talent I want no part of. Not anymore.

No more tunneling, no more headaches. No more hallucinations. At least, I hope they'll go away eventually—but I won't cause any more. I won't be able to help people. But I'll stay sane. I'll stay out of rubber walls. Any walls, maybe.

He puffs for a while. I hug my knees and watch the sky darken, the stars come out. I don't want to sleep, to lose a moment of this. I want to stay outside and watch the sky forever.

"Two things," he says. "First, most important: I have something for you."

He reaches into the pocket of his jacket, pulls out a folded blue piece of paper, and hands it to me.

I open it. In neat, twelve-year-old writing are the words *I love you, Jake.* Underneath, it says *We've missed you.*

I look at Dedushka. I almost can't say it. "Myka."

He tilts his head and smiles. "Your sister, she knows everything. She called me a month ago, to tell me she does not think you are dead. That it is fishy. She does not believe me when I say she must let you go." He shrugs. "So I tell her the truth. Then I tell her when you come to me." His eyes shine. "It was her plan, to use me as bait. If she does not hear from us by tomorrow night, she will go to the press, tell your story and mine. It was backup."

I feel a rush of giddiness, like being drunk. She didn't give up on me. She didn't believe I was gone, even when he told her to.

"And Mom?"

"Does not know. But I think she should, yes? It will be a risk. But I think we have all underestimated her."

"But they could be seen as threats to the government, or hostages." I clutch the note. "How can they be safe?"

He puffs, considering, the cloud of smoke a mushroom in the air. "They'll be watched, but no action has been taken, not yet. Your sister—and I—believe if we leave them be long enough, after this contact, they will be all right. I track them, like I did you. And in time, we will find a way."

After this contact. I look at the paper in my hand. She sent it as an object. I can go, right now. I can see her.

But I'm not supposed to tunnel anymore.

It's getting full dark, and the lake is turning mysterious, unknown. The insects are out, flitting around us.

"Go," Dedushka says.

I close my eyes, and go.

She's sitting at the kitchen table, at home, doing a jigsaw puzzle with Mom. I'm startled at first to see her hair cut short, to her chin. It makes her look different, older. Then I'm in her mind, easy. Like nothing ever happened.

She stops, breathes fast. She knows I'm there.

Myk. I'm out. I'm okay.

I feel her concern, a rush of stored-up worry. Even accusation. I said I was okay before, right before I went away. Before I left her behind.

I promise, I'm fine. I'm with Dedushka. Everything will be all right now.

She starts to cry, tears hot on her cheeks. Across the table Mom exclaims, worried.

Tell her everything, Myk. Tell her I'm sorry. Tell her I love her.

I have to go. I don't trust tunneling anymore.

Love you.

I pull away. My cheeks are wet too, and Dedushka's. We're quiet for a long time.

"There is a second thing," Dedushka says, when the night is full dark. His voice is so gentle I'm afraid. I grip the step, wait.

"Yakob—it is time you know. Your father is alive."

Everything stops. It's like being under the hood again: no sound, no sight, nothing but roaring blackness.

I blink. "What do you mean?"

"The death, it was faked. Like yours. Ivan is . . . it is difficult. It was for your safety, all of you. But he knew he was leaving. He told me so I could take care of things. Watch."

I'm back on that mountaintop in Colorado, holding my mother and sister at a grave marker, while the wind howls. I hate Dad terribly, for a second.

Only a second. I've done the same thing.

"Where is he?" I whisper.

"I do not know. With another organization. He said the CIA, the air force, did not even know of it. I tracked him to a base in Texas. But then he disappeared." He shakes his head sadly. "They have hidden him so well, or he has hidden himself—I do not think there is a way to find him."

I think instantly of the watch. The damned watch. If I'd known, I could've tunneled to him anytime I wanted. Anytime in the past two years, the past four months of hell. But I don't have it anymore.

"Do you have anything of his?" I ask urgently. "Anything personal?"

He frowns. "Not here. It is in my house in Standish, all the boxes are there." He chews on his pipe, thinks. "Or in your house in Herndon."

I set a hand on his arm. It's warm, alive. Like the tingle in my own blood, the excitement rising. The challenge.

"Dedushka," I say. "If we can get something of his, anything—I can find him. I can find him that second. And the two of us, we can get him. So none of us have to be underground."

Lukins stick together like glue.

And I guess I'm not done tunneling yet.

34

"Safe House" by Mintzkov

I run, dodging between the trees, the soft ground giving under my feet. There aren't dogs behind me, but I imagine dogs snarling and straining at leashes, sniffing me out. It helps me stay focused on running as fast as I can.

It's training. After four months of sitting on my butt in one room, I was massively out of shape. I've been running every day, as long as I can manage, to get some of that strength back. I want to be ready in every way I can when I get back out there.

Get an object. Find Dad. Rescue him.

Sounds simple enough when I say it to myself.

I come to a clearing by the lake, no trees, and sprint across the grass hard, pushing myself, my legs and arms pumping. It feels good, strong. Like I'm part of a rhythm, have a purpose.

It's been three weeks since I escaped, since I came here with

Dedushka. I still don't sleep inside the cabin. It gives me the shakes to *be* inside for long. And I know very well how hard Liesel and her people are searching for me. Especially since they figured out how I controlled Eric, how far I can really go. I honestly don't think she—or Eric—will ever stop searching.

I still feel awful about Eric. I've seen him, in tunnels to Liesel. He's wobbly, recovering from being shot. More, he's *pissed*. At me. They have him on official leave, investigating his actions. Concerned that he's still "compromised." But he's working with her anyway.

I don't even think he wants me underground anymore. I think if it were up to him, he'd shoot me dead on sight.

None of that stops me from making plans to go back out there, despite Dedushka's objections. He wants to keep me here, safe, forever. But now that I know Dad's alive, I can't just sit here and leave him alone. Not if he's locked up like I was.

"Whatchya running from?" Myka asks.

I slow, but don't stop, or look around me. I know it's just a hallucination of my sister trotting beside me somewhere. She comes often, more than anybody else. I dive into trees again, under cover. Keep going, find the rhythm. One two one two.

"They're gonna catch you," she says.

I stop, lean over to get my breath back. Myka stands there in front of me, only a foot away, arms crossed. Her hair long and braided, like it always was. A frown tugging at her mouth. Even Hallucination Myka is hard to ignore.

"They're not going to catch me," I pant. "We're safe here."

"I don't think so . . ." she says, sing-song. "I think they're gonna *find* you . . ."

I shake my head and run past her. She falls into a trot behind me. I keep going on my loop through the forest.

Not as relaxed as I was, though. There's no reason to listen to her. She's just a product of my mind. But somehow it echoes. I suddenly imagine coming back to find Dedushka on his knees, Liesel holding a gun to his head. I run faster. Almost there. Through the last trees, and . . .

Dedushka sits on the porch, an unlit pipe clenched in his teeth, reading one of his Russian novels. His beard ruffles in the breeze off the lake.

I breathe. He's okay. But I still can't shake off the worry, not until I check. I go straight for my bag and pull out Liesel's gun.

I sit on the porch and cradle the cold, heavy gun in my hands, distaste shivering through me.

I wasn't going to tunnel anymore. But it's smart to tunnel to her at least once a day, at different times. Just to make sure our safe house is still safe. I don't like touching the gun, knowing its power. I hate tunneling to Liesel. But I suck it up, close my eyes.

It's way faster than it used to be, easier. All that damn practice. I say it aloud.

Location: Virginia. Arlington. 3701 North Fairfax Drive, sixth floor, room 622. DARPA headquarters. The office is plain, big, room for two desks spilling over with folders, maps. A woman, midthirties, blond hair pulled back. She wears a black suit, a badge. She leans over a map spread out on a large, cluttered table, tracing a circle with her finger. Here. He's got to be in here, somewhere.

I focus on the map, try to see the detail. It's not as big a circle as I'd like it to be. Upstate New York, Vermont, Canada. Including Quebec, where we're sitting.

"Excellent," Eric says, behind her. She turns as he hangs up the phone. He smiles at her, brittle. His eyes are cold. "I think we can narrow that circle a little more."

"Excellent indeed." She turns back to the map, smooths it with her hand. "Not long now, Jacob. Not long at all."

I open my eyes.

Dedushka closes the book, sets it in his lap. Looks at me, silent.

"It's time," I say, my voice rising. "They're going to find us if we stay here. It's time to go."

I feel the weirdest mix of relief and absolute horror.

I flash back to Liesel's cell. I can still taste the stale air, the darkness of artificial light. Sitting there with my hands cuffed behind my back, powerless. Nothing but a tool. That's where they want me again, for the rest of my life.

I won't go back there. But I don't have to stay stuck here anymore, either. It's time to get Dad, so we can all three be together. I want to go *now*.

Dedushka takes the pipe from his teeth and examines the bowl carefully, like it's really important. "Perhaps not yet. They have a circle. A circle, it could be months . . ."

"Dedushka."

He meets my eyes. He looks old to me suddenly, uncertain. Vulnerable. I'm risking him too, going out there again. But I don't think we have a choice. We can't stay hiding here like rabbits until they beat down the door.

"Please," I say, low. "It's time."

He sighs, then sets the book and pipe on the table, and gives a short nod.

That's enough for me.

It doesn't take long—we've planned the heck out of this. I change clothes, pull on a baseball hat, and grab my backpack, Liesel's gun tucked safely inside. Dedushka has his bag. We hike to the motorcycle hidden deep in the trees, take the forest path out. We'll cross the border that way, and then do our best to disappear on the other side, make our way to Virginia again. To an object of Dad's, and then to wherever he is.

I hope Dedushka really does know how to avoid surveillance like he says he does—but I have to trust him.

I always trust him. And finally, finally, it's time to go.

We stop in Vermont, in a town called Saint Albans, to ditch the motorcycle and steal a car. We pull into a mall parking lot and troll the aisles, scouting. I let Dedushka choose the car, but I'm supposed to hot-wire it. He taught me how, theoretically at least. We're probably going to have to do it a lot. Not just cars either. To survive, to stay hidden, we're going to have to steal people's clothes, food, money.

I feel a twinge of guilt about it. These people didn't do anything to us; they're not involved in any way. And I'm selfishly fucking with their lives.

But I don't really have a choice there either. DARPA took my identity—Jacob Lukin is officially dead to everyone but Mom and Myka and Dedushka. I can't change that now. It's not like I can go get a job, apply for a credit card, start over. When I start over (if—no, when) it's going to have to go a lot deeper than that.

I wish I could really think that far ahead.

Dedushka pulls up next to an old, beat-up yellow Volvo wagon, cuts the motorcycle engine, and gives me a nod.

Old cars are easier, he says. Less fancy protection, key sensors and alarms and all that. Plus they're more likely to be unlocked, as long as we're not in a city, so we don't have to mess with a slim jim.

I look around . . . nobody nearby. Check the door handle. Unlocked. He's right.

Here we go.

I jump in, pull off the plastic panel, and search for the right wires. Red one for starter. There it is. I pull out the wire strippers from my pocket, strip it, and carefully touch the copper to the bundle of connected power wires. My hands are shaking. I'm totally sure at any moment someone's going to run over, yelling, and call the cops.

The engine catches, and I breathe. Dedushka stands next to the door, beaming.

"Well done, *malchik*. I will drive for now."

I climb across. He spits three times over his left shoulder, then gets in, and we take off.

That wasn't as bad as I thought. Maybe the Volvo owner will take the motorcycle we left parked, wires pulled and ready to start. Fair trade.

More likely I'm just trying to make myself feel better about it.

Dedushka heads east, aiming for the highway. We should be able to use this car for at least a few hours before we have to dump it too. Tonight we'll go hole up somewhere for a while, away from satellites. From what I could see in tunnels, they're actively scanning cameras, data, for any sign of us, 24/7. We don't want to give them an easy path to find.

It's quiet in here, compared to the roar of the motorcycle.

"Should I tunnel to her?" I ask. "See if they know anything?"

He shrugs. "*Nyet*. An hour or so."

For some reason being in the car doesn't give me claustrophobia like walls do. I guess because you can't lock me in a regular car, not like that. It's the being trapped part that starts all the panic feelings.

Worry about right now, Jake. Not tomorrow, or tonight, or what we'll do once we see where Dad is.

I watch the small-town scenery fly by the window, churches and stores and pastel houses with flags hanging out front and sprinklers shooting off. A couple kids running through in their bathing suits. It feels like none of it, none of that normal, everyday life, has a thing to do with me anymore.

"Yakob," Dedushka says, with a glance. "It is right that I should tell you, some. Now is good time."

I raise my eyebrows. I hope I know what he means. I've been asking questions about his powers, his past, for weeks, but it's like trying to pry a boulder.

"If something happens," he says, "you should know. At least the start of it."

I swallow, ignore the *if something happens*. “Know what?”

He sighs, grips the steering wheel, a tattered black leather cover. “It was in Russia, in 1958 . . .” He stops and glances at me, his face stony. “No. I do not wish to tell this part of the story now. It is too much. Enough to say that . . . your talent is with touch, with people’s things. Mine was voices.”

I wait, watch him. Suddenly he stares hard at the rearview mirror. My guts clench. Did they find us already? How? I spin, scan behind us. Nothing unusual. “What do you see?”

After a couple minutes he relaxes. “*Nichevo*. Anyway, voices.” He waves his hand. “Like you and tunnel, but not quite. When I hear voice of someone who has died, I was taken over with last moments of this person, how they died, where. I feel it all.” He shudders. “Not pleasant, Yakob. I have died so many times, in so many people. Always it is sad.”

He stares ahead, chewing on his lip.

“Wow. I’m sorry, Dedushka.” Tunneling only to dead people. If it’s anything like that soul-sucking cold I feel when I touch dead people’s objects, I don’t know how he can stand it.

Then I realize what he’s really telling me. “Was. You said was. You don’t have it anymore?”

He shakes his head slowly. “This is what I want you to know. I was not born with it, *malchik*. It was created. It started with me. And we found a way to make it stop.”

My head spins. You can *stop* it? I try to think what it would be like not to have this ability I was born with. To truly be a normal person.

Wait. I would be useless to them, wouldn’t I? I wouldn’t be a pawn anymore.

“How?” I ask, my voice cracking. “Can I make it stop?”

He blows a long breath. “There was a serum. It is possible. But I do not think there is serum left, anymore.” He looks at me for a long minute, and sets a hand on my knee. “We did not know it would continue, that you would have power too.”

"Who's *we*?"

He gets that look on his face, wistful, kind of goofy. "My Milena and I. Your Babushka."

I nod, look out the window again. There are a million things he's not telling me in this story, massive blanks. Who created this power in Russia in 1958? Why did he and my grandmother have a serum to stop it? And what about Dad?

I want to ask. I want to grill him on the details, find out more about this serum. But it doesn't work to push Dedushka. He closes right up.

We hit the outskirts of Burlington, and he squints at the signs. "We go to get an object of Ivan's? You are sure this is what you want?"

"Yes," I say firmly. No matter what else happens, that's the plan. The goal. Dedushka moves into the lane to go southeast, toward D.C. And then I ask, because I can't help it. "Does Dad have a power too?"

Dedushka flinches. "I am sorry, Yakob. I will tell you, but it is a difficult story, and I must think how to tell. I will say it is . . . my choice that makes all this. That makes you like this, in danger. Your father apart. I would take it back if I could, a hundred times."

I sigh. "It's who I am. Who I've always been. You don't have to apologize for that."

He turns back to the road, and I can tell he's not going to say any more. It's enough, I guess. For the moment. Even though he didn't answer how it happened. Or about Dad. I have to trust him that he'll tell me what I need to know eventually.

We ride, silence cushioning us. I try to imagine life without tunneling. Without this. *Is* it who I am? Who would I be, without it?

Free?

35

"Accidents" by Fishboy

We sleep in the car, under an overpass. It's easier and safer than negotiating a hotel, and hidden from satellites. Somehow, I actually sleep. In the morning we eat apples and Dedushka's homemade granola bars, and I tunnel to Liesel. I can't tell exactly what's going on—she's bustling down a hallway—but something's changed. The activity level has picked up. It's early, but the place seems full of analysts buzzing excitedly, and Liesel is out of breath, almost panting in anticipation.

I can't tell for sure, but I think they might know we're out, on the run.

I don't tell Dedushka. I don't want to freak him out.

Next I tunnel to Myka. She's still in bed, her own bed at home, but awake. God, home seems so far away.

Hey, I say in her mind. *Is it there? Did you leave it?*

We set up a dead drop of a little air force tie tack of Dad's—he used to wear it all the time, so it should work. I can't wait to get my hands on it. I'm so close.

'Course. It's been there for a week. I checked yesterday. When are you coming?

I pause. *You can't be there, Myk.*

Shame floods across, tangled with frustration. I was right. She had been planning to crash, to see me. My little sister, always a touch too smart for her own good.

It's the worst thing you could do, I say, dead serious. *Myka. They are watching you every second. You would lead them right to us.*

I could get around them, she says, hopeful.

No.

Her hurt stabs through me.

Promise me, I say.

She's silent.

Myk. Promise.

Fine. She stares out the window at the big elm in our backyard. I can hear the birds in it, chirping and fluttering around. I could hear them from my room too on summer mornings. *I miss you.*

You too.

I pull away. I don't like saying good-bye to her, to Dedushka. I never do.

"It is set?" Dedushka asks.

"Set. The library."

We steal another car, an ancient rusted-out pickup. I hot-wire it faster this time, mostly because the panel is gone and the wires are already hanging out. The rumble of the questionable engine is so deafening that we couldn't talk if we wanted to without shouting—but I don't want to talk. All I want to do is get to the Reston library and have Dedushka go in and pick up Dad's pin. I want to put a fat checkmark on that part of the plan and get on to the next part. Rescuing Dad.

We're taking a risk having the drop so close to home. The house is under heavy surveillance, and there are still tails on both Mom and Myka. They may be increased if they know we're out. But we're not going to the house. I wanted it to be a public place where Myka went on a regular basis already, so no one would question her going there. Since she practically lives at the library when she's not at school, especially in summer, this was perfect.

As long as she doesn't show up today. I'm still a little worried about that. But I hope she's smart enough to know better.

We're less than ten minutes away. I practically bounce in the seat. I'll know. Finally, I'll *know* where Dad is. How he is. For the first time since I thought he died.

Hallucination Eric pops up, squished next to me on the seat. "Hey, look at you! Rabbit is running!"

I grit my teeth. It takes all my will not to move away, not to acknowledge he's there.

He puts a hand to the back of his head and then examines his fingers, slick and red with blood. "Why Jake," he says, falsetto, "what have you done?"

Hallucination Eric is always sarcastic and mean. Real Eric wasn't, most of the time. I wonder if he is now. I haven't seen enough of him to know.

"You really should just kill me next time. Maybe then I'll leave you alone." He winks. "But probably not."

I look stubbornly out the window, then at the watch I borrowed from Dedushka. Five minutes.

"You're no fun anyway," he says. "Mad as a hatter. I think I'll go visit your little sister."

"Shut *up*!" I yell right in his face. "Leave me *alone*!"

But of course he's not there, and I'm yelling at Dedushka. He slams on the brakes, startled. The old truck skids, the back end swinging to the right in a sickening lurch, and we smack right into a parked car. The heavy truck crumples the car, a horrible, squealing crunch.

Then the truck stalls, and everything is silent. We sit there side by side, staring ahead.

"Are you all right?" I ask, shaky. "Sorry."

He sighs a long breath, blinks, and lets go of the steering wheel, stretches his fingers. Glances at me. "I am all right. That car, not so very much."

He creaks open the driver's door and goes to look. I get out too. It's bad. It's a Prius. The whole left side of the back end is smushed. The truck is fine, hardly a dent on it.

"What do we do?" I whisper. It's not like we have insurance. It's a stolen fucking car.

He shrugs. "Leave."

But a man in a tie tumbles out of the office building in front of us, wild-eyed, careening down the steps. "What have you done to my car?"

"Guess not," I say under my breath.

"Go," Dedushka says. "Go and get it. It is two blocks away. This will take time to deal with. I will be here."

"But . . ."

"You will be fine," he says. "Just be quick. Careful."

"I'm waiting for an answer, old man," the guy says, rough. "What the hell did you do?"

I look at Dedushka once more, as he turns up the Russian act and starts speaking broken English to the man, and I take off.

I run the whole two blocks. It's pretty big for a regional library, gray marble, an arch above the front door. It gives me a familiar twinge to see it. I used to be here constantly too, back when I thought I was going to be a historian, do research for a living.

Christ, what if the librarians recognize me? This was beyond stupid. Dedushka was supposed to be the one doing the drop—no one would know him. I pull the baseball cap down. I'm going to have to sneak in.

I watch the entrance for a while. All I see are people I don't know going in and out. Fine. Okay. Go.

I try to walk normally, casually, through the scanners. From the front door I can see the librarian's desk. She looks up, eyes on the door, on me. But I'm lucky—it's not someone I know. I don't know how I would have explained it if it was.

It feels like the walls are closing in on me already. Trapping me.

I pick up the pace, cut to the left and head past the children's room. It's huge, one of my favorite parts of this place. When I was little it was mostly just picture books and stuff, but they've added to it a lot.

Myk and I talked about hiding the pin in a picture book, something like *Where the Wild Things Are* that I read to her over and over when she was little. But it's too heavily trafficked, with little kids who see small, hidden things. Too unpredictable. I head past it, up the stairs to Nonfiction.

Damn, I'm up stairs now, separated from the outside. How easy it would be to lock me in here. I breathe deeply, force myself to relax. It's a huge, public building, Jake. You're fine.

I see Genealogy, where I used to spend a lot of time working on my senior project. I feel a tug even now. What if I could disappear into that aisle and everything would be back the way it was six months ago? When my biggest worry was whether I'd get into Stanford, and whether Rachel Watkins liked me. But back then I thought Dad was dead too. Gone forever.

I pass the aisle and head to Chemistry, Myk's domain. Run a finger over the call numbers, my pulse pumping. 540 Asi. 540 . . . there it is. *Asimov on Chemistry.* Myk loves this book. I pull it out. The book's old enough that there's still a pocket in the front where the card used to go. I feel inside, and there it is, solid in my hand. Dad's tie tack, a small gold air force logo. There's a folded note too.

I open it. Myk drew a picture of a bottle of Elmer's glue. Underneath she wrote *soon*.

Glue. Our family ritual. Dad's.

I wish I could tunnel to him *now*. But I can't do it here.

As if to prove my point, a guy in a tracksuit comes around the corner and stops at the other end of the aisle. He glances at me before turning to the shelf.

An agent?

I shove the note in my pocket, but keep the pin in my hand. I don't want to let go of it. I'll go with Dedushka later, in a safe place. I duck my head and go out the aisle, trot down the stairs.

"*Jake?*"

Her voice—I know that voice—freezes me. There's shock in it, and disbelief.

I turn slowly, even though I know I shouldn't.

Rachel. Right there in front of me, in front of the kid's section, staring. Her eyes shining with tears.

36

"Rachel" by Thomas Cunningham

"It is you," she whispers. "But you're . . . you're . . ." She steps forward, one hand stretched out, like she thinks I'm a ghost. Or wants to prove I'm not.

"Dead?" I smile, sort of. Sad. "Not quite."

"Oh my god. I went to your funeral." Her hands tremble. Mine do too, but I keep them clenched tight by my sides. So I don't accidentally reach for her. God, she's gorgeous. I had her like a still picture in my head, or the hallucinations. They don't match up to the real thing. I know this is bad, dangerous for her, for me. But part of me is happy to see her. One more time.

"I'm so sorry . . . Rachel . . ." The pin scratches my palm, reminding me that I can't stay here. I can't do this. Dedushka's waiting, and someone could be coming any minute. I shift, look over my shoulder. "I have to—"

"No." She crosses the gap, grabs my hand. Fierce. Her hand is hot in mine. "I'm not letting you disappear with no explanation. What happened to you?"

"I can't—"

She clenches her jaw and looks up at me, pinning my hand in hers, her eyes still wet. "You leave without talking to me, and I scream."

I go still. "What?"

"You're trying to avoid attention. I can see it. I'm not letting you leave here without telling me where you've been, what really happened." Her voice hitches. "I'll scream, and you'll have to stay here until they sort it out, and I bet you don't want that."

I look at the librarian who's got her eye on us. The claustrophobia's getting bad too. I feel the tremors tickling under my skin. I can't stay here. But I definitely can't let her scream. "Let's go outside."

She studies me carefully. "Promise you'll tell me? You won't bolt?"

I was going to bolt. I have no idea what to tell her. But I sigh. "Promise."

She squeezes my hand, keeping her grip on it, and we go through the doors like that. Holding hands like a couple.

Once outside, I do a once-over quick for any danger—and for somewhere we can talk without attracting attention. She pulls me around the corner. We're behind bushes, but I can still see the entrance. Not bad.

She lets go of my hand, and for a second mine feels cold. I tug the baseball cap lower over my eyes. I glance at her face—tight, waiting. Her hair's in a braid over her shoulder. That strand of hair is loose again, almost touching her lips. But her eyes . . . her eyes are so confused, hurt.

Damn it. I don't know what to say.

"It's because of that thing you did at the party, isn't it? Tunneling?"

I inhale sharply. With everything that happened after, I'd forgotten she knew about that. Witnessed it. "Yes."

How strange to tell the truth.

"You're in trouble. Were you not supposed to do that or something? Is it secret? Can I help?"

I meet her eyes. She's leaning forward, intent. Right now, she reminds me of Myka. Laser focus. She's already switched from bewilderment to puzzling it out.

More than anything I hated lying to my sister, to Rachel, to everyone. Hated leaving them. And what did it help? Where did it get me, all the lying, protecting DARPA? I don't want to lie anymore.

"They've been keeping me locked up in a government facility," I blurt. "Spying for them. They pretended I was dead, set it all up."

She purses her lips. Her cheeks are flushed, bright pink. "And you escaped."

I think she thinks I'm crazy. Lord knows I sound crazy.

"Yeah. My grandfather helped me escape." I scan the entrance again for anyone suspicious. It's clear. "But I have to go."

"They're looking for you?" She plucks a leaf from the bush next to us and folds it over and over, her eyes still on me. "But why are you back? What are you going to do now?"

"I'm going to find my dad."

It's a mistake telling her that. I know it as soon as it leaves my mouth. It was dumb to tell her anything, but that was spectacularly dumb. I guess I'm rattled, seeing her. If Liesel ever thinks to talk to Rachel . . . crap.

Her gaze is sharp again. "I thought your dad was dead? I remember . . ."

"He isn't." I shake my head. "Like I'm not. It's complicated."

She drops the leaf—it spins to the ground—and leans forward again. She's so close. She's wearing a summery short skirt, her legs so long, tan. "Take me with you."

That wipes all thoughts of legs out of my head. "Why would you want to . . . ? *No*. No way in hell."

"I graduated," she says, sounding all reasonable and sane, and like I didn't even answer. "I don't have anything going on all summer. Not until I go to California for college. My dad's gone. My mom's a mess—crazed. We're not getting along at all. I could *help* you." She reaches up and gently, hesitantly, touches my cheek, and my pulse goes psychotic. "My dad's gone, and doesn't want to be found. Let me help you find yours."

I want her to keep touching me. I don't want this to stop, to be alone again. But.

"You don't understand. It's not like hiding from the principal, or a couple security guards or something. These are people who—" My voice trails off.

Across the parking lot I see Myka, blithely walking to the library, a backpack bouncing on her back. *Myka*. I want to shout at her, hug her—protect her—all at the same time. A hundred yards behind her, there's an agent. In tan slacks and a short-sleeve shirt, the bulge of a shoulder holster underneath. Another agent on the other side of the street, a woman. Her hand in her purse. They're so obvious, I don't even think they're trying to hide. They're both actively scanning the area. I'm suddenly sure they're going to see me, sense me. I duck down to the grass, pull Rachel with me.

"Trouble?" she asks, low.

I glance at her. The panic must be clear in my face, because I see it shift to hers.

"Them."

I need to run. Without actually running, or alerting anyone's attention. I need to leave Rachel and Myka here, safe, and find a way to—

"Come on," she says, and grabs my hand again.

It flashes through my head that she's going to kiss me. Like she did, but more, like they always do in TV shows to hide. On TV, no cops or bad guys think of looking at a kissing couple. But she doesn't. She tugs me up and pushes me back and to the side, into a little space I didn't even see behind a stucco wall.

It's a line of recycling bins, hidden from outside view, with a tiny entrance on that side. I turn back to her, surprised, and her mouth curves. She looks excited, alive.

"I'm working here this summer. Well, I was." She keeps pushing me, all the way along the building, until the wall ends at the back of the library. We stop. The passage dumps into a sidewalk, then a thick cover of trees. There's a street beyond. I can get out this way easy, without anyone seeing me. Circle back around to Dedushka. Then all I have to do is tunnel to Dad, find out where he is, and head out.

Wait, *was* working here?

"You can't come with me," I say. Quiet, but clear.

"I'm coming with you," she says in the same tone.

I face her. I'm almost a foot taller than her, but it feels like she has the upper hand. "You wouldn't scream. Not when you know what would happen. They'd take me back, Rachel."

She flinches, but maintains eye contact. "I wouldn't. You're right. But I'd follow you." She swallows, hard. Her eyelashes are wet. "I will follow you. And won't it be less obvious if I'm with you, than trailing behind while you try to ditch me? They won't be looking for a couple."

We stare for another long minute, neither of us giving.

"You're back," she says very low, her voice breaking. "I thought you were dead."

God. I can't fight her now. I'm doing the same thing, going after Dad, not letting anything stop me.

Maybe she can help with Prius dude if Dedushka hasn't handled it. Use some of those girl wiles. But then I'll say good-bye and leave her here, and go with Dedushka. She is *not* coming any further than that.

We run. Side by side, like we're jogging together. She smiles up at me. It's like she thinks this is an adventure, like she's Veronica Mars and she's going to save me, easy as pie.

I don't smile back. Nothing is easy anymore.

When we get close I see Dedushka sitting in the truck reading a novel, parked a few spaces down from the accident. The munched Prius is still there, but the owner is gone.

I stop half a block away, before Dedushka has seen me. Us.

"This is it," I say. "You have to leave me here." I frown. I don't know how to do this. "Thank you."

She slips her hand into mine again. "I told you I'm coming. Lead on."

I yank my hand away, suddenly angry. Her and Myk, both of them. Endangering themselves, endangering me. Why don't they understand?

"You don't get it," I explode. "I have been *locked up.* By the government. For four months. I didn't see the sun, Rachel. I didn't step outside for *four months.* They used me—" I close my eyes for a second, breathe. "For all sorts of things I'd never tell you. And it would've gotten worse. It *will* get worse, if they find me. This is *real*."

She watches my face, solemn.

"People have been shot. Right next to me. Because of me. I don't want that to happen to you, okay? I want you to be a normal part of my—" I pause, searching her dark eyes, but push on. "My past. Not part of this . . ." I wave my hand.

Dedushka pulls up next to us, the truck rumbling. Glaring at me through the windshield. He points at the door. I glance at Rachel—quiet, her lips pressed together—and open it.

She steps up and in, sliding next to Dedushka.

"No!" I yell, over the deafening engine. "Get out!"

"Get in, foolish," Dedushka growls. "We will sort this later." I get in, shut the door, and he takes off, shaking his head. "Shouting in the street. Do you try to make people look?"

We drive. No one says anything until we're well away in a neighborhood. Dedushka pulls the truck over and parks, cuts the engine. Then he turns and looks at me. At Rachel.

"How'd you manage the Prius?" I ask. Distraction for a moment.

Dedushka shrugs. "Play dumb and pay money. That cost us much of our cash. Now you explain . . ." He gestures at Rachel, sitting between us. She folds her arms defiantly.

I open my mouth, but she answers. "I saw him, and made him bring me."

Dedushka's eyebrows rise in a way that reminds me of Pete. *Idiot.*

My cheeks go hot. What does he think, I decided to bring my girlfriend along? That I didn't try to stop her? "She threatened to scream. And then Myka was there, and agents, so she helped me get out."

His eyebrows snap down at the word *agents*. "Yakob. How much did you tell her?"

I sigh. "Everything."

He swallows. "She knows what we are doing here?"

"I'm right here," Rachel cuts in. Her neck is mottled red. "I know you're trying to find Jake's dad."

Dedushka bangs the steering wheel, swearing in Russian, and Rachel jumps back against me. Then he takes his pipe from the dashboard, shoves it in his mouth, and sucks on it, unlit. He speaks around it, his eyes moving from Rachel to me. "She must come with us."

"*What?*"

She flashes me a grin.

"No," I try. Has he lost his mind too? "It's not safe."

"It is not *safe* to leave someone behind with knowing," Dedushka snaps. "If Myka was there, they will watch video, from the library.

They will see you, this girl. The satellites follow you to the truck. They will know who she is in an hour. If she stays, they question her." He takes out the pipe, studies Rachel. "*Interrogate*. She must come."

For the first time, Rachel looks a little scared. Good, I think perversely. She should be scared. But it's not good. None of it is.

"Your name?" Dedushka asks. His gentle voice.

"Rachel Watkins," she answers soft.

"You like my Yakob?"

"*Dedushka,*" I say, and Rachel shifts. It's hard for her not to be touching one of us in this truck.

Dedushka barks a short laugh. "Why else she wants to come?"

We both stare forward, awkward, through the windshield. I'm aware of her breaths, her leg against mine.

"Your sister is okay? Did you find your father's tack?"

I nod, open my hand. I was squeezing so hard you can see the print of some of the stars on my palm. "I did. And Myk's fine. Just . . . stubborn." Like Rachel.

"So," he says with a nod. "Go already. It is safe here, for a few moments. We must know where we head next."

I look at the tack, small in my palm. I'm afraid I'll see something horrific, Dad being tortured or hurt. That he's unreachable. Worse, that he's dead. If I feel that cold nothingness for him I'll fall apart again.

But I can't give in to fear. Besides, this isn't only for me—or even Dad. It's for Mom, and Myka. And Dedushka. And Rachel, I guess.

I glance at her—she's watching me curiously—then squeeze my fist around the pin again, close my eyes, and go.

A man, tall, with dark curly hair, clean shaven, his face lined. New Mexico, southeast corner, not far from the border with Texas. Not near any towns at all. An underground base. He's wearing a short-sleeved dress shirt and slacks, sitting behind an uncluttered metal desk. There's another man across from him, a dignified man with silver hair . . . I've seen him before, somewhere . . . their heads bent together over something on the desk. A report of some kind, a chart with a stuttering set of lines—

There's a loud knock and I open my eyes, startled out of it. There's a uniformed cop standing there, knocking on my window.

Adrenaline shoots through me, mixed with confusion from jolting out of the tunnel. But Dedushka nods, calm. "Open it."

I crank down the window. It protests, squeaking the whole way. The cop doesn't even wait till it's all the way down.

"Can't park here," he says, gruff. "Residential parking only. Move along."

There's a headache coming. I feel it shoving its way into my head. "Dedushka," I say, weak, pressing the heel of my hand to my forehead.

He starts the truck and pulls away as fast as he can manage.

I can't stop it. I try. I have tried. But once it starts, there's nothing I can do. I writhe in the seat, brace my feet against the floorboard, waiting for it. I at least think to shove the tack deep into my pocket, so I won't lose it when it happens.

"What's wrong?" Rachel asks, her voice high. "Jake?"

The full pain hits, and it's all I can do not to scream. I squeeze my head between my hands and clench my jaw and think *don't scream don't scream don't . . .*

Until I pass out.

37

"Simple Twist of Fate" by Bob Dylan

I wake up on something soft. I open my eyes. Rachel's face hangs over me, concerned. Her hand moves rhythmically through my hair. "Hi," she whispers.

I'm lying on her lap. I try to sit up fast, but the headache pounces as soon as I move. It's easy for her to push gently on my chest, settle me back where I was. I groan. I can't help it.

"Are you sure we shouldn't give him some of that medicine?"

"*Nyet,*" Dedushka answers, sure, from somewhere in front of us. "Not unless we must."

I look at the ceiling, trying to puzzle together what's going on in spite of the roar in my head. A car, but not the truck. The backseat. We're moving.

"Where are we?"

She looks out the window. "Going through Beckley, West Virginia. We're heading to New Mexico, to your dad." She puts her hand in my hair again, rubbing my head with the tips of her fingers, looking down at me. I want her to stop—I don't want her to be here, in danger, and I still can't believe she forced her way into this madness—but I also *don't*. It helps. Her fingers are strong, certain. I barely keep from giving in and closing my eyes again. I focus on her face.

She seems different. More serious. "Your grand—" Dedushka makes a sound from the front seat, like a warning growl, and she half-smiles. "Your *dedushka* and I had a long talk while you were out. I understand better now, everything that happened. Everything that's going on."

I can't have a conversation lying on her like this. I push up, more slowly this time, the headache pulsing, and she lets me. I slide over to the other side. "You shouldn't be here."

"I know." She looks away. Out the window it's ridiculously green, crammed with trees, and raining, drops racing each other down the glass. "I'm sorry. I didn't really understand. I didn't mean to complicate it more."

She puts one finger to a drop, and I have a sudden, strong memory of pushing my hands flat against the smoky glass door in my cell, pounding to get out. I let out a long breath. I'm not inside that hellish place anymore. I'm here, in the world, with Dedushka and Rachel. On my way to Dad. How can I complain?

"It'll be okay," I say.

The look she gives me is pure relief. It does something to me too, releases something, a band around my chest snapping. Or melting. Maybe I can be happy. Someday. Maybe I don't have to be guarded and watchful and alone the rest of my life. The headache ebbs a little, and I actually smile. She smiles back, shiny like before . . . all of this.

"How long was I out?" I ask. "And how on earth did you get me into a different car?"

She laughs. "Awkwardly. I'm glad no one was watching. And a little over four hours. You passed out, and then you slept. I wanted to give you that medicine, but he said no."

Like she summoned it, a hallucination of Liesel appears in the seat between us, in her business suit and everything, prim and proper. "Who's this?" Liesel asks, strident. "Someone else for me to target? Wonderful. You make my job easier all the time."

I frown, ignoring her.

"Pretty girl." She leans over Rachel, her hand almost touching Rachel's face, and I cringe. "Needed some company, did you? Well, I can't guarantee a double cell. But I will get you back, Jacob. Soon."

I squeeze my eyes shut. It's harder to ignore them out here with other people around. She's still there when I look again. And Rachel, watching me on the other side of her. "Hallucination?" she asks.

I grit my teeth and nod. What must she think of me? Headaches, hallucinations. I'm a fucking wreck. Liesel leans in to me, her eyes close to mine. "We're tracking you," she whispers. "Soon."

She disappears, the happy feeling gone with her. I don't know what I was thinking. I can't relax. Yes, I'm not locked up right this minute, but Liesel will never stop looking. And now she's hunting Rachel too.

"Dedushka, give me the gun, please."

Rachel starts. She probably thinks I've gone nuts again, am going to shoot her. Or myself.

Dedushka's eyes flick to mine in the rearview mirror. It's too soon after the headache, and we both know it. But I wouldn't ask if I didn't need to. He grunts, slides one hand down into my bag, and hands Liesel's gun over the back seat.

Rachel doesn't say a word.

I ignore the dregs of the headache, hold the gun in my hands, and go. I do it out loud.

Location: Virginia. Arlington. 3701 North Fairfax Drive, sixth floor, room 622. She's at the desk by the window, on the phone, looking out over the busy street below. The desk by the door is empty. She cradles the phone against her ear as she types, tries to scan the real-time images on the other monitor. "Yes, Sergeant. I understand. Thank you. Keep looking."

Eric comes in, stopping in the doorway, and she hangs up the phone. "Not yet," she says. "We've got eyes on the 40 West, the 81, and the 64. Nothing. They might have gone north again. We're still looking for stolen cars."

"They might have gone undercover," he answers, frowning. "He might have spied on one of us and knows where we're looking."

She sighs, and I feel her surge of irritation. "Every time I get optimistic I remember he could be watching, anytime. Jesus, he could be making you or me say things, and we wouldn't even know it."

"I knew it," Eric says, irritably. "I just couldn't do anything about it."

"True." She taps her fingers against her skirt. "But Dr. Tenney didn't know. So it might depend on the extent of his activity." She sighs. "I need that boy in a lab."

"Soon," Eric answers. He looks severe, harsh. More like the Eric in hallucinations. "They'll make a mistake, moving this way, and we'll catch them. They have the girl with them too. That makes it harder to hide." His lip curls. "This time he'll never get away again."

I come out of it. The first thing I do is drop the gun back in the bag—I can't get it out of my hands fast enough. Only when it's out of sight do I look at Dedushka. He frowns, clutching the wheel.

"We were going to travel on the 64," he says. "From Charleston."

"Well," I sigh, "We can't. We can't keep doing the car switch either. Not if they know we're stealing cars."

"We could take a train," Rachel says.

She seems totally unfazed by the tunnel, the gun, even her first glimpse of the hunters. She's just working the problem.

I don't know what I thought she'd do, exactly. Cry? Freak out? She's not like that. That's why I liked her in the first place.

"Like a passenger train?" I ask.

She shakes her head. "Freight. My grandpa used to hop freight cars, back in the day. He said it was easy." She looks wistful, for a moment. "My dad always said that's where he got his wanderlust."

"It is not so easy now," Dedushka says, thoughtful. "But it is possible. I know how. There is hub in Charleston."

"Okay then," I say. I may not be able to relax, but at least I have help now. Partners. "We'll take the train."

We sit on the pavement behind huge stacks of boxes in the Charleston train yard, waiting for it to get dark enough to move, waiting for the train. They're assembling a big one a couple tracks over, and Dedushka's source—a homeless guy he met, who also showed us the hole in the fence—claims it's westbound. All we have to do is wait for the right time: after they check the cars, as it's pulling out, and hop on. I hope it'll be that easy.

But it'll be a while. Dedushka's napping, and Rachel's stretched out too, her eyes closed.

I wouldn't mind sleeping either, but I need to do my tunnels. Not Liesel this time, though. Myka. And Dad.

Myka first, always.

Myka. 902 Van Buren Street, Herndon, Virginia.

Home.

She's on her bed, reading a fat fantasy book, twisting her hair with her other hand. She's all wrapped up in the story . . . but as soon as she feels me she slams it shut, drops it on the bed.

Jake. Thank God.

You okay? I ask. *Is Mom okay?*

Yes. I just—I went to the library. To see you. Guilt floods through. *I was afraid I messed it up.*

I don't let her sense that she did, a little. Rachel probably wouldn't be here if I hadn't seen the agents.

Don't worry. I try my trick to soothe her, relax her, like always. *We're fine. We'll be okay.*

Be careful, she says, not soothed at all. *Did you find Dad?*

Yes. He's all right. Going to get him.

I feel her jumble of emotions. Relief, mostly. But she's mad at him too. Like she was with me, but more. *Check with me every day. Please.*

I will. Be safe, dorkus.

I pull away and lie on the pavement for a bit on my back, breathing.

Every once in a while it smacks me that this isn't going to just go away, even when we get to Dad. That I am *never* going to be able to be Jake Lukin again, never go home.

One minute at a time.

I take out Dad's tack. Maybe tunneling to him will make me feel better. He's what I'm working toward, what I still have left. I close my eyes, let the warmth come.

He's in the underground base in New Mexico. He sits at a table, a young man across from him, hair buzzed like a soldier, but in a white T-shirt and jeans. There's a gray plastic tub between them. The young man has his eyes closed, cupping something in his hands. The young man frowns and scrunches his eyes shut while Dad watches, leaning as far as he can against the table, his feet tapping lightly on the floor. The man opens his eyes. "Sorry, sir. Still nothing."

Disappointment fills Dad, sour, familiar. "That's all right, son. We'll keep trying."

I don't understand. Is that . . . an object? Is Dad giving someone else objects, trying to make that guy tunnel? Why would he do that?

Jesus, why would he do that?

The soldier leaves, and Dad sits for a second, staring at the object, a tennis ball. He picks it up, rolls it in his hands. It's possible. He's seen it. Why is it so hard?

I come out of it. I don't think I want to see anymore.

I can't be sure. But what if Dad isn't being experimented on, like me, like Dedushka? What if he's doing the experiments? It looked like he was on the other side of the table, trying to get someone like me to tunnel.

But he *knows* how messed up that is. He's warned me all my life not to let the government see, not to let anyone know. Why would he encourage anyone to—

Wait. Maybe the military or the government *did* find out about my tunneling, two years before I thought they did. Maybe Dad went away to work with them, help them find out how to do it, instead of letting them take me. He could've made a deal to protect me.

I feel better instantly. It makes sense. I hate the idea of him working with anyone to try to make other people tunnel. But it explains both why he left in such a brutal way, and why he would be encouraging someone to tunnel now.

I have to talk to Dedushka.

When Rachel heads off to find somewhere to pee, I wake Dedushka.

"Yakob," he mutters, throwing his arm over his face. "If the train is not ready, I do not want to hear."

"I tunneled to Dad."

He lowers the arm, squints up at me.

"And . . . I saw something weird."

I have his attention. He sits up, scoots back slowly against a box, groaning as he goes. "The girl?"

"Gone for a few minutes."

He yawns. "And so?"

"I don't think he was the subject, Dedushka. I think he was running a test. Trying to get some guy to tunnel. He was all disappointed when it didn't work."

Dedushka's face hardens. "*Deerma,*" he says under his breath.

"Someone must've known about my tunneling, and he made a deal," I say fast. "To protect me. Right?"

He sighs, folds his gnarled hands in his lap. "I fear, *malchik,* it is more messy than that."

"Messy?"

He drops his chin. Sighs again. "Okay. I tell you the whole thing, the quick version. It was 1958. In Russia. I was seventeen years old, a pup. Poor as a clod of dirt, and that is all we had, my family, a farm with dirt and no potatoes." He stares off into the train yard like he's somewhere else.

A hallucination of Eric plops himself on the ground next to Dedushka. He sets his chin in his hands like he's listening, captivated. I watch him to reassure myself he's a hallucination. Dedushka can't see him. He keeps going.

"The army men come by and offer to take me with them, give me money and take me away from farm, so I go. Of course I go. To Moskva they take me and others, to the big screaming city. But we do not go to fight wars for Khrushchev, like we think. We do not get uniforms—we do not even get pay. We are taken to a building with many levels, under the ground where it is dark when the lights are off, where it is concrete and cold. It is explained that they will do experiments, that they try to improve the powers of the mind. Set off unused areas of brain. We will be superhuman, they say, and still they will pay us when we are done and we will go home with piles of money. As better people. New people.

"I am foolish, and I sign. What else would I do, at seventeen?"

He doesn't look at me, but I know he's thinking I signed too—in a different way. I did.

"I let them inject me with needles, let them do tests. For months, different medicines, different tests. I feel sick sometimes, but they take good care of me."

Eric grins at me and flips me off. I concentrate on Dedushka.

"We go on, months, and then I start to notice I am different. Most times I am fine, usual. But when they do tests, they play me voices on the tape recorder, and it starts to happen."

"The voices," I say. "With dead people."

He gives me a stern look, like an offended owl. "I tell this story."

"Sorry. I'll shut up."

"Yes." He looks down at his hands again, touches the plain gold wedding ring he still wears even though Babushka has been dead for thirty years. "It is not working how they want, but they still find ways to use it. *You* know. But it is terrible, these dead visions. And I am only one it works with. My friend Vladimir, Milena . . . I meet her there . . . they have medicine same as me but nothing happen. Milena, she overhear that the others will be sacrificed, they are not useful, know too many things." He meets my eyes. "Sacrificed means killed."

I nod. It doesn't shock me anymore, what these people do. All of them.

"We make plan to escape. Vladimir, me, Milena. Together. Milena has idea to take serum with her. To use to bargain, if we need it. Instead when we get to America she goes to school for chemistry. She work on it, years, until she made an antidote. She made it stop in me, these horrible dead things."

"She was a chemist? Like Myka?"

He smiles, full. "Like your sister, *da*. Myka is very like Milena."

I smile back. Eric vanishes, with a grunt. Thank God. They seem to be shorter lately.

Rachel walks quietly up behind Dedushka. She puts a finger to her lips, to show I shouldn't interrupt his story. I stare at her for a moment, decide she's probably not a hallucination. And it's okay to let her hear the rest. She's in deep already.

"That's why you never liked TV or radio or movies," I say, suddenly understanding. "Dead people's voices."

"Dead people everywhere." He shakes his head. "*Da*. I still do not like, in case it happen again."

"And then what?" I ask. "What about Dad? What's his power?"

Dedushka stills. A cricket chirps behind us, loud. We can distantly hear the people moving the train, talking to each other.

"Your papa does not have an ability like you," he answers. He puts both hands to his cheeks and rubs his beard hard. His voice drops. "He always wanted one."

Oh. Ever since I found out he disappeared more or less voluntarily, I'd assumed Dad was like me. That he had a power like mine he'd always hidden, and he'd been forced to use it in some way like I had. That we'd get together and be some sort of super family.

Crazy, I guess.

"He's normal?"

"Ivan is very smart," Dedushka answers. "Dangerous smart." He shrugs. "Again, like your sister, perhaps. But . . . as I say, Yakob, he wanted one his whole life. Desperate want. So this thing he is doing—"

Rachel shifts, jarring a box, and Dedushka whips his head around faster than I thought he could. She walks forward, cool, and sits next to me, curling her arms around her knees.

He stands stiffly, stares down at us. "Enough for now. I must go walk, stretch these old muscles before this train jump." He turns away without another word, and disappears behind the boxes.

Which leaves me and Rachel. Alone, for the first time since she helped me escape. Sitting close enough to touch. It makes me nervous. Silly, considering everything else I have to be nervous about. Now including Dad, and whatever's up with him . . .

I glance at her sideways. Does she even remember the kiss? It's burned in my brain. I don't even know how often I've thought of it over the past few months. Relived it. And here she is, real. Next to me.

"I'm not sorry," she says.

I blink. "Not sorry? About what?"

She scoots over another inch, so our legs really are touching. It makes me dizzy instantly. "That I came. I know it's dangerous, and stupid. But I . . . I was so happy to see you. Alive." She touches my cheek again—delicate—and moves closer. "I never thought . . . do you remember when I kissed you?"

I lean in and kiss her in answer. It isn't the same as my memory. That was a surprise, and new. This is right. Warm and soft and *her,* electric, sparks fizzing all through my blood. It's like we fit together. I melt into her, into the kiss, in a different way than tunneling. This moment. *Finally.*

There's the unmistakable click of a gun hammer. Then another, and another.

We freeze, both of us breathing in unison, foreheads together.

"Mr. Lukin. So nice to find you."

Rachel's eyes go wide, scared. I drop my hand from her neck and pull back slowly.

"That's it," the voice says. A deep voice, smooth. A man. "No sudden moves. I can see you've done this before."

I turn, still slow, and shift so my body is between the man and Rachel. He's tan, good looking in a flashy way, short black hair peppered with gray. In a dress shirt and pants. Oh, and he's pointing a gun at me, and there are three goons behind him, all built like trucks, all with guns trained on us.

He steps toward me, keeping his eyes on mine. "Yes, very good. Cuff his hands in front of him, so he can't tunnel anywhere." One of the goons comes and yanks me to my feet, snaps my wrists into metal cuffs.

Just like that, back where I was.

"I want you to understand how serious I am, Mr. Lukin," the man says. "I am not one of your government pansies who has to follow rules. I have no rules. If I want to kill you, if I want to kill this girl—" Rachel makes a squeaking sound. Again I try to shield her. "I will do it. There is no one to stop me."

I swallow hard. Somehow I believe him. But if he's not government, not Liesel's, who is he?

"I also know, in detail, exactly what you can do," he continues. "And I'm not going to let you trick me like you did them. Until I sell you to the right bidder, you're not going anywhere I don't tell you to go. In your head or otherwise. Got it?"

Sell me?

I nod slowly. I wonder where Dedushka is. Hopefully safe away from this. And Rachel—

"Now what shall I do with the girl?" he asks, tapping his cheek. "Kill her, or bring her with? I so hate these *choices*."

"Don't hurt her," I say, hoarse. "Leave her here."

"That wasn't one of the options." He tilts his head at one of his men, and I tense. But the guy comes forward, snaps another set of handcuffs on Rachel. "She might be useful . . . as leverage."

I breathe. It's something. As long as we're not dead, and we're together, there's a chance.

I try to look back at her, but I'm pulled forward by the elbows, face-to-face with the man. His chin juts out, too big, and he has thick, dark eyebrows. But mostly I see his eyes. Bright, bright blue. Totally insane.

I should struggle, think up a plan. But he's right—I can't tunnel like this, not now, and this guy genuinely, utterly scares the crap out of me.

"Nice to meet you," he says. "I'm Mr. Smith. I know what you're thinking . . . and you're right. It would've been much better for you if Liesel Miller had found you first."

He gestures to his men, and they walk me and Rachel with them through the boxes, out the gate of the train yard, and into the back of a waiting car.

I never would have believed it, but I think he might be right.

As soon as we pull away he opens a little box and takes out a syringe. Before I can even say no, the sharp end is in my arm, and the cold tingle blasts through me. That's all.

38

"The Jig Is Up" by Quasi

I come to on a plane, strapped down into a seat, my cuffed hands on a table in front of me. It's some kind of a private jet, the seats in sets of four facing each other. Mr. Smith is across from me, his crazy eyes steady, watching. Two of his goons are in the aisle seats, blocking us in.

I check, panicked, for Rachel. She's awake and okay, across the aisle with the third guy, facing me. She's strapped down too. I meet her eyes. She's terrified.

Hell, I am too. I squirm against the straps. But I'm on a plane. I really can't go anywhere.

Through the little windows I see the sun, just coming up in a blaze of orange. I don't even know when it is, where we are. We might be out of the country already.

The claustrophobia hits bad, my whole body starting to tremble. I'm completely trapped.

"What do you want from me?" I try to sound bold, like Bond or something, but I don't think I do.

Mr. Smith tilts his head. He has a strong nose, sharp lines from his nose to his mouth, to that standout chin.

"Oh, I want *you,* Mr. Lukin. I've been looking for you since you escaped Montauk. You will fetch such a pretty price."

This is the "private people" Liesel always warned me about. But I didn't think they were real. I imagine all the people this guy could sell me to. *Jesus.*

"I've taken your bag, with the gun. Was that Liesel's?"

I don't answer. I stare at my hands, trembling on the table, the cuffs rattling. Liesel mentioned a Mr. Smith, in the park. Does he *know* her?

"A gun and an object. A twofer. Well done." He actually does sound impressed. "But you don't need that anymore. As I said, I'm not sloppy like she is, so you won't get away from me. I've taken everything from your pockets. There will be no tunneling. Understand?"

I still don't respond.

"Look at me," he snaps, in a voice that makes me look. "No tunneling. Now. Mr. Lukin." He sits forward in his seat. "I know your father is alive. Where is he?"

I gape at him. How could he possibly know that? Liesel didn't even know that.

Don't admit anything.

I slowly shake my head.

"No?" he says, his voice toxic. "No what? No, he isn't alive—because I know very well he is, hiding in a hole somewhere—or no, you're not going to tell me where he is?"

I swallow hard, meet his eyes. "I'm not going to tell you anything."

"You're not?" His eyes shift. "Really. Somehow I don't believe you."

He looks at Rachel. The guy with her pulls a knife—a huge, sharp knife—and presses the tip into her cheek. She screams.

That woman. That woman I tunneled to, so long ago, the knife slicing her cheek open . . . I strain against the straps again. I can't reach him.

"It's fairly simple, Mr. Lukin," Smith says. "You two seemed quite intimate when I found you. Surely you don't want her sliced into bits. Face first, too. Would you like to tell me now what I want to know?"

Not Rachel. Not like that woman. "*Please*. Stop."

He shrugs. "No need to beg. It's very easy. You tell me what I want, you do exactly what I want, and your girlfriend—oh, and your sister and your mother, I can get to them too—will be fine. *Where is your father,* Mr. Lukin?"

"Jake," she gasps, "don't tell him." The guy presses the knife, and a drop of blood drips down.

I don't want to tell him. I don't want to give him any more than he has, give up the dream of finding Dad, give up *Dad*. But Rachel, right here, wins over that. She's my responsibility.

"In a base about ninety miles southeast of Roswell, New Mexico," I say, low, my eyes on her. She bites her lip, tears tracking down her cheeks, washing away the blood. "I can give you coordinates."

"Excellent. See how well we work together? Tell me the coordinates, and we're done here. For now."

I tell him. He writes them down with a flourish.

"Put the knife away," I say. "Leave her alone."

He nods to the minion with Rachel, who slides his knife into a case and comes and takes the paper. Mr. Smith says something in his ear, and the big guy nods and heads for the front of the plane.

"Are we going to my dad?" I ask hopelessly.

He flashes me a patronizing look. "Don't think that because

we're such good friends now I'm going to tell you any of my plans. Unlike everyone else you've been dealing with, I'm not stupid. But thank you, Mr. Lukin. You have been most helpful." He stands, turns to the two guys next to me. "Don't let him move his hands." He pulls a phone out of his pocket, waggles it. "Let the bidding begin."

As soon as he's gone I turn toward Rachel. "I'm so sorry," I say.

"No talking," one of the guys snaps.

She studies me for a long minute, like she's judging me, or deciding something. Then the corners of her mouth lift just slightly. Not anywhere near a smile, but tempering the frown. She looks away, out the other window, the tears on her cheek reflecting the lights.

I hate that she's here, her life in actual danger, because of me. I can't get her out of it, not yet. But there's something I *can* do. A start.

I close my eyes, but not to sleep. Mr. Smith knows I can tunnel with objects, and he knows I can control people. He even knows about Dad. What he doesn't know—what no one but me and Dedushka and Myka know—is that there is one person I can tunnel to without any object at all. I've done it before. I have to, now.

I focus on Dedushka, on everything I know about him: his weird, bristly, paranoid habits, his fishing and technology-avoiding obsessions, his love for my grandmother, his ring. His huge, constant love for Myka, for me. I can't picture him fishing like last time, but I picture *him* as hard as I can. *Dedushka,* I call in my mind. *Please, Dedushka. I need you.*

I feel a breeze across my face, the smell of beer.

Thank God.

I try to sense where he is, what he's doing. With him it's like I go in the reverse way from everyone else. Interior first, then outward.

He's in Knoxville, Tennessee. On a street not far from the train yard, passing by an Irish pub. It's warm, even at six in the morning, and damp. It will be hot today. But it does not matter. He needs to find a ride to New Mexico before the morning is out. Wherever Yakob is, he will know to get there, meet there.

Worry for me prickles through, and I wish I could talk to him. But I don't have time to waste to make him write a note to himself, make him realize I'm there. I have to do this the fast way.

I take him over, fill him completely. It's easy with him—there's no resistance. I don't know if he knows what I'm doing now, but he will, once I'm gone.

I look around him, searching for what I want. He's on a street of cafés, crowded with people drinking coffee, and there's got to be . . .

There. A girl at a table closest to the sidewalk, leaning in to her boyfriend. Her phone sitting on the table at her elbow, ignored.

I take it with Dedushka's fingers as I make him walk past, walk on. She doesn't even notice. I have to get out of sight, but I don't have long.

I'm sticking, already. I haven't been in anyone this deeply since Eric.

I go around the corner, into a little alley behind the pub. Tap out the number of Myka's cell.

"Hello?" she says, tentative. Groggy with sleep.

The phone is tapped, of course. All their phones are tapped. "Myk," I say, in Dedushka's voice. "It's me, dorkus. Go to the zoo, you and Mo . . . your mom both. Go now."

There's a small pause. "I understand," she says. "We'll go to the zoo today."

I hang up, throw the phone down the alley. "Roswell," I say, in Dedushka's voice, hoping he can hear it. "If I can."

I tear myself away. I keep my eyes shut, though, and try to control my breathing. So no one will even know I was gone.

Zoo is a code word, worked out in tunnels while I was at the cabin. The emergency distress signal. Myk knows if I—or Dedushka—tell her to go to the zoo, it's done. They're blown, in danger. They have to duck surveillance and run. Disappear.

She's smart, and we had a plan. She'll do it right. They'll vanish, and be safe. When I'm clear of this, somehow, we'll meet up again.

And if I never get clear of this? I told Dedushka I'd go to Roswell, but I don't know how I can get away from this guy. What if he really sells me to someone else?

They'll be safe anyway. Maybe Dad won't be, after what I had to do. I *hate* that. But I saved Mom and Myka, and Dedushka knows I'm still alive. I'm better than I was a few minutes ago.

Next I have to worry about Rachel.

I realize I'm not trembling anymore. The jitters, the physical fear of being trapped, is gone. It vanished when I saw Rachel threatened, realized we're in this together. I can't afford to have jitters. It's not just me anymore.

I don't know how long we're on the plane after that. A few hours, maybe? He gives us some food, water. Time stretches like it did in the cell, like it did when I was handcuffed, waiting for Liesel.

Hallucinations of Liesel, then Eric, come to visit. I don't know why my brain keeps choosing them over everyone I love, but there they are, both of them raging in their own ways that I'm here with Smith instead of with them. That this is why I should be in custody in the first place. That I'm a traitor to my country because I escaped them and let this happen.

I wish I could punch them, swipe them. Make them go away. But I can't move.

It's a perverse relief when Smith saunters down the aisle and takes his seat. At least something will *happen,* maybe something I can use. Though Rachel shrinks back in her seat at the sight of him.

I have to get her out of this.

Smith ignores her, eyes bright on me. He watches me for a few minutes, silent. Then he grins. Like a crocodile.

"You have just made me a very wealthy man, Mr. Lukin." He waves at the luxurious jet. "Well. Wealthi*er*."

"Happy to help."

He laughs. "I'm sure." He's definitely in a different mood. Giddy. "I'm almost sorry to have you go. I'm quite sure you would prove useful to me right here. And you're such a joy to have around."

"Where are we going?" I ask, casual.

"You? You're going night-night again. Next time you wake up you'll be in the care of your new owner." He gestures to one of the goons, who pulls a case out from under the seat. Smith snaps it open, shows it to me. A needle, ready to go.

The panic slides back, and I feel sick. No. Not again. "I'm not going anywhere without Rachel."

"Yes," she cries. "Send me too. He—needs me to work now. I help him."

He glances at her, curious. "That is patently false. But a fine lie, on short notice. And you're going, but not for that reason. I recommended that the new owner take you too, as . . . incentive for Mr. Lukin to work his best. It was agreed."

I try to launch myself at him again. I can't get far out of the seat, but I swing my arms up, try to clock him with the handcuffs.

He signals with one finger, and one of the guys grabs me, holds me down while the other one plunges the needle into my arm.

I look at Rachel, focus hard. Maybe I can be stronger than the drugs. Maybe I can hold out this time, find a way. . . .

Rachel's face, tearstained, her jaw set, is the last thing I see.

39

"Dad" by Goldfinger

When I come to this time it takes a couple disorienting seconds to realize I'm blindfolded, my hands still cuffed. Though there's something about the air that gives me a bad feeling. It's heavy, motionless. Underground air.

I want to cry. If I'm stuck again, back at square one . . .

No. I've learned a lot since then. I sit up straight, rattle the cuffs. "Hello?"

The door opens, shuts. Someone is in here with me. I hear the breathing, soft. I have the wild thought that it's a predator—a wolf, or a mountain lion—before my brain kicks in and reminds me it's worse than that. It's probably my *owner*.

There's rustling at my cuffs, a click, and the weight is lifted off. I rub my hands over my free wrists, instinctive. Then fingers come up to my blindfold, lift it up. I blink in the light of a white, bare room. Into eyes that are just like mine.

"Dad?" I whisper it, as if saying it aloud will break him. He seems real, but he might just be a hallucination, one my brain cobbled together.

"Jake," he says, in his round, familiar voice. He's real. He clasps my hands, looks into my face sadly. "What have you done?"

Right. All of this, everything, is my fault because of the party, because I did what he told me not to. Wait, no. Liesel *drugged* me at the party. I think I've done all right, considering.

But I don't argue. "Is Rachel okay? Why am I here?"

He lets go, lets his hands dangle between his knees. Like he always did. I can't believe he's here, alive, in front of me. At last.

"She's fine. Sleeping. As to why you're here—" He sits back in the white plastic chair, studies me. "Do you know where 'here' is?"

"An underground base. I don't know why, but—I saw you trying to make someone tunnel."

"Ah." He looks a lot older in the two and a half years since I've seen him, the lines etched in his face. "You tunneled to me. Yes. And you told Gareth Smith where you found me?"

"He threatened Rachel."

He sighs, runs a hand through his hair. It's longer now than he ever had it, the first time he hasn't been in the military. It probably makes him look more like me.

"I understand. Well, he's smart enough to know that I'd be the highest bidder for you, Jake. But that man won't stop there. If I'm right, he's already sold the information about where I am, where you are, to someone else. Maybe Liesel—but that won't be a problem. It's the others we have to worry about. We have to get out of here, soon."

Crap. I'm still not safe, even here. And I've brought them to Dad too. None of this is going how I thought it would. Where's the relief? The happy reunion? It feels . . . wrong.

"How do you know about Liesel?" I ask.

He shakes his head, sharp. "Not now."

I'm so tired of hearing that. "What is this place, Dad? Why are you in an underground base trying to get people to tunnel?"

He stands, his hands in his pockets, and turns away. I can't see his face. "This is my base." It's so quiet I strain to hear it. "My project."

"Making tunnels like me?" My eyes fill, and I remember the memorial marker again, huddling with Myka, Mom, and Dedushka. My breathing seems amplified. I hear it loud in my ears. "You left on purpose? You pretended to die, left us alone, to come here and try to make *tunnels*?"

He turns. "It's not that simple. You don't understand how critical this project is, could be, to national security . . ." He trails off. "But you do understand. They found you."

I feel my face crumple. "Four months. Underground, being their puppet."

He closes his eyes and just stands there for a long moment, like a statue. "I tried so hard to keep you out of it."

I stand too, so we're face-to-face. We're the same height now. "But you didn't. And you're trying to make more like me? Don't you think one person with this curse is enough?"

"Curse?" His voice is shocked. "Jake. It's a gift. A gift I would do anything for."

I take a step closer. Curl my hands into fists. I can't believe how much my chest aches right now, like it might cave in on itself. "How much did you know? About me? About what they were doing to me?"

There's a long pause. Another head shake. "Nothing, I swear. Not until you escaped, and then the general told me. I was very upset. But I think—he realized you might come to me."

The general. That's who I recognized in the first tunnel to Dad. The general from that first tunnel in Dad's office.

He puts his hands on my shoulders. "He'll pull Liesel off now. Now that you're here, we're together. We'll work together. We'll have to be underground—not here, but there are other bases—"

I pull back sharply, and his hands fall. I can't believe he'd even say that.

"I'm not tunneling for you. Or anyone. I'm not staying underground anymore."

He looks at me like I've lost my mind. "Jake. There isn't a choice. Now that they know, everyone knows. Gareth Smith will try to sell you to foreign governments, terrorists. Maybe he already has. I'm sorry, but you can't be up there anymore. Neither of us can."

The ache twists deeper, sharper. Ever since I knew he was alive, all I wanted was to find him. Save him. Reunite our family. And he wants *this*?

"I'd rather take my chances out there," I say violently.

He doesn't say he won't let me, that I'm a prisoner, a tool, to him too. My own father. But it's there in the look he gives me.

"Take me to Rachel," I say. "I need to make sure she's all right."

"And that." He thrusts his hands in his pockets again, like he's making fists too. "I can't believe you brought a civilian—"

"*I'm* a civilian. I'm staying a civilian."

We stare at each other, eye to eye.

"Very well," he says. "You can go see the girl—"

"Rachel."

"Rachel," he repeats. "And then we need to evacuate with everyone else. In the chopper we can discuss what to do."

In the chopper?

Those words seal it for me. He's just like them. Like Liesel and Eric and Ana and the rest. Now that I'm exposed, in his hands, there will be no discussion. He already has it planned out, and as soon as I set foot in that chopper my fate's decided. On to another bunker. Forced to tunnel over and over for their purposes. Worse, he'll probably use me to try to make more like me. Make himself like me. And then I can really never be free; no one can. He—they—probably want Dedushka too.

Rachel and I have to get out of here before any of that happens.

He takes me to a barracks-type room a few doors down, all set up with a twin bed and a dresser and all. There's a lock on the door—from the outside. The overhead fluorescents are off, but there's a desk lamp on the nightstand, glowing yellow. Rachel's sprawled out on the bed, asleep.

As soon as I'm through the door I turn, shut it in his face.

I hope they don't lock us in. But it wouldn't be for too long anyway if we're evacuating.

"Rachel," I whisper. She looks so peaceful, I hate to wake her. But we may not have this chance again. Still I stand there for a second, looking. Her hair spilling across her neck, her eyelashes dark against her cheeks. The tiny smudge where the knife cut her.

I sit on the edge of the bed, touch her arm. "Rachel. Wake up."

She bolts upright, startling us both. She stares at me in confusion.

"It's okay. It's me. You're all right." I touch her arm again, to soothe her.

She surprises me by throwing her arms around me, hugging tightly.

"You're okay," she murmurs, her mouth against my neck. "I didn't know."

I hug back, with all my attention, for a minute. Then I make myself pull away.

"We have to get out of here," I whisper, heads close. "It's my dad—but he's one of them. They're going to try to put us on a helicopter. But we can't get on. If we do, that's it. We're done."

She thinks for a minute. "Distraction?" She rubs her fingers over my chin, rough with stubble. "You know I can act."

"Good call. Can you run?"

She leans her forehead against mine, like we were before. "First place, four hundred meters."

I thread my hands in her hair. It's come out from the braid, thick and wavy. "Distract, then run," I whisper. "It's all we've got."

The door opens. "We don't have time for that," Dad says, bland. "It's time to go."

We stay together a moment longer, share one more meaningful look. Then I kiss her on the cheek, on that tiny scratch, and we go.

40

"Run" by Kill It Kid

Dad lets us use the bathrooms, and then we follow him down a maze of hallways that look remarkably like the ones in Montauk. Enough to give me shivers. Rachel notices, takes my hand. She squeezes it, then winks up at me.

Smart. We can signal each other that way, when it's time to run.

Dad turns to check on us, glances at our linked hands. His face stays blank. But he drops back, walking next to us instead of in front. There's just enough room in the hallway. He has to make room whenever other people—all scurrying around preparing for evacuation—pass by. A few glance at us curiously. I wonder how much I do look like him, now.

"Jake," he says quietly. He stops, faces me square. "I didn't want any of this to happen. You know that, right?"

Rachel's finger traces my thumb gently. Giving me enough support to ask my questions.

"How do you know Liesel, Dad? And . . . Gareth Smith?"

He flinches. Looks over his shoulder. Then he lowers his voice. "We all worked together. A joint project. Pentagon, DARPA, CIA, a couple other agencies. Liesel and Gareth were junior scientists working with me. Exploring paranormal abilities, their use in intelligence gathering. Counterintelligence. Dr. Miller continued my work, after I . . . left."

"And Smith became a . . . what? A black-market dealer in people?"

He leans in. "We cannot allow him anywhere near you again, Jake. Liesel will stop when the general tells her to. He won't. He scents blood in the water—more money—and he won't let it go, if he can get to you." He starts walking again, and we have no choice but to move with him. "We'll be exposed, for a little while. But once we're in a new base, we should be all right. You should be safe."

I don't answer that. I squeeze Rachel's hand, and she squeezes back. If all goes well, we'll have to brave the risk of Smith on our own. Dedushka will help. I'll tunnel to him as soon as we're clear of Dad.

Sounds simple enough when I say it to myself.

We go up one set of stairs, then another. Then down a hall and up five more flights.

Dad stops in front of stairs below a heavy metal door, says into a radio that we're ready. He waits for an all-clear. Then he climbs the stairs, pushes it up and open. We follow, first Rachel, then me.

I'm outside again.

It's night, which I didn't expect for some reason. I've lost so much time lately I had no idea. But it's the desert in July. It's probably better for all these people to travel at night. It's a lucky break for us too.

Dad looks back, then leads us across a long stretch of hard-packed dirt. The chopper is on a pad about half a mile away, the engines already running, deafening. There isn't anyone else around. But I scan the landscape, and my heart sinks. I don't see how we can make it. It's nothing but flat scrub in every direction, not even a road. There's nowhere to hide. Yeah, it's dark, but we'd have to get a fair distance away before that would help. Especially with their chopper. Dad could call people on his radio and be after us in seconds.

Still, we have to try. I stop about halfway to the chopper. Dad stops too, eyebrows up, already suspicious. Time for distraction. I squeeze Rachel's hand.

She swings a small bottle out of her pocket with the other hand, and sprays something right into Dad's eyes, then kicks away his radio, off into the darkness.

He screams and falls to his knees, clawing at his face. I stand there for a second, totally deer-in-the-headlights. That's Dad. She just hurt *Dad,* so we could escape from him.

"Come *on*!" Rachel cries.

I force myself to turn away, and we run.

We trot evenly through the dark. It's only a half moon tonight, but there's a ridiculous number of stars, so it's easy enough to see, to avoid holes. It's cool, though I know it won't be once the sun comes up.

We're over a mile away, and no sign of anyone after us yet. Or anything around us. But I thought I saw a light, so we're heading that direction. We need to put some distance behind us and then I can tunnel to Dedushka, figure out how to meet up with him.

I glance at Rachel, jogging next to me. "What was that? That you shot at him?"

"Drain cleaner," she pants. "It was under the sink in the bathroom." She stops for a second, hands on her knees. "He'll be okay. You just flush it out, and it'll be fine. I thought maybe distraction wouldn't be enough."

I picture Dad writhing on the ground, take a deep breath. "It was perfect. Ruthless, but perfect. We wouldn't have gotten away without it."

She smiles small, and we keep running.

I know about ruthless, after all. She just learned quicker. What would it have been like if she'd been with me the whole time?

"Your mom must be worried about you," I say. "They might have Amber alerts out and everything."

She makes a face. "Probably not. Mom is—strange. She'll probably tell them I ran away." She laughs. "Wait, I guess I did."

The light's getting closer. I see the shape of an oil well. It's not working, but there's a single light shining from a trailer on the lot. I wonder what they're up to.

It doesn't matter to us. What matters is there's an oldish gray truck parked near the trailer, right there for the taking. I point at it, and Rachel nods. She was with Dedushka when he stole a car.

It's too easy. I slip in, mess with the wires, and start it up, not as fast as Dedushka but fast enough. A guy runs out of the trailer after us, but by that time we're on the road. It turns into a main road, curves around northwest. Eventually there's a sign that confirms what I was hoping. We're heading toward Roswell.

We stop near a place called Artesia, in the fields on the outside of town. It's still dark, so nobody's around yet. Rachel switches behind the wheel—in case we have to leave in a hurry—and I sit in the passenger seat, focus. Tunnel out loud.

Dedushka. I reach toward him, toward all I know about him. That smell of tobacco and fish, his laugh when he tells old Russian jokes. His hands, calloused from fishing, from working.

His knees are not meant for this.

I'm in.

He kneels, in the dark, on damp grass, his hands up high. South Park Cemetery, Roswell, New Mexico. There's a gun to his head.

"I'm going to keep asking until you tell me where he is," growls a voice.

Dedushka looks up, back. Eric stands over him, his face twisted like I've seen it in hallucinations. "I have told you. He was taken," Dedushka says, mildly.

"I know he was 'taken,'" Eric spits. "By John Lukin, who appears to be alive, yay for everyone. Except we're not supposed to even look for Jake now. We're supposed to leave him alone. And I will not *settle for that." He touches the back of his head, gingerly. "I need to see him."*

"I am not in contact with Yakob," Dedushka says. His arms start to tremble, holding them up like this. He cannot take it long.

"Bullshit." Eric yells. He sounds completely unhinged. "I'll kill you if he doesn't come meet me."

He looks down into Dedushka's eyes, and I swear he's looking at me. That he senses me, somehow.

I come out of it, my whole body shaking. "Dedushka," I whisper.

Rachel starts the truck. "We'll get there in time. We'll get to him."

We have to.

41

"Full Circle" by Otherwise

Rachel drives fast—we get there in just over half an hour. We fumble a little on where the cemetery is, with no phones or GPS, and I don't want to ask. It's not great to ask for directions when you're driving a stolen car. Eventually we find a sign, and make it to the gates. Two stone pillars, with fancy wrought iron gates between them, swung open.

It's 5:30 according to the bank clock we drove by. It must be almost dawn.

"Stop here," I say.

She pulls over next to the gates, stops. Frowns. "I'm not waiting here."

I lay my hand over hers. Her skin is cool, and she's shivering a little. "You have to. I already have to worry about Dedushka. I can't risk having both of you there. Eric seems insane."

"But I can *help,*" she says. "I can't just sit here and—" She sighs. Turns her hand over, under mine. "And worry."

"I'll be all right. But I have to get to Dedushka."

She grits her teeth. "Okay," she whispers.

"Keep the truck ready. In case we need to run. And you—take off if it goes wrong, okay?"

We share one last, long look—she covers her mouth with her hand, but she nods quick—and then I slip out the door.

I jog down a long, straight driveway lined with trees. Really long, nothing on either side but dirt fields. There's no sign of the sun yet, but the sky is starting to lighten, the dark less dense.

I'm starting to wish I'd had Rachel drive me this far, when I finally get to the graves. This is a huge cemetery.

I think of cataloging all these graves, telling their stories like I used to. Like Oak Grove Cemetery in Virginia. The days with Pete, then Eric. It seems like a lifetime ago.

I suddenly recognize the trees, the area, from my tunnel to Dedushka, down the second side road. I see a car. Then I spot them, a ways back from the path. Dedushka's sitting on a bench under a tree. Eric stands behind him, twitching, holding a gun to Dedushka's head.

I run, at first. As I get closer I slow to a walk, careful.

"Doesn't this bring back fond memories, mate?" Eric shouts. "You and me, together?"

I step forward. Dedushka watches, solemn. "Put the gun down, Eric," I say.

He snorts, his eyes wild. "Oh, now you're going to tell me when to use my gun? I'm the one in charge here. I'm the agent. You—you're just a rogue asset."

I keep walking slow. Put my hands up. "Not anymore."

His face hardens. "Right. I'm not an agent anymore, because of you. They're probably going to fire me. And you think you're free. You found your daddy and now you can do whatever you want."

I meet Dedushka's eyes. He probably has an idea how untrue that is.

His beard moves very slightly with his breath. "Go," he mouths. "Walk away."

I shake my head.

"Stop!" Eric says. "That's close enough."

I stop ten feet away. Not close enough to do anything useful. "What do you want?"

Eric rubs at the back of his neck. "I *want* you to undo what you did. But I'll take an even trade. You for the old man. It's very generous, since they really want you both. And this time—you're not going to pull any of your crap. Not going to *use* me." His lips curl. "I liked you, you know. I didn't have to do the tennis thing. I was trying to make it easier for you."

"You worked to keep me a prisoner and a slave," I answer, cold. "Easier is not enough."

"And you made me look like a traitor!" he shouts. "You got me shot. You made me lose my job."

We stare at each other.

"Tunnel through one of those gravestones," he says. "I want you to make yourself weak, and sick. Then I'll leave the old man here, and you'll come with me."

"I can't do that."

"You can't?" His voice goes higher, and he shoves the gun hard against Dedushka's head, into his thick white hair. "You want me to blow his head off, right here in front of you?"

"I'll go with you," I say slow. "But I'm not tunneling to dead people first."

"Do not," Dedushka says. "I am old. Leave now, Yakob."

"Shut up!" Eric yells. "Do it!"

A car comes screaming down the main road, dust barreling behind it. It pauses at the turn, then takes it, heads our way.

Behind it, slower, I see the truck following. Rachel. *Stay away,* I want to tell her.

"Who is that?" Eric moves closer to Dedushka, looking wildly all around him. "Who did you bring?"

I think of using the distraction to get in there and pull Dedushka away, but I don't think I could do it. The way Eric is right now, I think he'd shoot.

"No idea," I answer honestly.

The car flies toward us, the brakes squealing as it stops, swings a little sideways. Liesel pops out of the door, her gun (a new gun) aimed at the three of us.

Crap.

"Eric." She moves slow, steady, toward us. "Put the gun down."

What? I figured she was coming to help him. To be on his side.

"Stay back!" Eric calls. "I've almost got him."

"You don't want to do this, Eric," she says, in that sweet voice I hate so much. She looks the same as always, hair back, professional. "Put the gun down now, and I can pretend this never happened."

Her eyes flick to me. "Jacob."

Like we're old friends.

At the end of the side road Rachel has the truck turned and waiting, idling.

"He can't just get away with it," Eric says. Almost whining. "You need to study him. Don't you want to study him?"

Again, a glance at me, though she keeps creeping toward Eric. She's even with me now. I could reach out and touch her. Though I'd rather touch a snake. "I might still. I put in to work with John, now that I know about his lab."

Hell, no. Reason number five billion and one not to go back to Dad.

"But it's time for you to move on, Eric. Other cases. Other projects."

Suddenly Eric swings the gun up, points it at me. "I'll kill him. Right here. Then he won't use anyone again."

I stare down the barrel, like I did in the cemetery so long ago. It's worse this time. This time he's serious.

But I'm not the same person anymore.

In one movement I duck, leap forward, and tackle him at the knees. We both go down hard. He kicks out, trying to get me off him. I jump sideways to try to get his gun arm, to get it away so he can't shoot anyone. . . .

There's a massive bang, and I cover my head, total instinct. He must have shot the gun. But I don't feel anything, no pain. I sit up, checking for Dedushka. He's fine, still motionless on the bench, watching.

Eric is on the ground, flat, next to me. A hole in the middle of his forehead.

Liesel lowers the gun like it's suddenly heavy. "I couldn't let him shoot you," she says, almost to herself. "Not you."

There's a moment where we stay there, still, looking at each other. Everything that's happened, so much. Before Dad, it was me and her.

And Eric.

I jump to my feet, grab Dedushka, and run. I don't look back. She'll take me in again. To Dad. To labs and sunless rooms and tests. Tunneling for the rest of my life.

"Wait!" she calls. "Jacob, wait!"

My shoulders twitch. But no shot comes.

It's not far to the truck, and Dedushka manages to keep up, panting next to me. Rachel throws open the door from the inside and we hop up and in, slam the door behind us. She takes off, spraying gravel.

I look back. Liesel's standing over Eric, staring down, gun hanging at her side.

I remember him joking with Chris, sitting in the mausoleum

with me. Playing tennis at Montauk, on the court he rigged. Laughing.

With his wife and his babies.

Dead. Gone.

I feel numb, like everything around me—trees, sky—is unreal. A hallucination that'll wipe away any minute, and I'll find myself sitting with Eric in a cell.

Dedushka sets a hand on my shoulder, and I look at him, at Rachel, safe.

"*Malchik,*" Dedushka says, quiet but urgent, "I contact my friend Vladimir yesterday. There is still serum, to stop this thing. He has hidden it, but it is there. It may need fixing, for you, but there is a chance . . ."

"You could make it stop?" Rachel asks, hope spilling out of her voice.

I don't answer, not yet, the enormity of it overwhelming me. This is real, this moment. And we could make it stop. Then no one would be after me at all, ever again.

I could live a normal life. Not Jake Lukin, maybe. But a normal person, above ground. A real person. Without guns and handcuffs and ruthlessness.

We drive through the streets of Roswell, the three of us safe as the sun comes over the horizon.

42

"The End" by Jason Reeves

We sit in a gas station parking lot in Daleville, Virginia, watching the trail. I'm behind the wheel, Rachel next to me in the passenger seat, Dedushka taking a nap in the back. This car—well, van—we actually bought with cash, so nobody will be reporting it stolen. We can keep it for a while. And it's big enough for everybody.

If they come.

I go over it again in my head. It's the right day, definitely the right crossing. If they stick to the schedule. Of course they may have had to change the plan. Or gone slower than they thought. Or had something horrible happen to them.

"They'll be here," Rachel says, calm.

I flash her a tense smile. It makes all the difference, her being here. Not being alone. Of course we don't know what's going to happen at the end of the summer. After we do this we're going to go to this Vladimir guy in Florida, get the serum. See if it works.

I wanted to get Myka first. She might be able to help with it, anyway.

If all goes well, if the serum works, Rachel will go to Berkeley in the fall, like she planned. There won't be anything for anyone to hold over her if there's no reason to take me. She could claim she had a wild summer exploring the U.S. (true) and now she's resuming her life.

She says she might want to take a year off anyway. That this has been valuable experience of the political system, the behind-the-scenes working of the government, and she's not sure if she's ready for it to end.

Then she laughs, and I kiss her, and we don't talk about it anymore.

But if it works—if it really works—maybe I can figure out a way to go to Stanford too. Maybe Dad can help if I'm wiped clean of this ability and not a temptation for him.

I see it there, the future I want. It's possible. If they come . . .

"There," Rachel says. "Someone's there."

I see Myka first. She bounces with each step as she walks along on the dirt trail. Her hair pokes out under an army-green ball cap pulled down low, a backpack on her shoulders. Mom's behind her. She looks tired, disheveled, but good. They've been walking the Appalachian Trail for three weeks now, since I called them. Just two more hikers, anonymous. Easily lost among the rest.

Except now they're found.

Myka stops at the edge of the road, hand over her eyes, searching. I open the door, step out. Stand where she—they—can see me.

I hear Myk's *squee* from across the street. She grabs Mom's hand and they run across, straight into my arms. All three of us, in a jumble of arms and grins and exclamations.

Dedushka and Rachel get out too and watch us, laughing.

Will Dad come after us before we get the serum? I hope not. I like to think that he knows it's wrong, that he'll go back to his original plan of keeping me out of it.

He and Liesel can keep trying, but I doubt they'll make another tunnel.

Mr. Smith is another thing, but Dedushka says he can help me stay out of sight, stay above ground. Until the serum works, and then I'm out of this for good.

I close my eyes and hug Myka, Mom. We don't even need to do Glue, not anymore. If we can stick together through all that craziness, we can stick together through anything.

We will. Mom, Myk, Dedushka, Rachel, me. Maybe we are kind of a super family after all.

Together, at last. And almost free.

Acknowledgments

My journey to publication has not been quick or easy in any sense—which means there are more people to thank, friends and family who stuck firmly by my side and helped along the way. Thank you, to all of you. Persevering with writing long enough to get published requires a community of support, and I can never really thank you enough. If I miss you somehow here, know that I still appreciate you.

First, to the one who was there first, my mom, and to my much-loved stepdad, Doc: your encouragement means everything.

To Michael and Sophie, who live with this craziness every day even though they didn't choose it: I love you most, always. I wouldn't be anywhere without you.

To Kate, who was the second person to love Jake as much as I did, and who wouldn't give up on finding a home for him: you're not just an agent, but my champion (my ninja superhero champion).

To Brendan, who gave Jake's story a home. It wouldn't be book-shaped without you! Thank you for getting Jake so well. To all the fabulous Thomas

Dunne and St. Martin's crew for their excellent work: Nicole Sohl, Greg Collins, Stephanie Davis, Janna Dokos, Marie Estrada, Bridget Hartzler, Jeanne-Marie Hudson, Jessica Katz, Young Jin Lim, and everyone else behind the scenes. Thank you for transforming my words from a story to a Real Book.

To the Compuserve Forum, where the Kick-Ass Writer Chicks were born, and to the Surrey International Writer's Conference. Thank you Diana Gabaldon, my first writing mentor. Your reassurance early on was so important to me. Thank you especially Kathy Chung, Rose Holck, Julie Kentner, and Vicki Pettersson. Thank you to Janet Reid, for loving Jenna.

To Team Sparkle—Linda Grimes, Emily Hainsworth, Tiffany Schmidt, Victoria Schwab, Courtney Summers, and Scott Tracey—who wouldn't let me give up even when I was the only one still without a deal. Look! We made it!

To Liz Briggs and Krista Van Dolzer, the other two triplets, for all the e-mails and IMs. To other fellow kt lit lovelies Sara Beitia, Ellen Booraem, Matthew Cody, Erin Danehy, Trish Doller, Carrie Harris, Renee Nyen, Stephanie Perkins, Rebecca Petruck, Amy Sonnichsen, Amy Spalding, and Kate Linnea Welsh. Fellow nerds, unite!

To all the Fearless Fifteeners for your endless and necessary support, and especially to the admins who helped me make everything run for our debut year: MarcyKate Connolly, Lauren Gibaldi, Kathryn Holmes, Cordelia Jensen, Jen Klein, Stacey Lee, Moriah McStay, Heather Petty, Cindy Rodriguez, Jenn Marie Thorne, Krista Van Dolzer, and Jasmine Warga. And Ilene for keeping me company at BEA.

To all the many, many writer and publishing friends who've e-mailed and posted and tweeted and hugged (virtually or otherwise) over the years. You inspire me every day: Dahlia Adler, Kendare Blake, Joanna Bourne, Heather Brewer, Patricia Briggs, Bill Cameron, Leah Clifford, Julie Cross, Kari Lynn Dell, Julianne Douglas, Sarah Beth Durst, Jamie Ford, Miriam Forster, Kelly Jensen, Mike Jung, S.J. Kincaid, Stephanie Kuehn, Yi Shun Lai, Claire Legrand, Melissa Manlove, Lish McBride, Gretchen McNeil, Jodi Meadows, Martha Mihalick, Molly O'Neill, Sarah Prineas, Diana Peterfreund, C.J. Redwine, Chandra Rooney, Shana Silver, Nova Ren Suma, Capillya Uptergrove, Joanna Volpe, Laura Whitaker, Kiersten White, and Cat Winters. I know the list is long, but every one of you has been critical in some way. You make me bubble-happy.

To my first and forever inspirations: Douglas Adams, Susan Cooper, Madeleine L'Engle, and Mary Stewart.

And last, but not least, to Chuck.